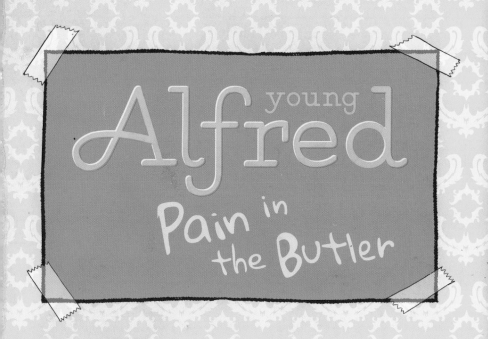

young

Alfred

Pain in the Butler

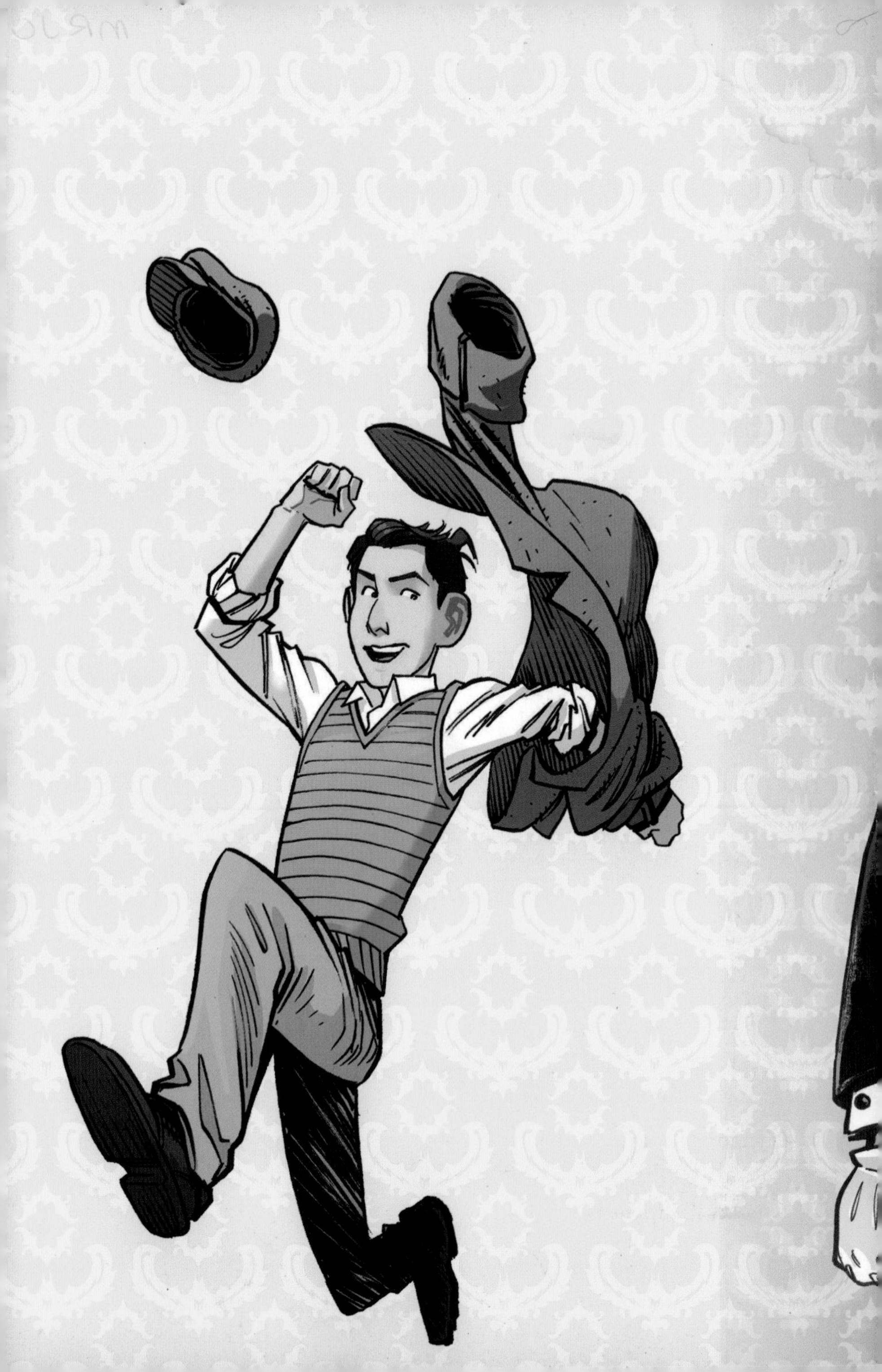

young Alfred

Pain in the Butler

WRITTEN BY
Michael Northrop

ART BY
Sam Lotfi

COLOR BY
Kendall Goode

LETTERING BY
Wes Abbott

SARA MILLER EDITOR
STEVE COOK DESIGN DIRECTOR – BOOKS
AMIE BROCKWAY-METCALF PUBLICATION DESIGN
TIFFANY HUANG PUBLICATION PRODUCTION

MARIE JAVINS EDITOR-IN-CHIEF, DC COMICS

ANNE DePIES SENIOR VP – GENERAL MANAGER
JIM LEE PUBLISHER & CHIEF CREATIVE OFFICER
DON FALLETTI VP – MANUFACTURING OPERATIONS &
WORKFLOW MANAGEMENT
LAWRENCE GANEM VP – TALENT SERVICES
ALISON GILL SENIOR VP – MANUFACTURING & OPERATIONS
JEFFREY KAUFMAN VP – EDITORIAL STRATEGY & PROGRAMMING
NICK J. NAPOLITANO VP – MANUFACTURING
ADMINISTRATION & DESIGN
NANCY SPEARS VP – REVENUE

LOGO DESIGN **SYDNEY LEE**

FSC
www.fsc.org
MIX
Paper from
responsible sources
FSC® C002589

DC Comics, 4000 Warner Blvd., Bldg. 700,
2nd Floor, Burbank, CA 91522
Printed by Worzalla, Stevens Point,
WI, USA. 6/16/23.
First Printing.
ISBN: 978-1-77950-971-0
Library of Congress Control Number: 2023937770

CHAPTER 1
The Butler
and the Bat

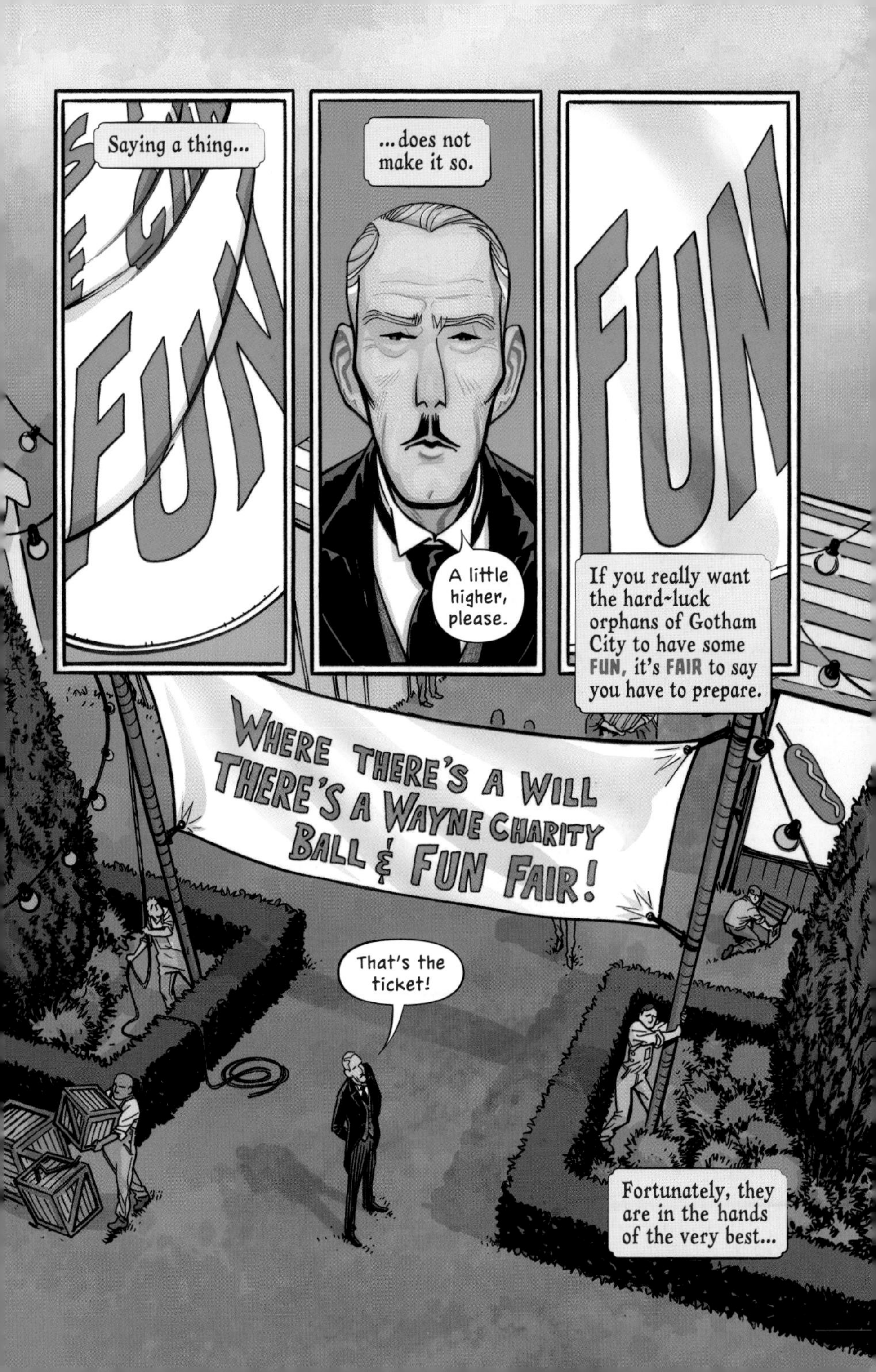
Saying a thing...
FUN
...does not make it so.
A little higher, please.
FUN
If you really want the hard-luck orphans of Gotham City to have some FUN, it's FAIR to say you have to prepare.
WHERE THERE'S A WILL THERE'S A WAYNE CHARITY BALL & FUN FAIR!
That's the ticket!
Fortunately, they are in the hands of the very best...

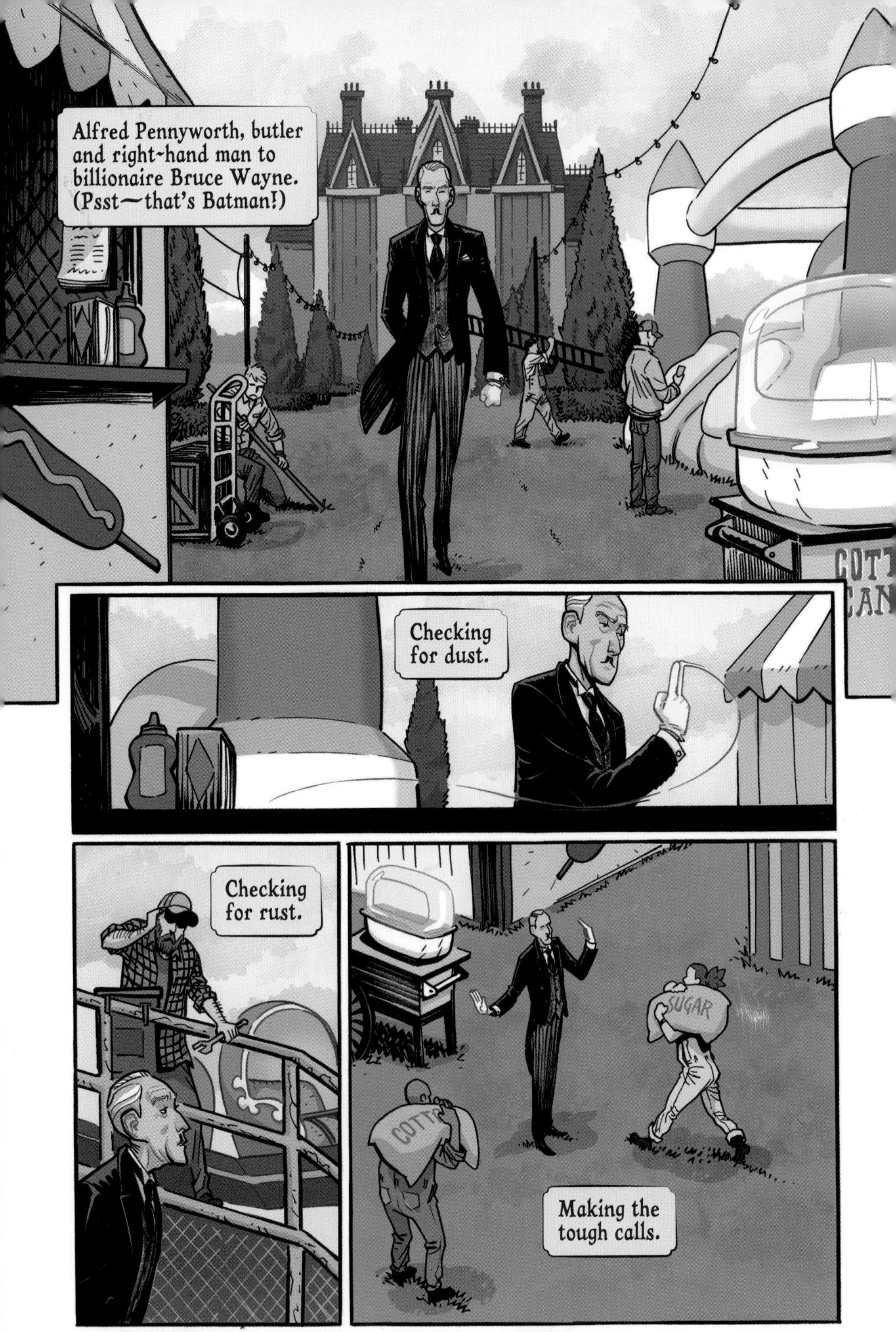
Alfred Pennyworth, butler and right-hand man to billionaire Bruce Wayne. (Psst—that's Batman!)
COTT
CAN
Checking for dust.
Checking for rust.
SUGAR
COTT
Making the tough calls.

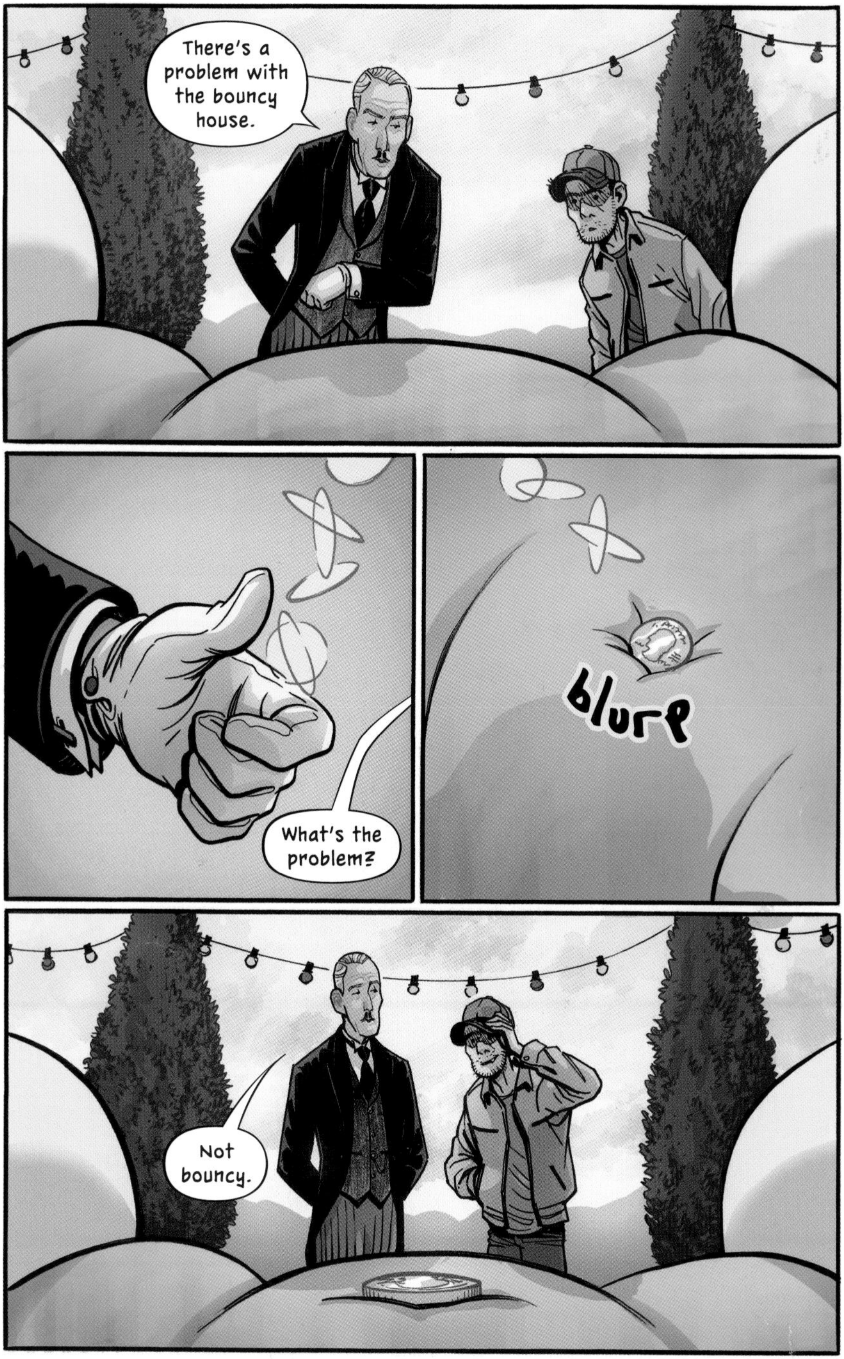
There's a problem with the bouncy house.
What's the problem?
blurp
Not bouncy.

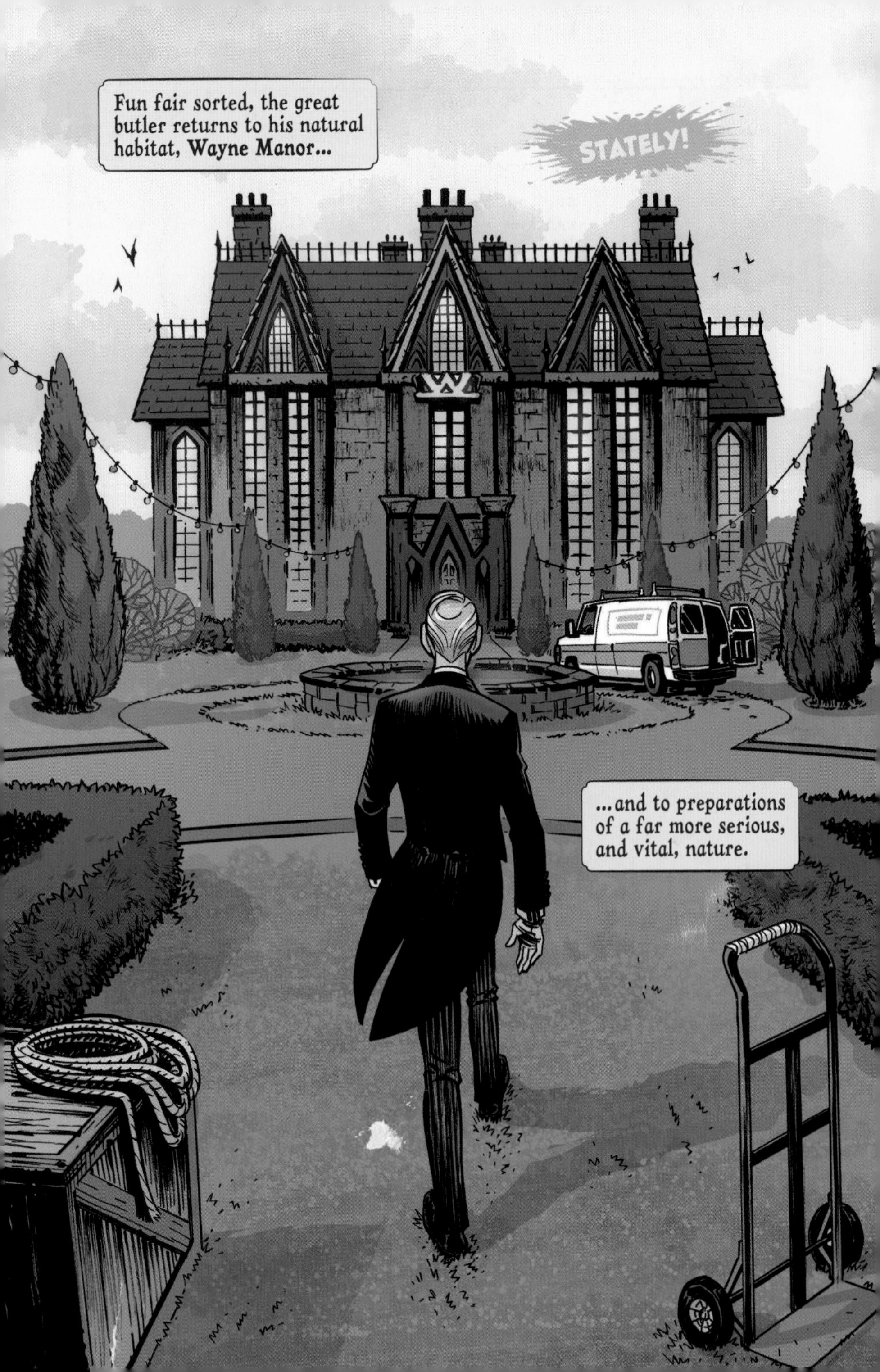
Fun fair sorted, the great butler returns to his natural habitat, Wayne Manor...
STATELY!
...and to preparations of a far more serious, and vital, nature.

A squirrel in a tree. A bear in a cave. A butler in a ballroom.

You are the finest hostesses, busboys, and cater-waiters in Gotham.

And you shall need to be!

≥gulp≤

Tonight's fundraiser must be *flawless.* The city's orphans are depending on it!

HIGH STAKES!

Food for summer, school supplies for fall, heat for winter.

VRRRRRRRRRR

RRRRRRRRRR

RRR

That money must... be...

RRR

...raised tonight.

VRROOM

Now, if you'll excuse me, I'll leave you to it.

Wow.

The G.O.A.T.*

*Greatest of All Time

11

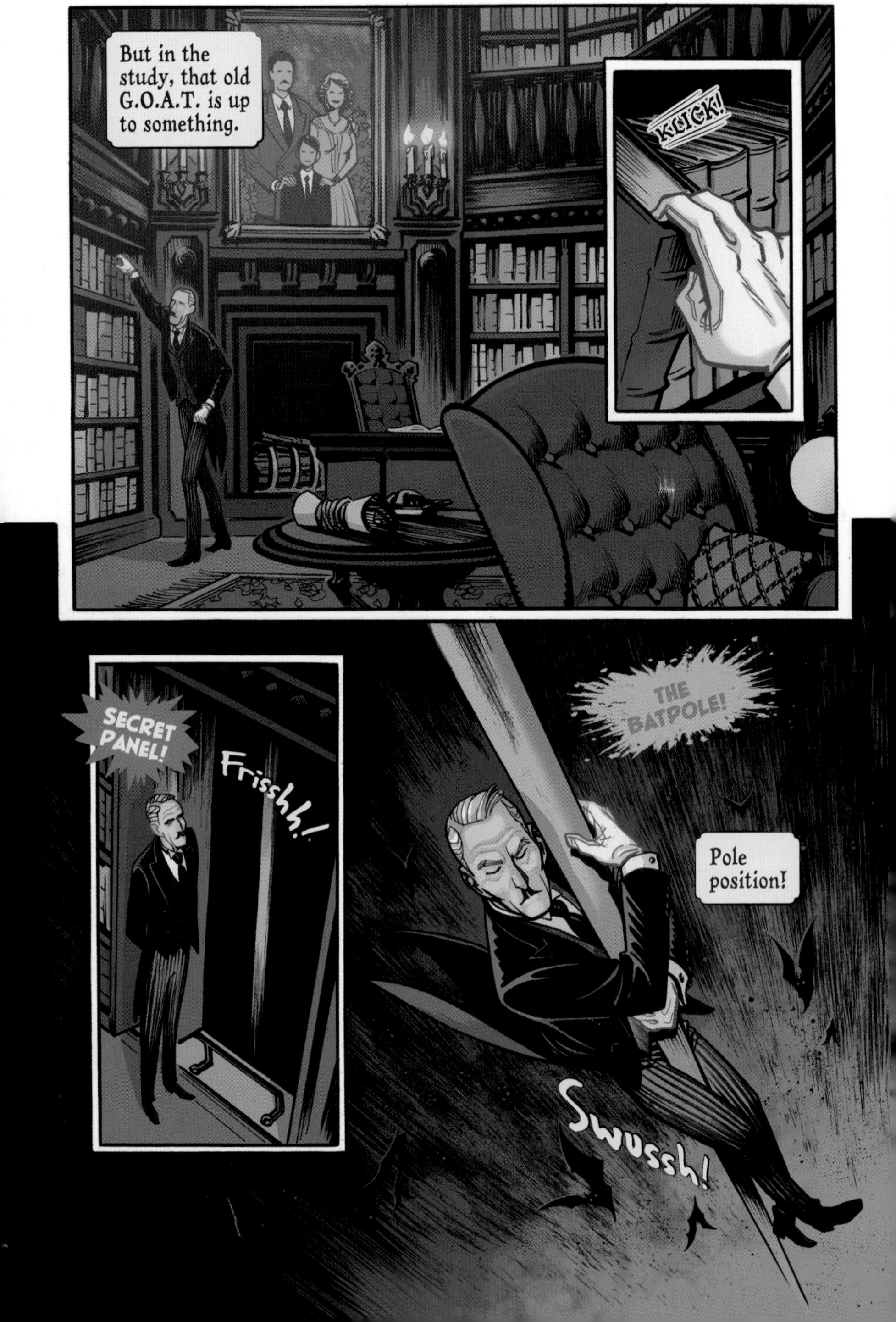
But in the study, that old G.O.A.T. is up to something.
KLICK!
SECRET PANEL!
Frisshh!
THE BATPOLE!
Pole position!
Swussh!

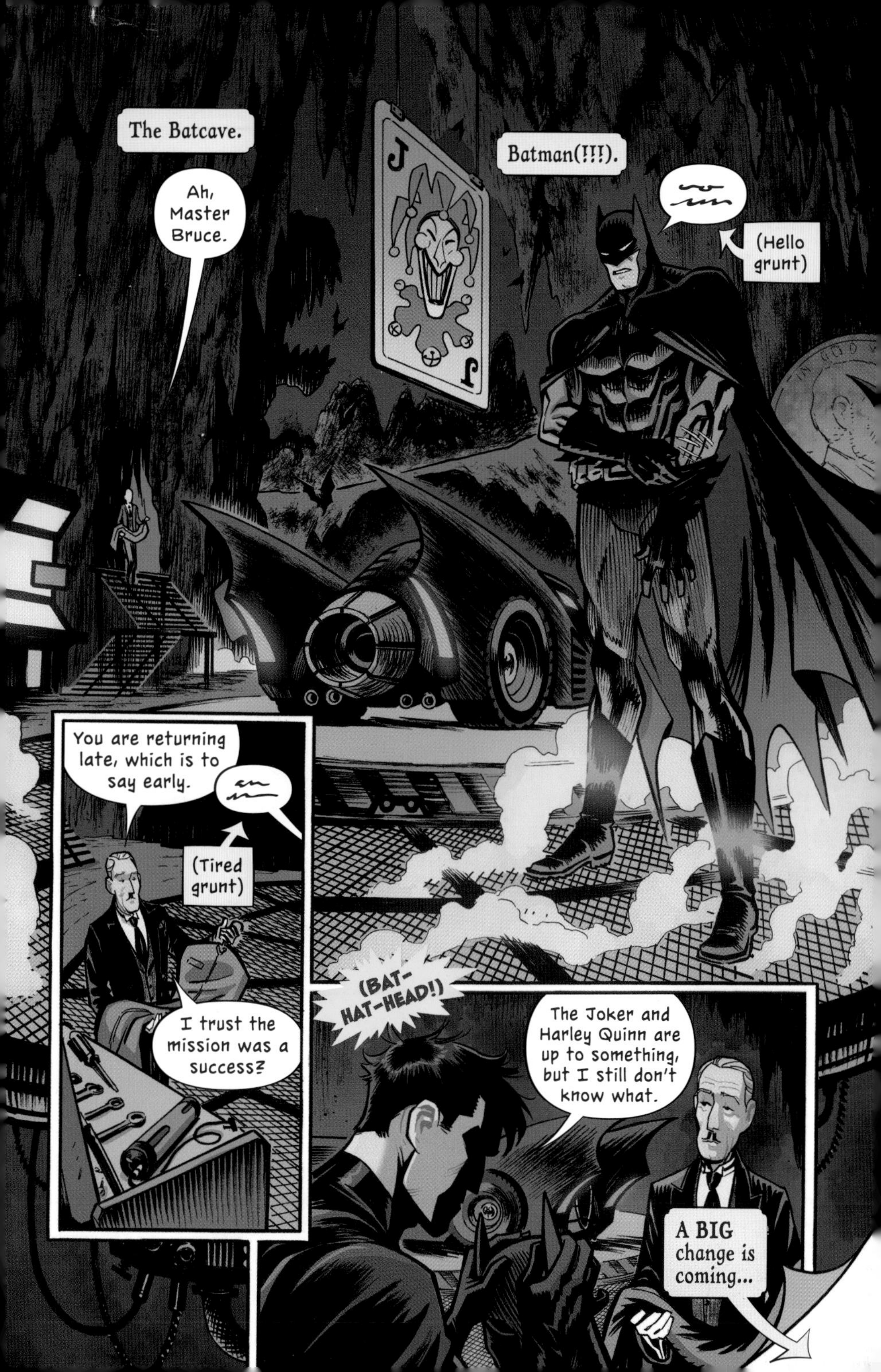

The Batcave.
Ah, Master Bruce.
Batman(!!!).
(Hello grunt)
You are returning late, which is to say early.
(Tired grunt)
I trust the mission was a success?
(BAT-HAT-HEAD!)
The Joker and Harley Quinn are up to something, but I still don't know what.
A BIG change is coming...

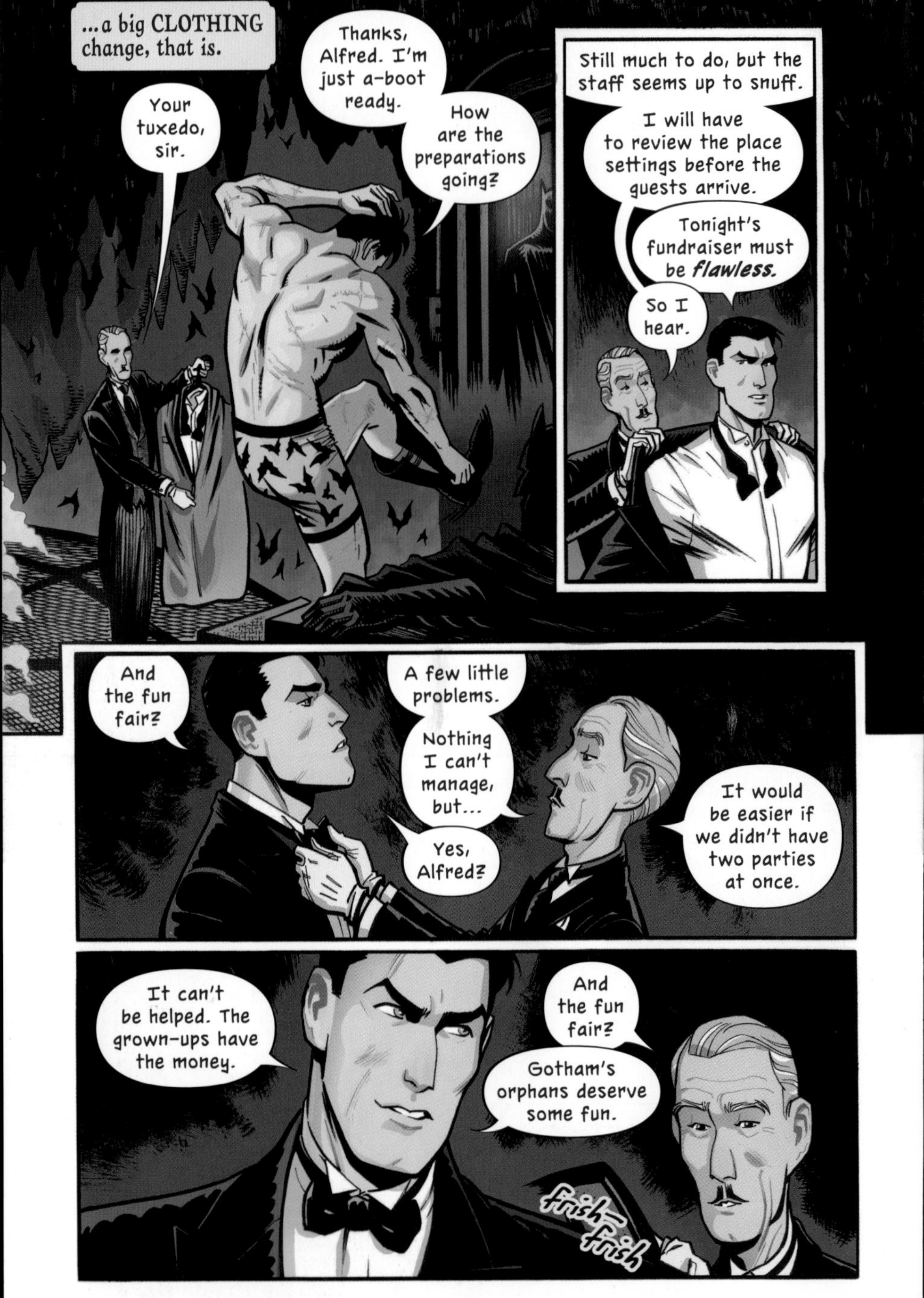
...a big CLOTHING change, that is.
Your tuxedo, sir.
Thanks, Alfred. I'm just a-boot ready.
How are the preparations going?
Still much to do, but the staff seems up to snuff.
I will have to review the place settings before the guests arrive.
Tonight's fundraiser must be *flawless.*
So I hear.
And the fun fair?
A few little problems.
Nothing I can't manage, but...
Yes, Alfred?
It would be easier if we didn't have two parties at once.
It can't be helped. The grown-ups have the money.
And the fun fair?
Gotham's orphans deserve some fun.
frish-frish

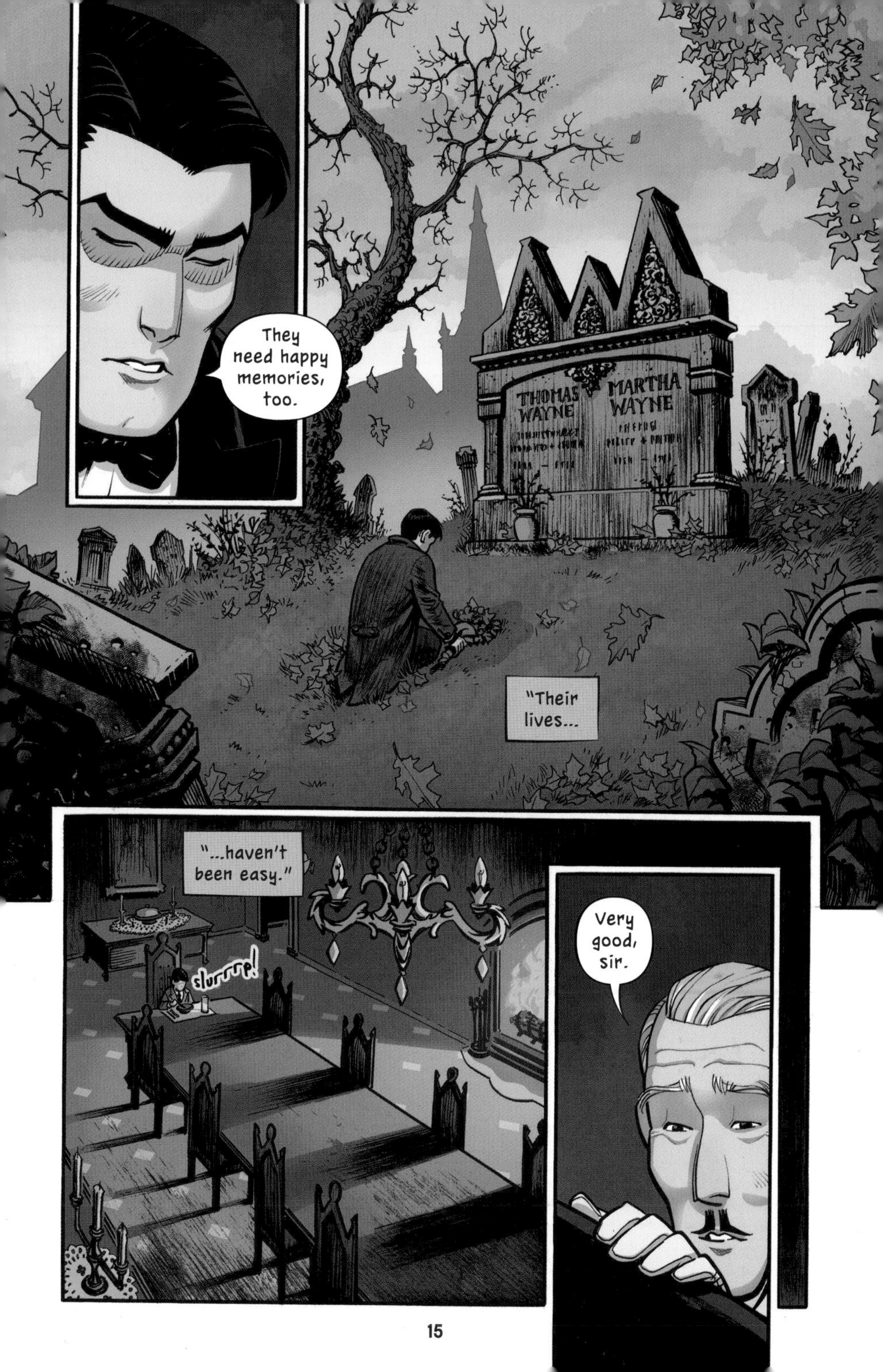

They need happy memories, too.
THOMAS WAYNE
MARTHA WAYNE
"Their lives...
"...haven't been easy."
slurrrp!
Very good, sir.

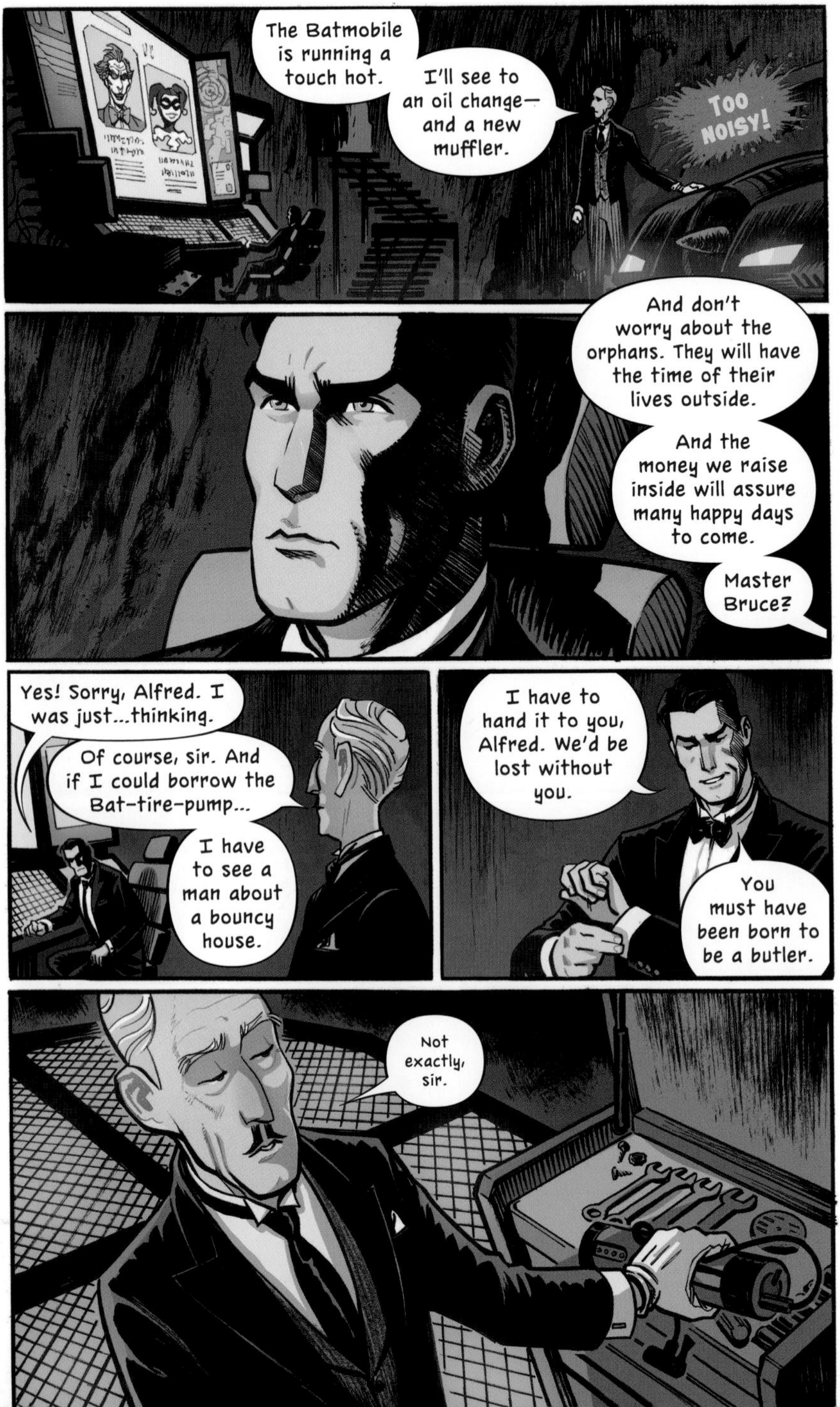

The Batmobile is running a touch hot.
I'll see to an oil change— and a new muffler.
TOO NOISY!
And don't worry about the orphans. They will have the time of their lives outside.
And the money we raise inside will assure many happy days to come.
Master Bruce?
Yes! Sorry, Alfred. I was just...thinking.
Of course, sir. And if I could borrow the Bat-tire-pump...
I have to see a man about a bouncy house.
I have to hand it to you, Alfred. We'd be lost without you.
You must have been born to be a butler.
Not exactly, sir.

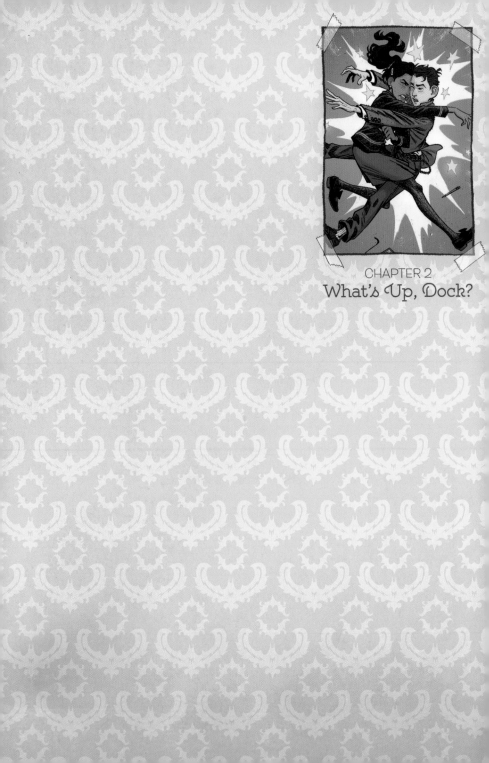

CHAPTER 2
What's Up, Dock?

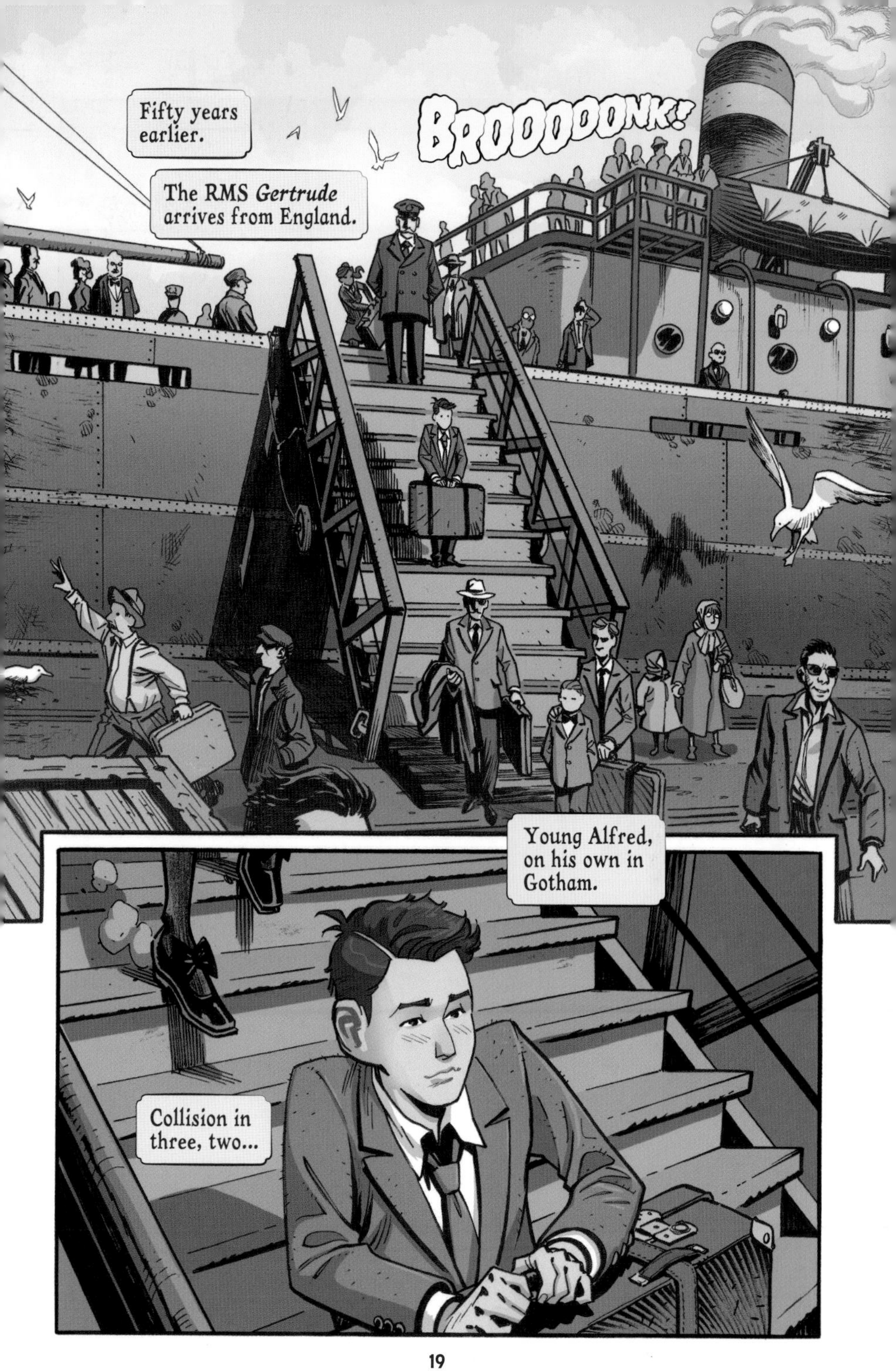
Fifty years earlier.
The RMS Gertrude arrives from England.
BROOOOOONK!
Young Alfred, on his own in Gotham.
Collision in three, two...

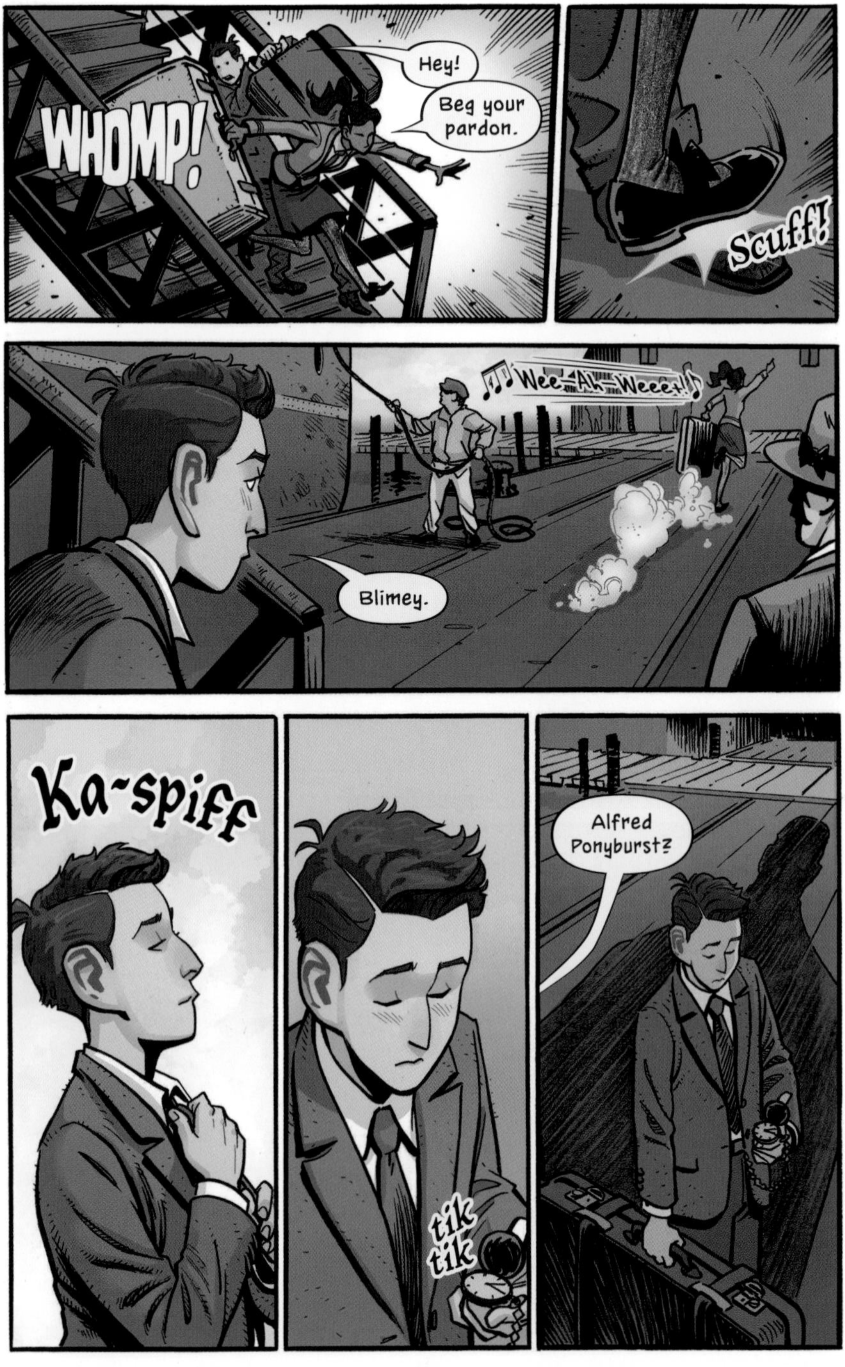

WHOMP!
Hey!
Beg your pardon.
Scuff!
Wee-Ah-Weeee!
Blimey.
Ka-spiff
tik tik
Alfred Ponyburst?

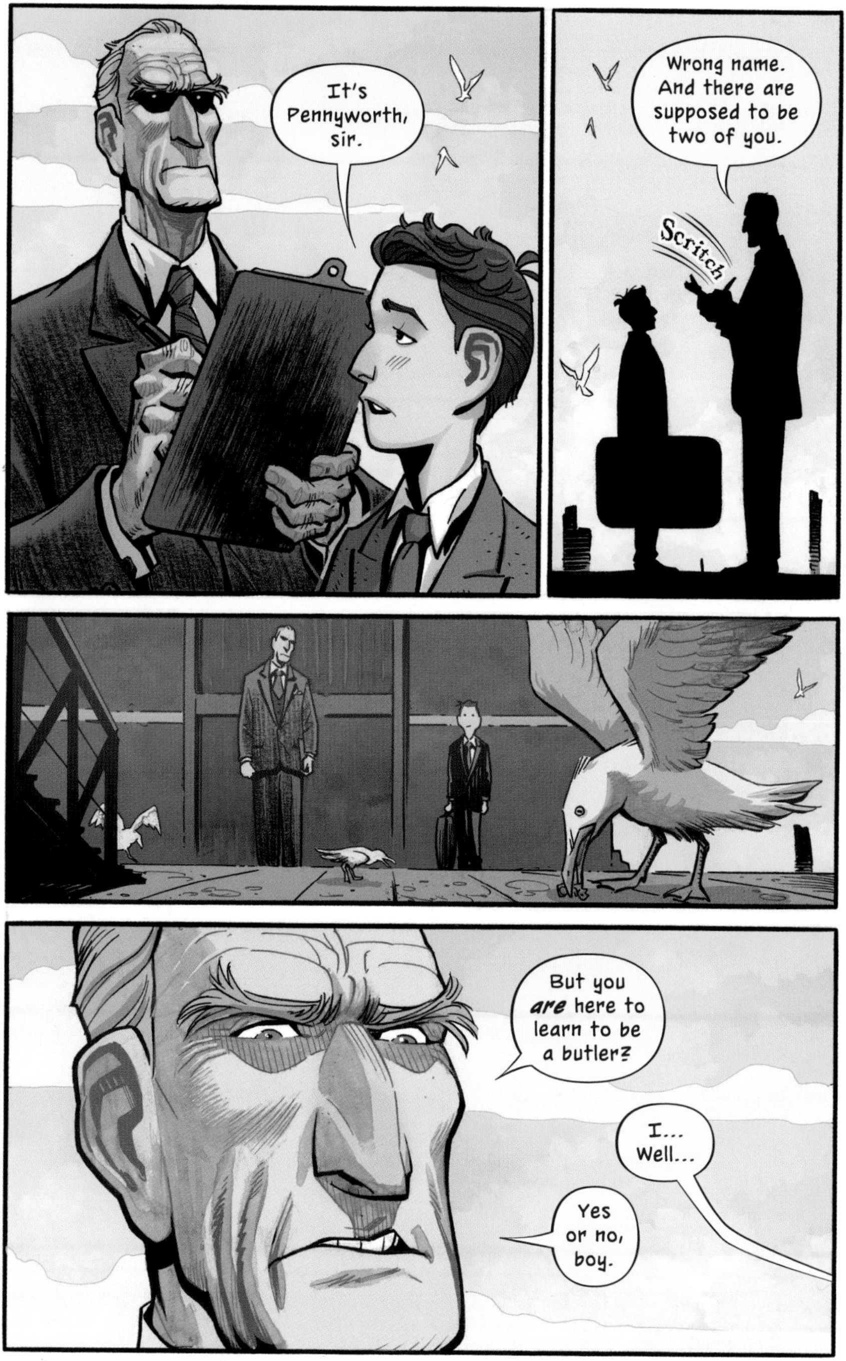
It's Pennyworth, sir.
Wrong name. And there are supposed to be two of you.
Scritch
But you *are* here to learn to be a butler?
I... Well...
Yes or no, boy.

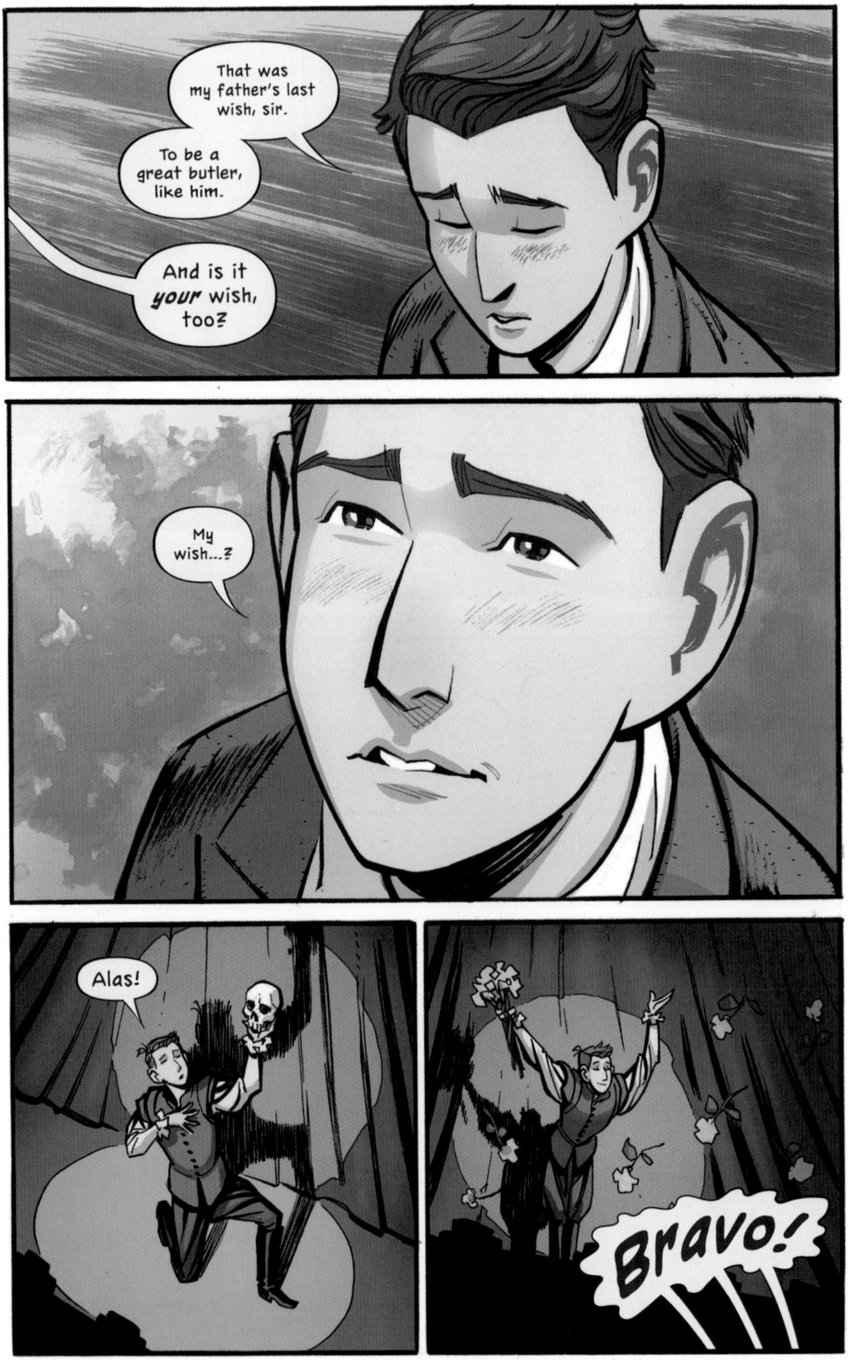
That was my father's last wish, sir.
To be a great butler, like him.
And is it *your* wish, too?
My wish...?
Alas!
Bravo!

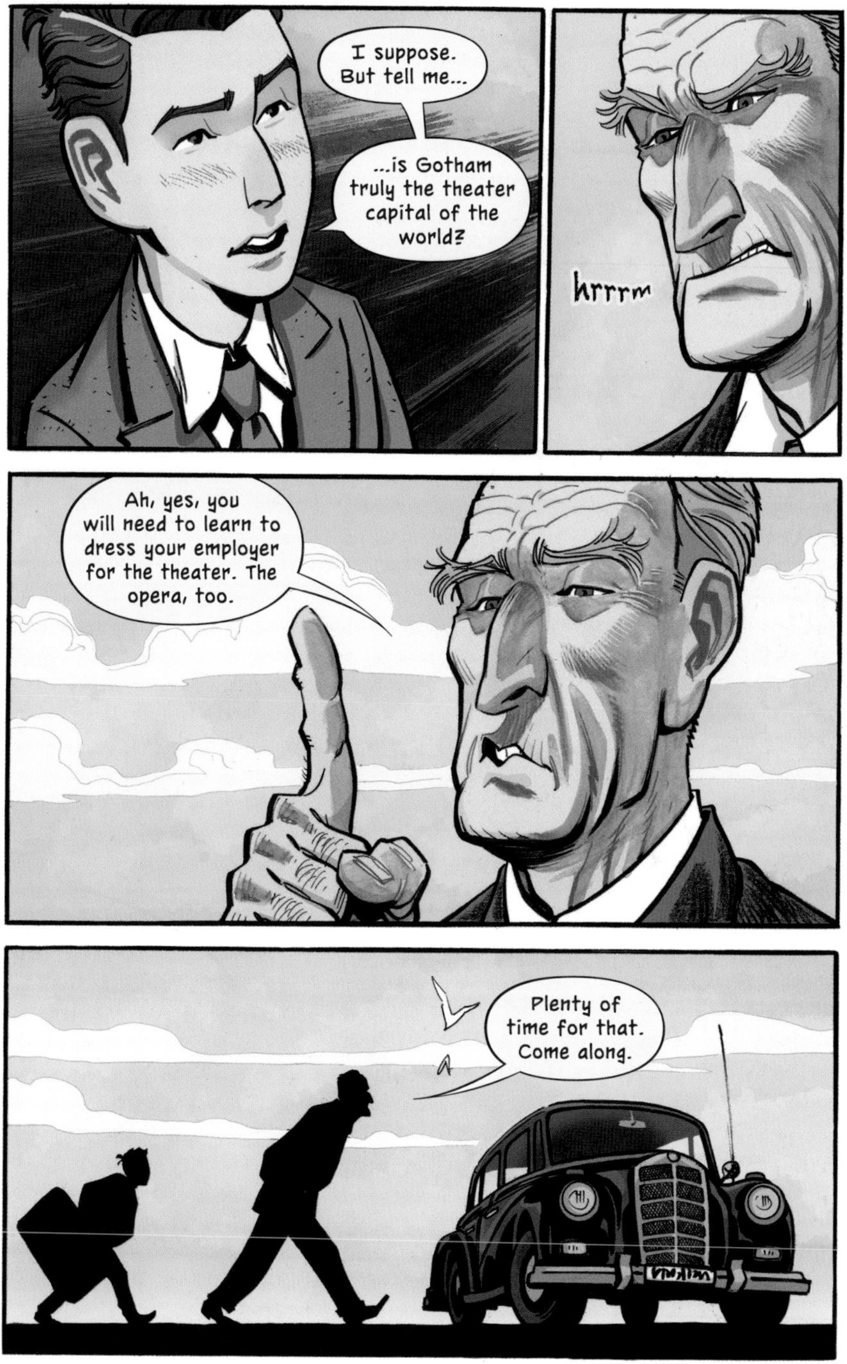
I suppose. But tell me...
...is Gotham truly the theater capital of the world?
hrrrm
Ah, yes, you will need to learn to dress your employer for the theater. The opera, too.
Plenty of time for that. Come along.

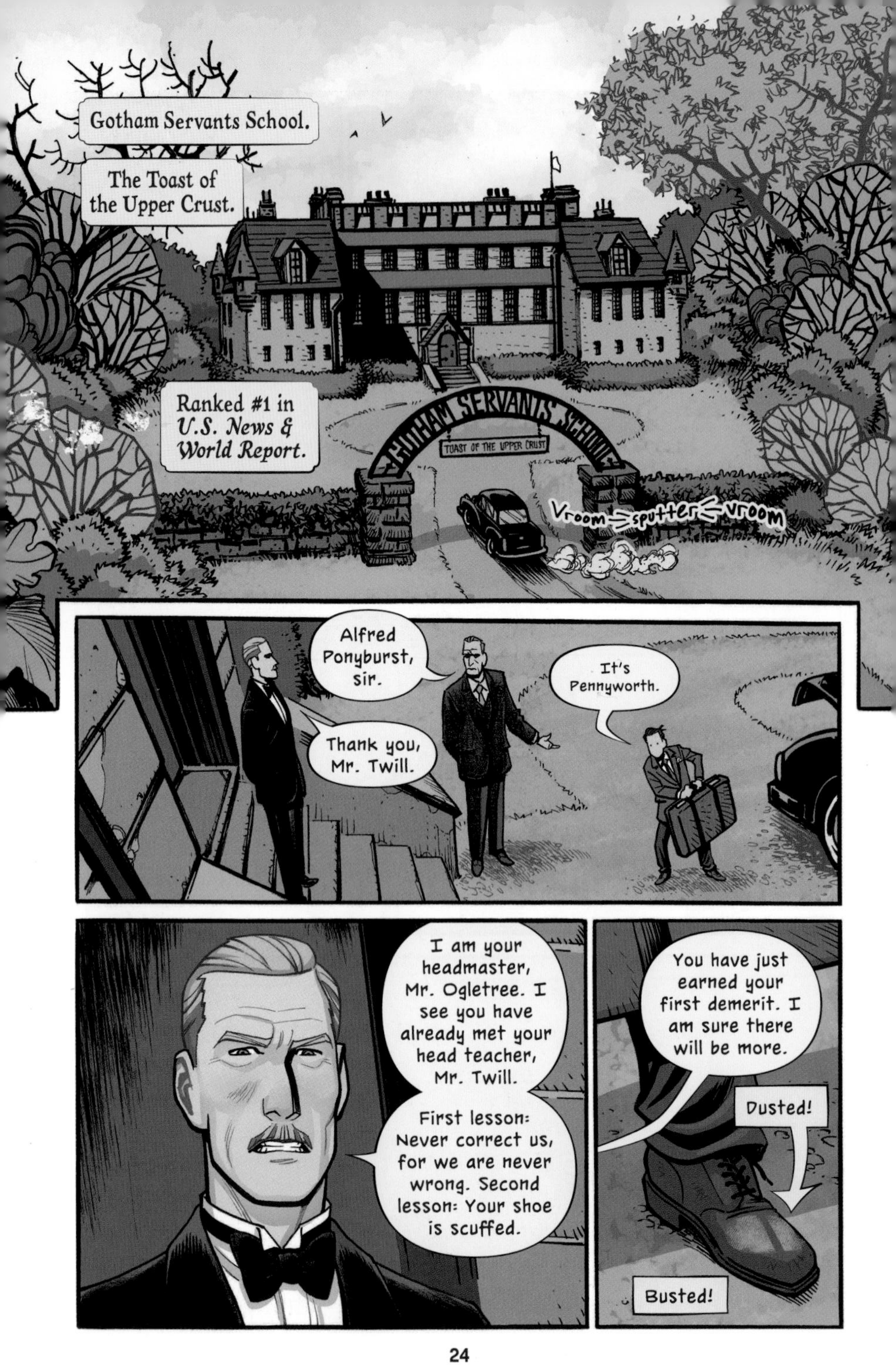

Gotham Servants School.
The Toast of the Upper Crust.
Ranked #1 in *U.S. News & World Report*.
GOTHAM SERVANTS SCHOOL
TOAST OF THE UPPER CRUST
Vroom sputter vroom
Alfred Ponyburst, sir.
It's Pennyworth.
Thank you, Mr. Twill.
I am your headmaster, Mr. Ogletree. I see you have already met your head teacher, Mr. Twill.
First lesson: Never correct us, for we are never wrong. Second lesson: Your shoe is scuffed.
You have just earned your first demerit. I am sure there will be more.
Dusted!
Busted!

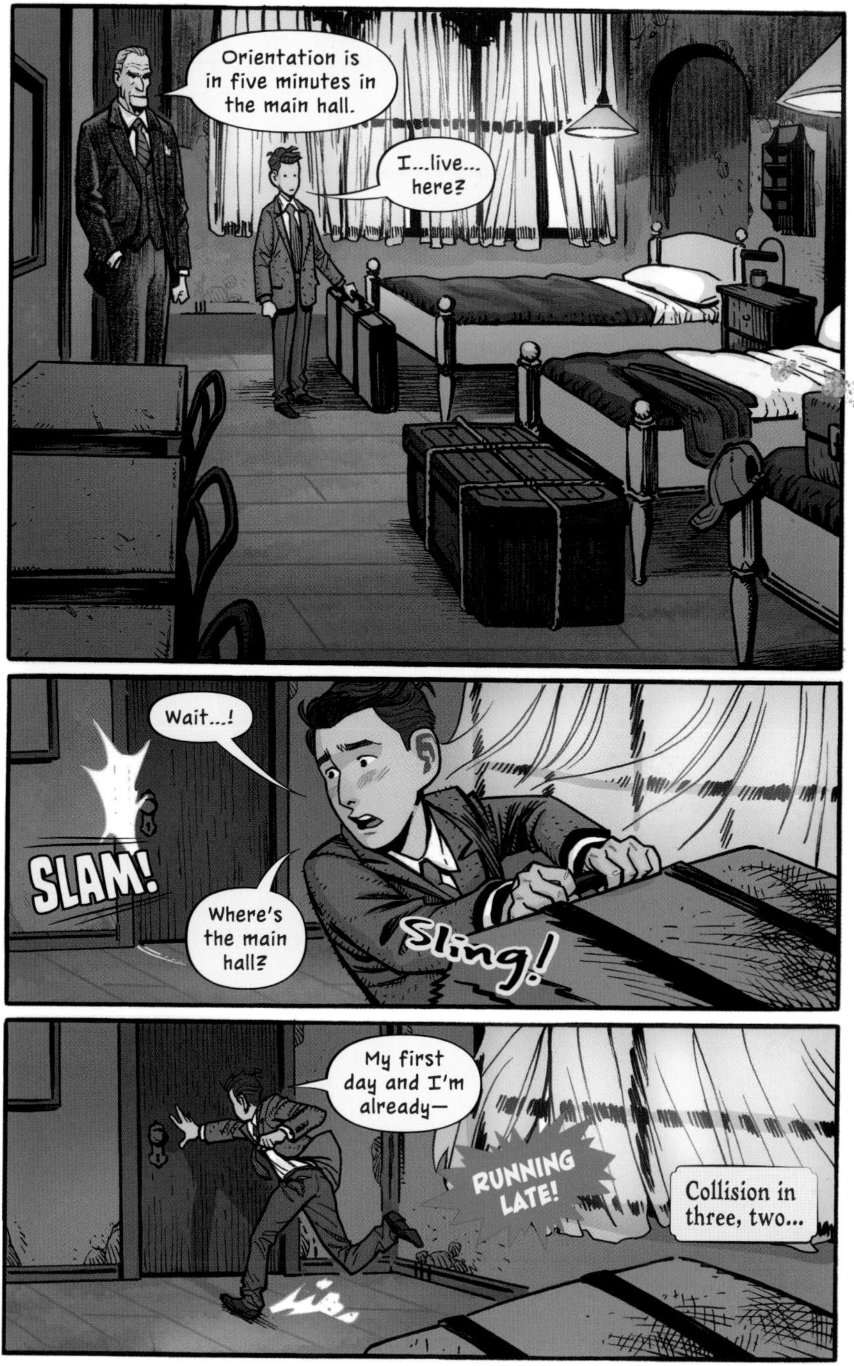
Orientation is in five minutes in the main hall.
I...live... here?
Wait...!
SLAM!
Where's the main hall?
Sling!
My first day and I'm already—
RUNNING LATE!
Collision in three, two...

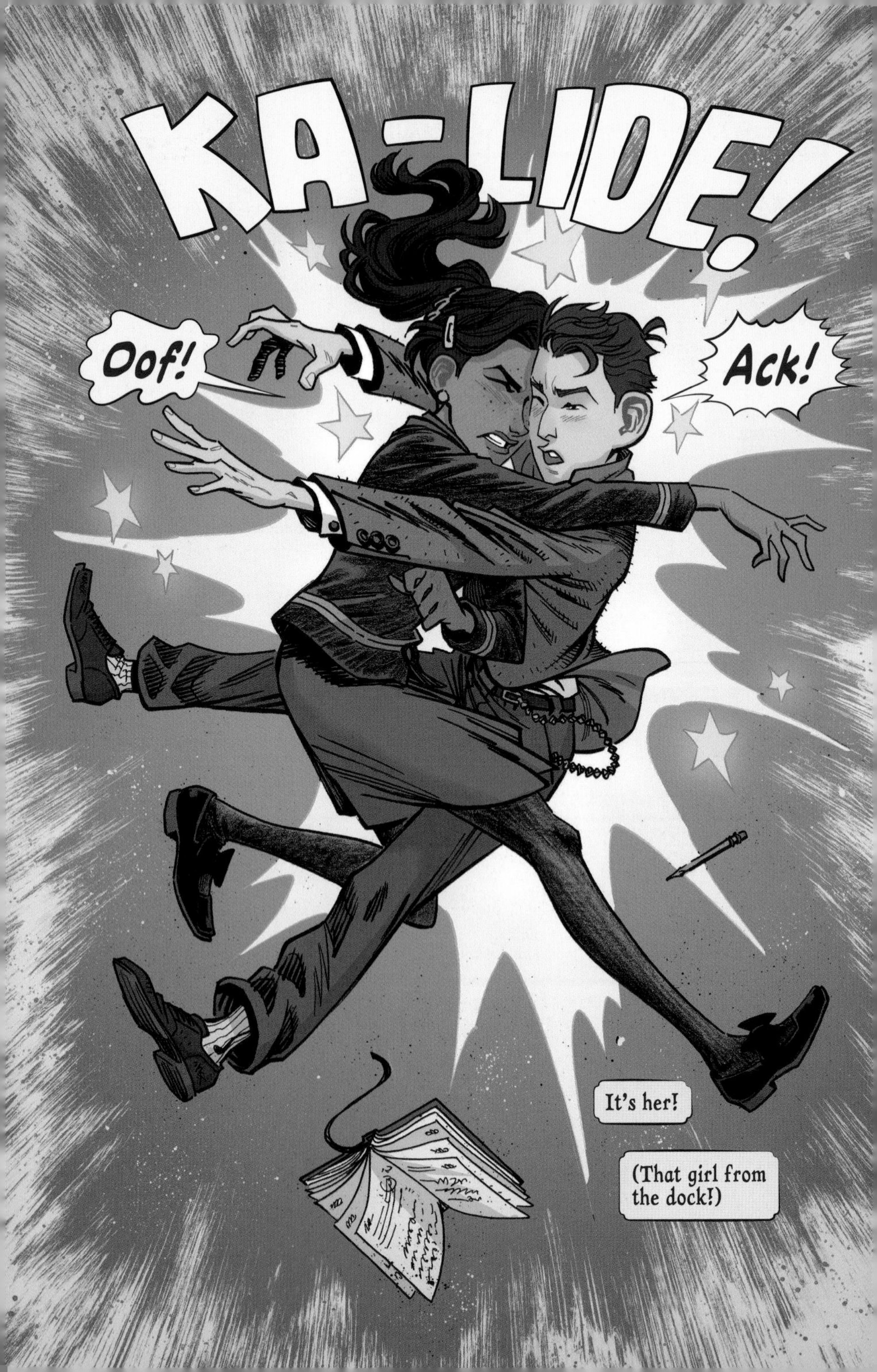
KA-LIDE!
Oof!
Ack!
It's her!
(That girl from the dock!)

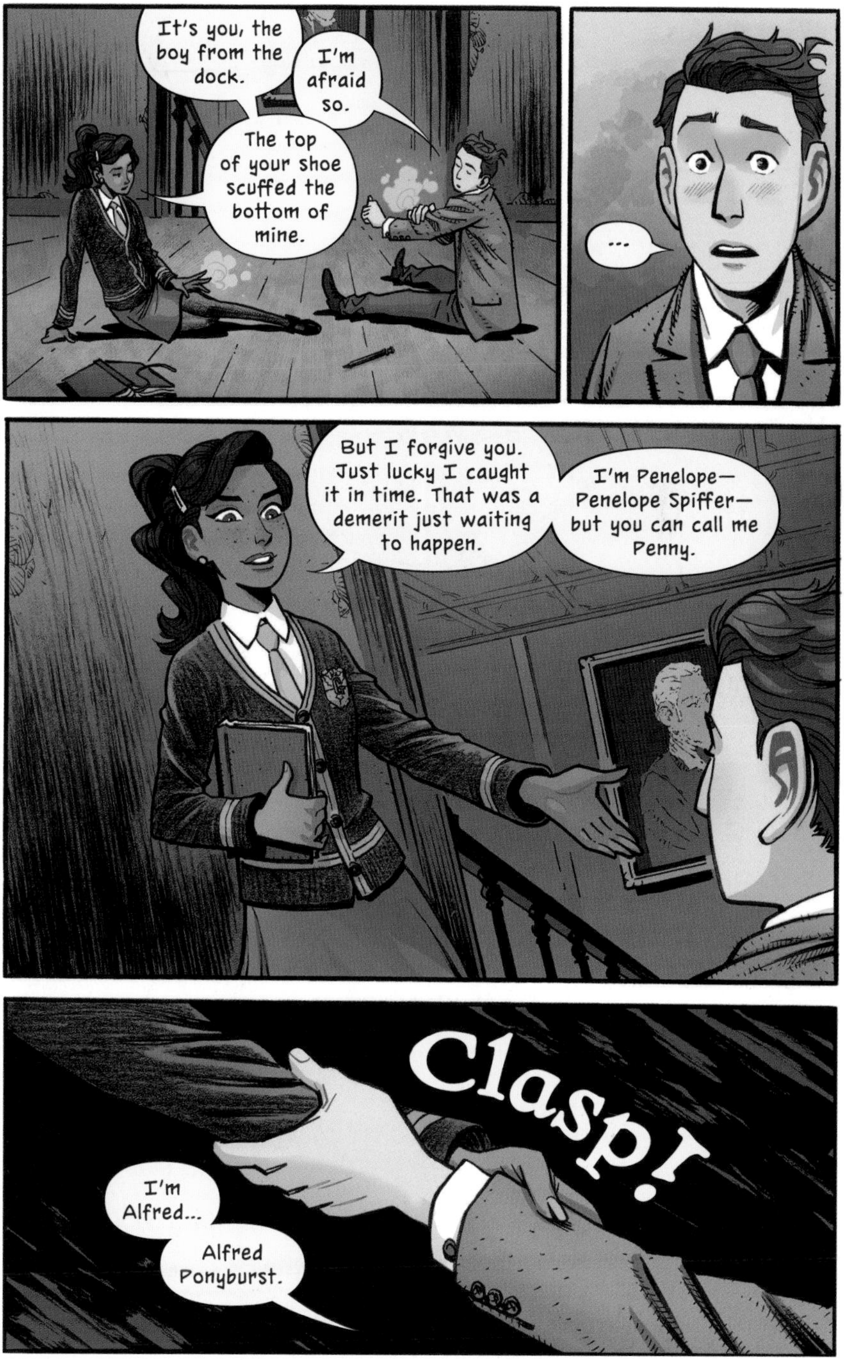

It's you, the boy from the dock.
I'm afraid so.
The top of your shoe scuffed the bottom of mine.
...
But I forgive you. Just lucky I caught it in time. That was a demerit just waiting to happen.
I'm Penelope—Penelope Spiffer—but you can call me Penny.
Clasp!
I'm Alfred...
Alfred Ponyburst.

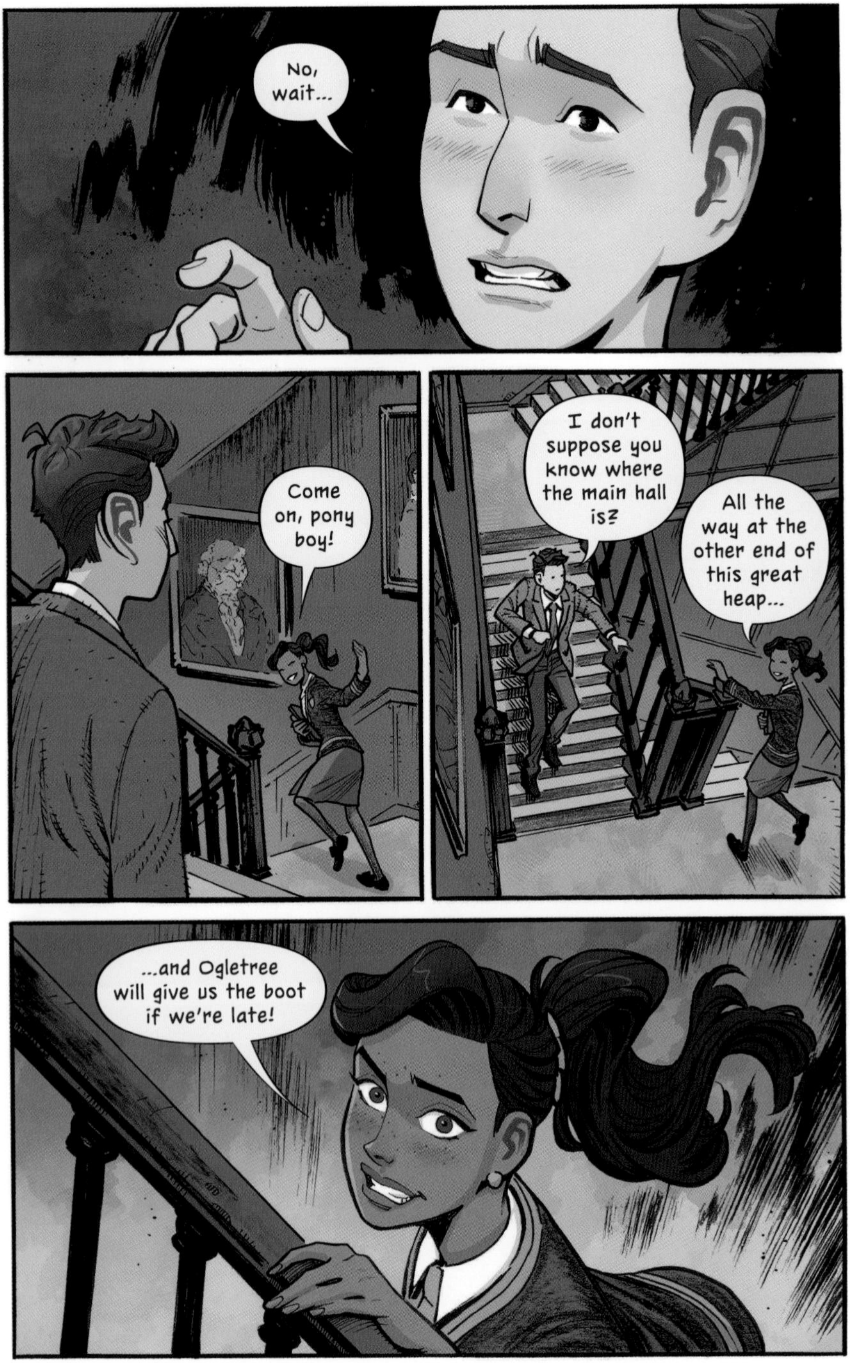
No, wait...
Come on, pony boy!
I don't suppose you know where the main hall is?
All the way at the other end of this great heap...
...and Ogletree will give us the boot if we're late!

CHAPTER 3
Disorientation

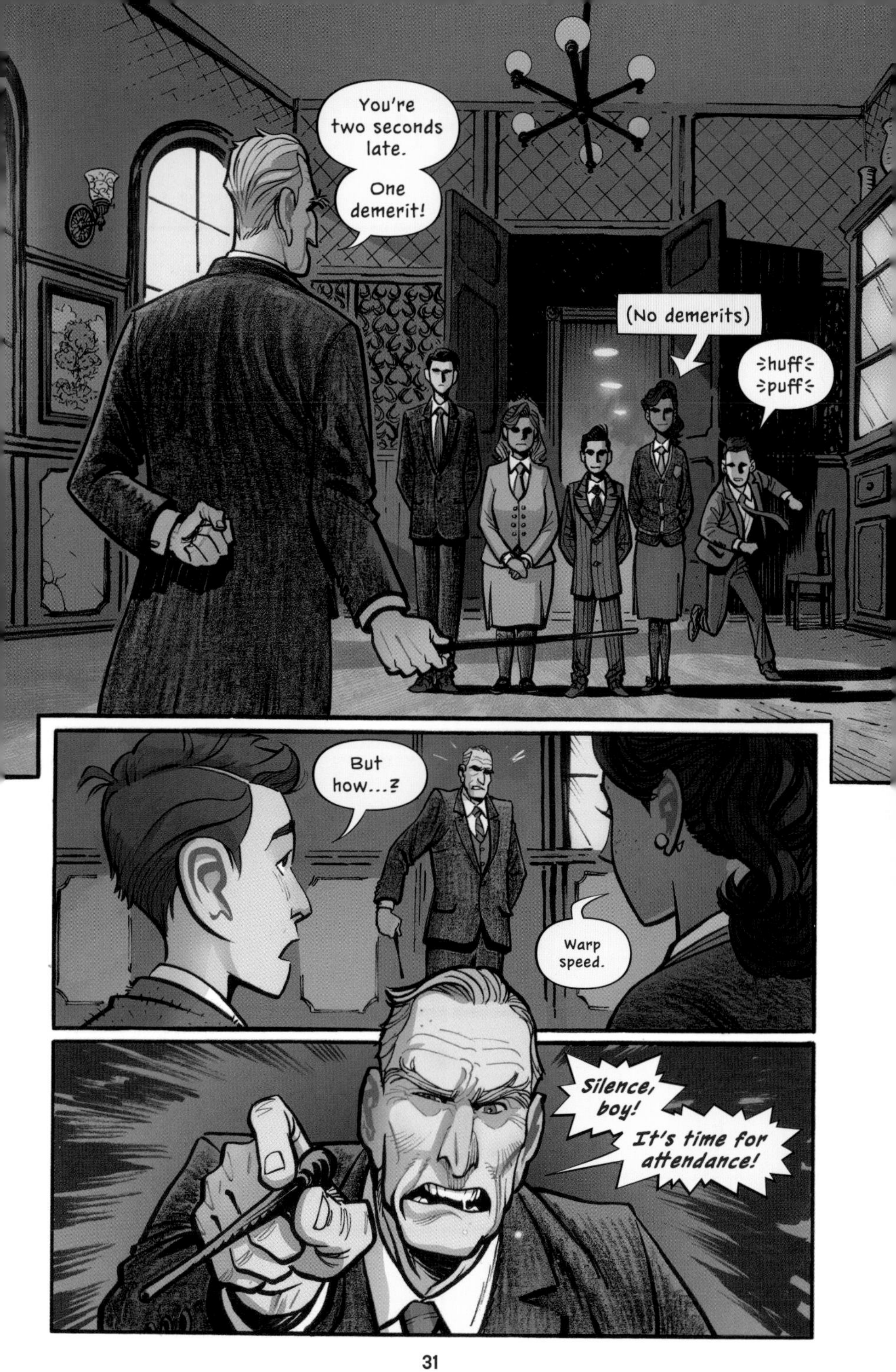
You're two seconds late.
One demerit!
(No demerits)
huff puff
But how...?
Warp speed.
Silence, boy!
It's time for attendance!

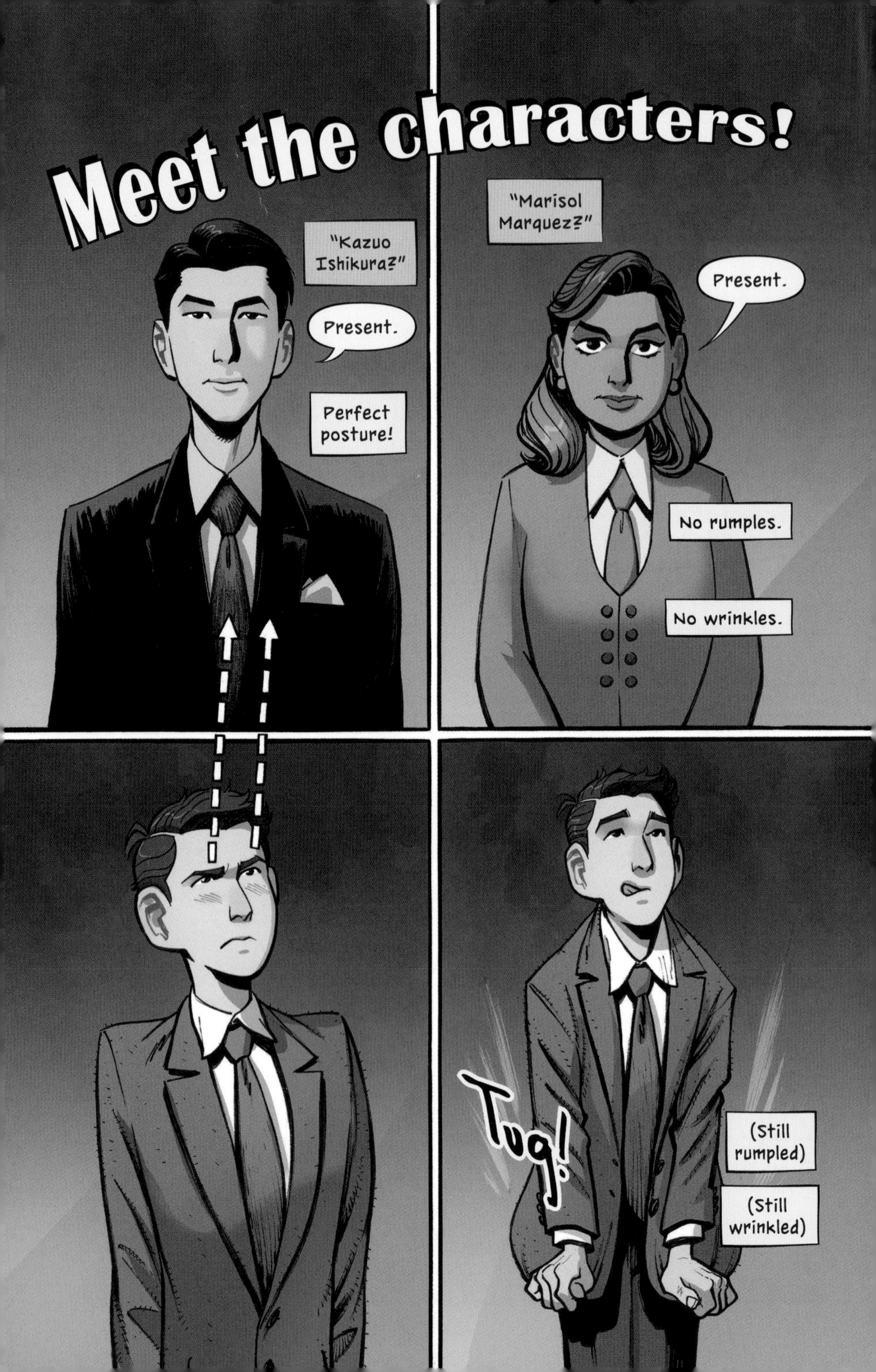
Meet the characters!
"Kazuo Ishikura?"
Present.
Perfect posture!
"Marisol Marquez?"
Present.
No rumples.
No wrinkles.
Tug!
(Still rumpled)
(Still wrinkled)

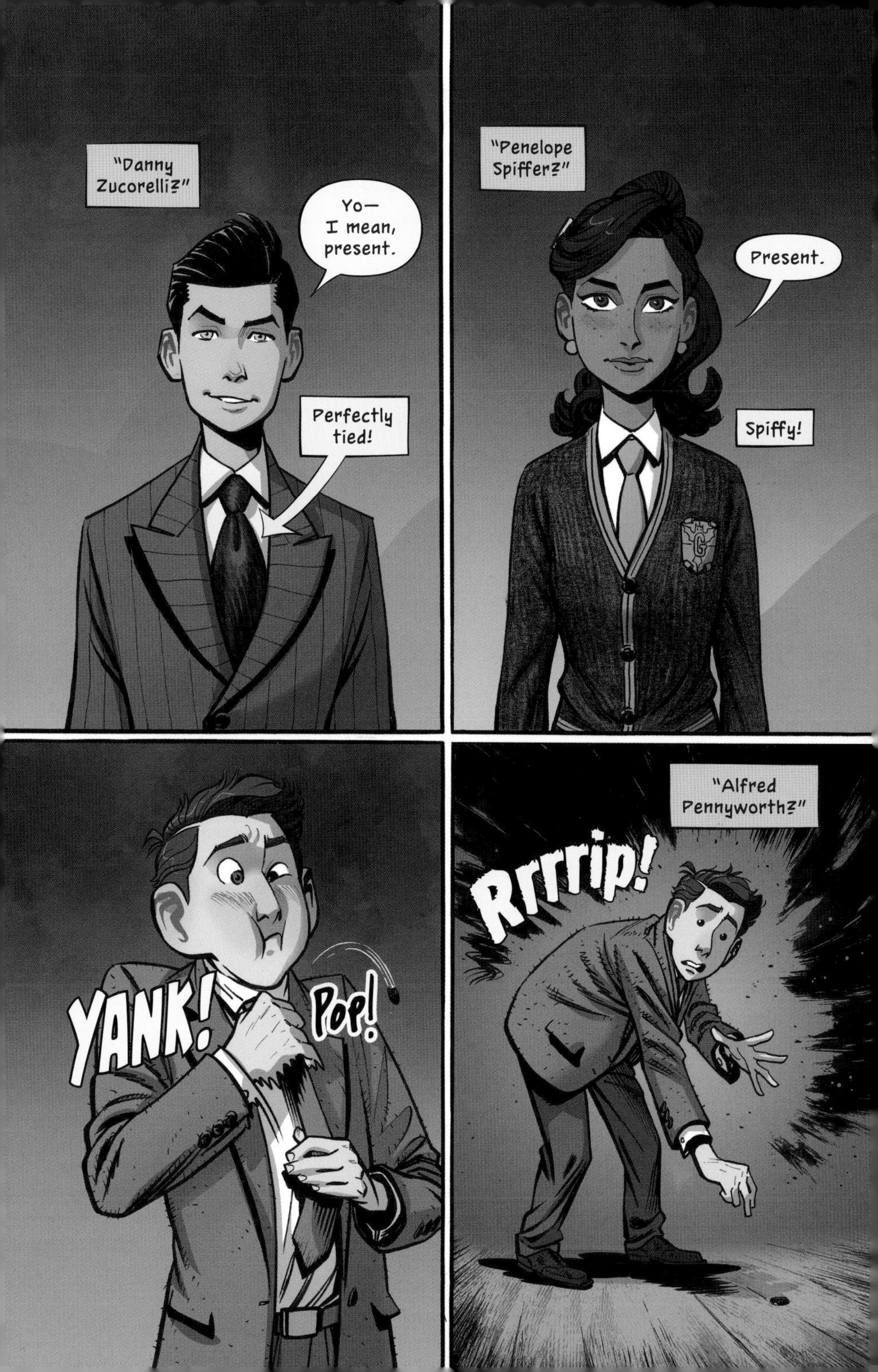
"Danny Zucorelli?"
Yo— I mean, present.
Perfectly tied!
"Penelope Spiffer?"
Present.
Spiffy!
YANK!
POP!
"Alfred Pennyworth?"
Rrrrip!

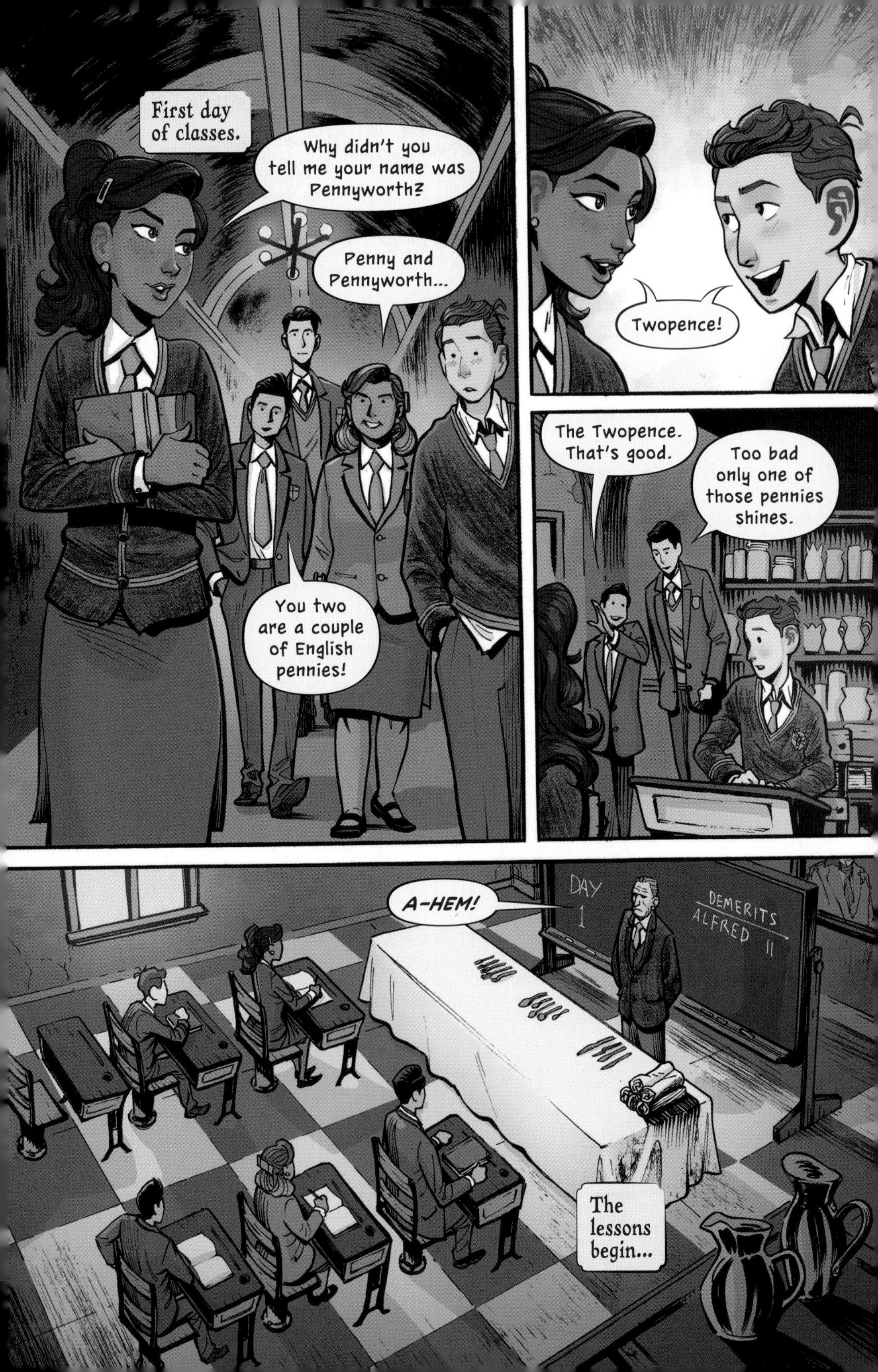
First day of classes.
Why didn't you tell me your name was Pennyworth?
Penny and Pennyworth...
You two are a couple of English pennies!
Twopence!
The Twopence. That's good.
Too bad only one of those pennies shines.
A-HEM!
DAY 1
DEMERITS
ALFRED II
The lessons begin...

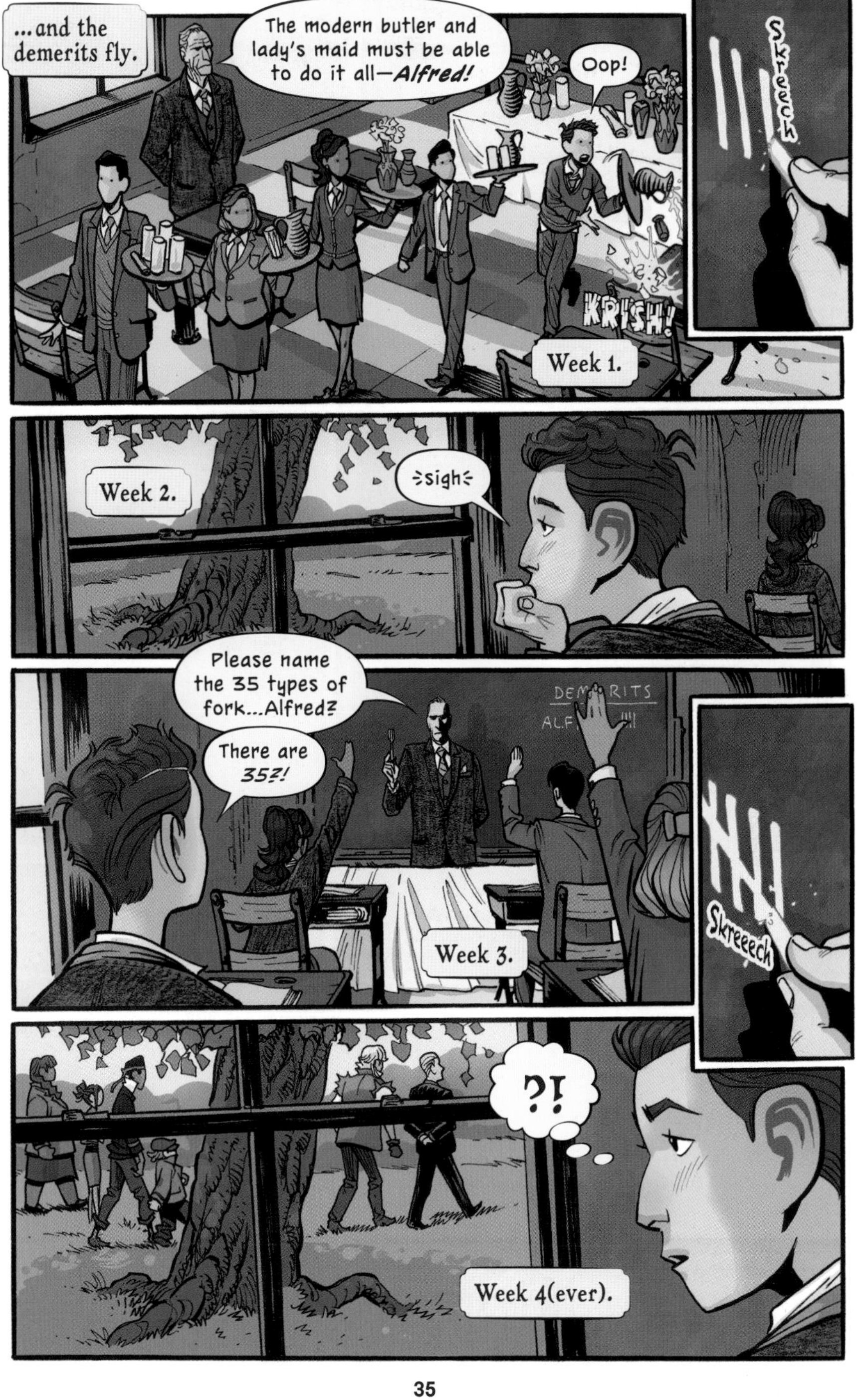
...and the demerits fly.
The modern butler and lady's maid must be able to do it all—*Alfred!*
Oop!
KRISH!
Week 1.
Skreech
Week 2.
sigh
Please name the 35 types of fork...Alfred?
There are *35?!*
DEMERITS
Week 3.
Skreeech
?!
Week 4(ever).

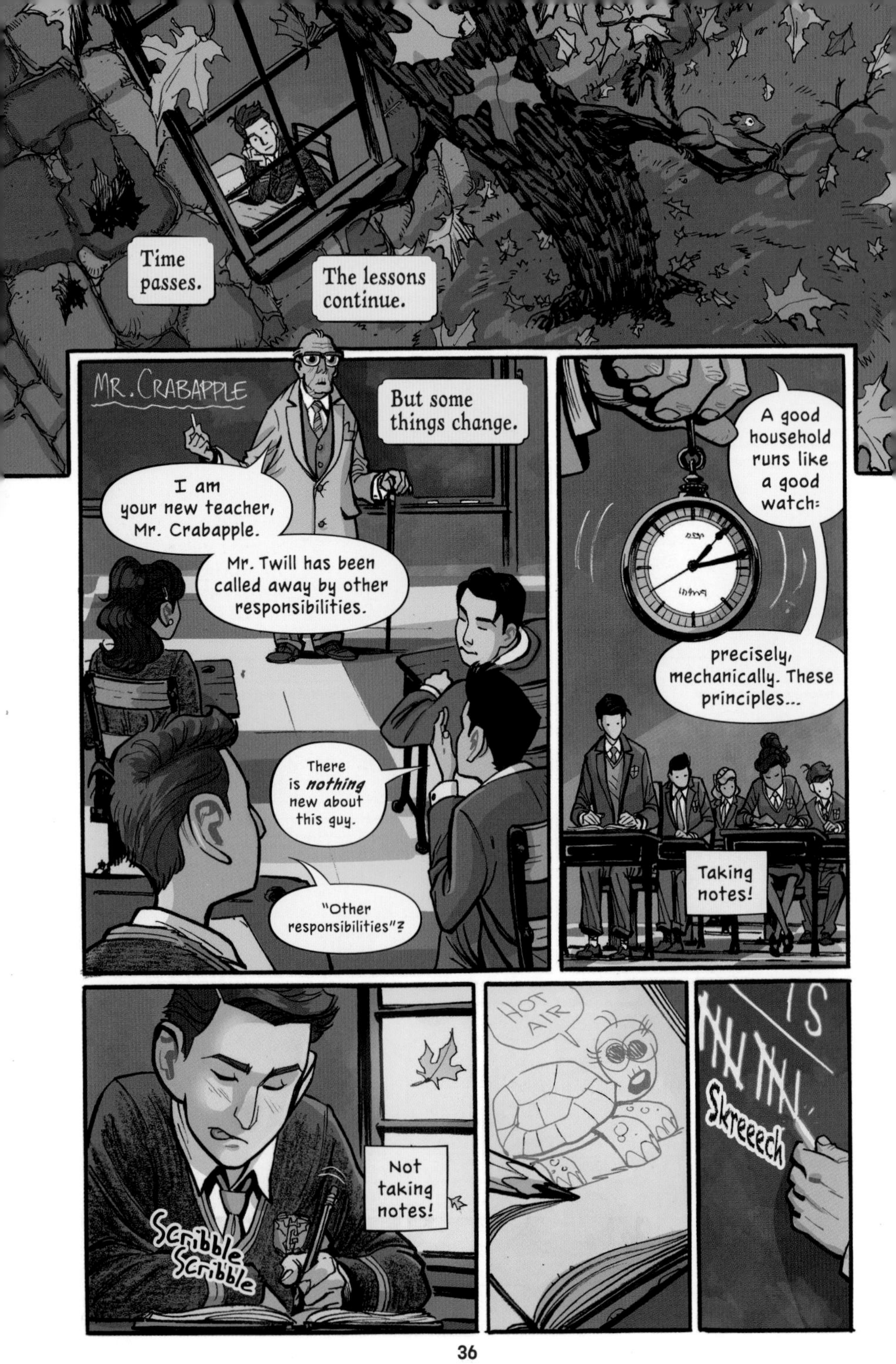
Time passes.
The lessons continue.
MR. CRABAPPLE
But some things change.
I am your new teacher, Mr. Crabapple.
Mr. Twill has been called away by other responsibilities.
There is *nothing* new about this guy.
"Other responsibilities"?
A good household runs like a good watch:
precisely, mechanically. These principles...
Taking notes!
Not taking notes!
Scribble Scribble
HOT AIR
IS
Skreeech

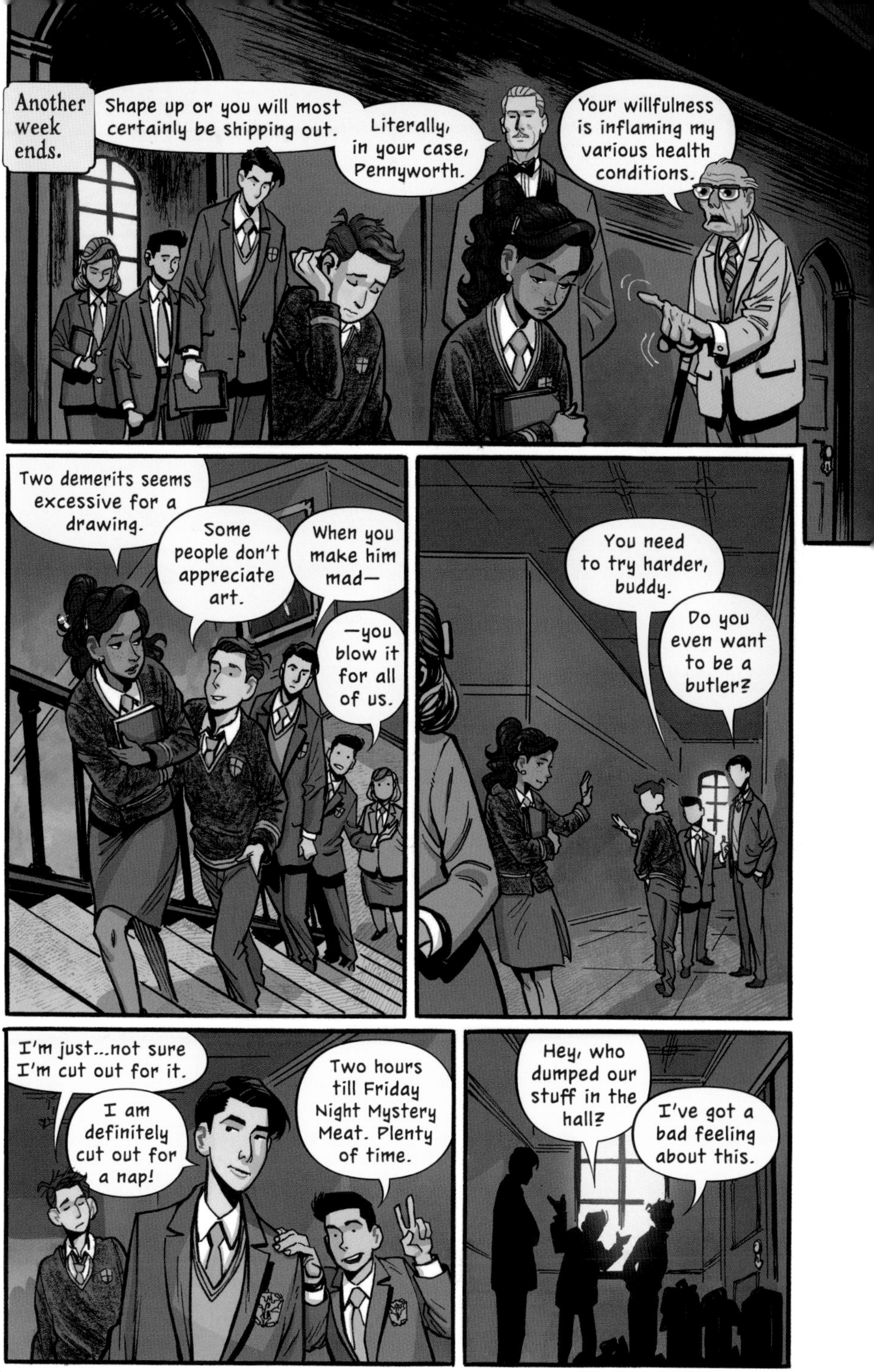
Another week ends.
Shape up or you will most certainly be shipping out.
Literally, in your case, Pennyworth.
Your willfulness is inflaming my various health conditions.
Two demerits seems excessive for a drawing.
Some people don't appreciate art.
When you make him mad—
—you blow it for all of us.
You need to try harder, buddy.
Do you even want to be a butler?
I'm just...not sure I'm cut out for it.
I am definitely cut out for a nap!
Two hours till Friday Night Mystery Meat. Plenty of time.
Hey, who dumped our stuff in the hall?
I've got a bad feeling about this.

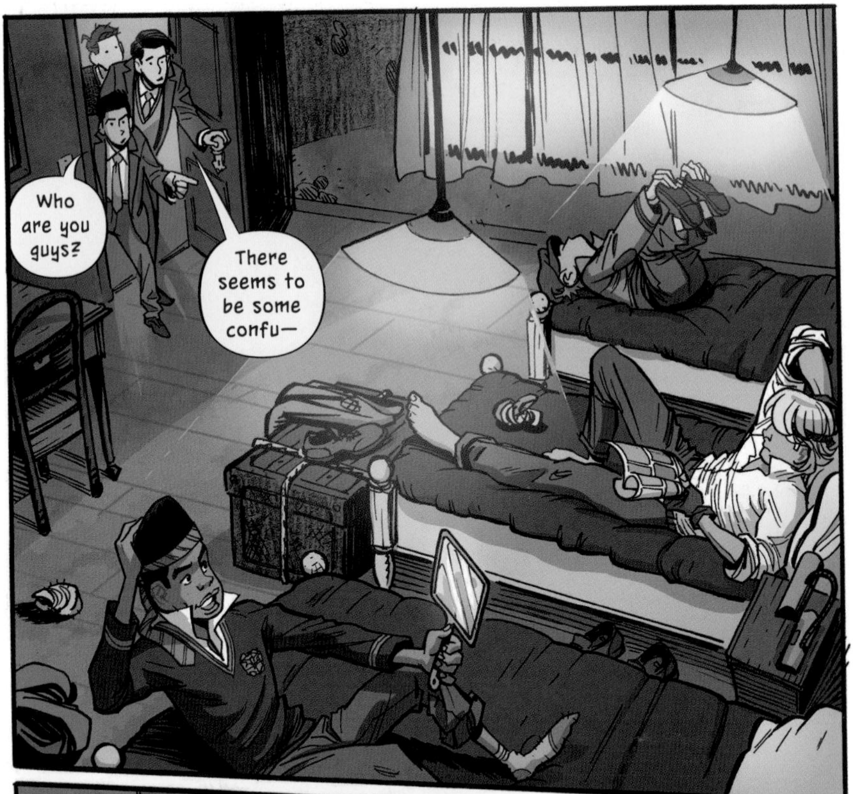
Who are you guys?
There seems to be some confu—

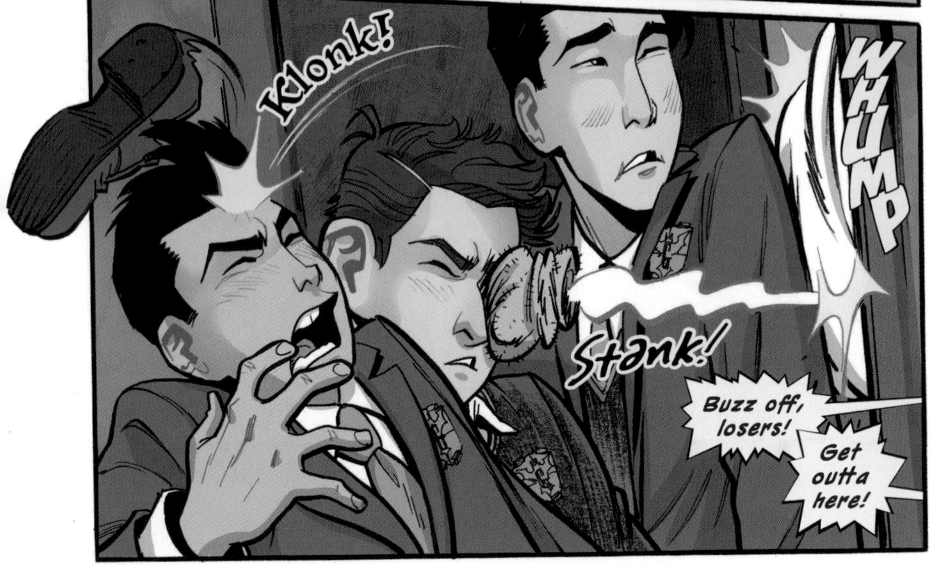
Klonk!
WHUMP
Stank!
Buzz off, losers!
Get outta here!

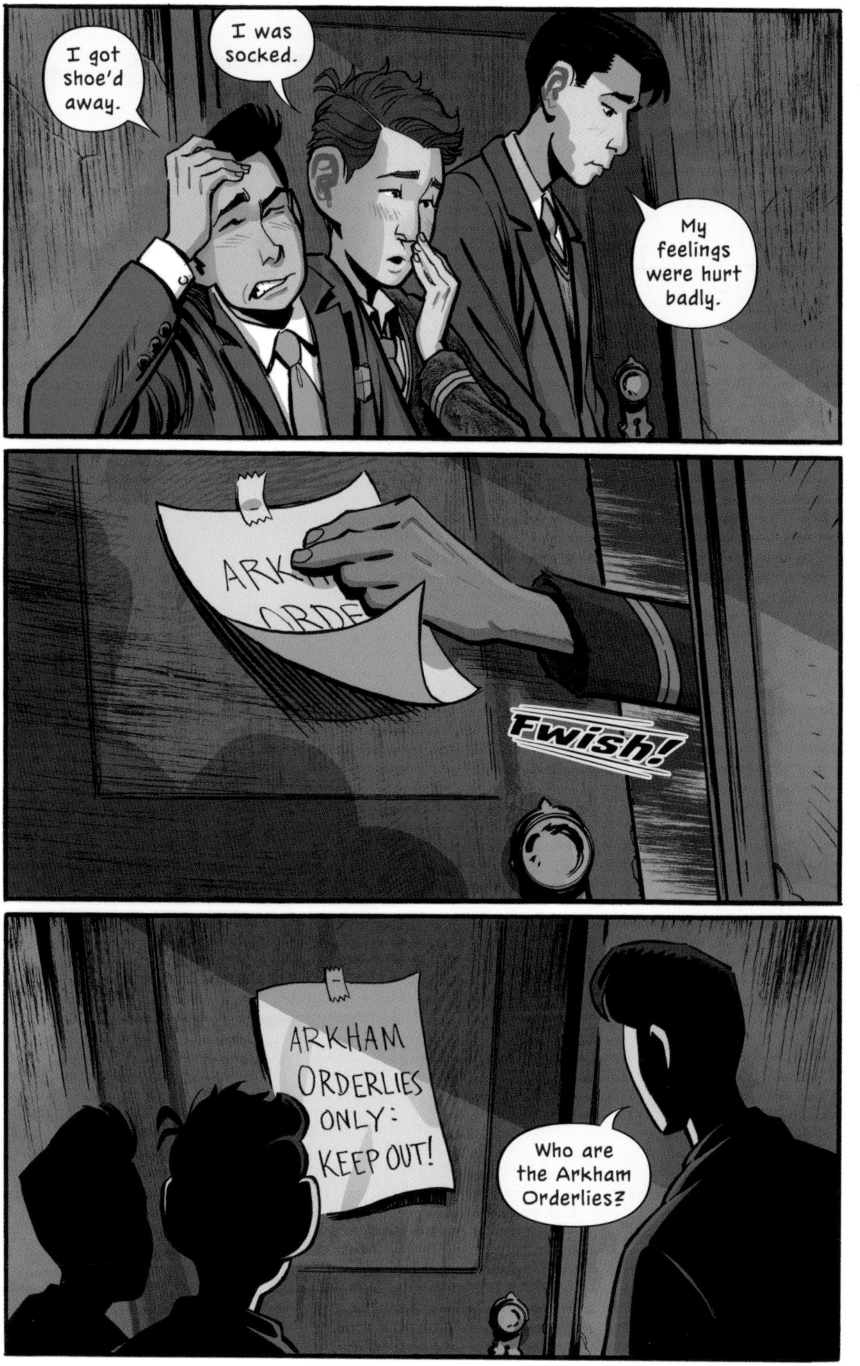
I got shoe'd away.
I was socked.
My feelings were hurt badly.
Fwish!
ARKHAM ORDERLIES ONLY: KEEP OUT!
Who are the Arkham Orderlies?

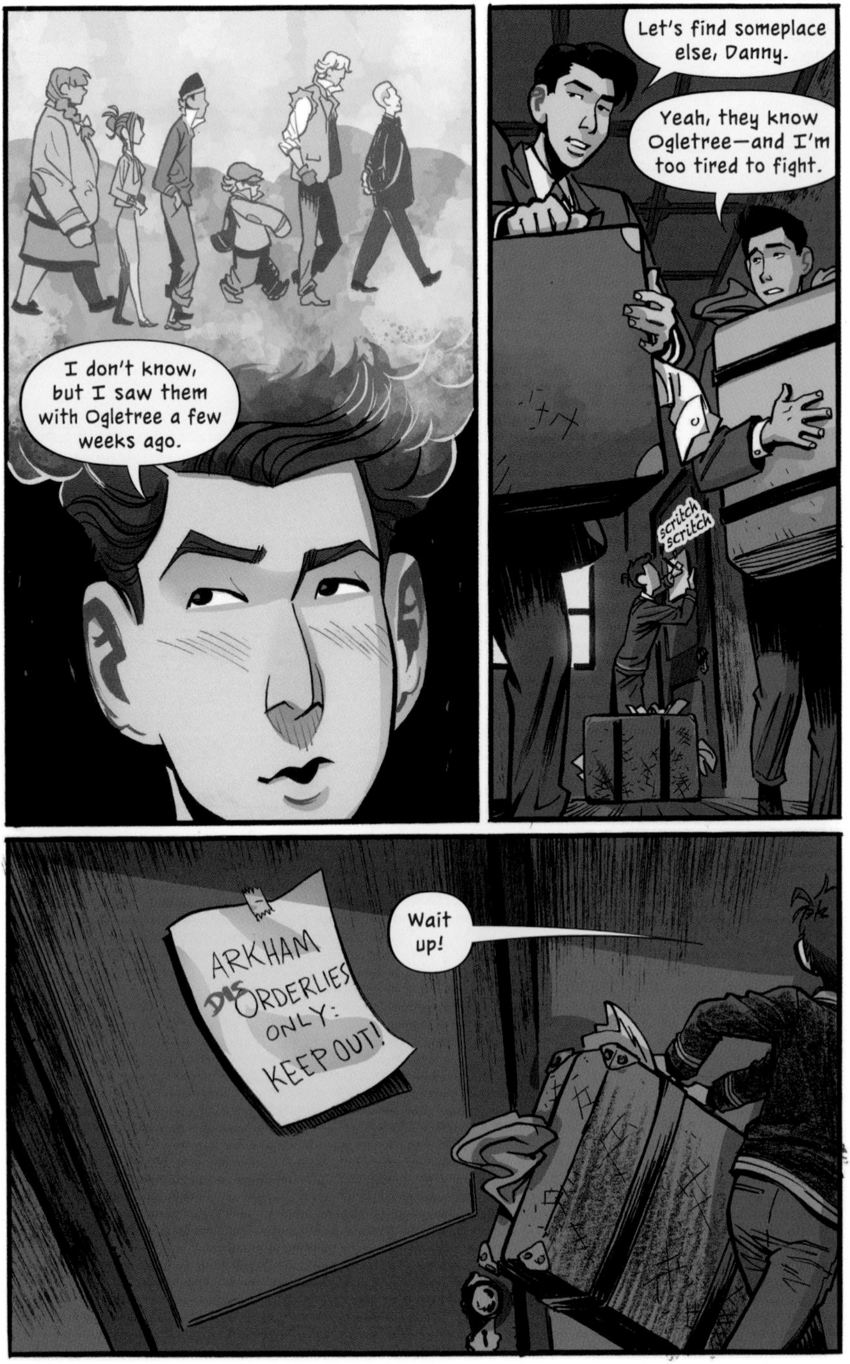
I don't know, but I saw them with Ogletree a few weeks ago.
Let's find someplace else, Danny.
Yeah, they know Ogletree—and I'm too tired to fight.
scritch scritch
ARKHAM DIS ORDERLIES ONLY: KEEP OUT!
Wait up!

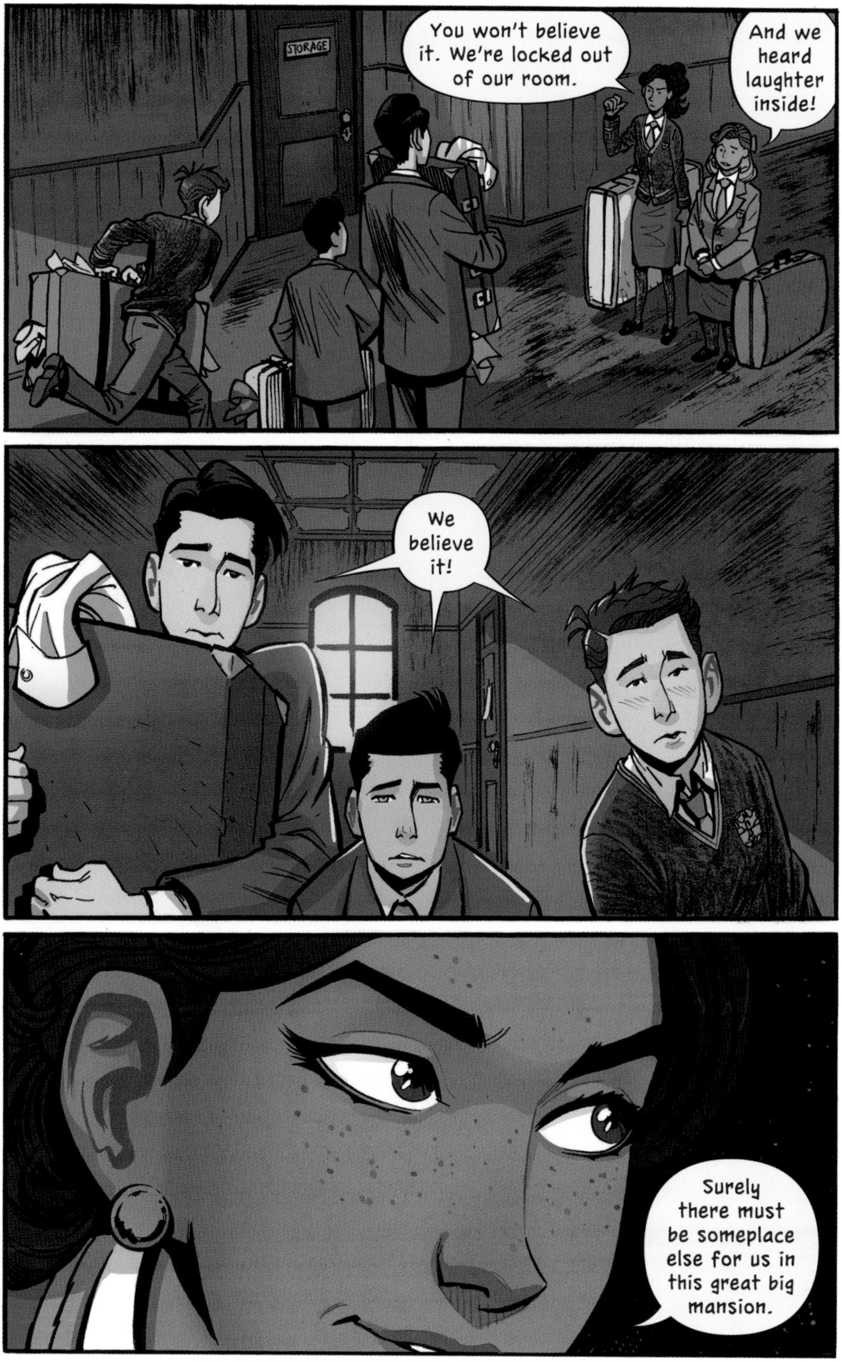
STORAGE
You won't believe it. We're locked out of our room.
And we heard laughter inside!
We believe it!
Surely there must be someplace else for us in this great big mansion.

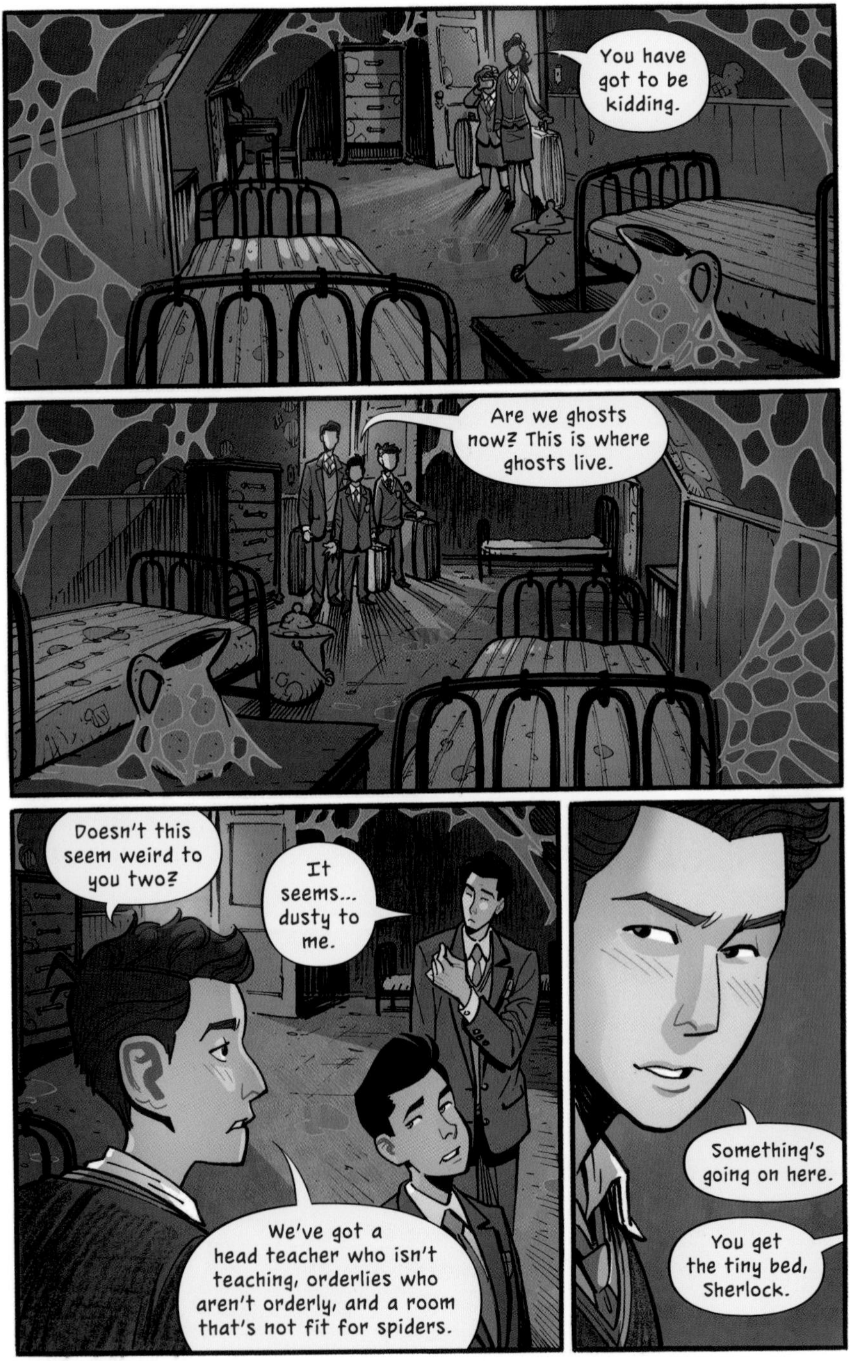

You have got to be kidding.
Are we ghosts now? This is where ghosts live.
Doesn't this seem weird to you two?
It seems... dusty to me.
We've got a head teacher who isn't teaching, orderlies who aren't orderly, and a room that's not fit for spiders.
Something's going on here.
You get the tiny bed, Sherlock.

CHAPTER 4
Teatime!

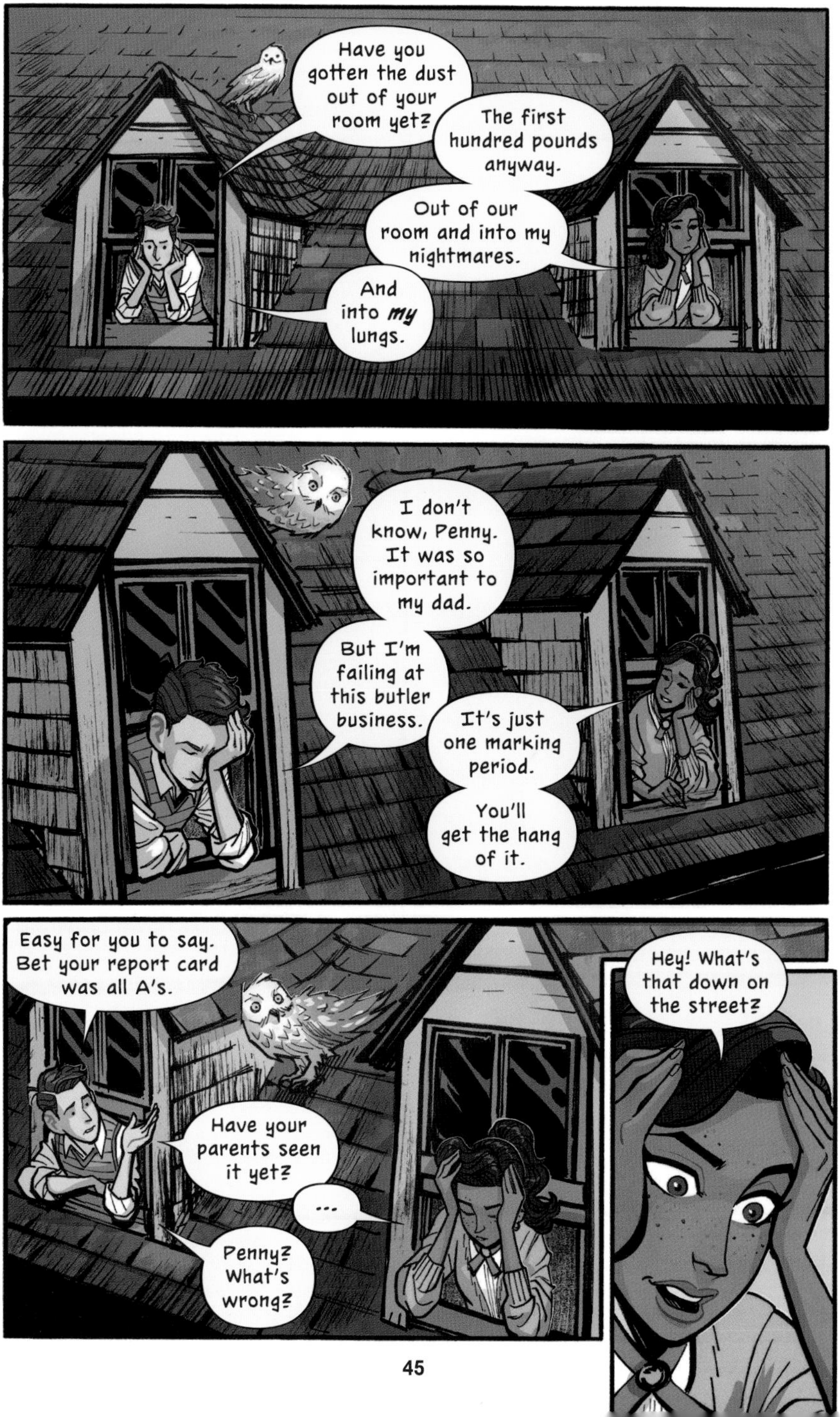
Have you gotten the dust out of your room yet?
The first hundred pounds anyway.
Out of our room and into my nightmares.
And into *my* lungs.
I don't know, Penny. It was so important to my dad.
But I'm failing at this butler business.
It's just one marking period.
You'll get the hang of it.
Easy for you to say. Bet your report card was all A's.
Have your parents seen it yet?
...
Penny? What's wrong?
Hey! What's that down on the street?

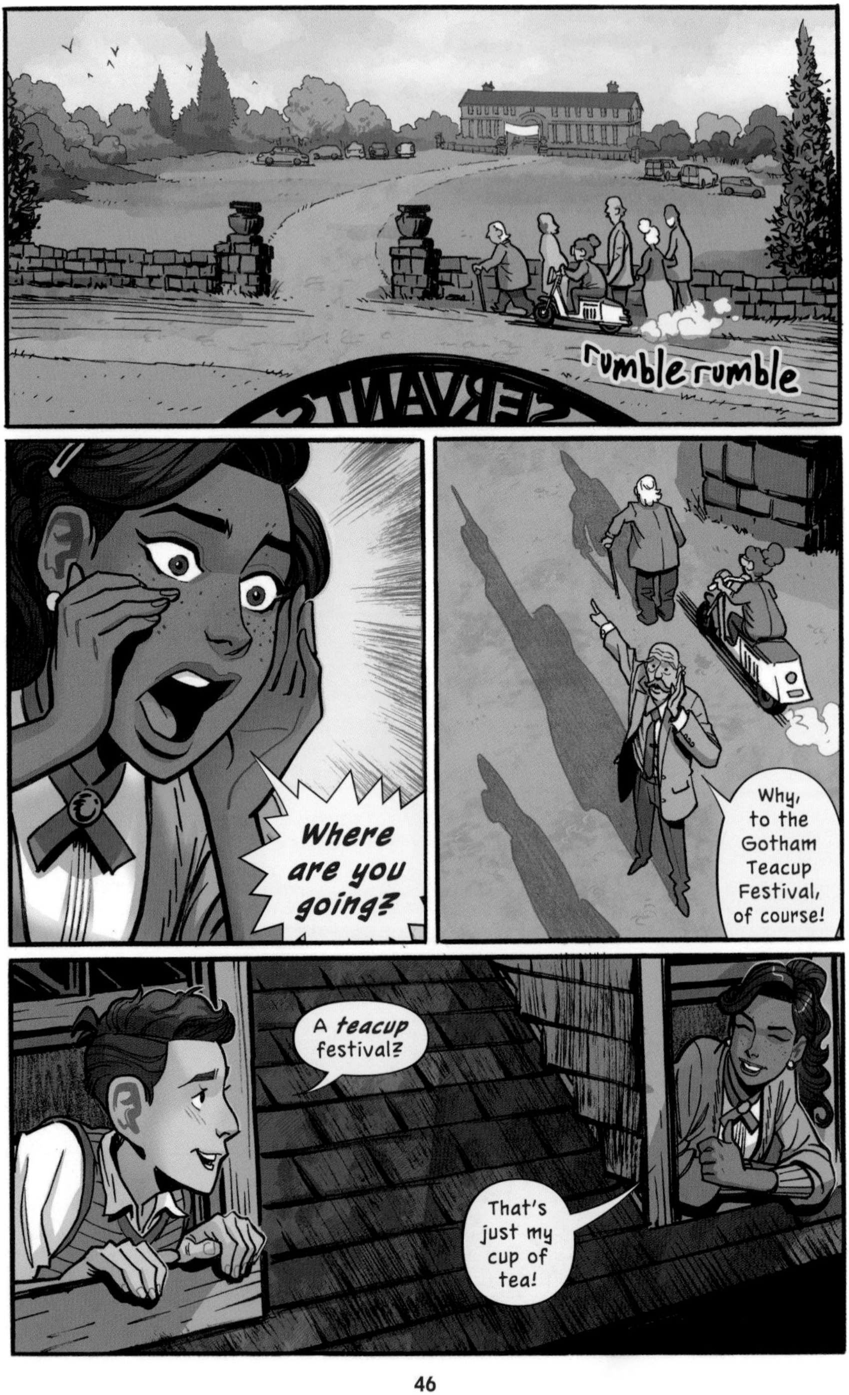
rumble rumble
Where are you going?
Why, to the Gotham Teacup Festival, of course!
A teacup festival?
That's just my cup of tea!

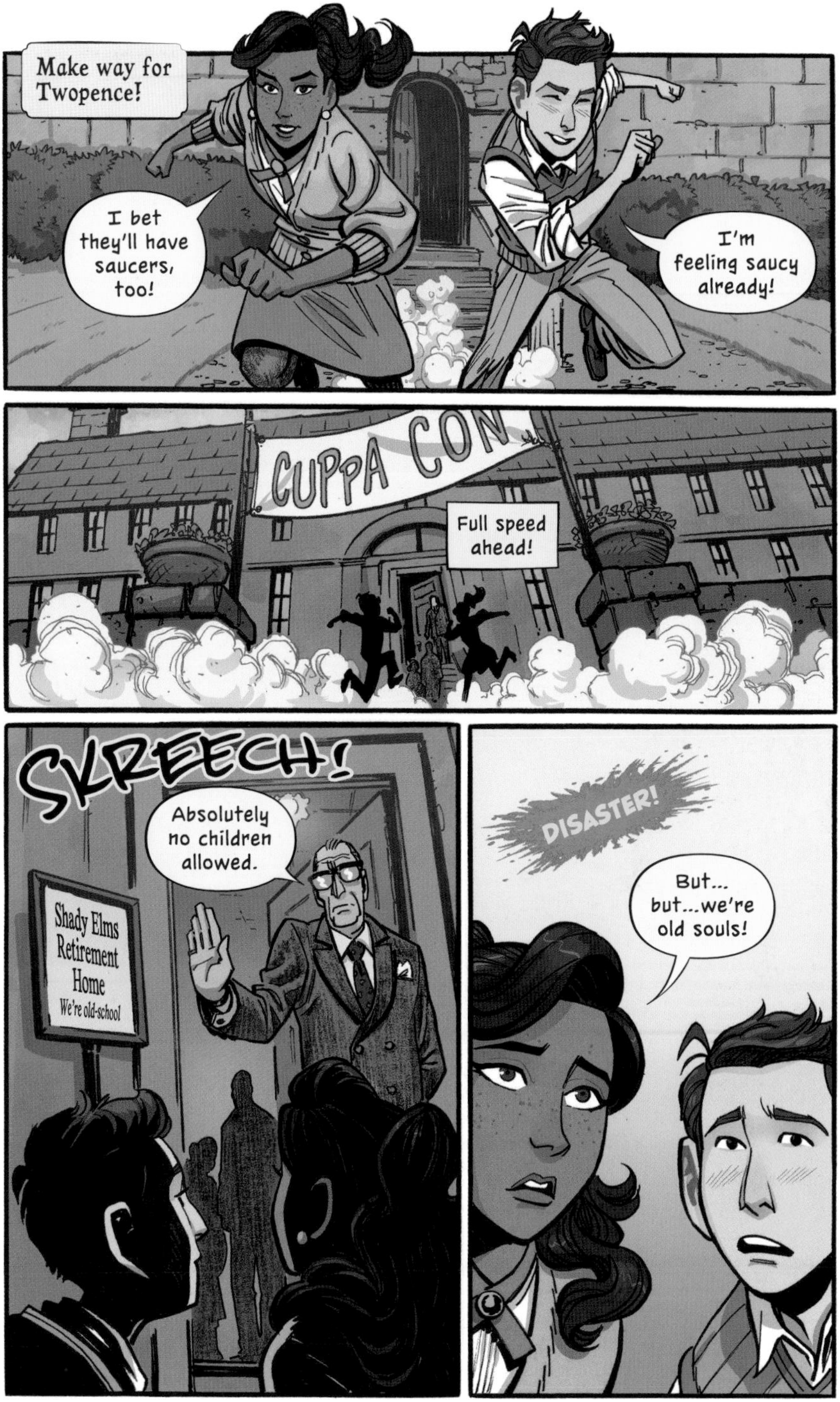
Make way for Twopence!
I bet they'll have saucers, too!
I'm feeling saucy already!
CUPPA CON
Full speed ahead!
SKREECH!
Absolutely no children allowed.
Shady Elms Retirement Home We're old-school
DISASTER!
But... but...we're old souls!

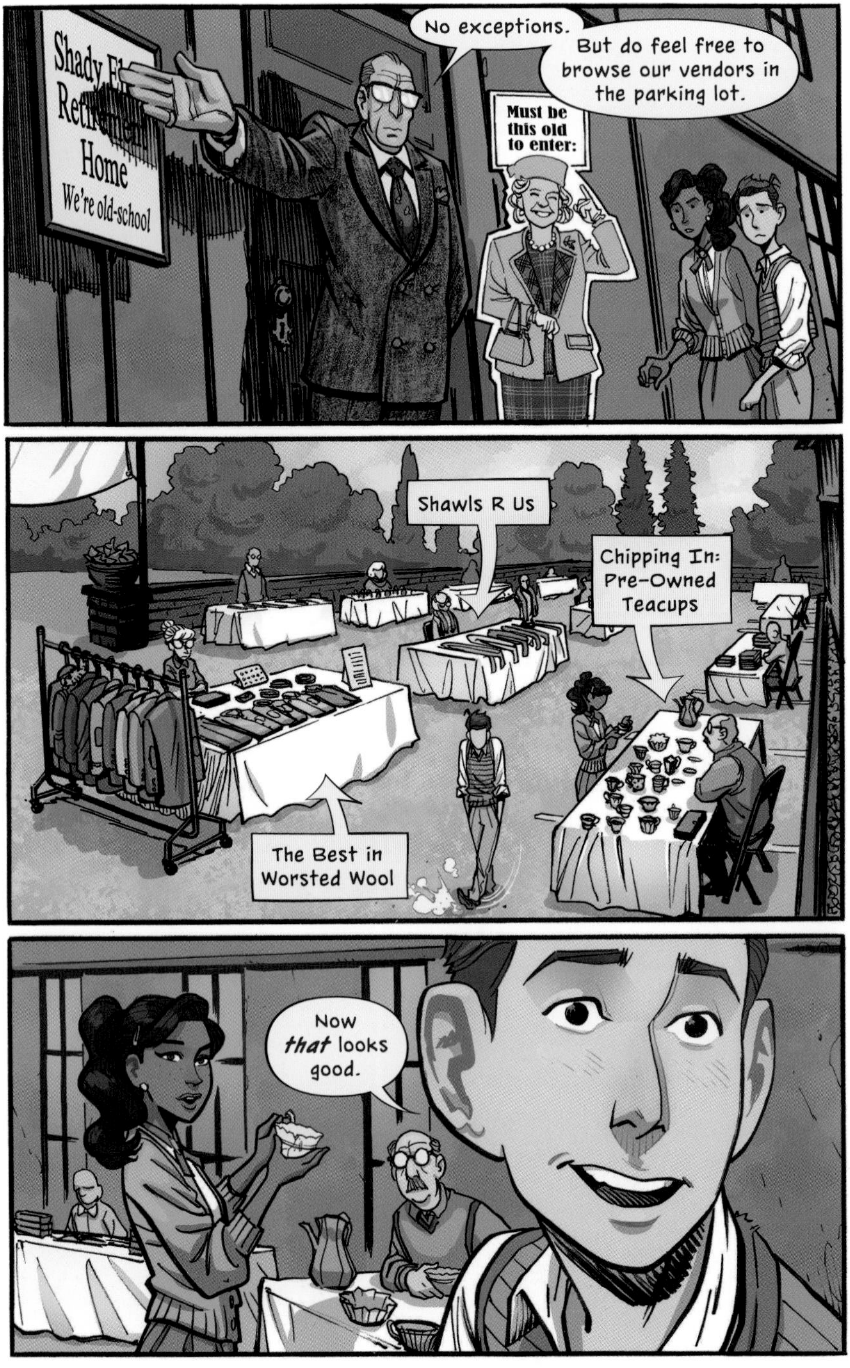
Shady
Home
We're old-school
No exceptions.
But do feel free to browse our vendors in the parking lot.
Must be this old to enter:
Shawls R Us
Chipping In: Pre-Owned Teacups
The Best in Worsted Wool
Now *that* looks good.

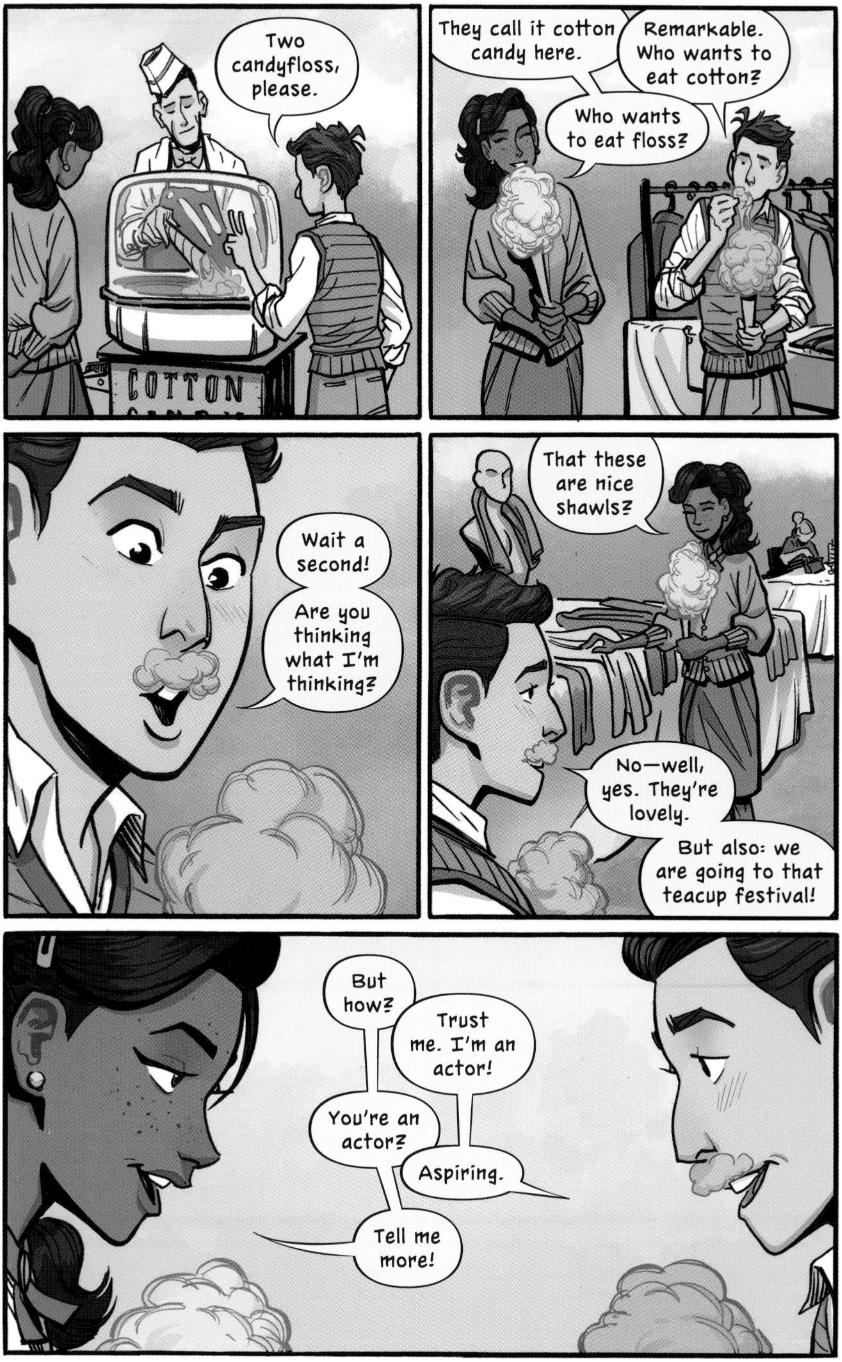

Two candyfloss, please.
COTTON
They call it cotton candy here.
Remarkable. Who wants to eat cotton?
Who wants to eat floss?
Wait a second!
Are you thinking what I'm thinking?
That these are nice shawls?
No—well, yes. They're lovely.
But also: we are going to that teacup festival!
But how?
Trust me. I'm an actor!
You're an actor?
Aspiring.
Tell me more!

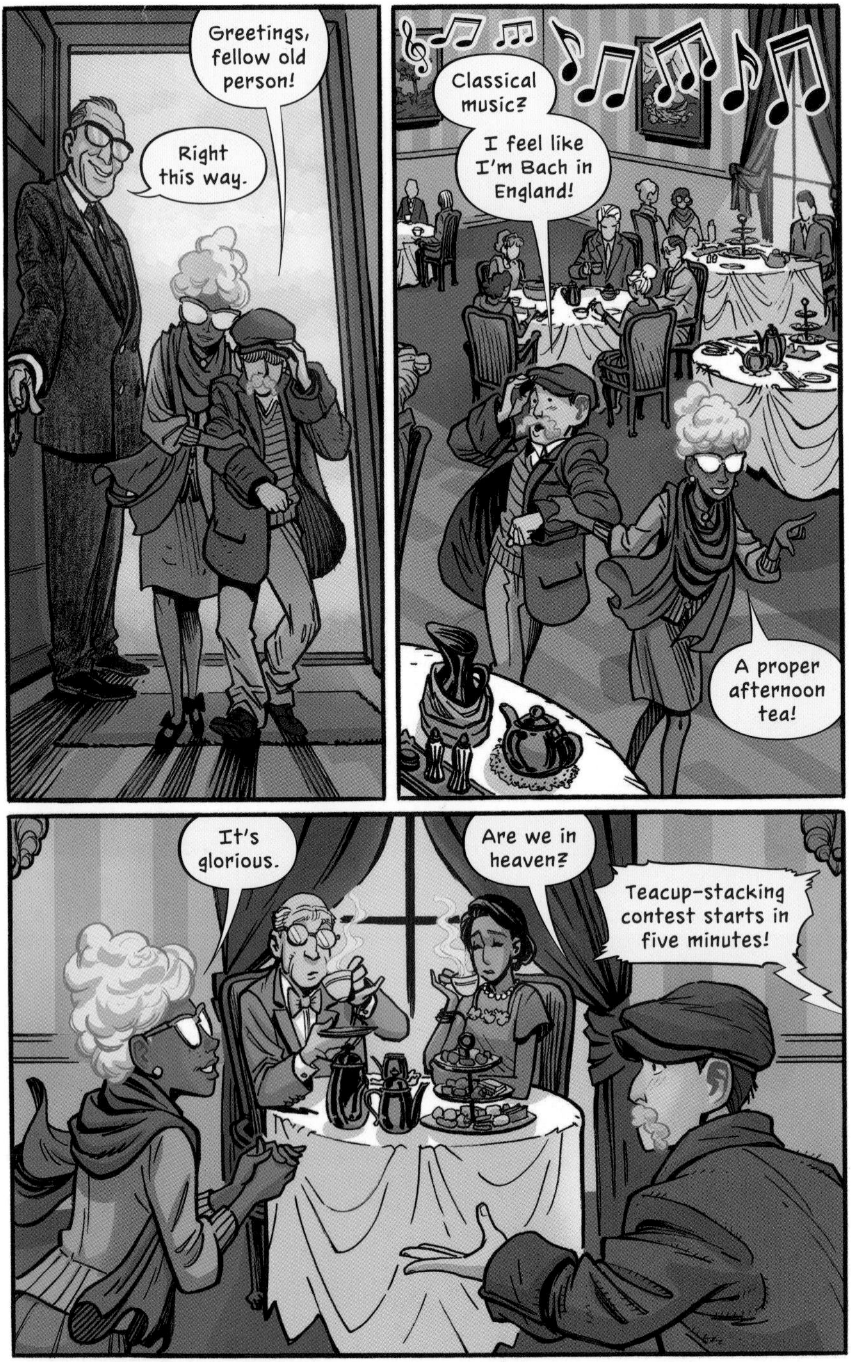
Greetings, fellow old person!
Right this way.
Classical music?
I feel like I'm Bach in England!
A proper afternoon tea!
It's glorious.
Are we in heaven?
Teacup-stacking contest starts in five minutes!

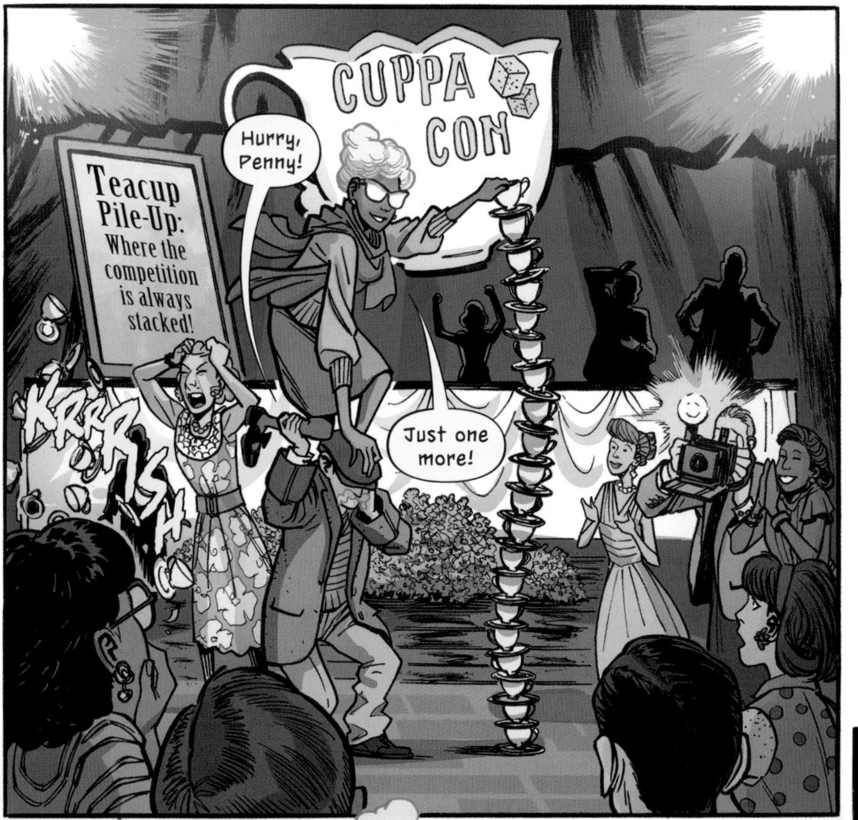
CUPPA CON
Teacup Pile-Up: Where the competition is always stacked!
Hurry, Penny!
KRRR RISH
Just one more!

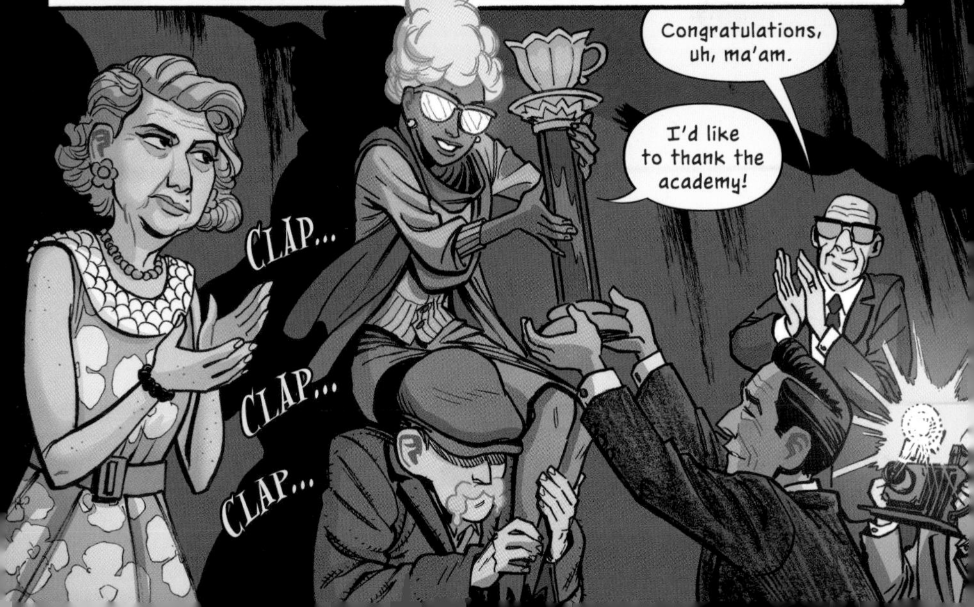
Congratulations, uh, ma'am.
I'd like to thank the academy!
CLAP...
CLAP...
CLAP...

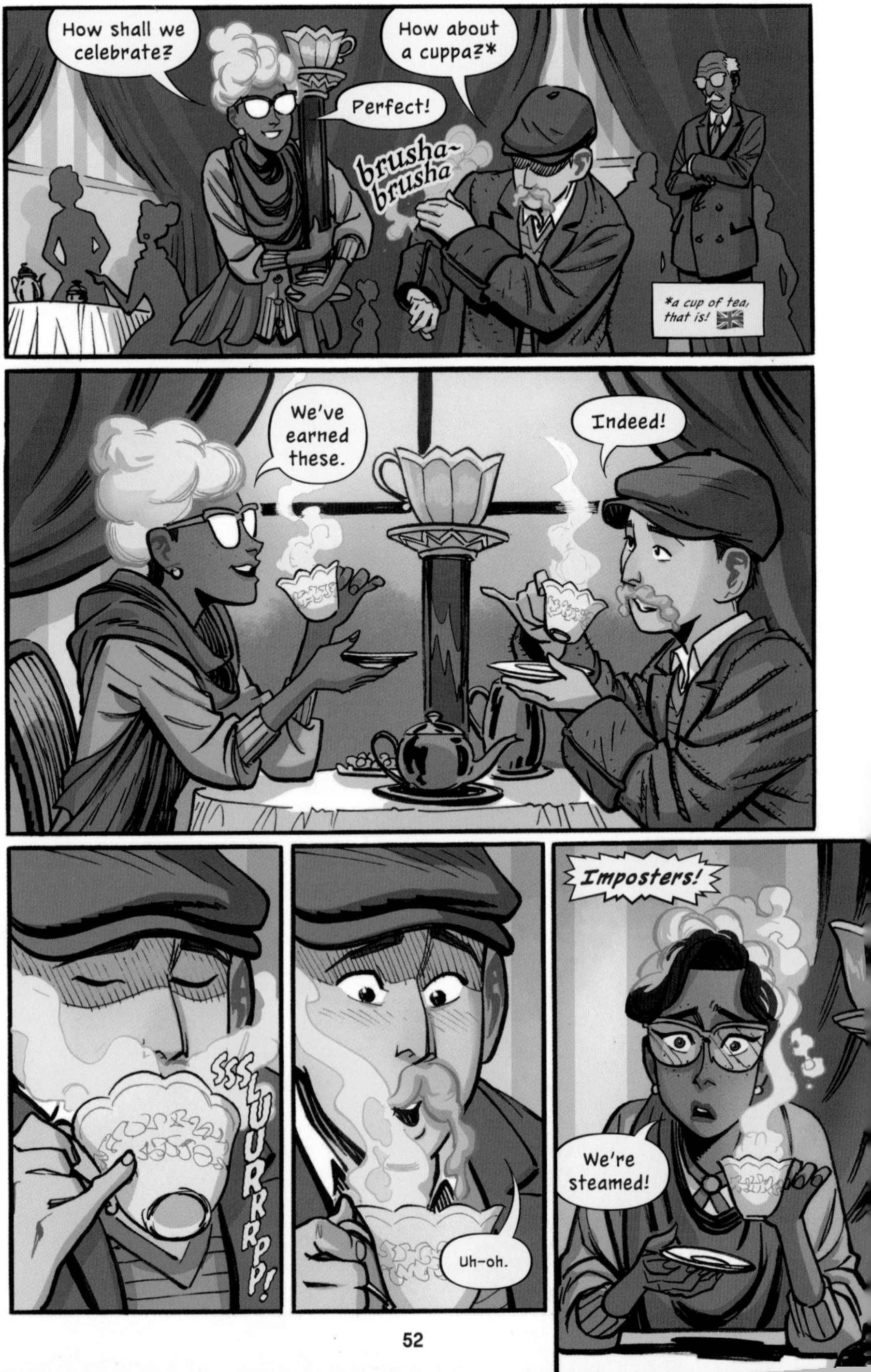
How shall we celebrate?
How about a cuppa?*
Perfect!
brusha-brusha
*a cup of tea, that is!
We've earned these.
Indeed!
SSSLURRRPP!
Uh-oh.
Imposters!
We're steamed!

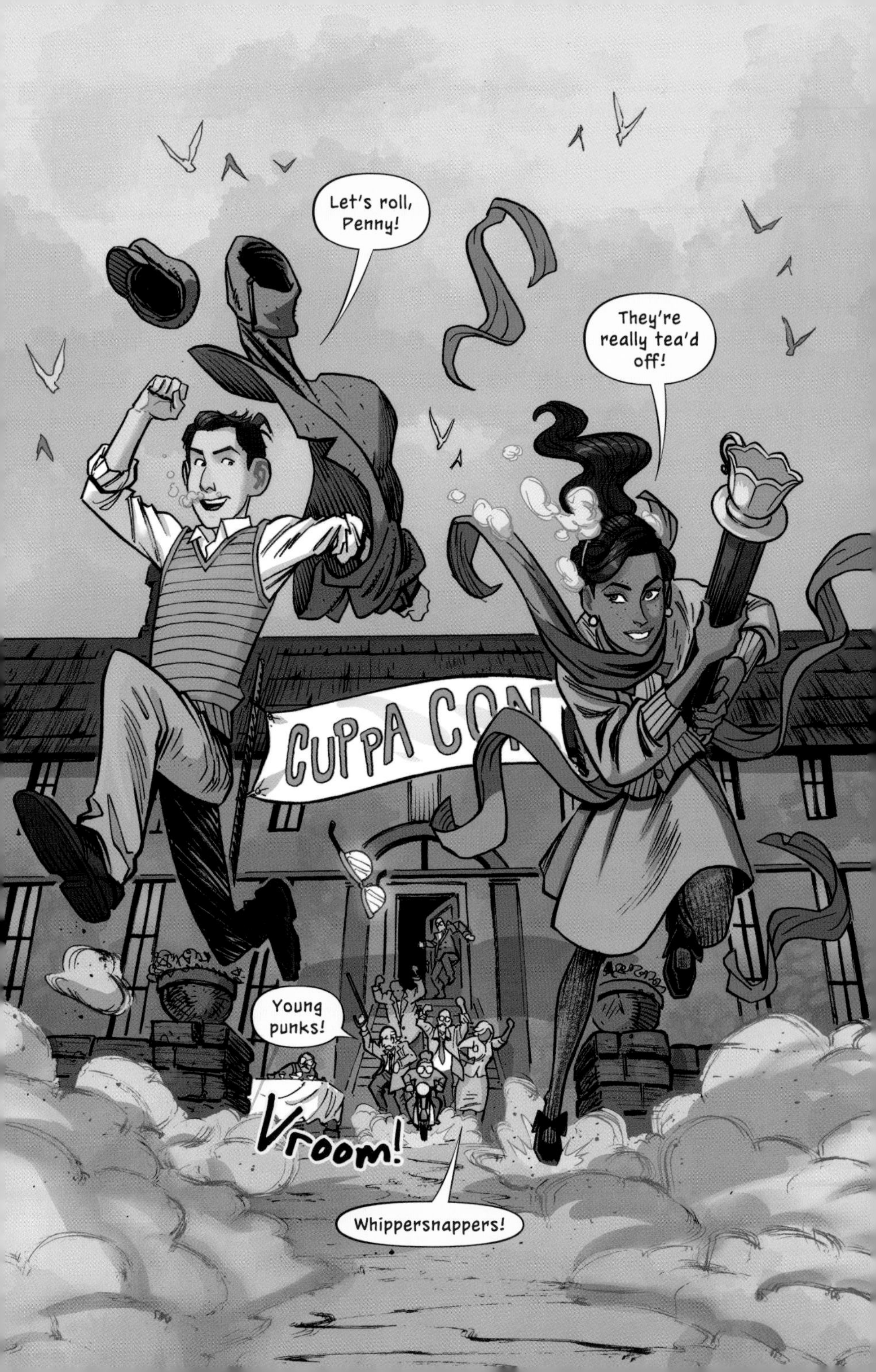
Let's roll, Penny!
They're really tea'd off!
CUPPA CON
Young punks!
Vroom!
Whippersnappers!

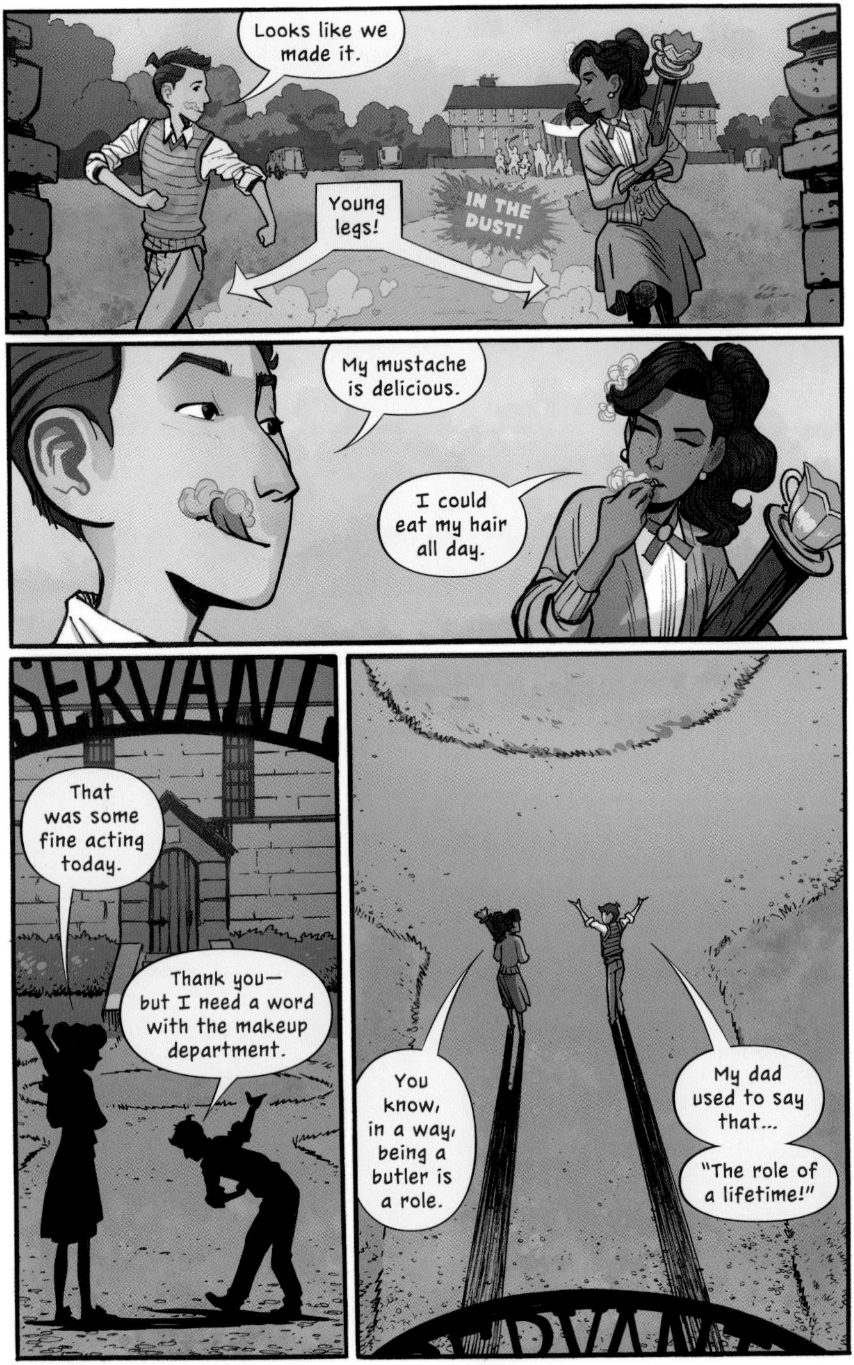
Looks like we made it.
IN THE DUST!
Young legs!
My mustache is delicious.
I could eat my hair all day.
SERVANT
That was some fine acting today.
Thank you— but I need a word with the makeup department.
You know, in a way, being a butler is a role.
My dad used to say that...
"The role of a lifetime!"

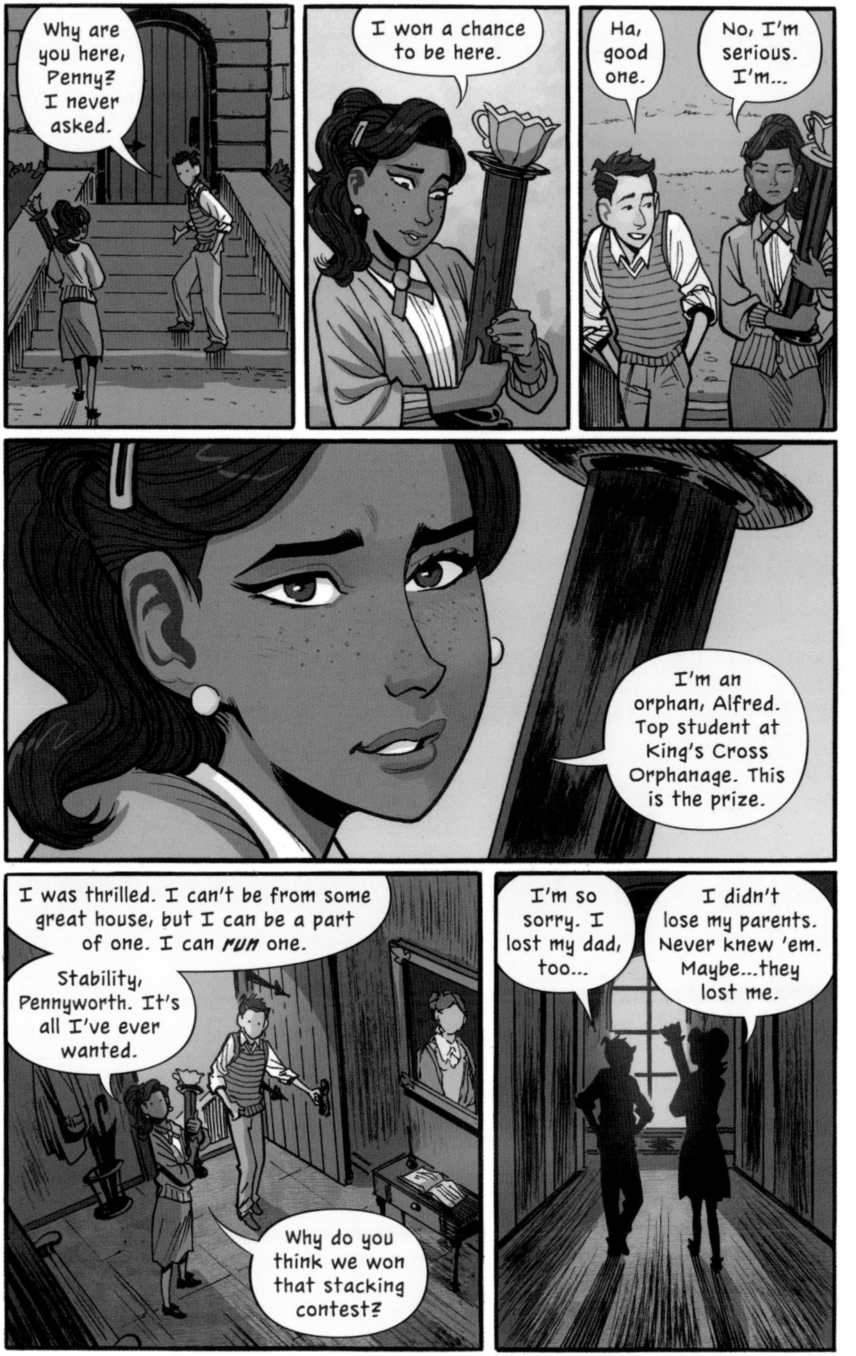
Why are you here, Penny? I never asked.
I won a chance to be here.
Ha, good one.
No, I'm serious. I'm...
I'm an orphan, Alfred. Top student at King's Cross Orphanage. This is the prize.
I was thrilled. I can't be from some great house, but I can be a part of one. I can *run* one.
Stability, Pennyworth. It's all I've ever wanted.
Why do you think we won that stacking contest?
I'm so sorry. I lost my dad, too...
I didn't lose my parents. Never knew 'em. Maybe...they lost me.

CHAPTER 5
"What's a
Pennyworth?"

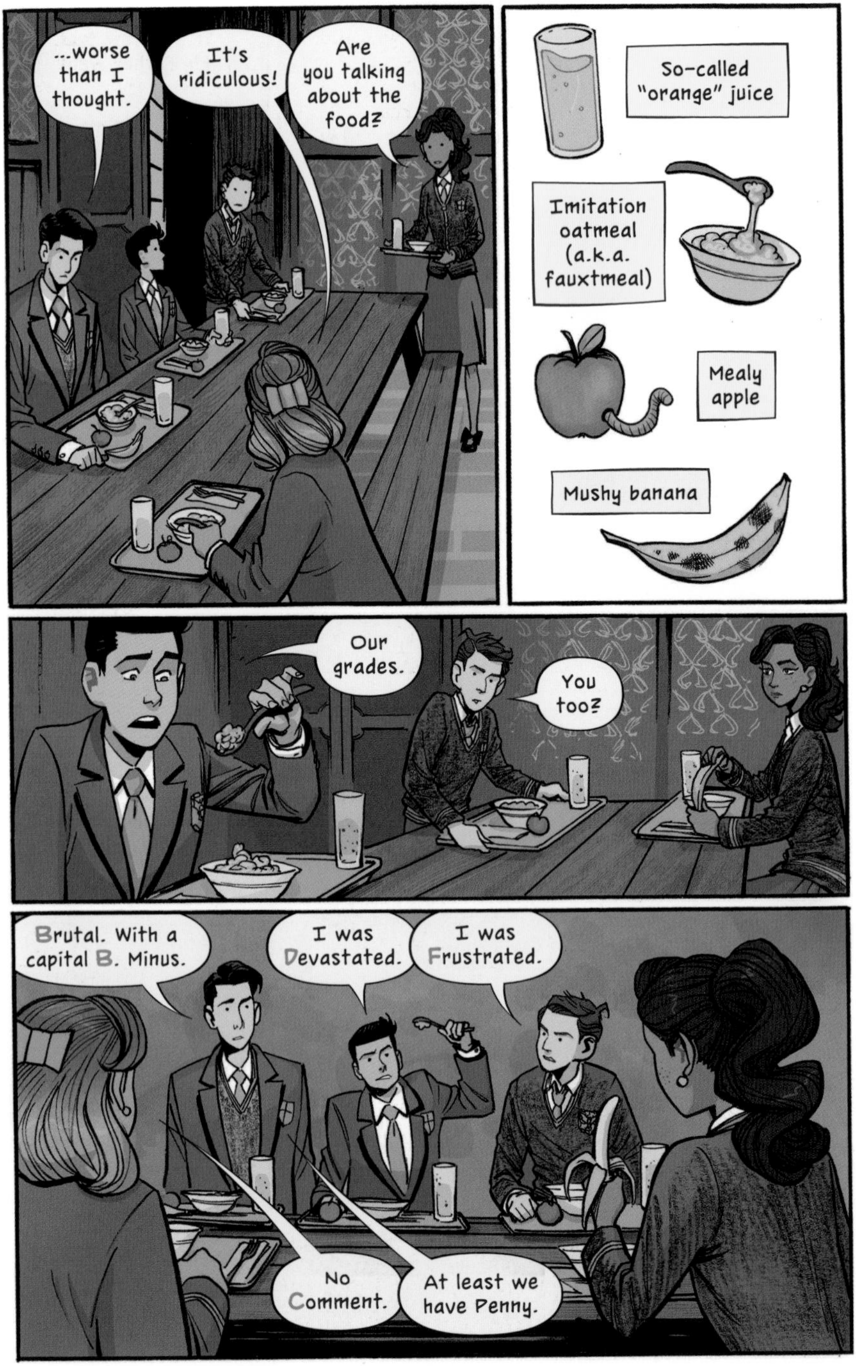
...worse than I thought.
It's ridiculous!
Are you talking about the food?
So-called "orange" juice
Imitation oatmeal (a.k.a. fauxtmeal)
Mealy apple
Mushy banana
Our grades.
You too?
Brutal. With a capital B. Minus.
I was Devastated.
I was Frustrated.
No Comment.
At least we have Penny.

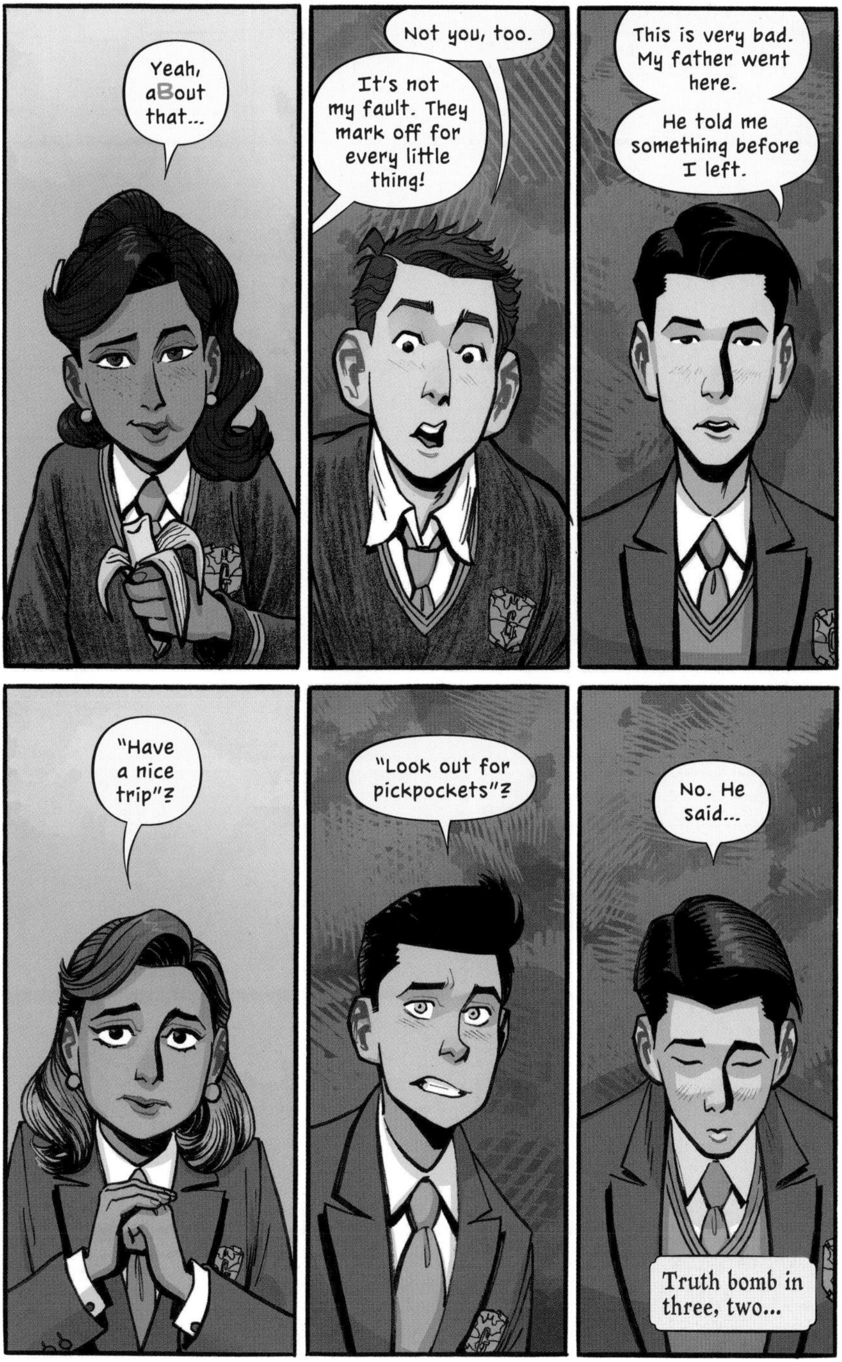
Yeah, aBout that...
Not you, too.
It's not my fault. They mark off for every little thing!
This is very bad. My father went here.
He told me something before I left.
"Have a nice trip"?
"Look out for pickpockets"?
No. He said...
Truth bomb in three, two...

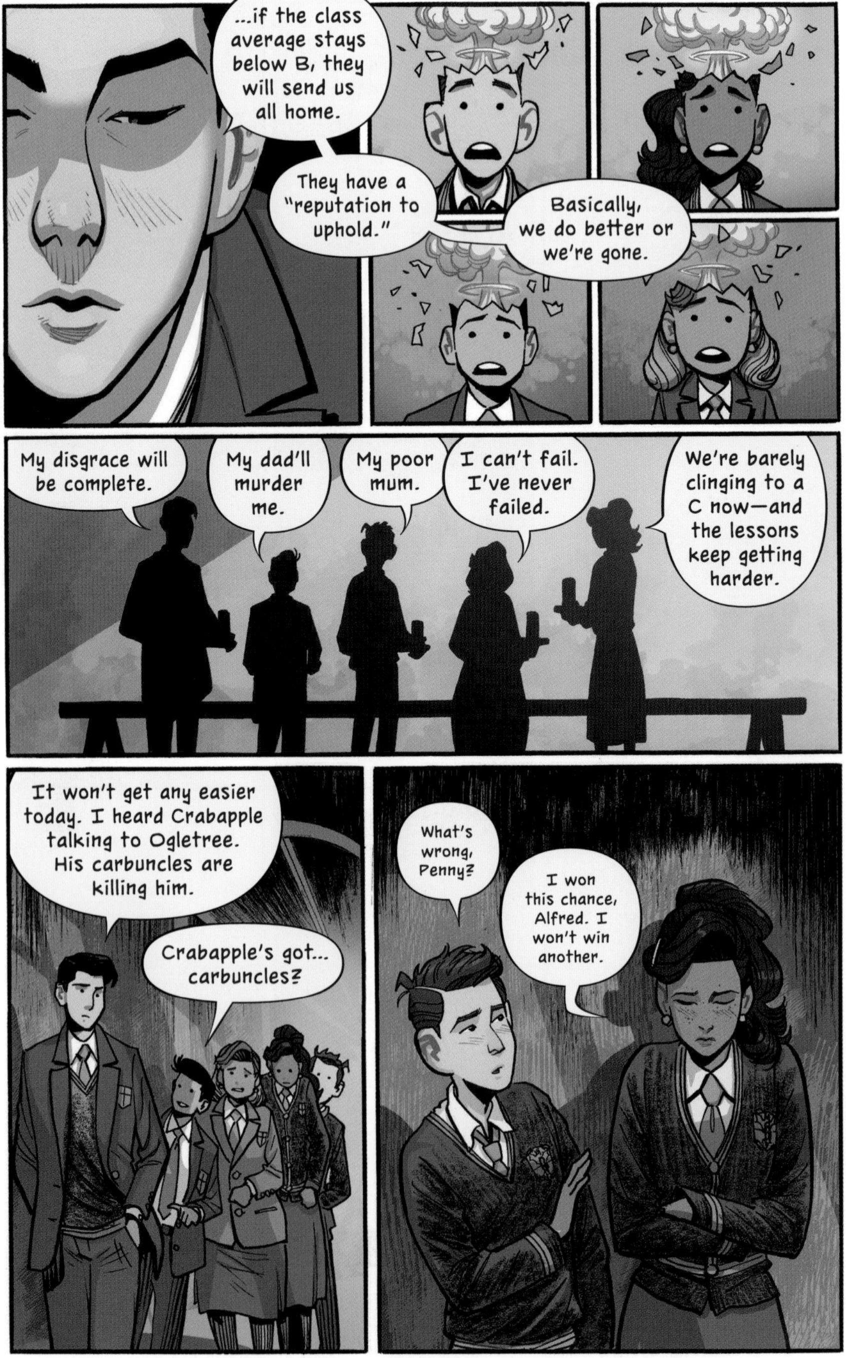
...if the class average stays below B, they will send us all home.
They have a "reputation to uphold."
Basically, we do better or we're gone.
My disgrace will be complete.
My dad'll murder me.
My poor mum.
I can't fail. I've never failed.
We're barely clinging to a C now—and the lessons keep getting harder.
It won't get any easier today. I heard Crabapple talking to Ogletree. His carbuncles are killing him.
Crabapple's got... carbuncles?
What's wrong, Penny?
I won this chance, Alfred. I won't win another.

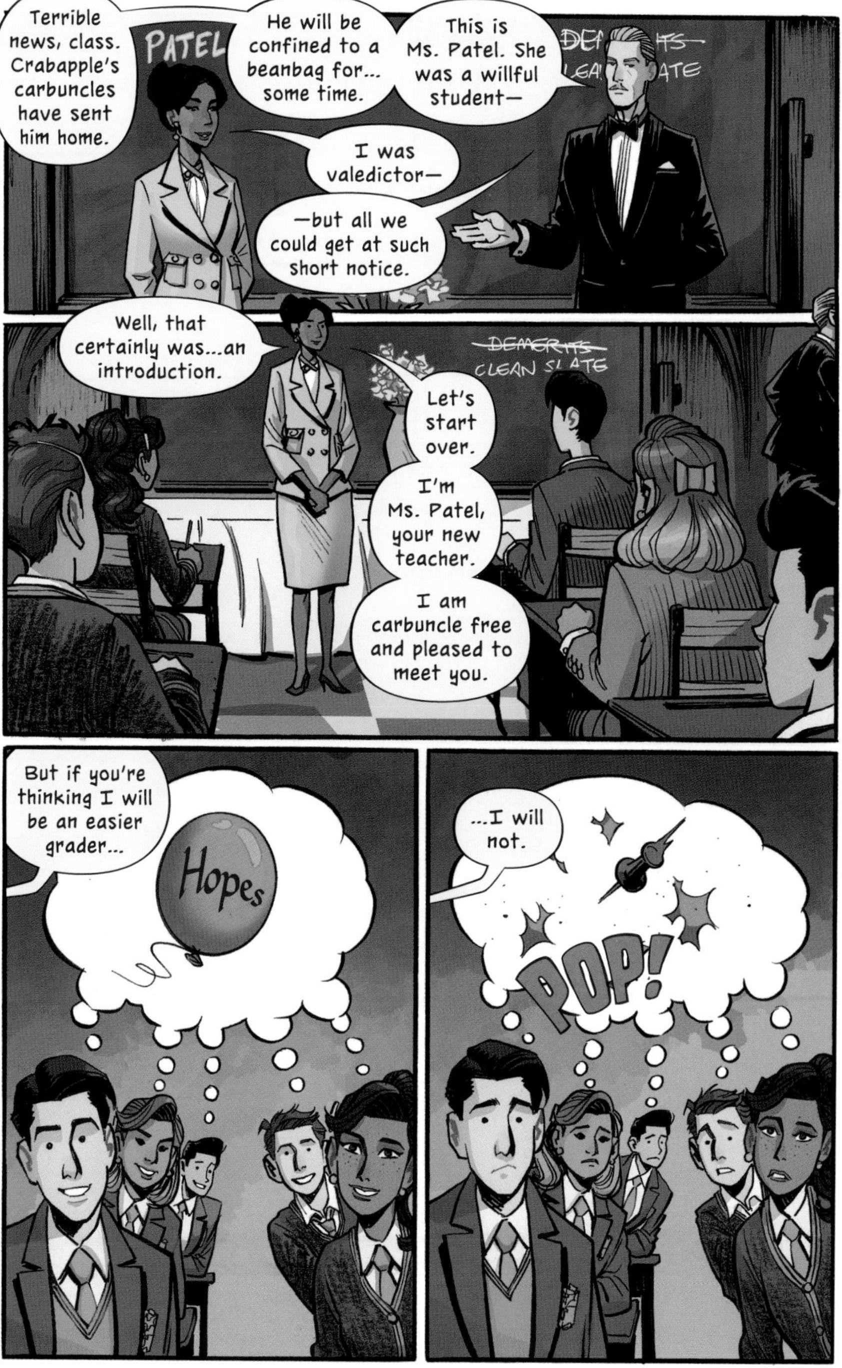

Terrible news, class. Crabapple's carbuncles have sent him home.
He will be confined to a beanbag for... some time.
This is Ms. Patel. She was a willful student—
I was valedictor—
—but all we could get at such short notice.
PATEL
DEMERITS
CLEAN SLATE
Well, that certainly was...an introduction.
Let's start over.
I'm Ms. Patel, your new teacher.
I am carbuncle free and pleased to meet you.
But if you're thinking I will be an easier grader...
Hopes
...I will not.
POP!

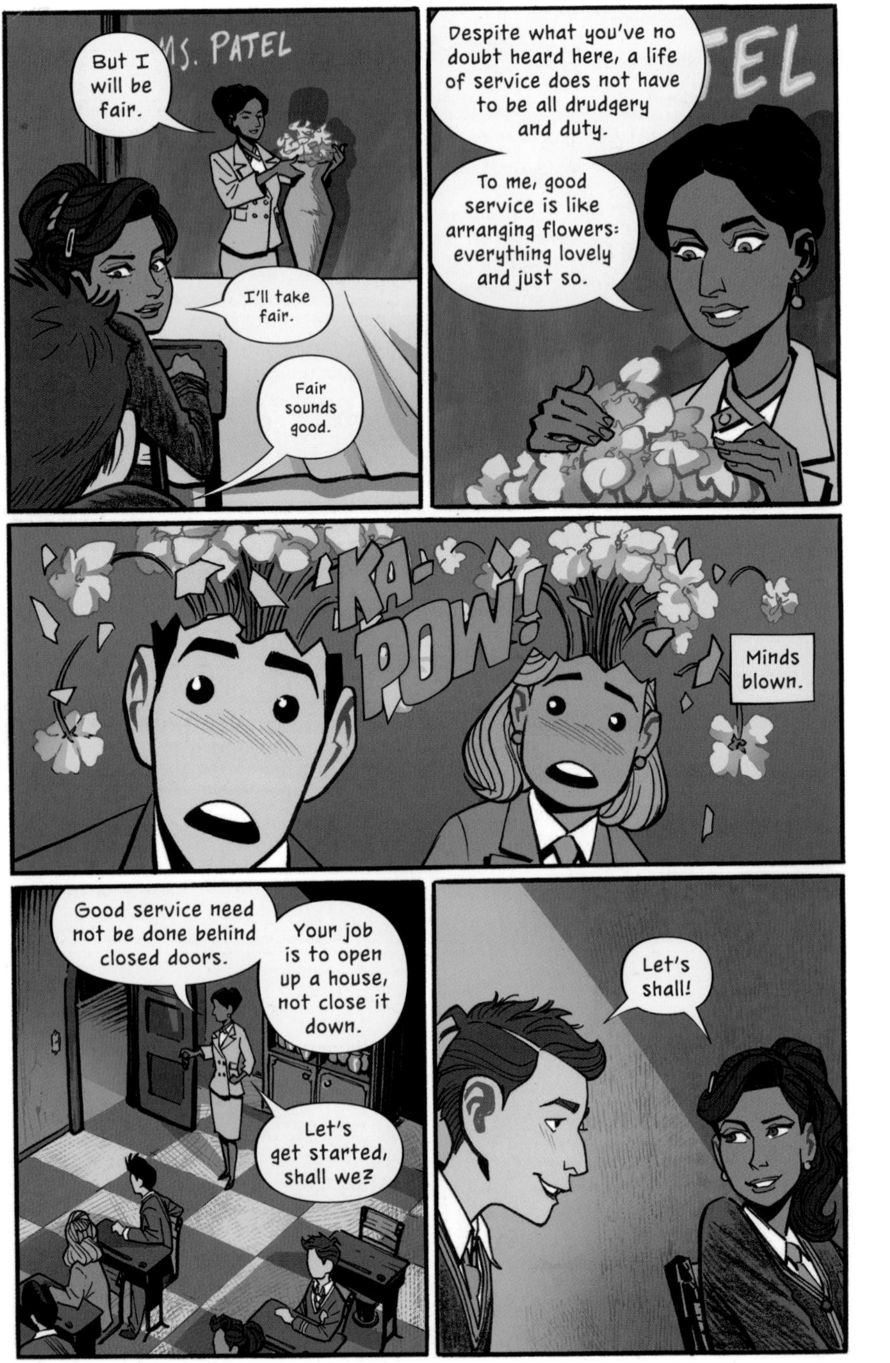
MS. PATEL
But I will be fair.
I'll take fair.
Fair sounds good.
Despite what you've no doubt heard here, a life of service does not have to be all drudgery and duty.
To me, good service is like arranging flowers: everything lovely and just so.
KA-POW!
Minds blown.
Good service need not be done behind closed doors.
Your job is to open up a house, not close it down.
Let's get started, shall we?
Let's shall!

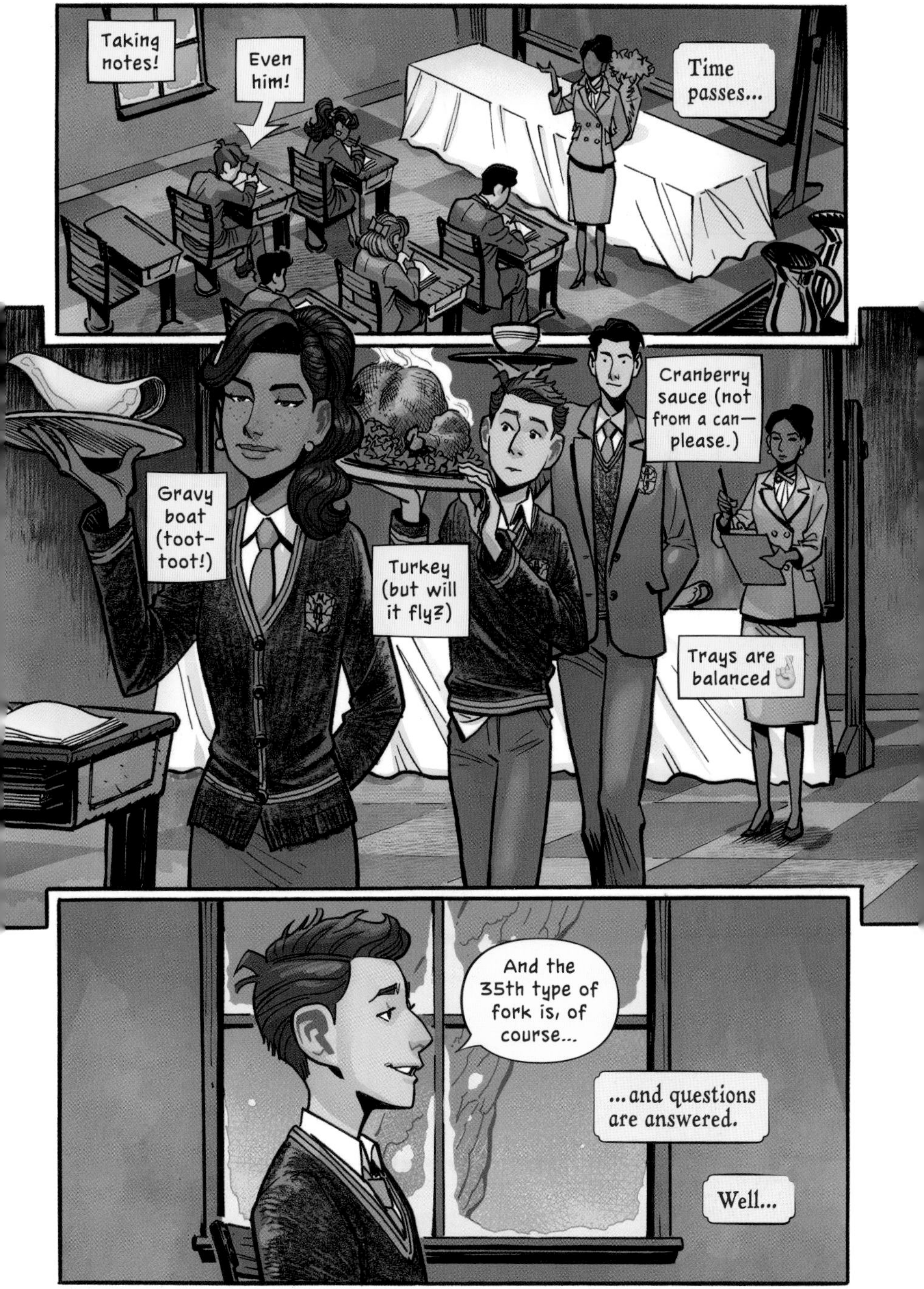
Taking notes!
Even him!
Time passes...
Gravy boat (toot-toot!)
Turkey (but will it fly?)
Cranberry sauce (not from a can—please.)
Trays are balanced
And the 35th type of fork is, of course...
...and questions are answered.
Well...

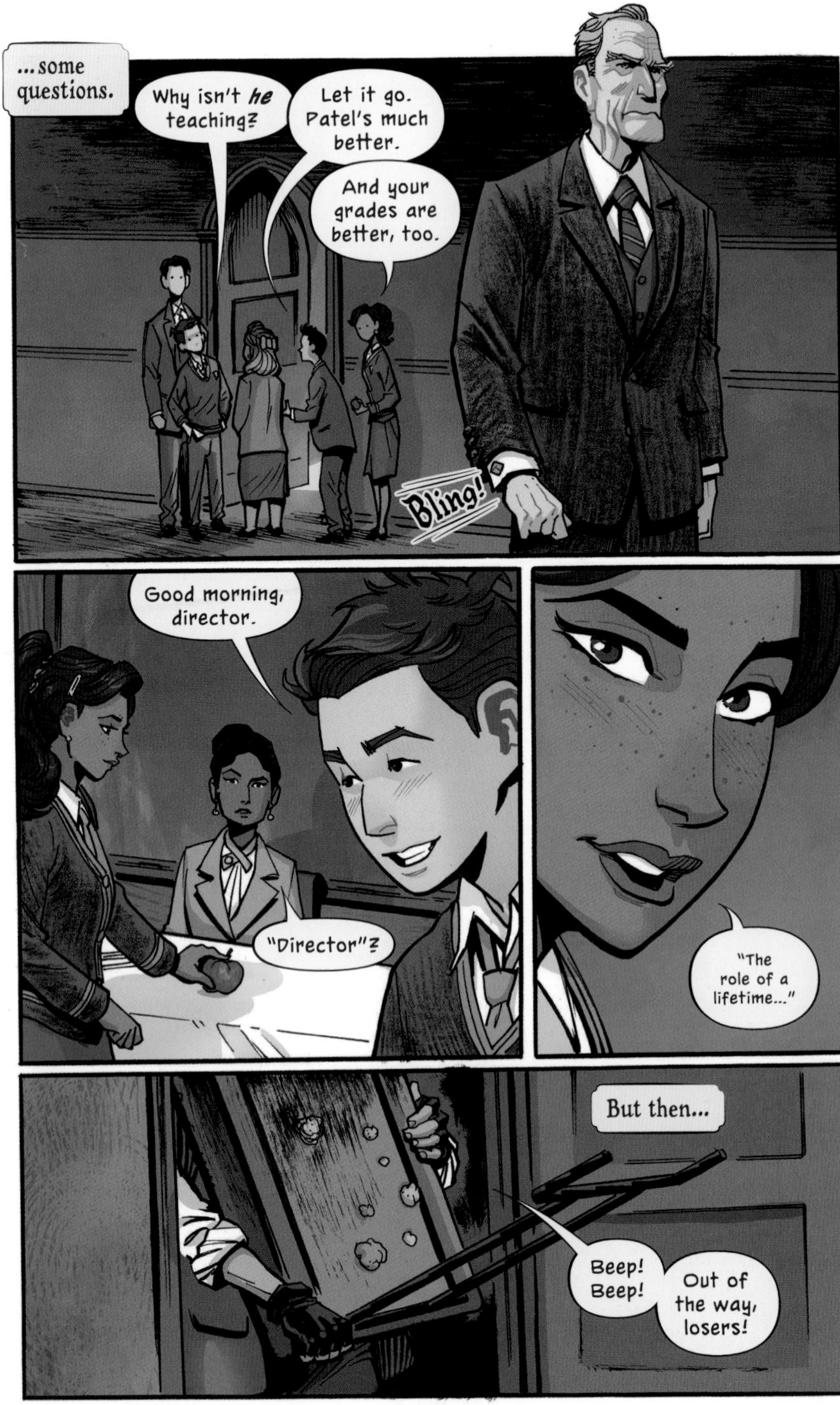
...some questions.
Why isn't *he* teaching?
Let it go. Patel's much better.
And your grades are better, too.
Bling!
Good morning, director.
"Director"?
"The role of a lifetime..."
But then...
Beep! Beep!
Out of the way, losers!

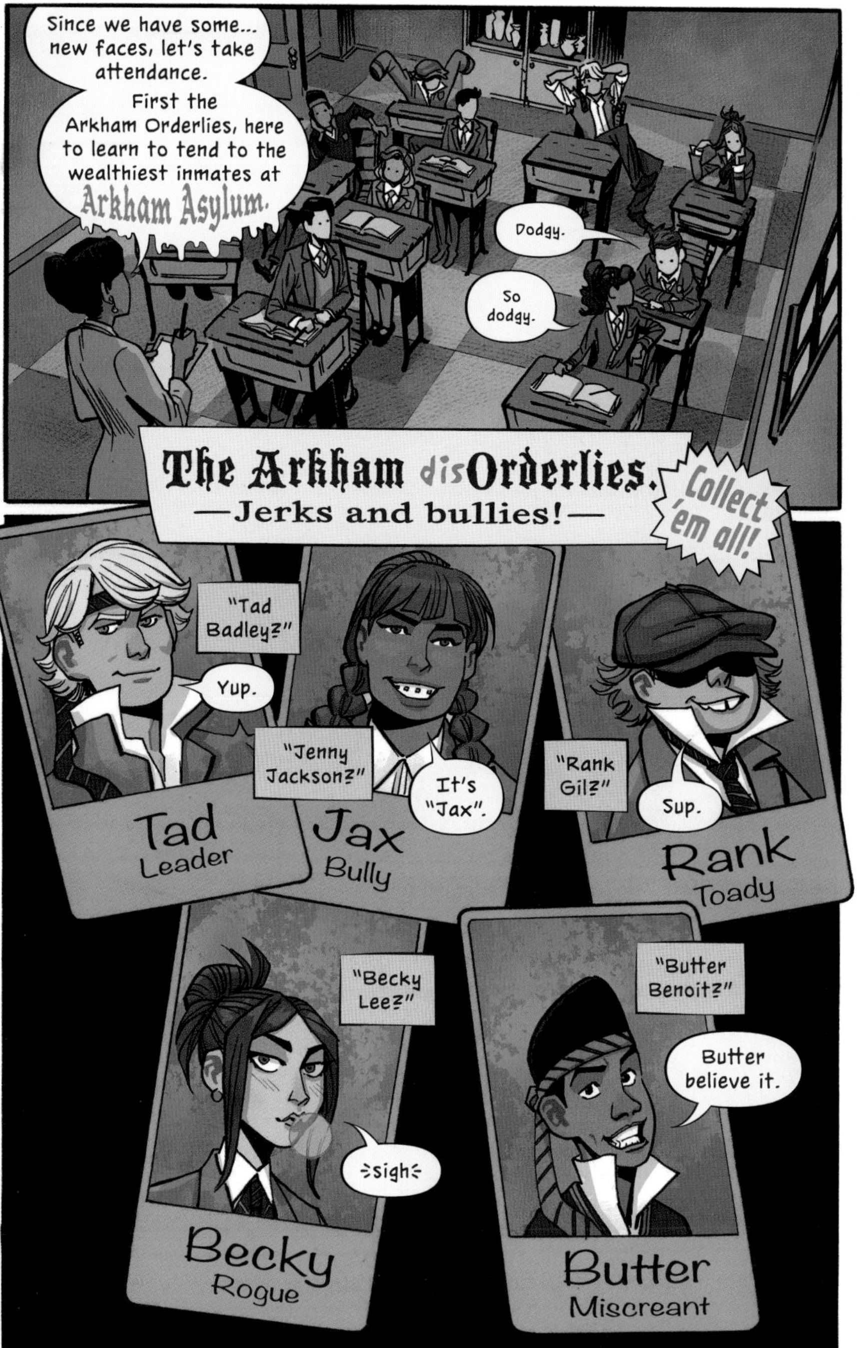

Since we have some... new faces, let's take attendance.
First the Arkham Orderlies, here to learn to tend to the wealthiest inmates at Arkham Asylum.
Dodgy.
So dodgy.
The Arkham disOrderlies.
—Jerks and bullies!—
Collect 'em all!
"Tad Badley?"
Yup.
Tad
Leader
"Jenny Jackson?"
It's "Jax".
Jax
Bully
"Rank Gil?"
Sup.
Rank
Toady
"Becky Lee?"
sigh
Becky
Rogue
"Butter Benoit?"
Butter believe it.
Butter
Miscreant

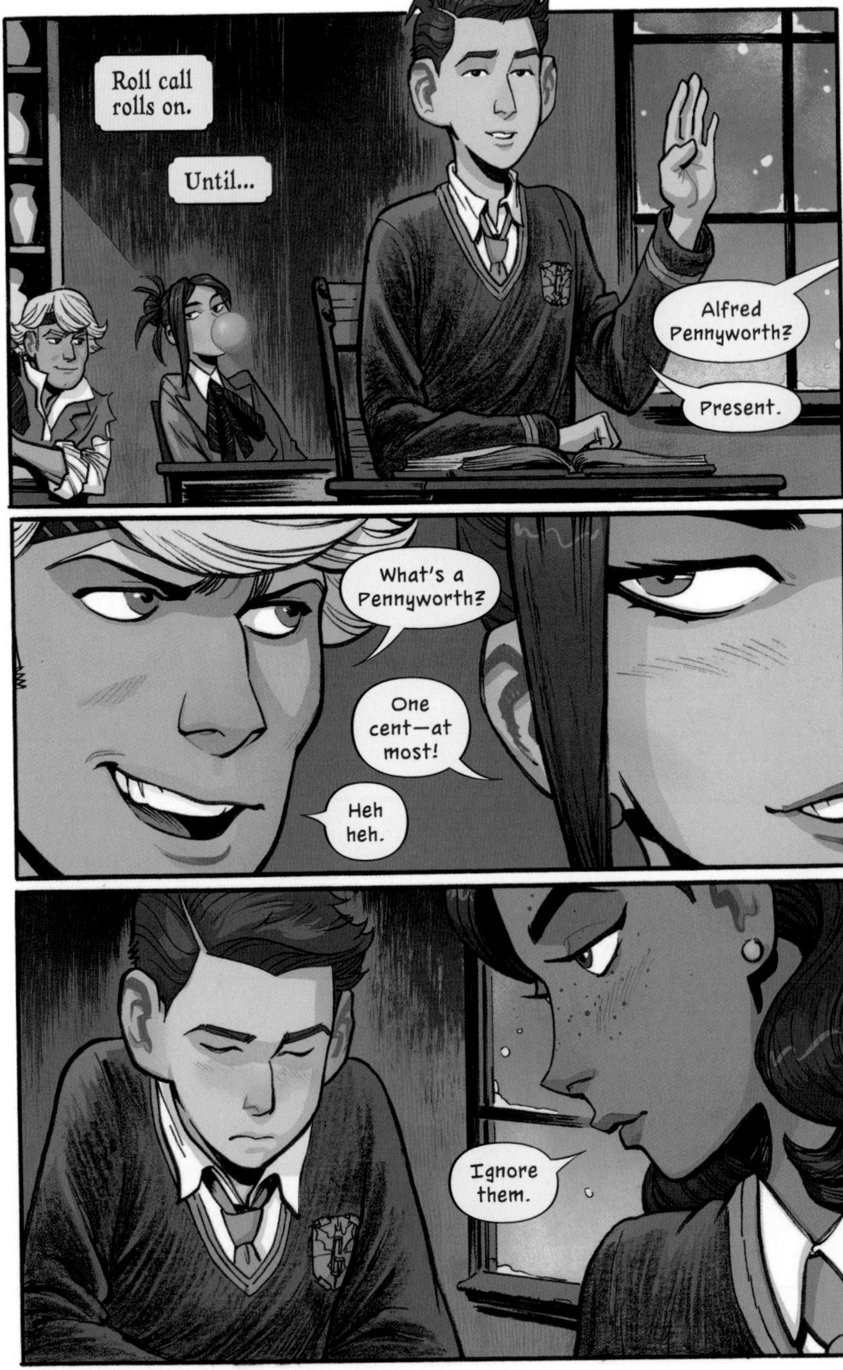
Roll call rolls on.
Until...
Alfred Pennyworth?
Present.
What's a Pennyworth?
One cent—at most!
Heh heh.
Ignore them.

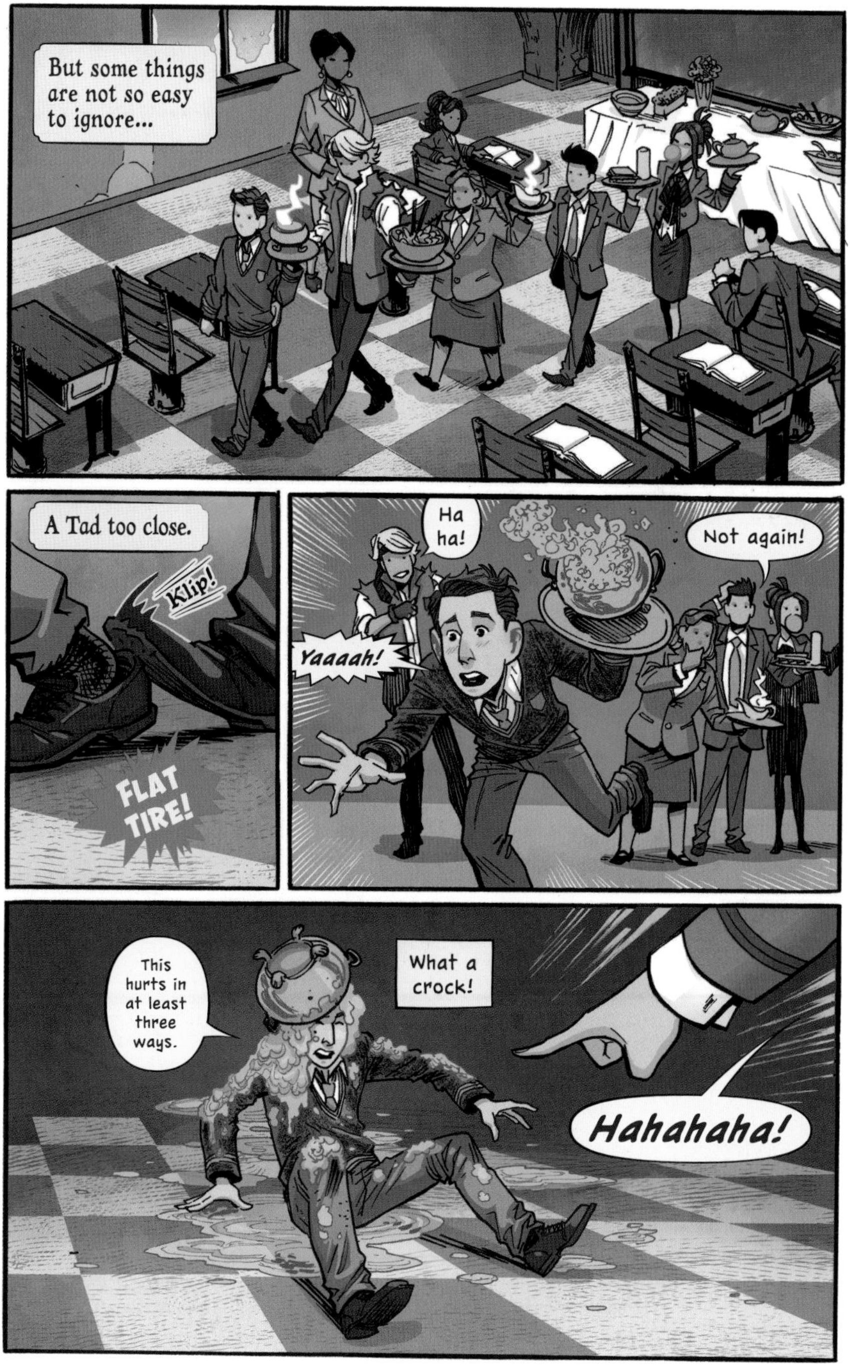
But some things are not so easy to ignore...
A Tad too close.
Klip!
FLAT TIRE!
Ha ha!
Yaaaah!
Not again!
This hurts in at least three ways.
What a crock!
Hahahaha!

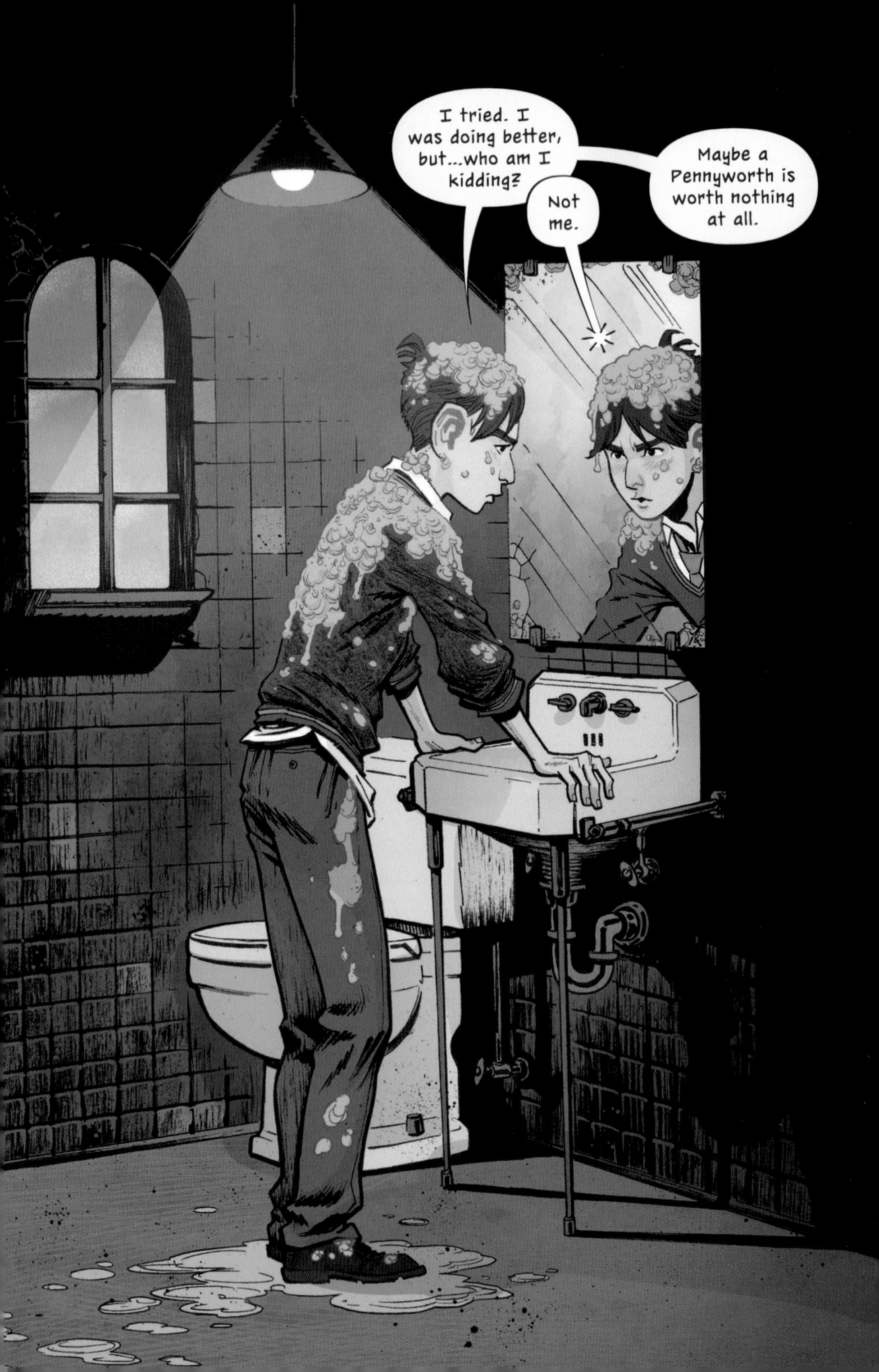
I tried. I was doing better, but...who am I kidding?
Not me.
Maybe a Pennyworth is worth nothing at all.

CHAPTER 6
Vile
Visitors

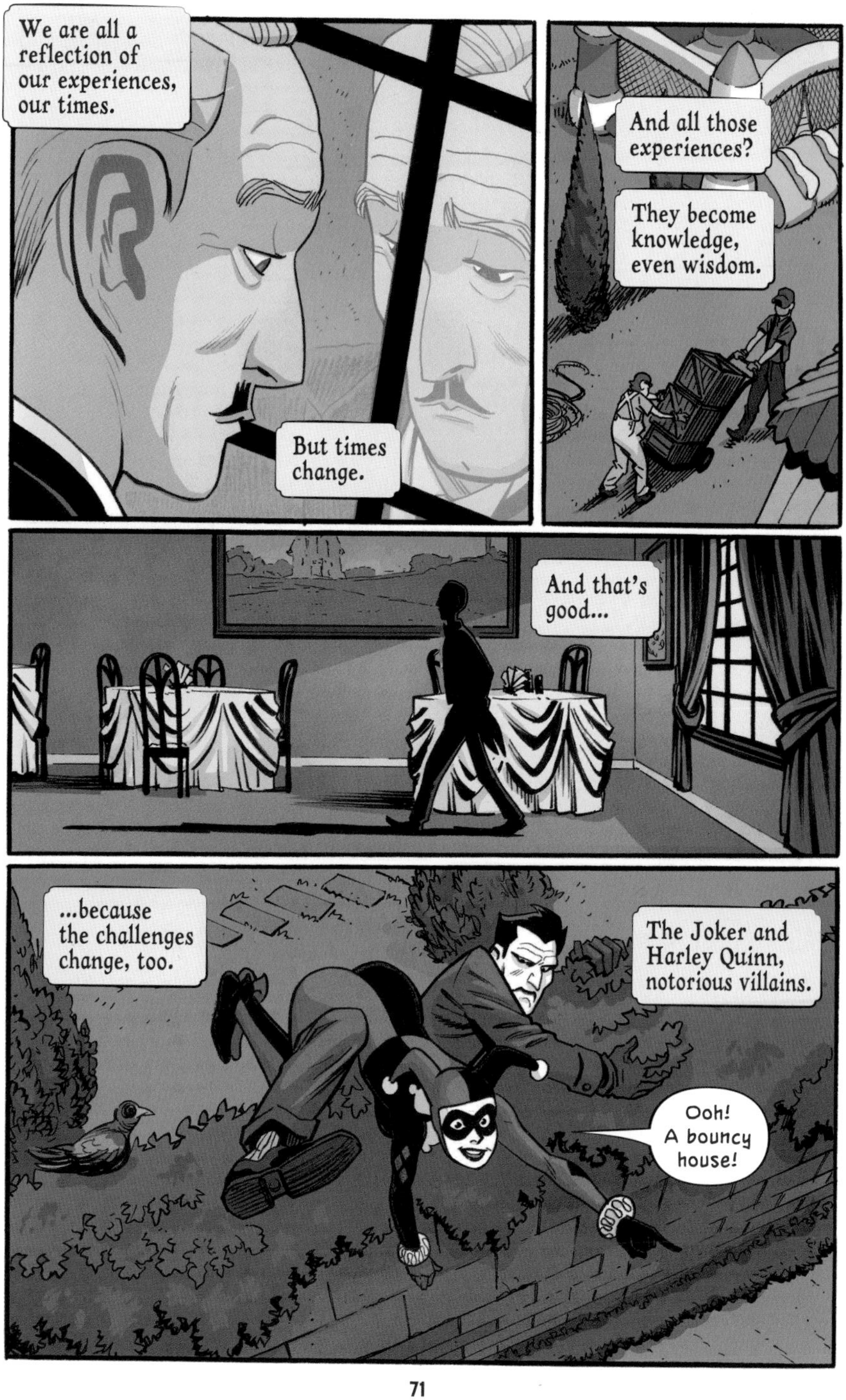
We are all a reflection of our experiences, our times.
But times change.
And all those experiences?
They become knowledge, even wisdom.
And that's good...
...because the challenges change, too.
The Joker and Harley Quinn, notorious villains.
Ooh! A bouncy house!

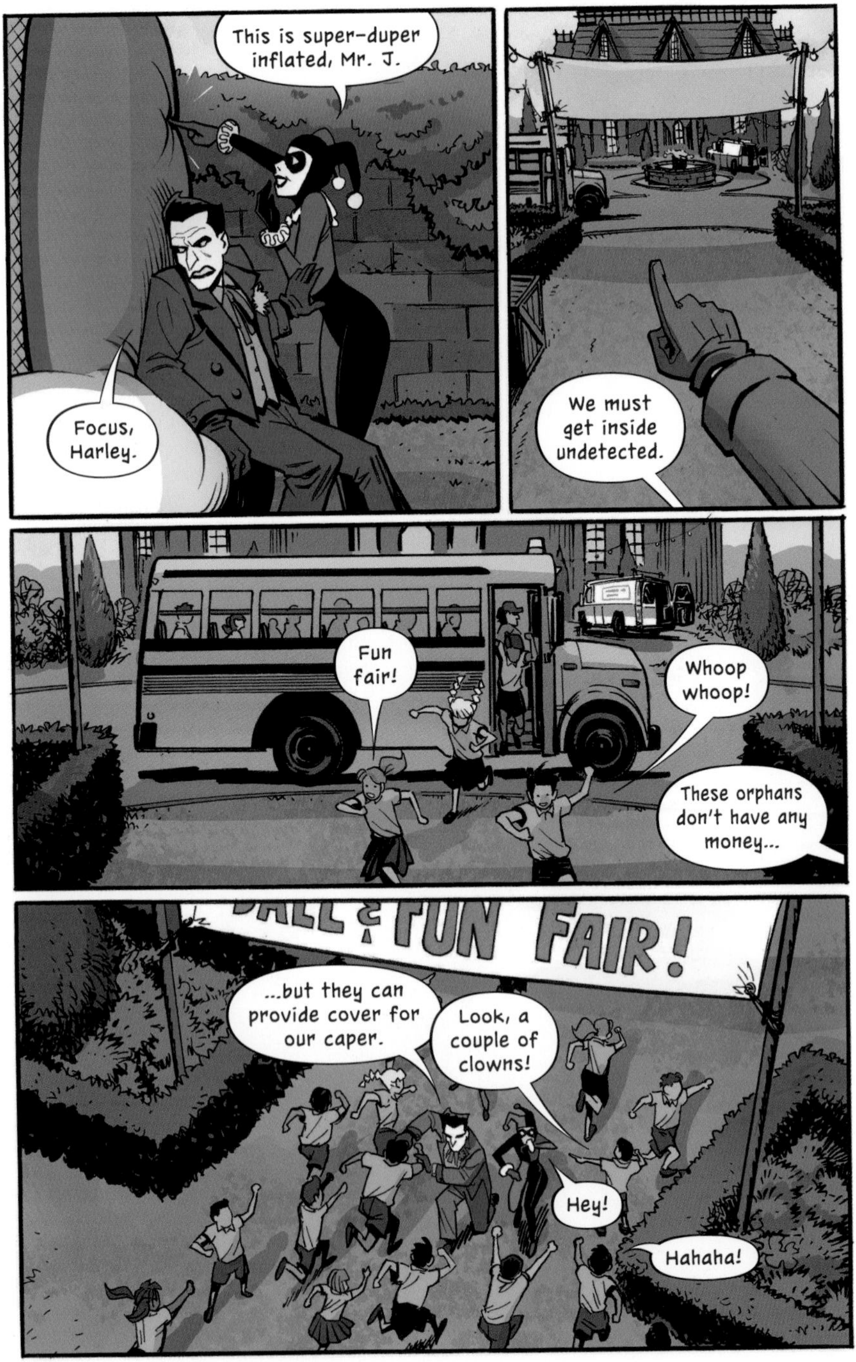
This is super-duper inflated, Mr. J.
Focus, Harley.
We must get inside undetected.
Fun fair!
Whoop whoop!
These orphans don't have any money...
BALL & FUN FAIR!
...but they can provide cover for our caper.
Look, a couple of clowns!
Hey!
Hahaha!

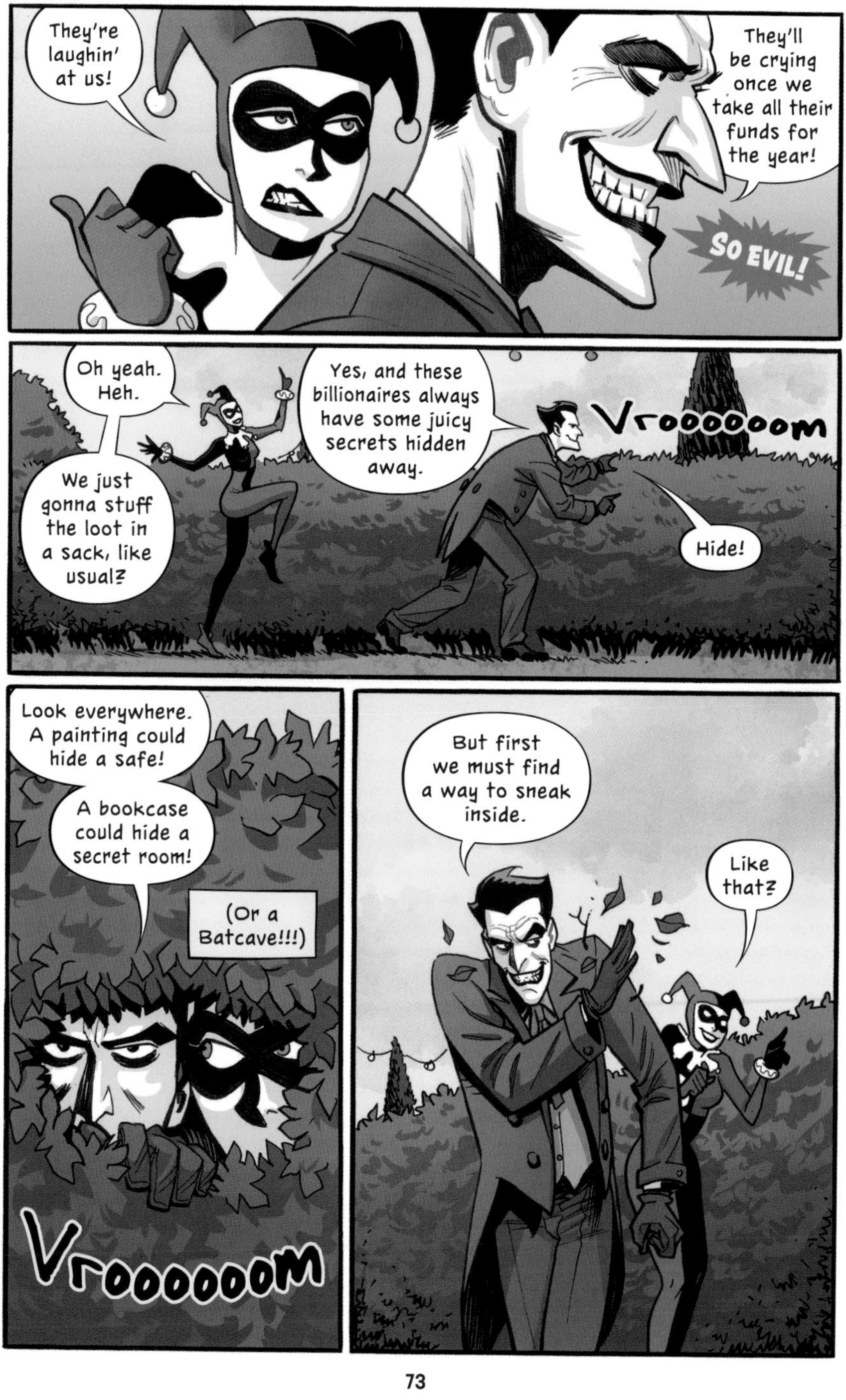
They're laughin' at us!
They'll be crying once we take all their funds for the year!
SO EVIL!
Oh yeah. Heh.
We just gonna stuff the loot in a sack, like usual?
Yes, and these billionaires always have some juicy secrets hidden away.
Vroooooom
Hide!
Look everywhere. A painting could hide a safe!
A bookcase could hide a secret room!
(Or a Batcave!!!)
Vroooooom
But first we must find a way to sneak inside.
Like that?

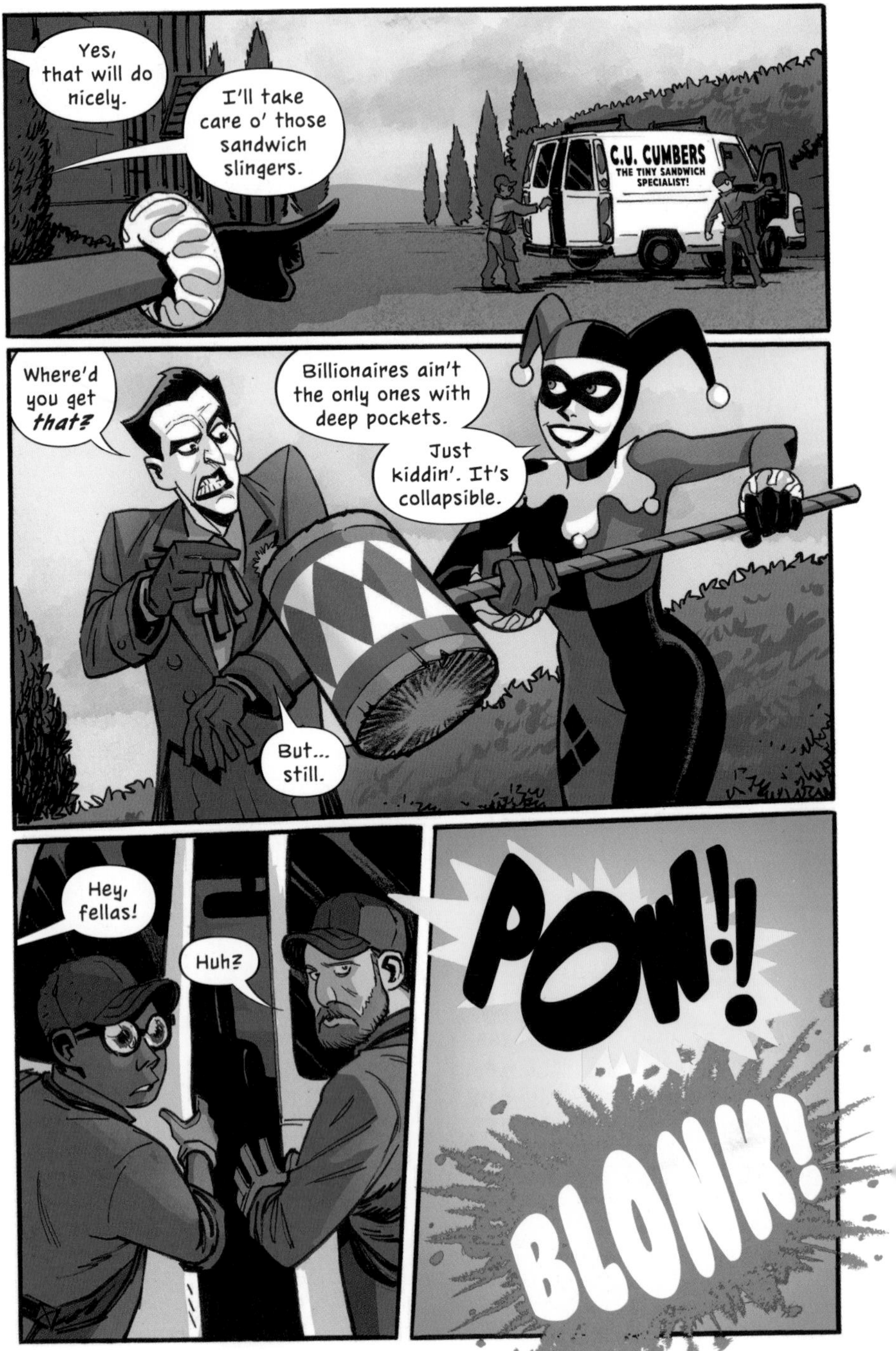
Yes, that will do nicely.
I'll take care o' those sandwich slingers.
C.U. CUMBERS
THE TINY SANDWICH SPECIALIST!
Where'd you get *that?*
Billionaires ain't the only ones with deep pockets.
Just kiddin'. It's collapsible.
But... still.
Hey, fellas!
Huh?
POW!!
BLONK!

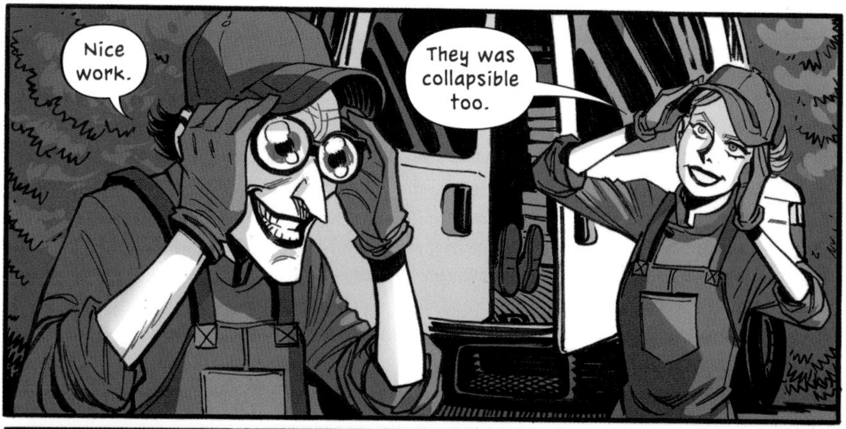
Nice work.
They was collapsible too.

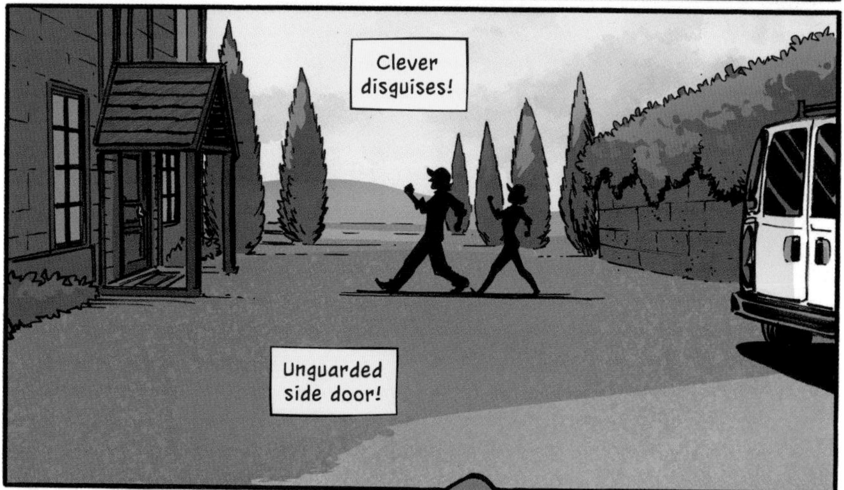
Clever disguises!
Unguarded side door!

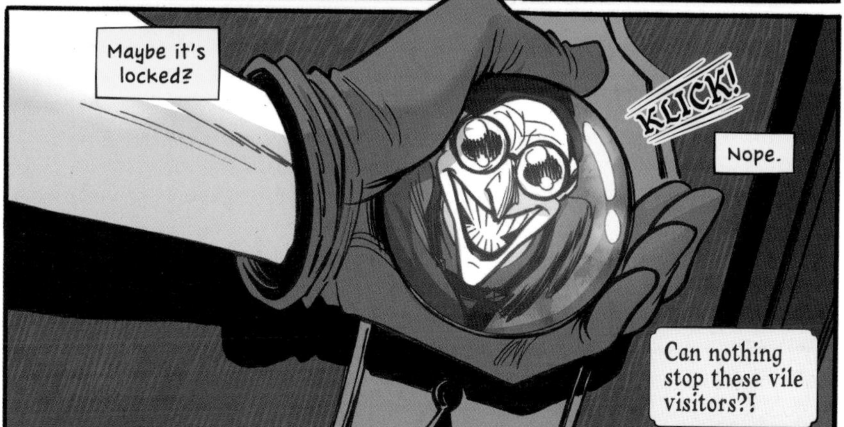
Maybe it's locked?
KLICK!
Nope.
Can nothing stop these vile visitors?!

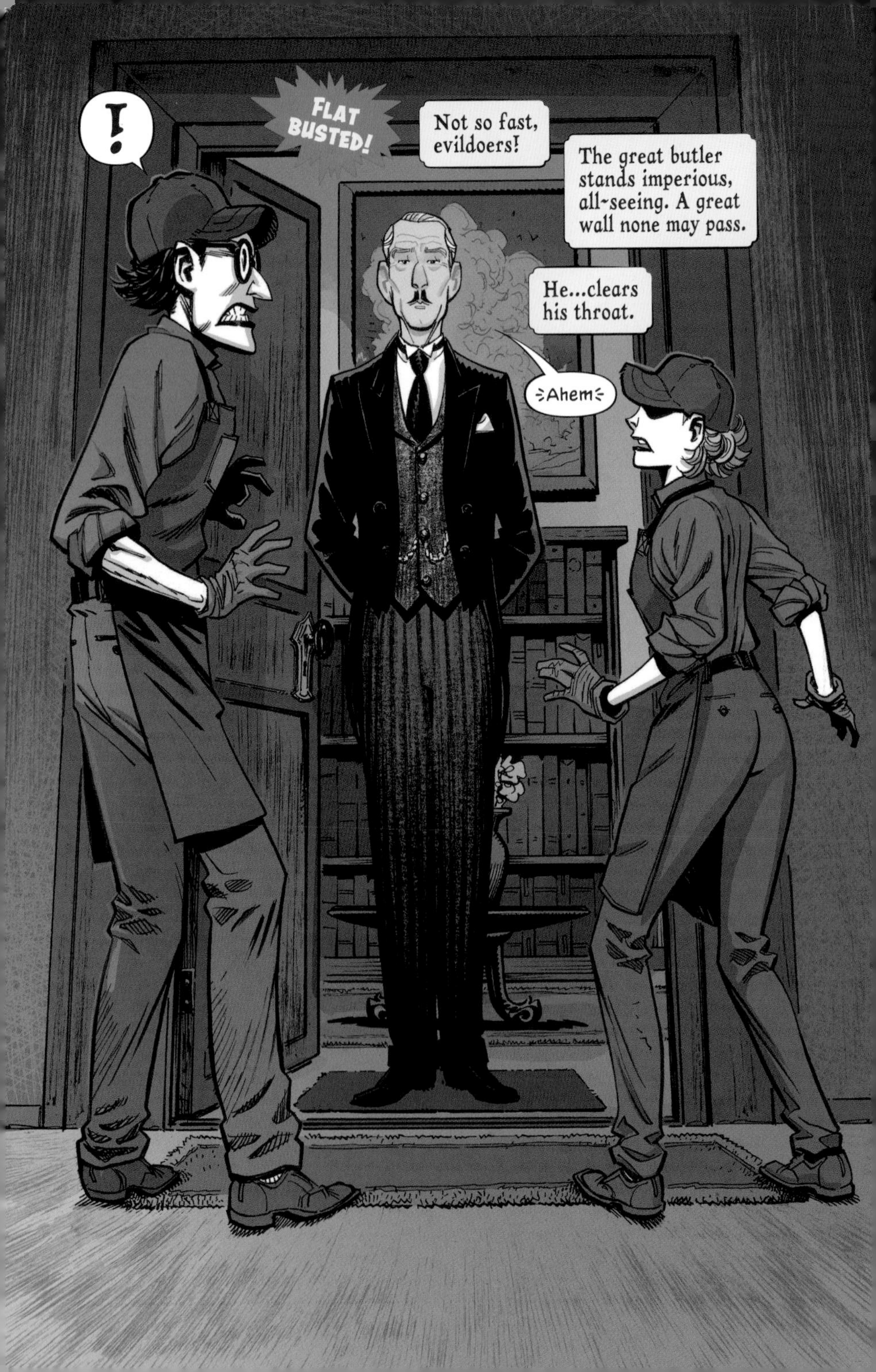
!
FLAT BUSTED!
Not so fast, evildoers!
The great butler stands imperious, all-seeing. A great wall none may pass.
He...clears his throat.
Ahem

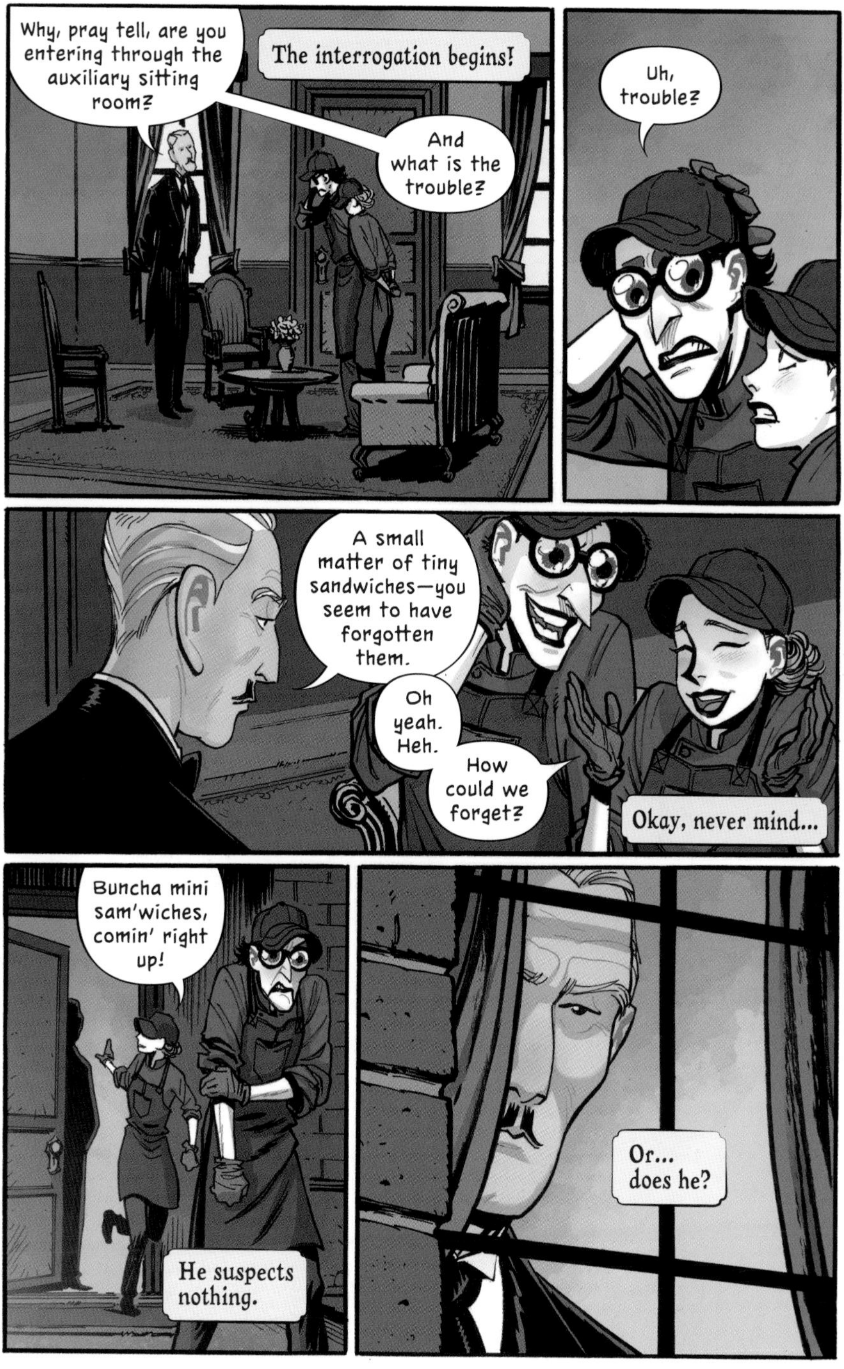
Why, pray tell, are you entering through the auxiliary sitting room?
The interrogation begins!
And what is the trouble?
Uh, trouble?
A small matter of tiny sandwiches—you seem to have forgotten them.
Oh yeah. Heh.
How could we forget?
Okay, never mind...
Buncha mini sam'wiches, comin' right up!
He suspects nothing.
Or... does he?

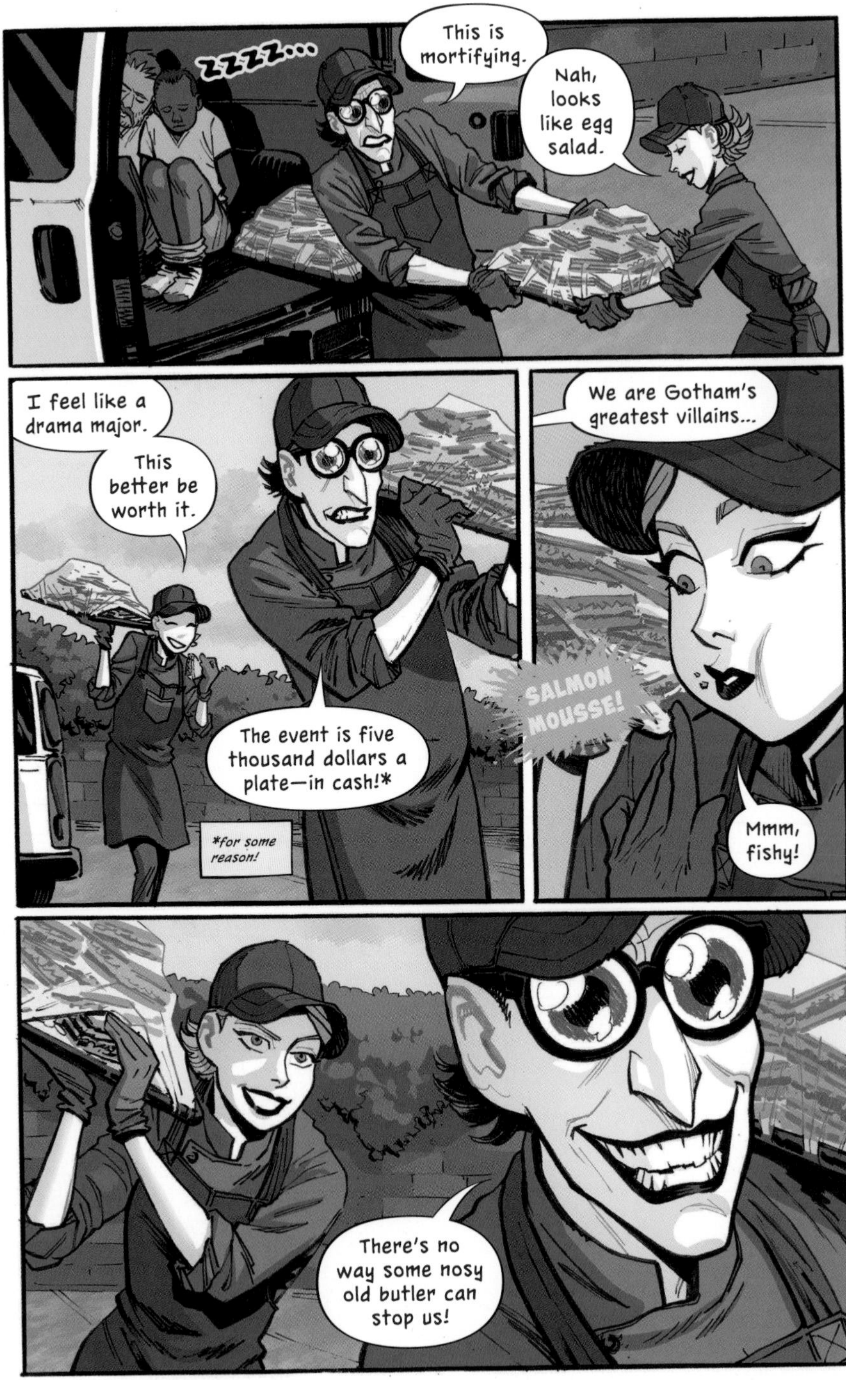
ZZZZ...
This is mortifying.
Nah, looks like egg salad.
I feel like a drama major.
This better be worth it.
The event is five thousand dollars a plate—in cash!*
*for some reason!
We are Gotham's greatest villains...
SALMON MOUSSE!
Mmm, fishy!
There's no way some nosy old butler can stop us!

CHAPTER 7
A Curious Discovery

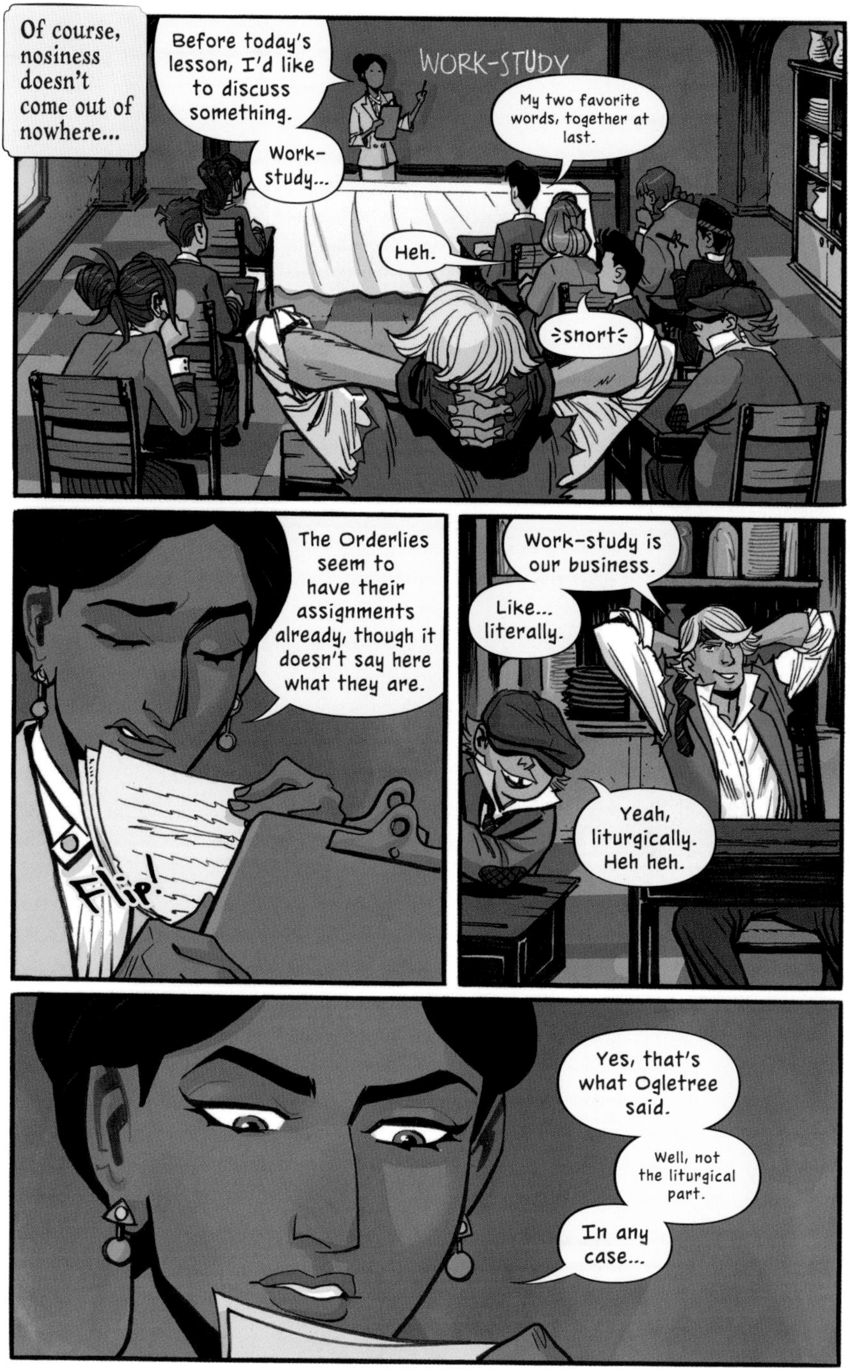

Of course, nosiness doesn't come out of nowhere...
Before today's lesson, I'd like to discuss something.
WORK-STUDY
Work-study...
My two favorite words, together at last.
Heh.
snort
The Orderlies seem to have their assignments already, though it doesn't say here what they are.
Flip!
Work-study is our business.
Like... literally.
Yeah, liturgically. Heh heh.
Yes, that's what Ogletree said.
Well, not the liturgical part.
In any case...

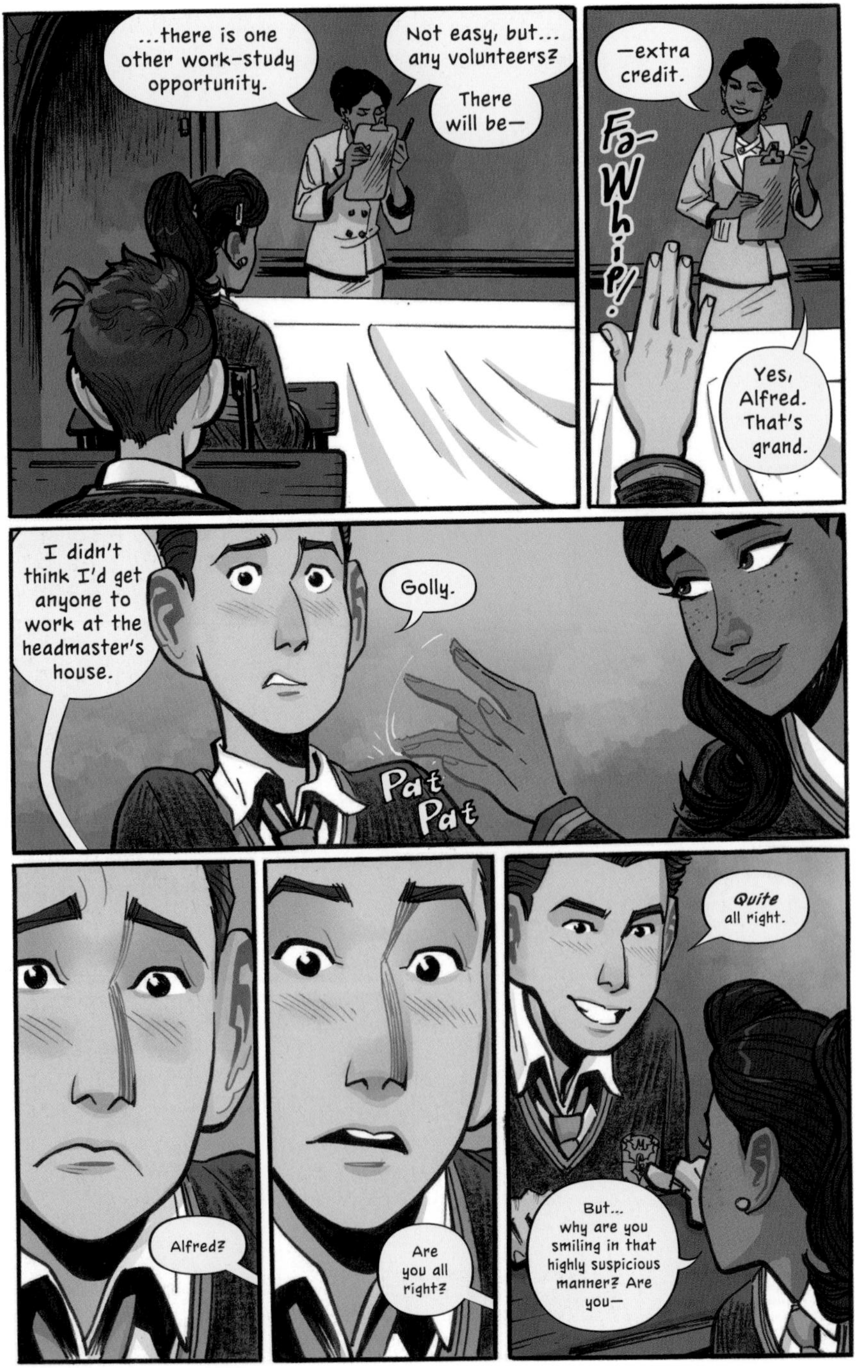
...there is one other work-study opportunity.
Not easy, but... any volunteers?
There will be—
—extra credit.
Fa-Whip!
Yes, Alfred. That's grand.
I didn't think I'd get anyone to work at the headmaster's house.
Golly.
Pat Pat
Quite all right.
Alfred?
Are you all right?
But... why are you smiling in that highly suspicious manner? Are you—

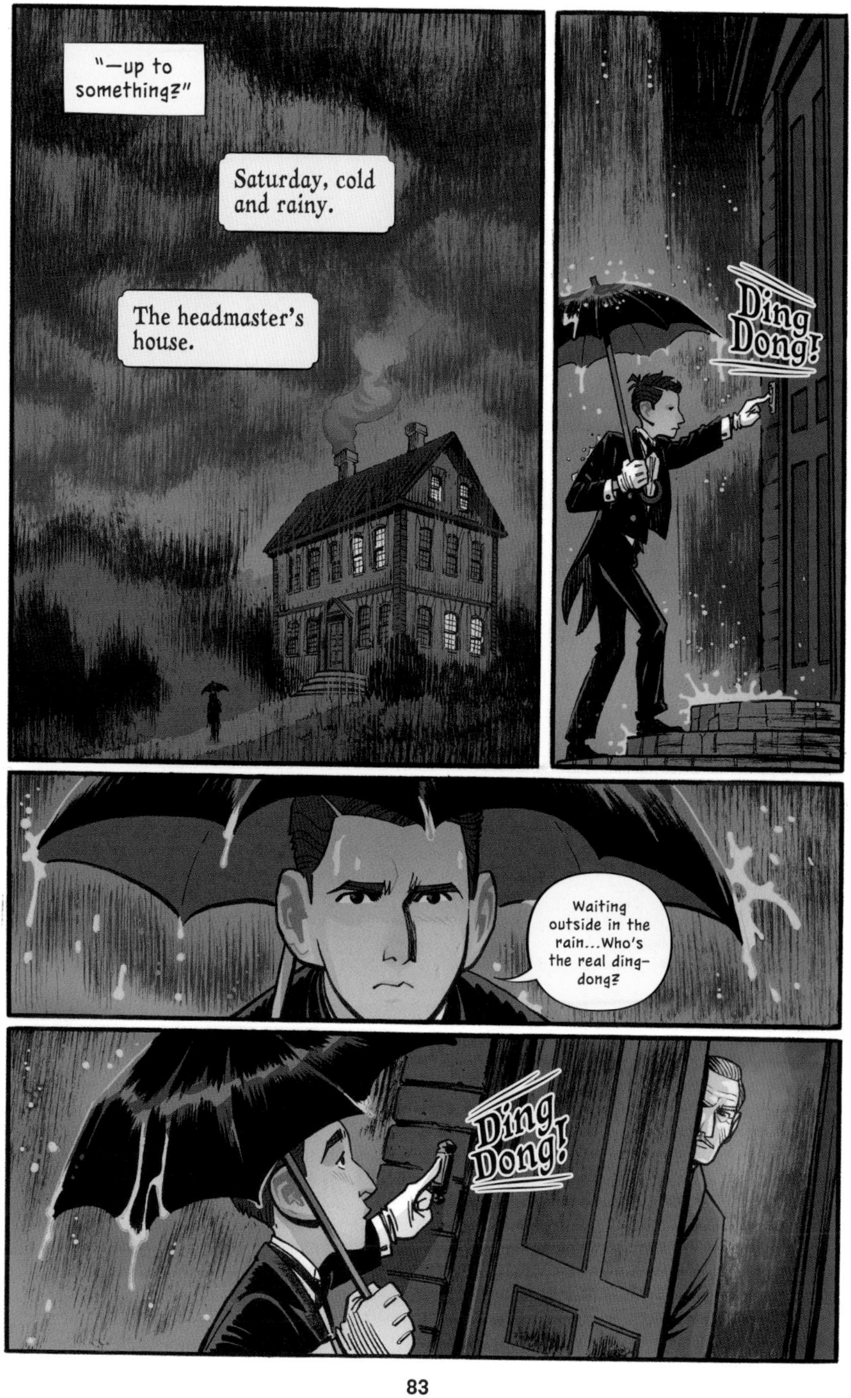
"—up to something?"
Saturday, cold and rainy.
The headmaster's house.
Ding Dong!
Waiting outside in the rain...Who's the real ding-dong?
Ding Dong!

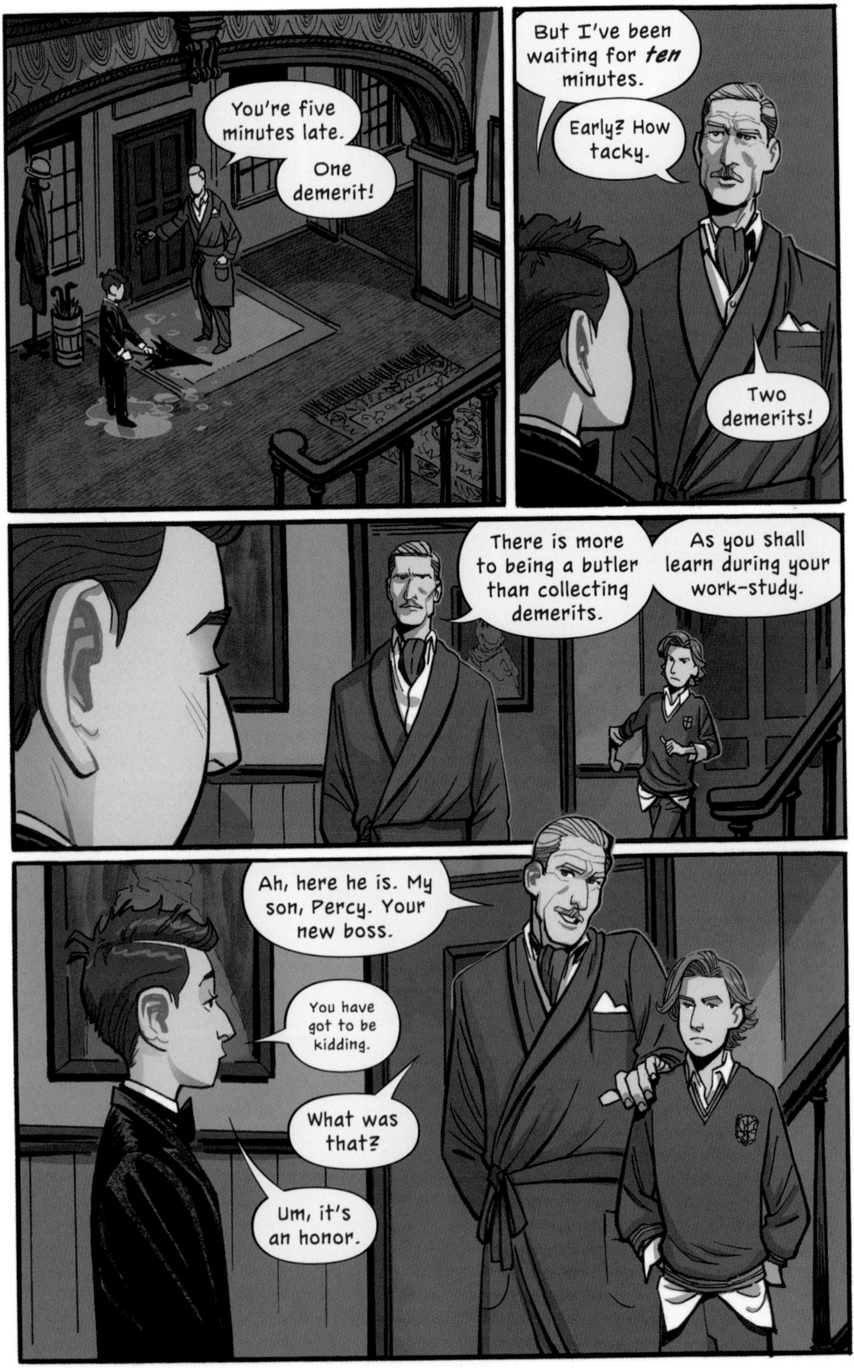
You're five minutes late.
One demerit!
But I've been waiting for *ten* minutes.
Early? How tacky.
Two demerits!
There is more to being a butler than collecting demerits.
As you shall learn during your work-study.
Ah, here he is. My son, Percy. Your new boss.
You have got to be kidding.
What was that?
Um, it's an honor.

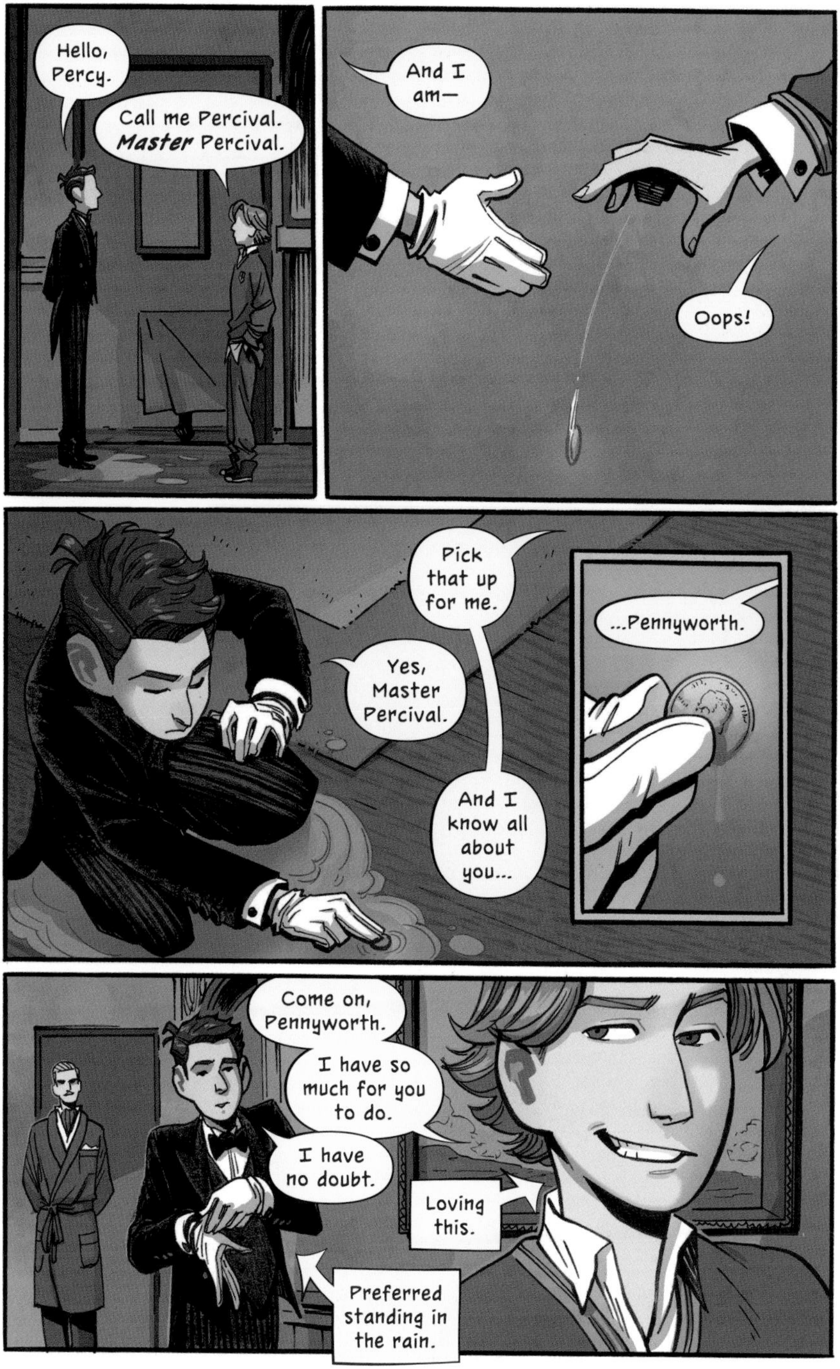

Hello, Percy.
Call me Percival. *Master* Percival.
And I am—
Oops!
Pick that up for me.
Yes, Master Percival.
And I know all about you...
...Pennyworth.
Come on, Pennyworth.
I have so much for you to do.
I have no doubt.
Loving this.
Preferred standing in the rain.

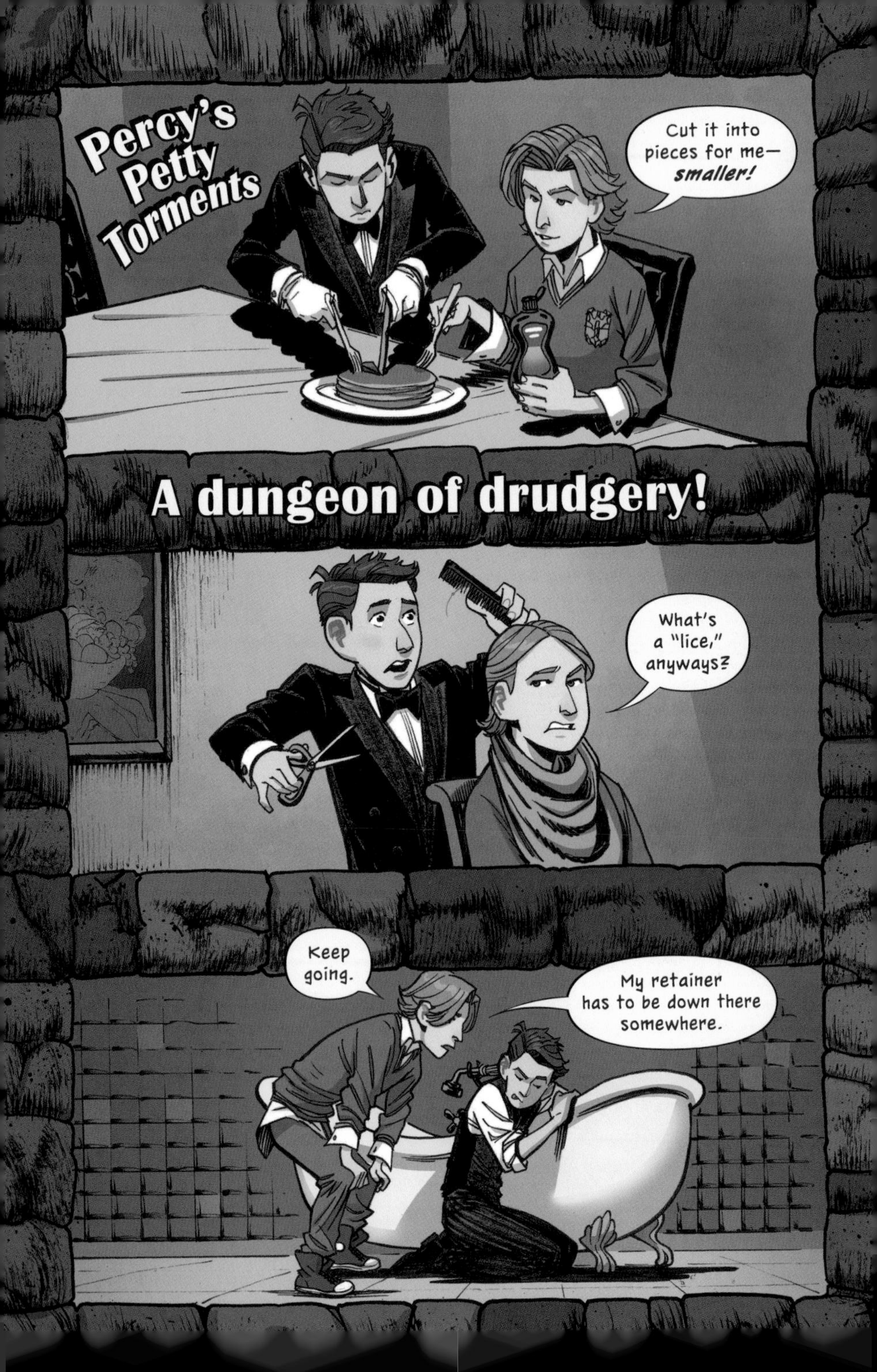
Percy's Petty Torments
Cut it into pieces for me— *smaller!*
A dungeon of drudgery!
What's a "lice," anyways?
Keep going.
My retainer has to be down there somewhere.

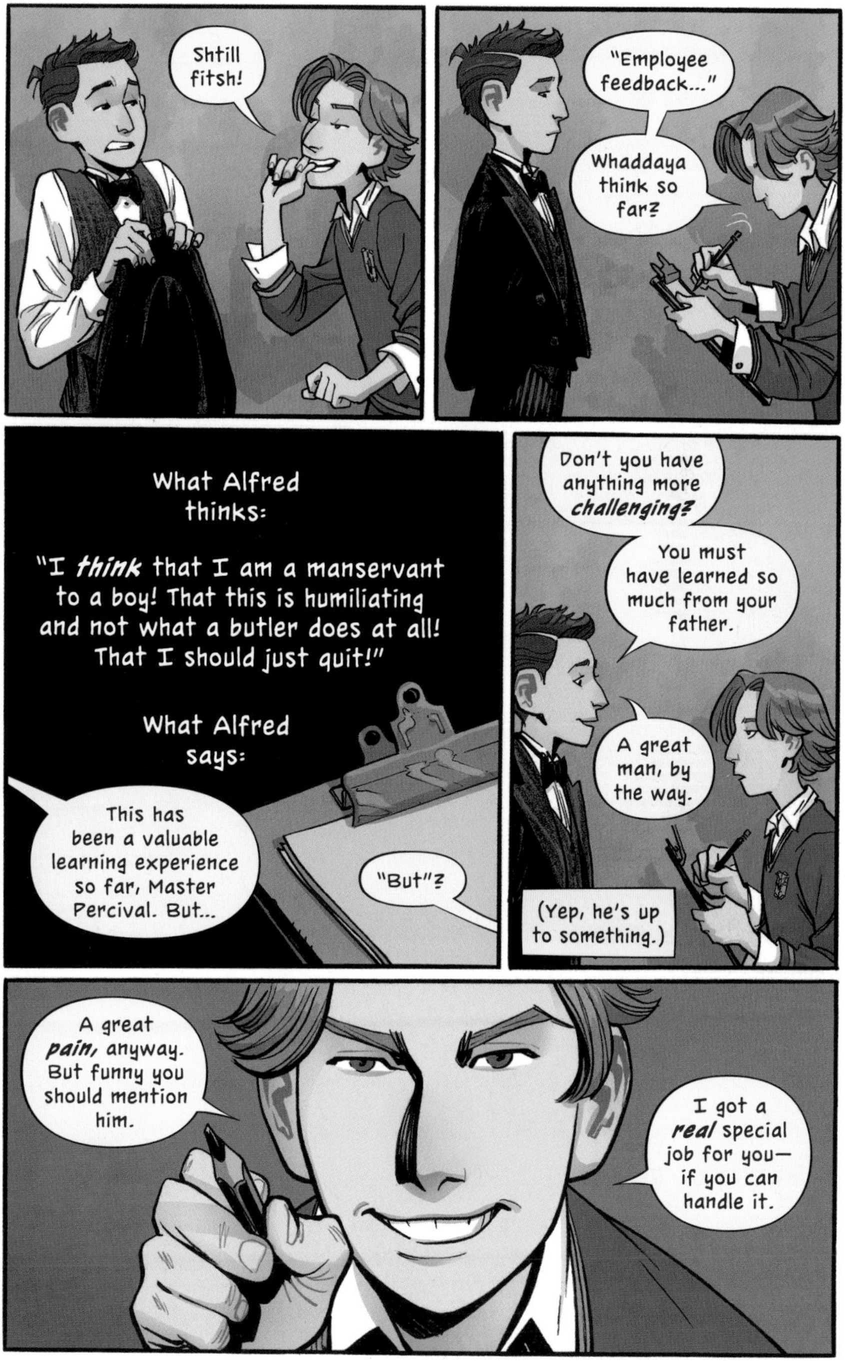
Shtill fitsh!
"Employee feedback..."
Whaddaya think so far?
What Alfred thinks:
"I *think* that I am a manservant to a boy! That this is humiliating and not what a butler does at all! That I should just quit!"
What Alfred says:
This has been a valuable learning experience so far, Master Percival. But...
"But"?
Don't you have anything more *challenging?*
You must have learned so much from your father.
A great man, by the way.
(Yep, he's up to something.)
A great *pain,* anyway. But funny you should mention him.
I got a *real* special job for you— if you can handle it.

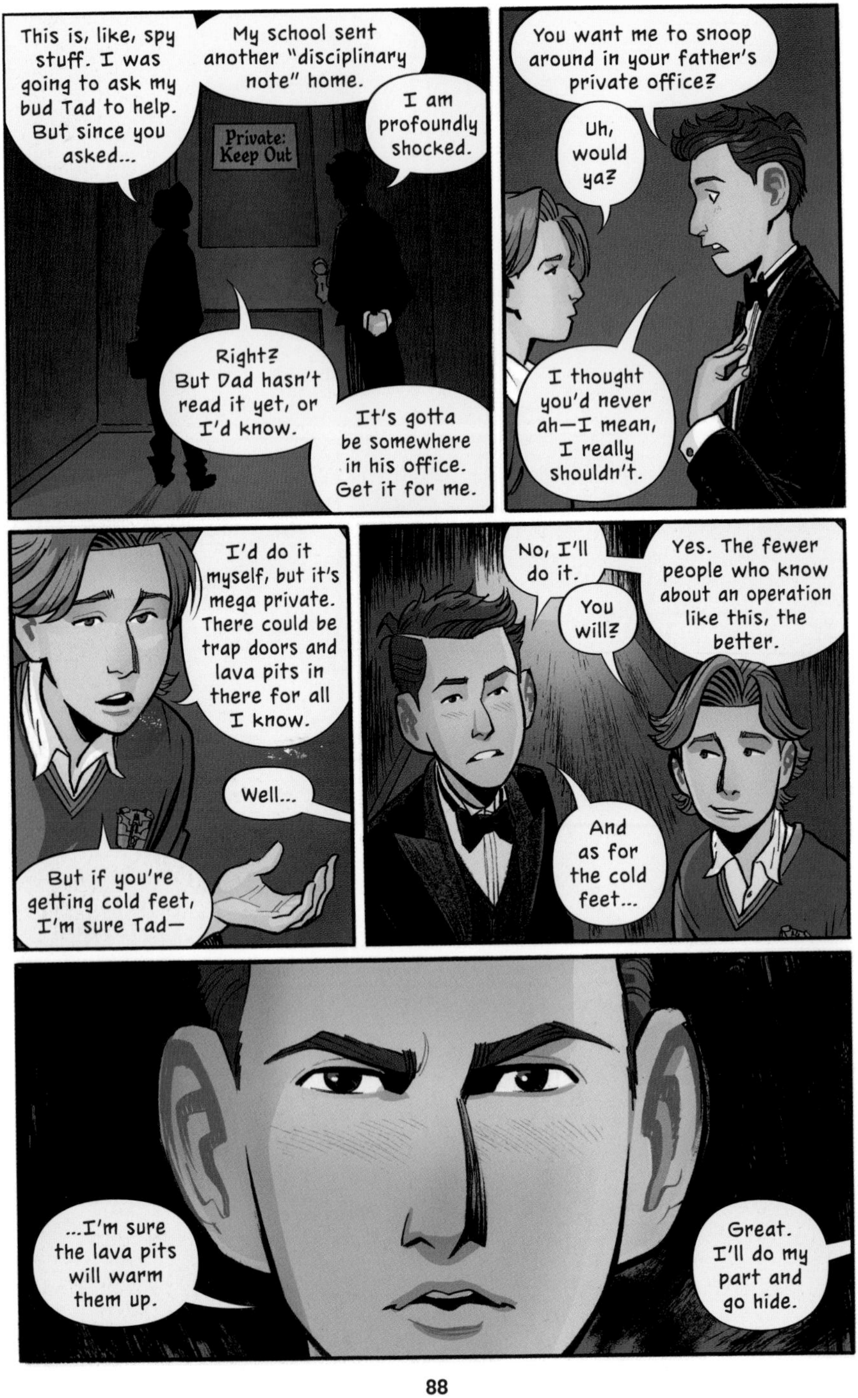
This is, like, spy stuff. I was going to ask my bud Tad to help. But since you asked...
My school sent another "disciplinary note" home.
Private: Keep Out
I am profoundly shocked.
Right?
But Dad hasn't read it yet, or I'd know.
It's gotta be somewhere in his office. Get it for me.
You want me to snoop around in your father's private office?
Uh, would ya?
I thought you'd never ah—I mean, I really shouldn't.
I'd do it myself, but it's mega private. There could be trap doors and lava pits in there for all I know.
Well...
But if you're getting cold feet, I'm sure Tad—
No, I'll do it.
You will?
Yes. The fewer people who know about an operation like this, the better.
And as for the cold feet...
...I'm sure the lava pits will warm them up.
Great. I'll do my part and go hide.

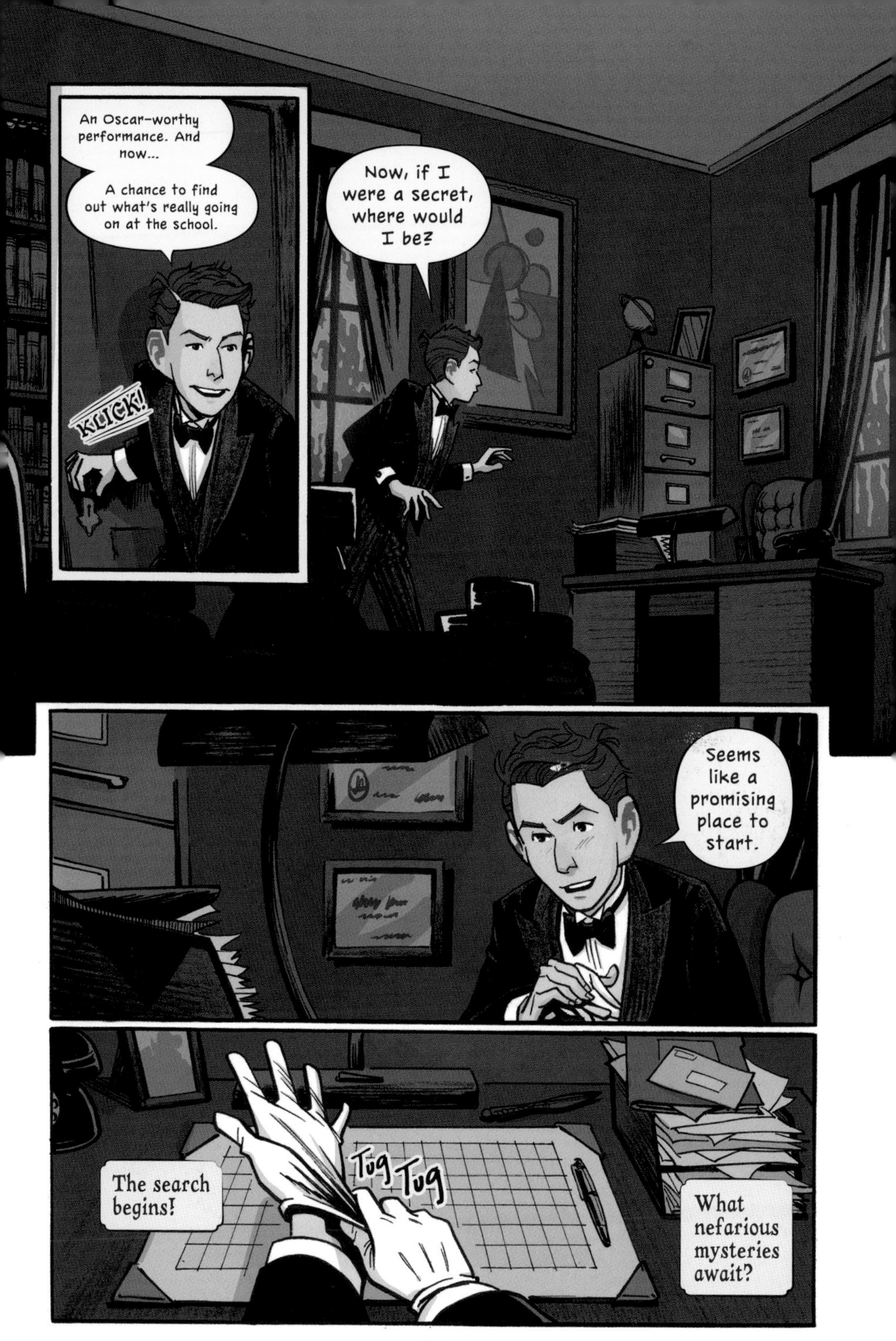
An Oscar-worthy performance. And now...
A chance to find out what's really going on at the school.
KLICK!
Now, if I were a secret, where would I be?
Seems like a promising place to start.
The search begins!
Tug Tug
What nefarious mysteries await?

Paperwork, mostly.

From the Desk of Basil Twill, Certified Public Accountant

An accountant... strange.

He certainly never loses track of those demerits.

ARKHAM SUCCESS CONFIDENTIAL

Ooh... "strictly"!

Making himself comfortable...

But just outside...

But just inside (and still quite comfortable)...

Regarding the placement of the Arkham Orderlies in the homes of Gotham's leading citizens for "on-the-job training."

Suspicious quotation marks!

Hmmm...

Percy! I'm—

—home!

SLAP!

CRAM!

Swip!

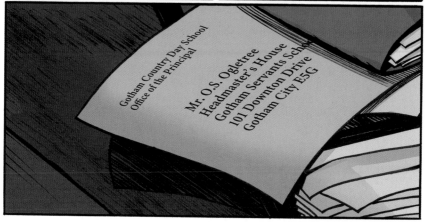

Gotham Country Day School
Office of the Principal

Mr. O.S. Ogletree
Headmaster's House
Gotham Servants School
101 Downton Drive
Gotham City E5G

Letter from Percy's school

UNMISSABLE!

Ah, there you are!

Private: Keep Out

That was too close.

Did you find the letter?

Couldn't get past the lava pit, I'm afraid.

CHAPTER 8
Dastardly Deeds!

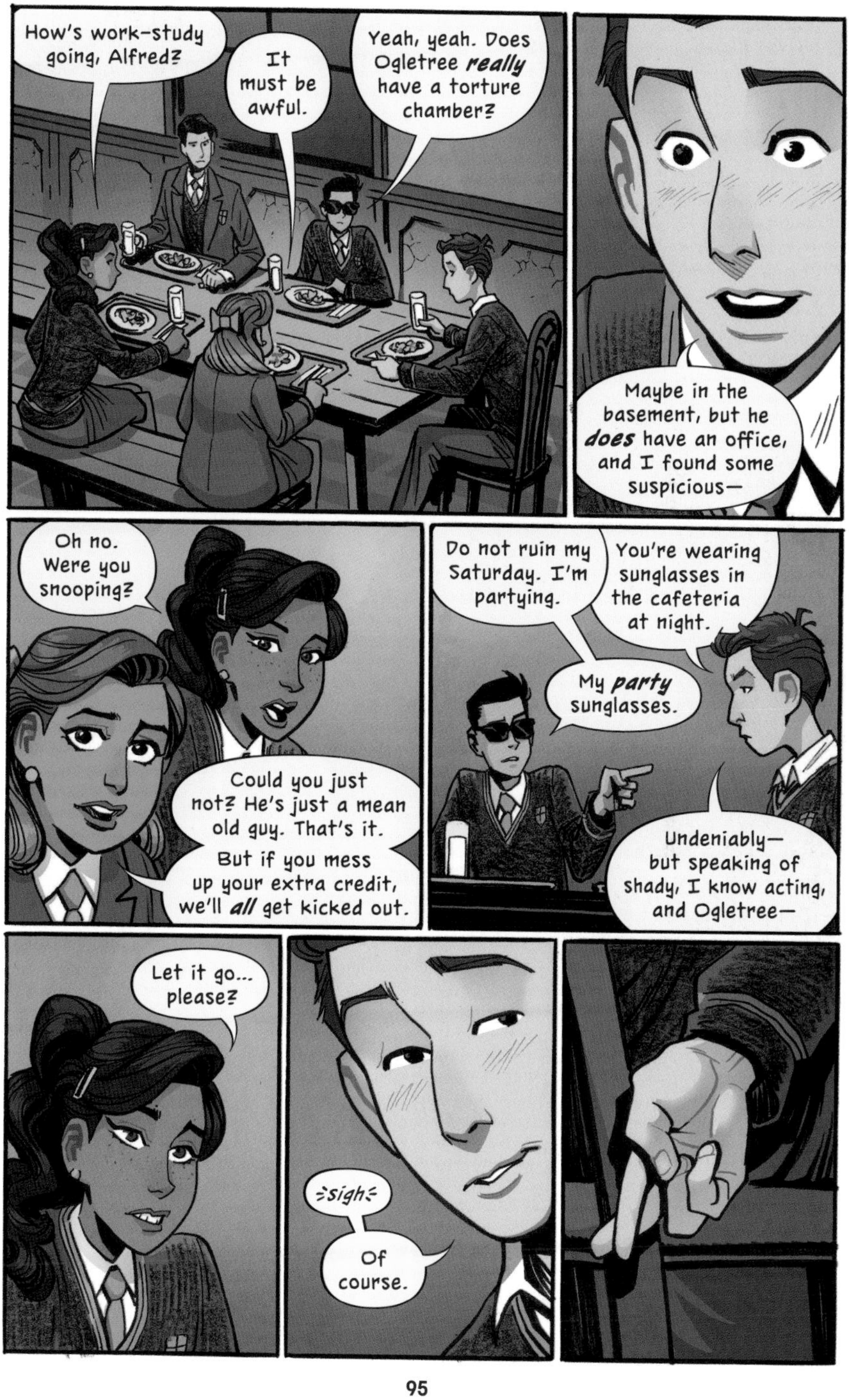

How's work-study going, Alfred?
It must be awful.
Yeah, yeah. Does Ogletree *really* have a torture chamber?
Maybe in the basement, but he *does* have an office, and I found some suspicious—
Oh no. Were you snooping?
Could you just not? He's just a mean old guy. That's it.
But if you mess up your extra credit, we'll *all* get kicked out.
Do not ruin my Saturday. I'm partying.
You're wearing sunglasses in the cafeteria at night.
My *party* sunglasses.
Undeniably— but speaking of shady, I know acting, and Ogletree—
Let it go... please?
sigh
Of course.

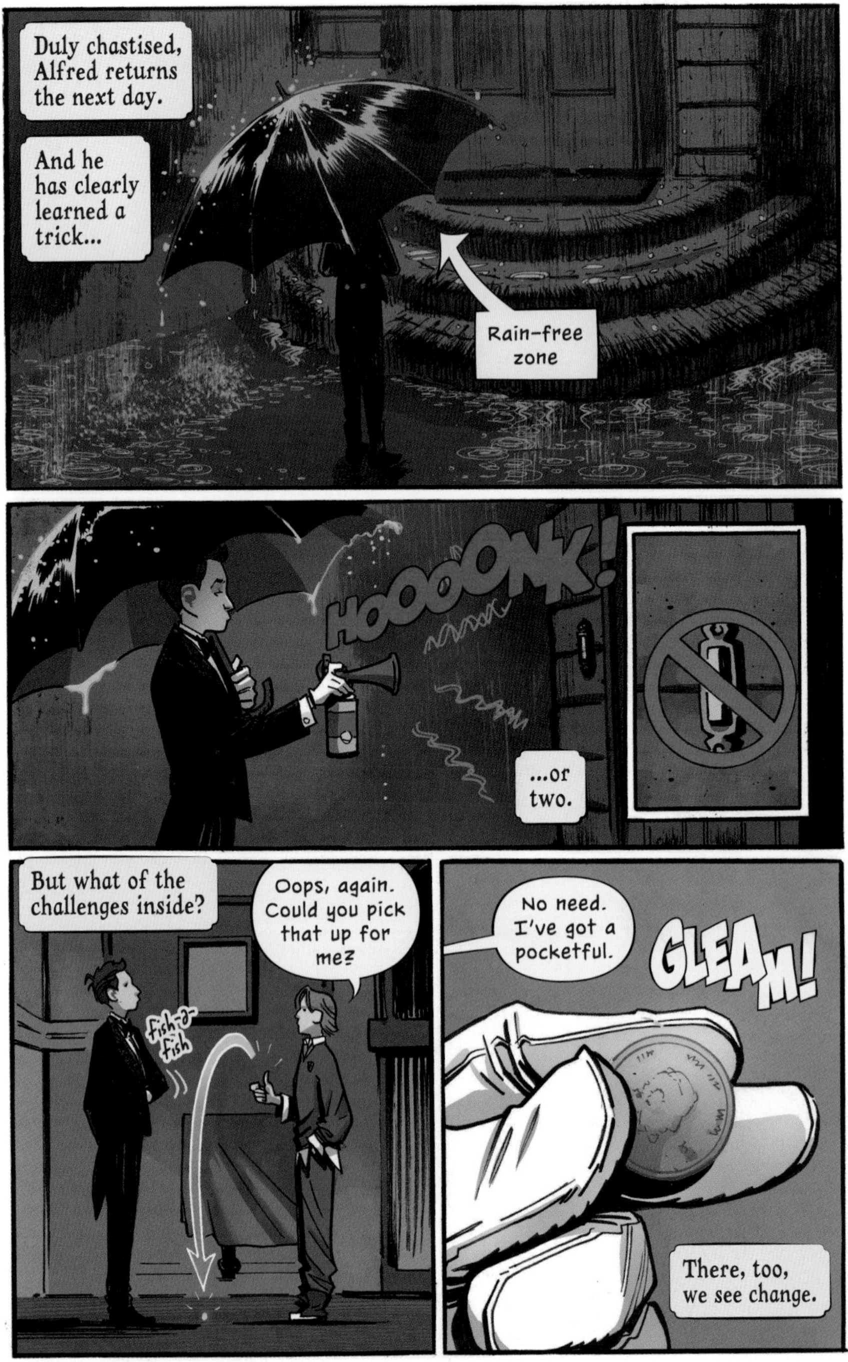
Duly chastised, Alfred returns the next day.
And he has clearly learned a trick...
Rain-free zone
HOOOOONK!
...or two.
But what of the challenges inside?
Oops, again. Could you pick that up for me?
fish-a-fish
No need. I've got a pocketful.
GLEAM!
There, too, we see change.

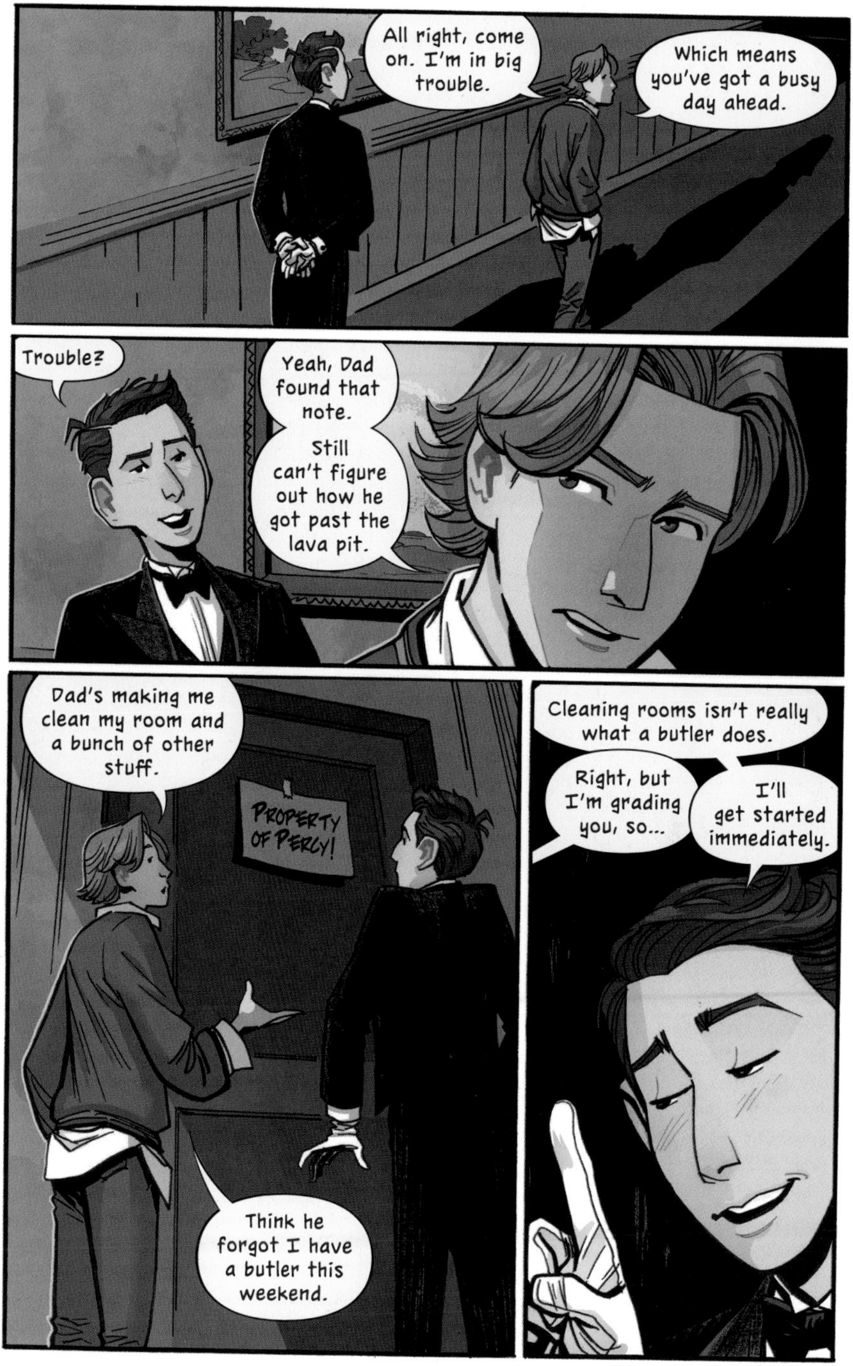
All right, come on. I'm in big trouble.
Which means you've got a busy day ahead.
Trouble?
Yeah, Dad found that note.
Still can't figure out how he got past the lava pit.
Dad's making me clean my room and a bunch of other stuff.
PROPERTY OF PERCY!
Think he forgot I have a butler this weekend.
Cleaning rooms isn't really what a butler does.
Right, but I'm grading you, so...
I'll get started immediately.

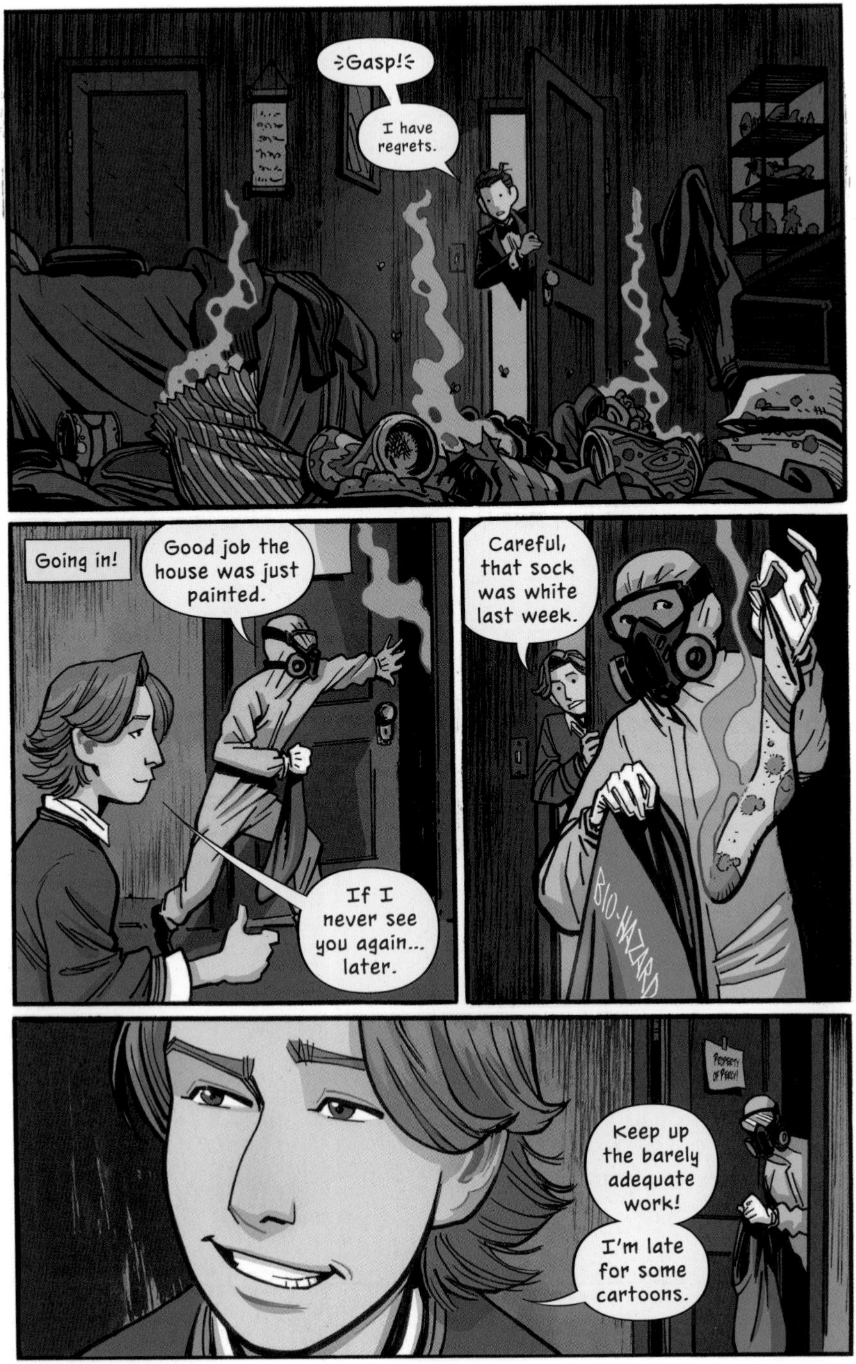

Gasp!
I have regrets.
Going in!
Good job the house was just painted.
If I never see you again... later.
Careful, that sock was white last week.
BIO-HAZARD
Keep up the barely adequate work!
I'm late for some cartoons.

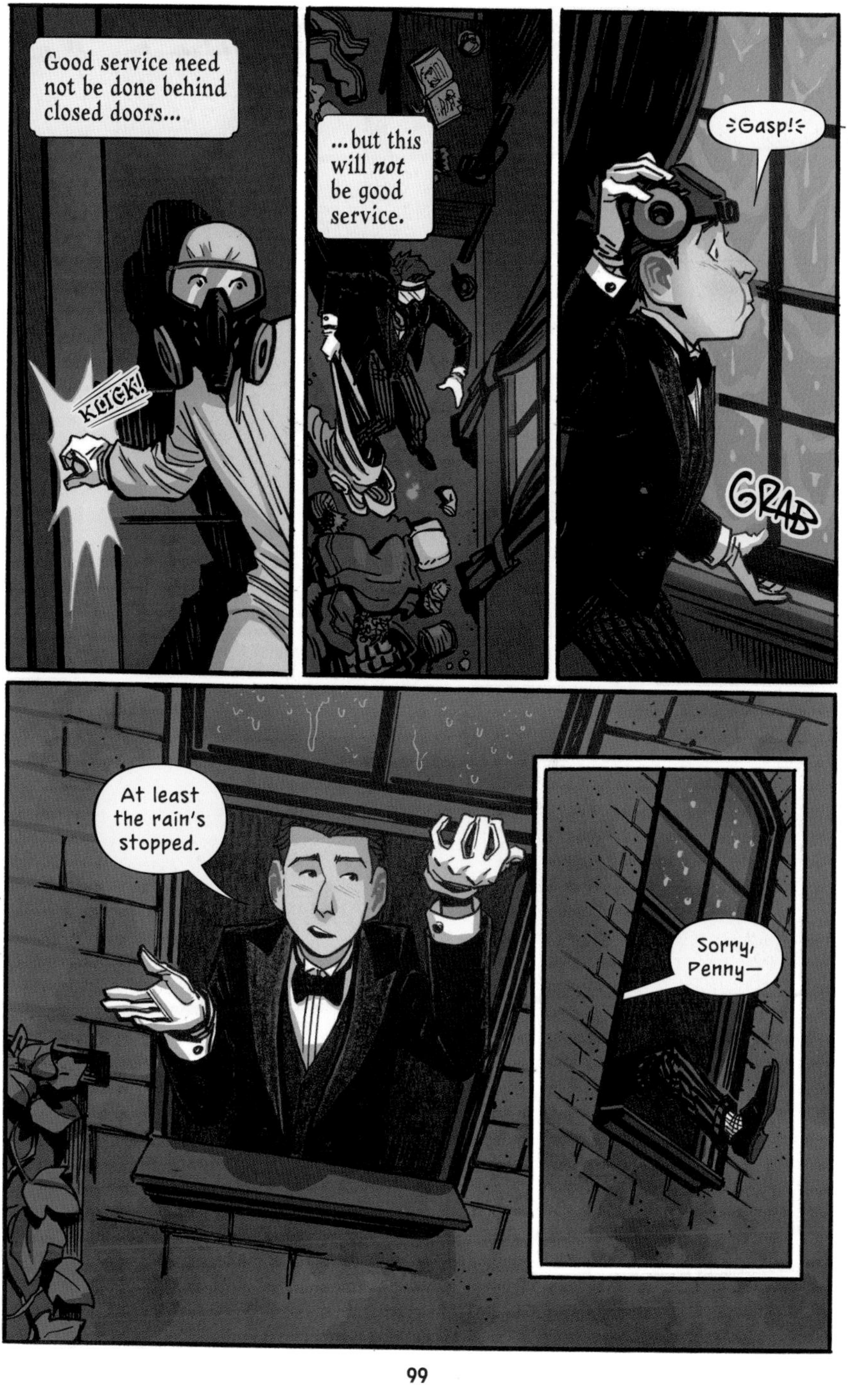

Good service need not be done behind closed doors...
KLICK!
...but this will *not* be good service.
Gasp!
GRAB
At least the rain's stopped.
Sorry, Penny—

—but I'm sure I'm right. And I know how to prove it.

Target: acquired.

(Ogletree's office!)

Good job I played that mountain climber in my old school's production of *The Sound of Music*.

Whoosh

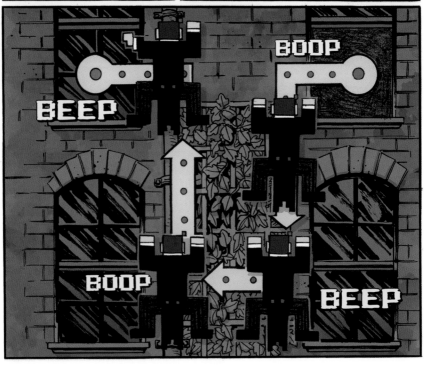

BOOP

BEEP

BOOP

BEEP

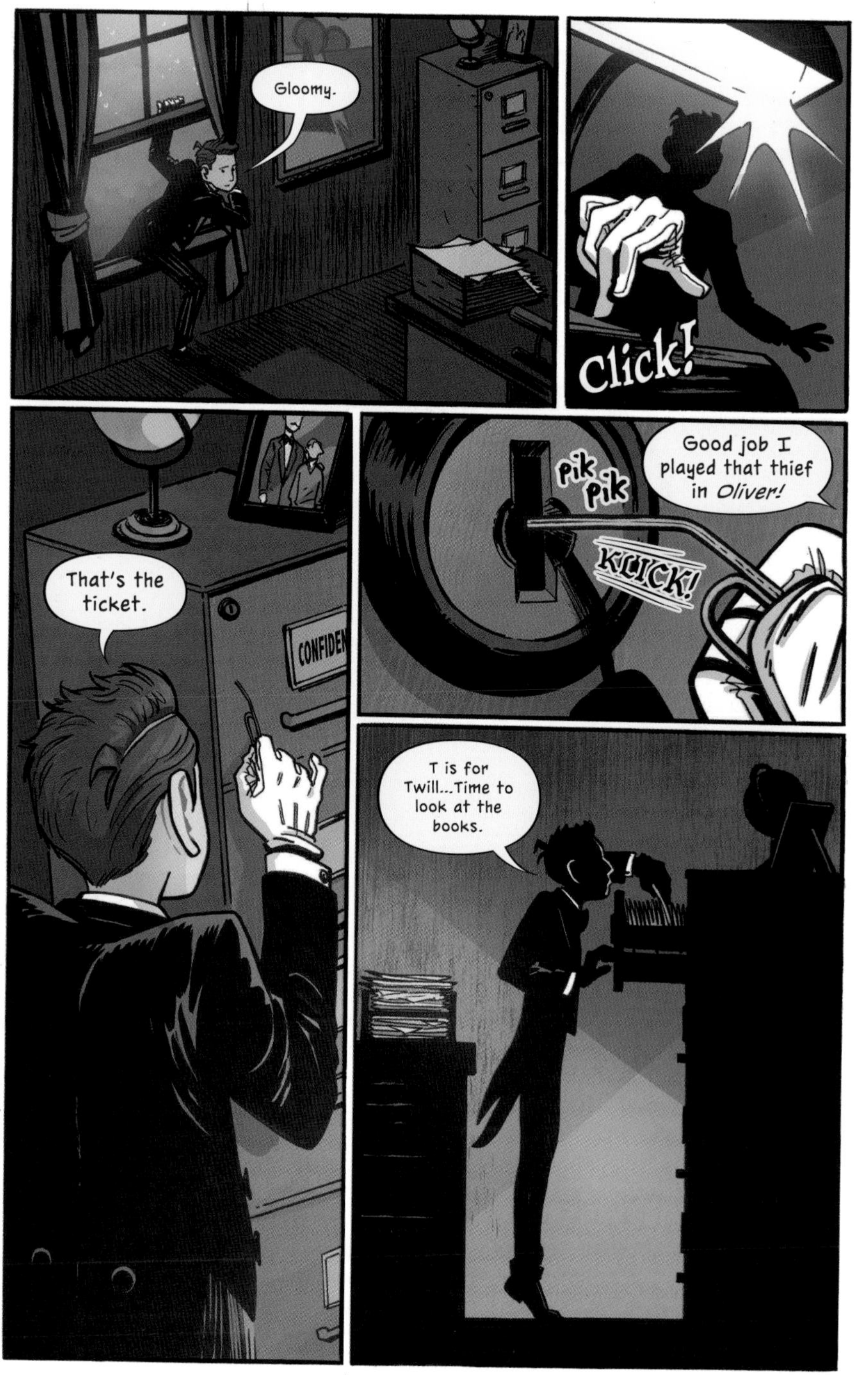
Gloomy.
Click!
That's the ticket.
CONFIDEN
PIK PIK
Good job I played that thief in *Oliver!*
KLICK!
T is for Twill...Time to look at the books.

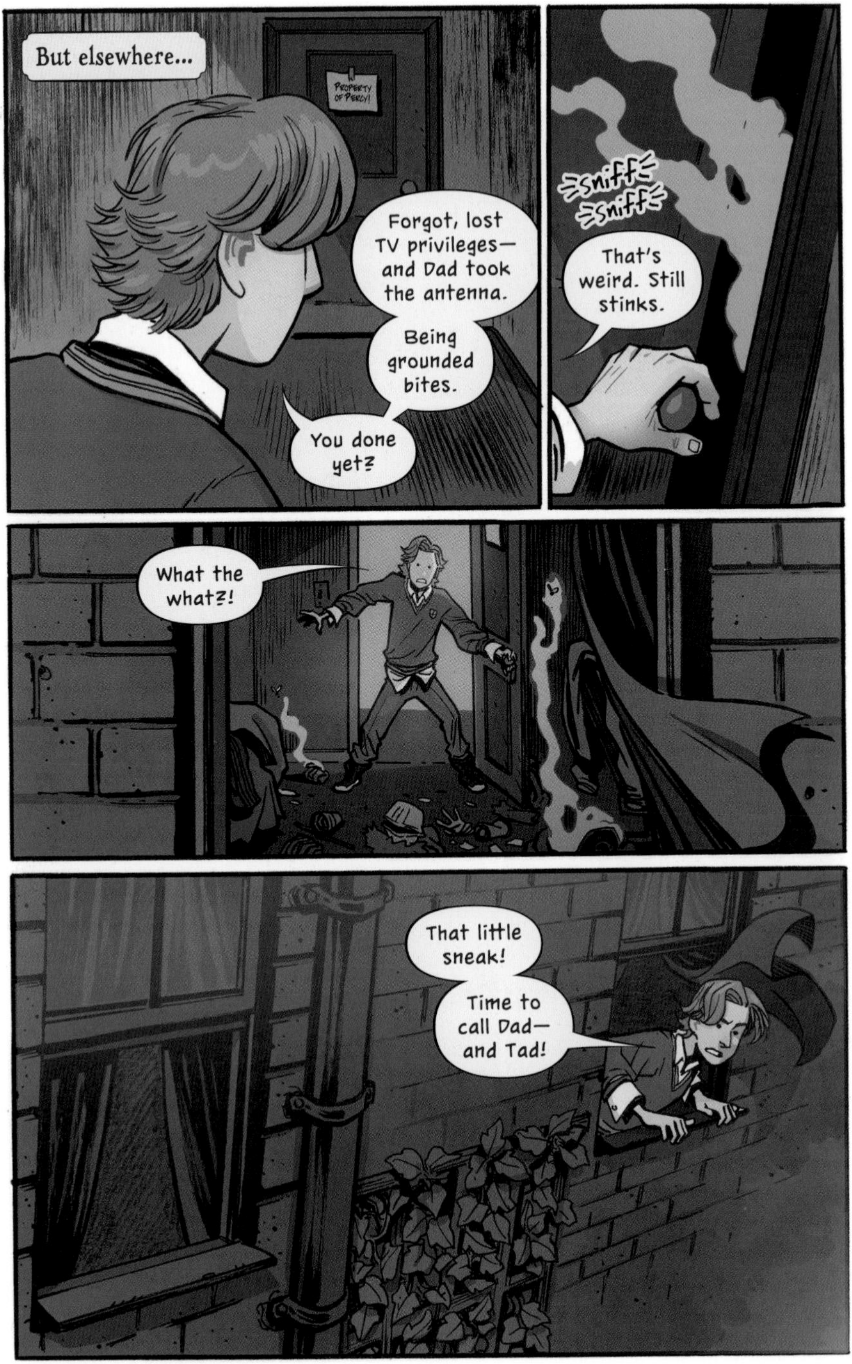

But elsewhere...
PROPERTY OF PERCY!
Forgot, lost TV privileges—and Dad took the antenna.
Being grounded bites.
You done yet?
SNIFF SNIFF
That's weird. Still stinks.
What the what?!
That little sneak!
Time to call Dad—and Tad!

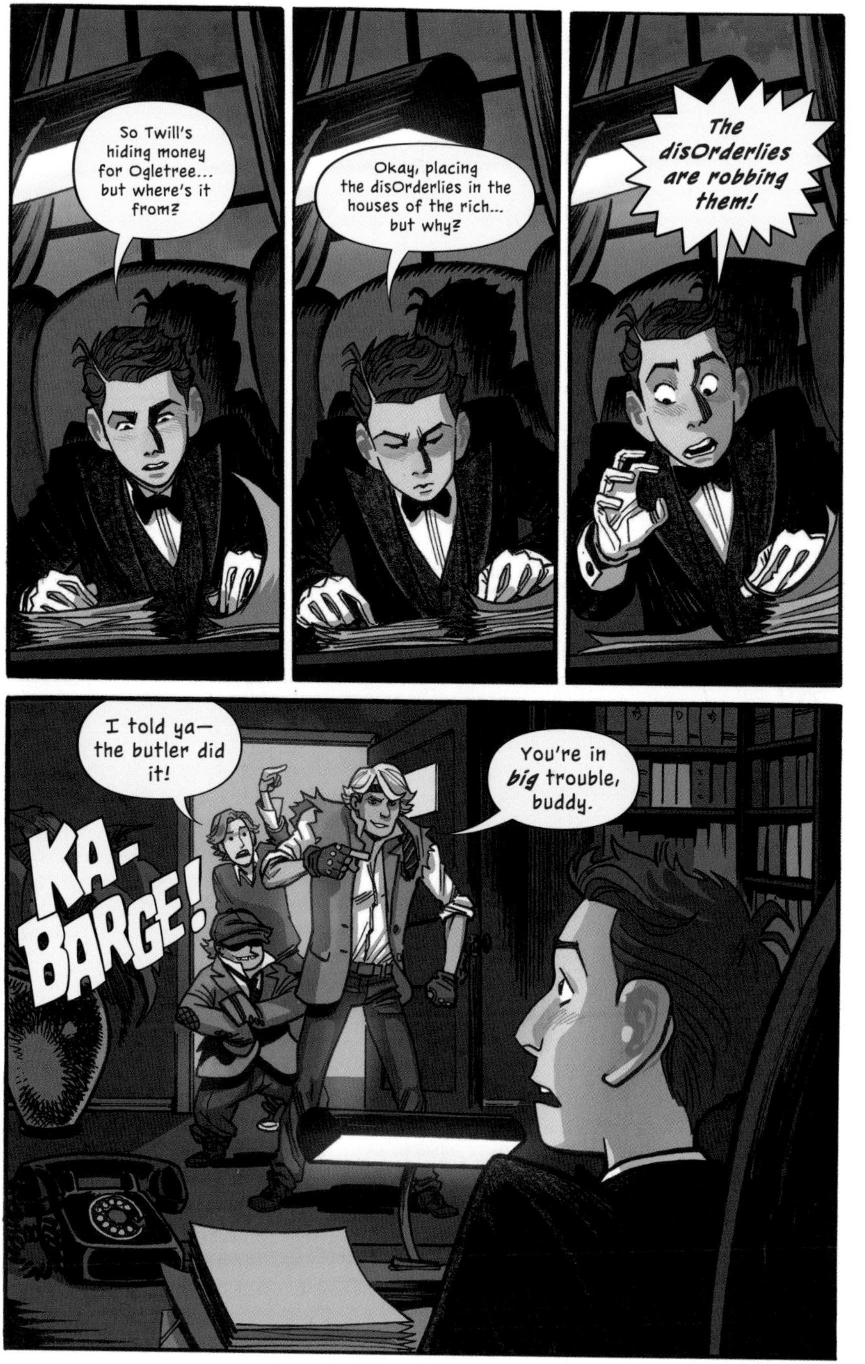
So Twill's hiding money for Ogletree... but where's it from?
Okay, placing the disOrderlies in the houses of the rich... but why?
The disOrderlies are robbing them!
I told ya— the butler did it!
You're in *big* trouble, buddy.
KA-BARGE!

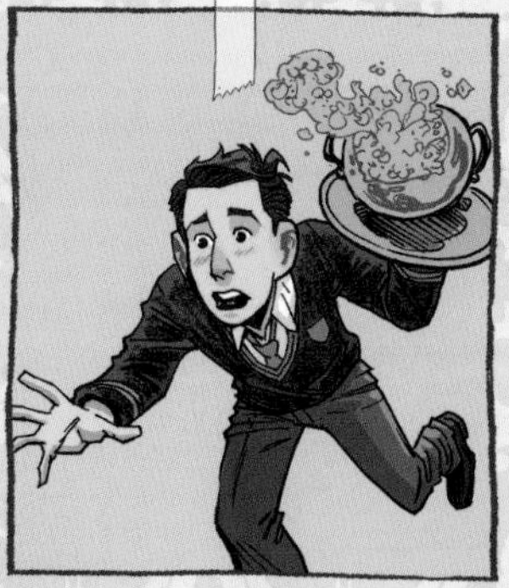

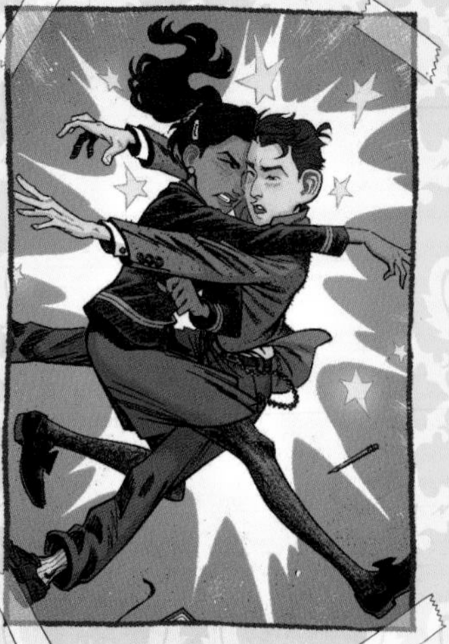

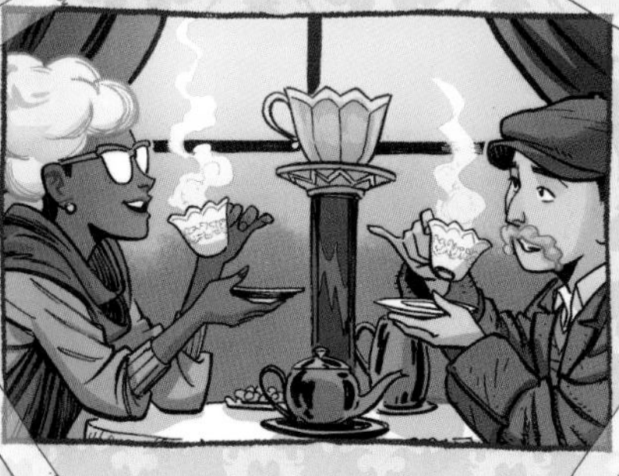

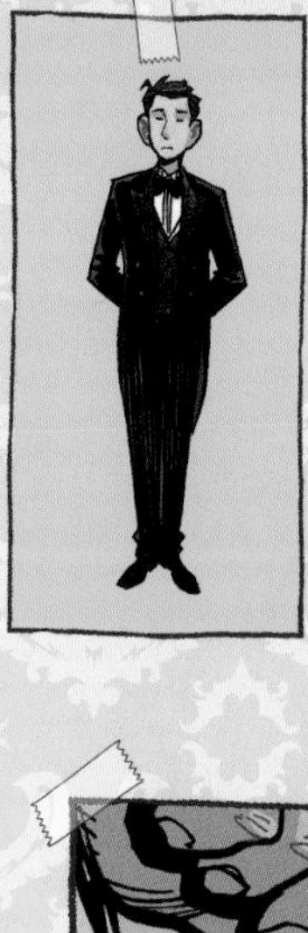

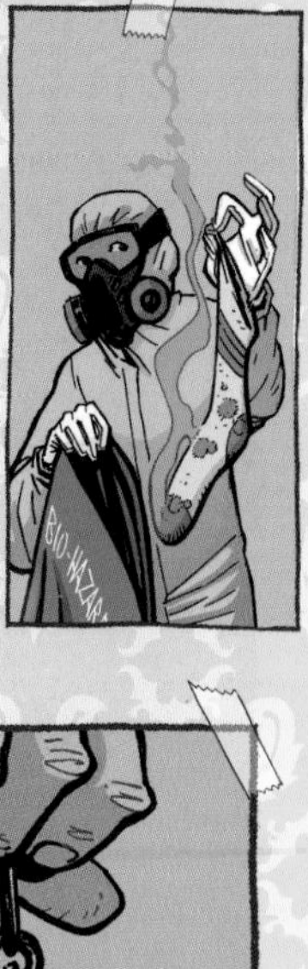

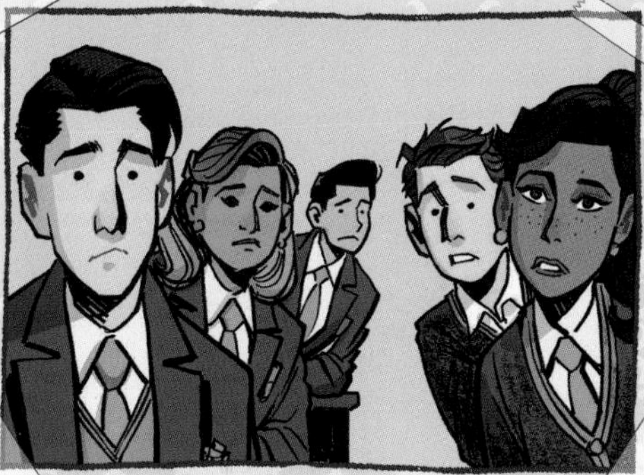

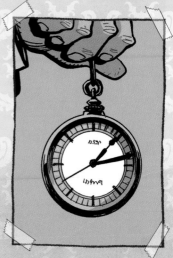

CHAPTER 9

Your Name Is Mud!

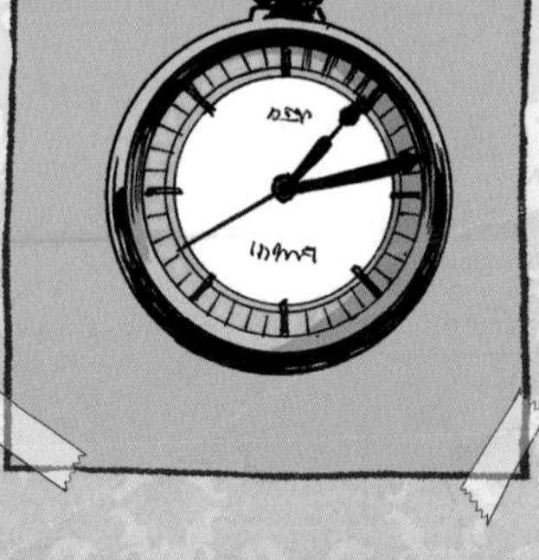

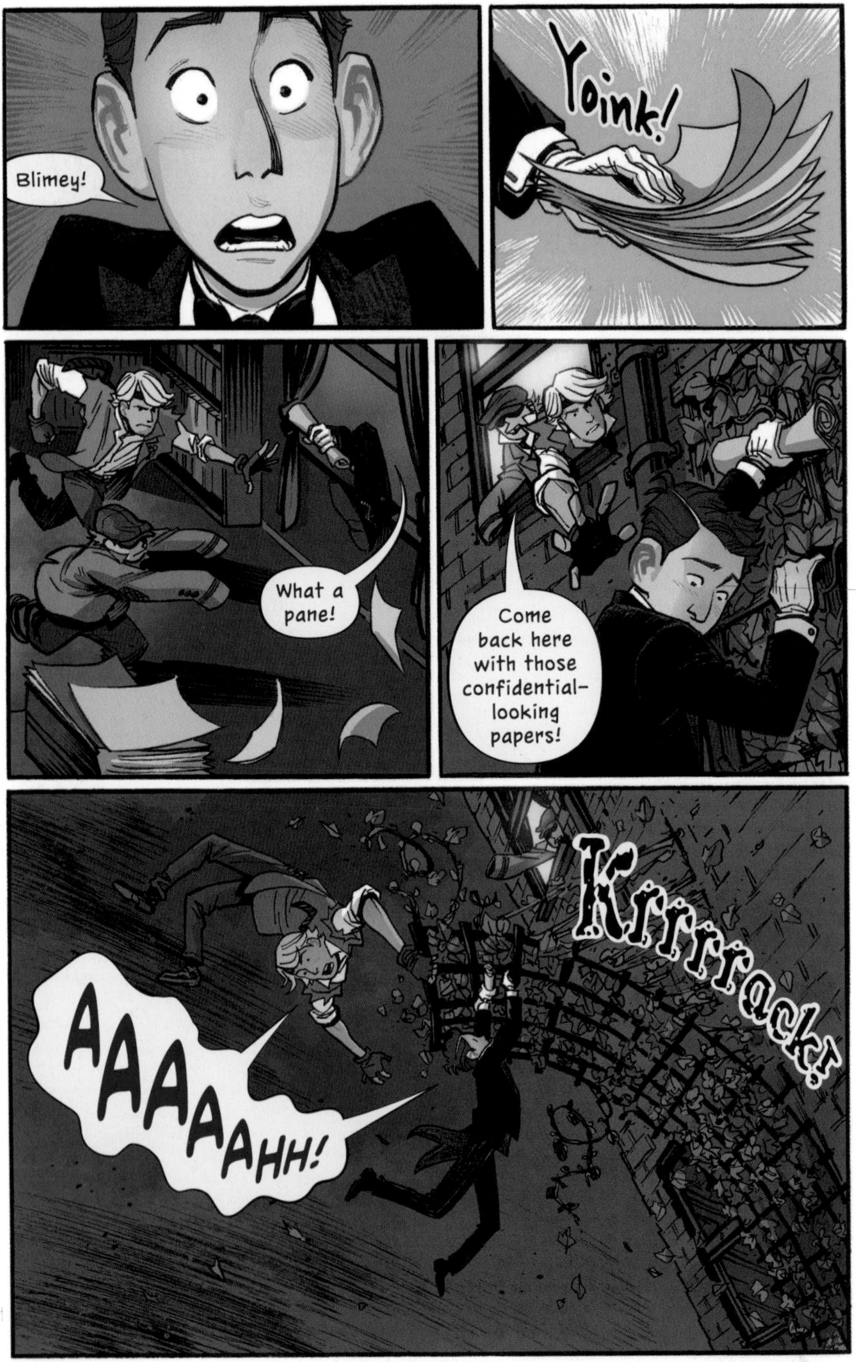
Blimey!
Yoink!
What a pane!
Come back here with those confidential-looking papers!
Krrrrack!
AAAAAHH!

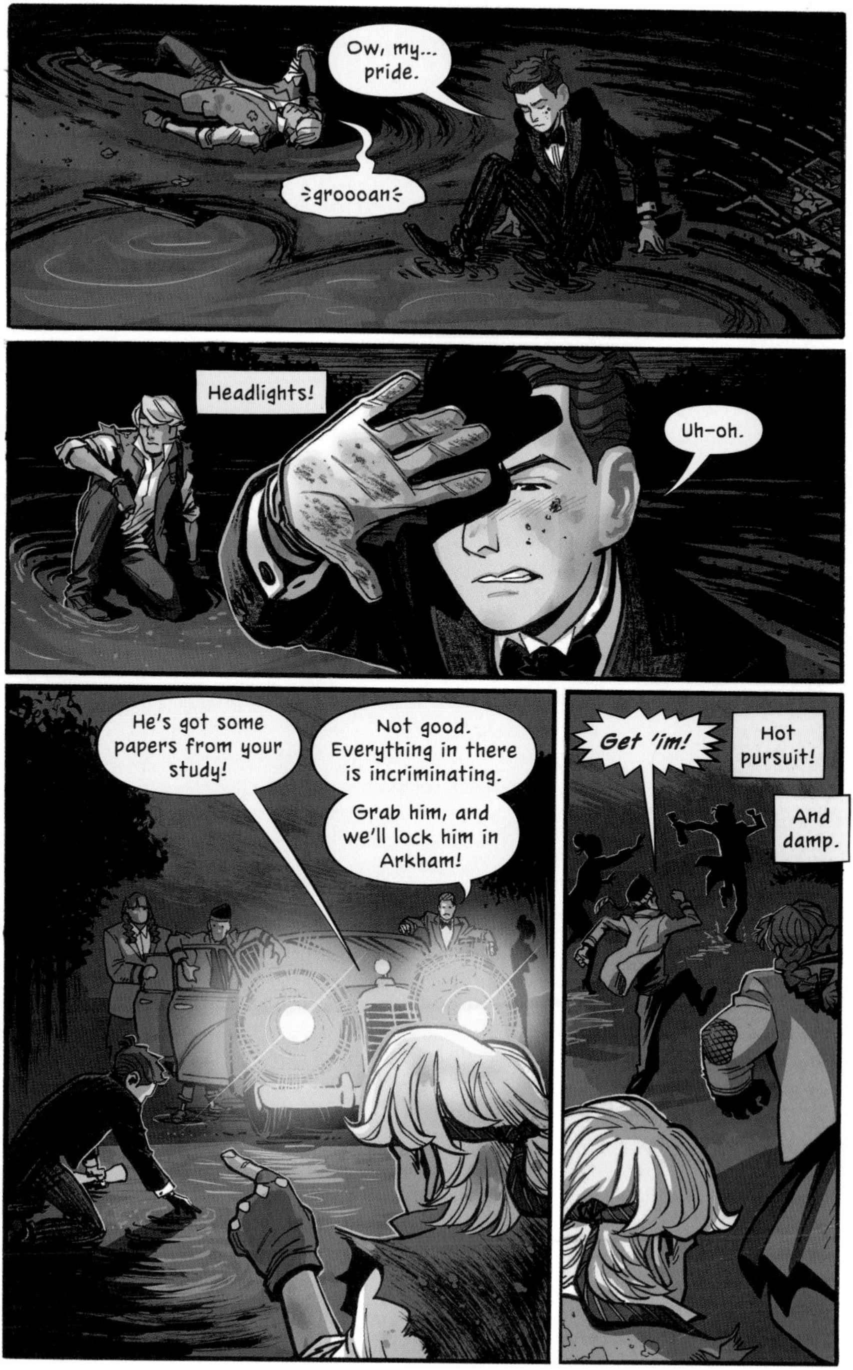
Ow, my... pride.
groooan
Headlights!
Uh-oh.
He's got some papers from your study!
Not good. Everything in there is incriminating.
Grab him, and we'll lock him in Arkham!
Get 'im!
Hot pursuit!
And damp.

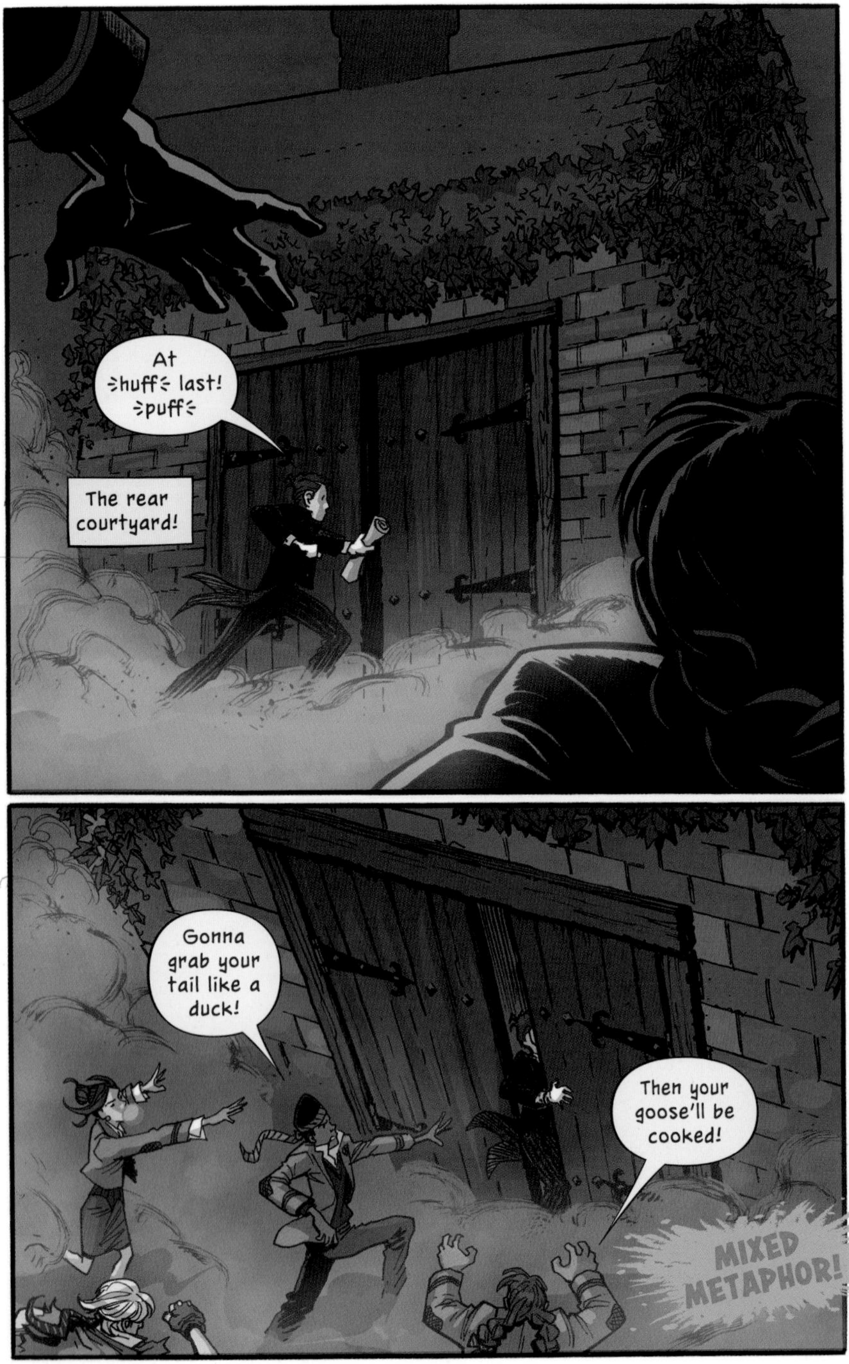

At ≈huff≈ last! ≈puff≈
The rear courtyard!
Gonna grab your tail like a duck!
Then your goose'll be cooked!
MIXED METAPHOR!

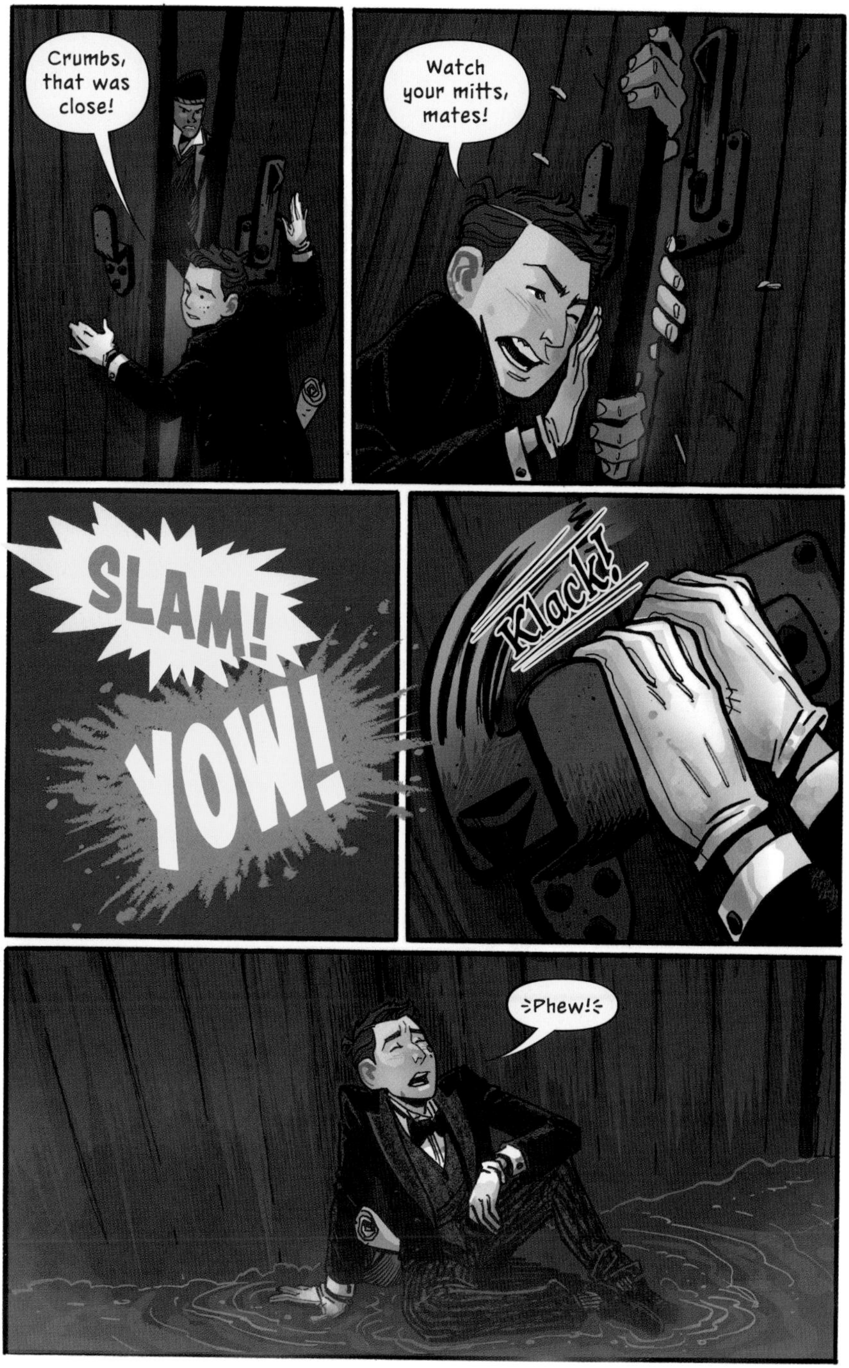
Crumbs, that was close!
Watch your mitts, mates!
SLAM!
YOW!
Klack!
Phew!

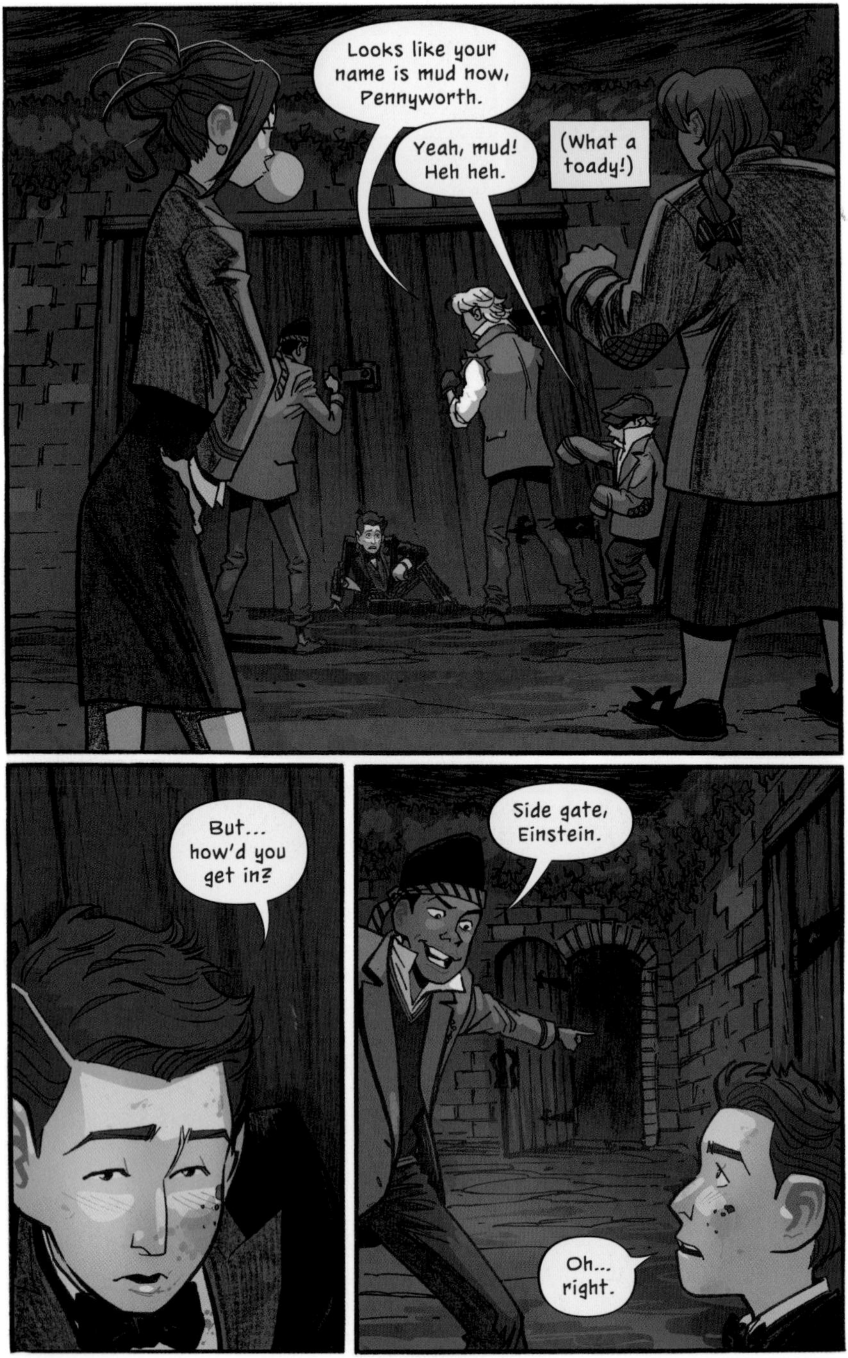
Looks like your name is mud now, Pennyworth.
Yeah, mud! Heh heh.
(What a toady!)
But... how'd you get in?
Side gate, Einstein.
Oh... right.

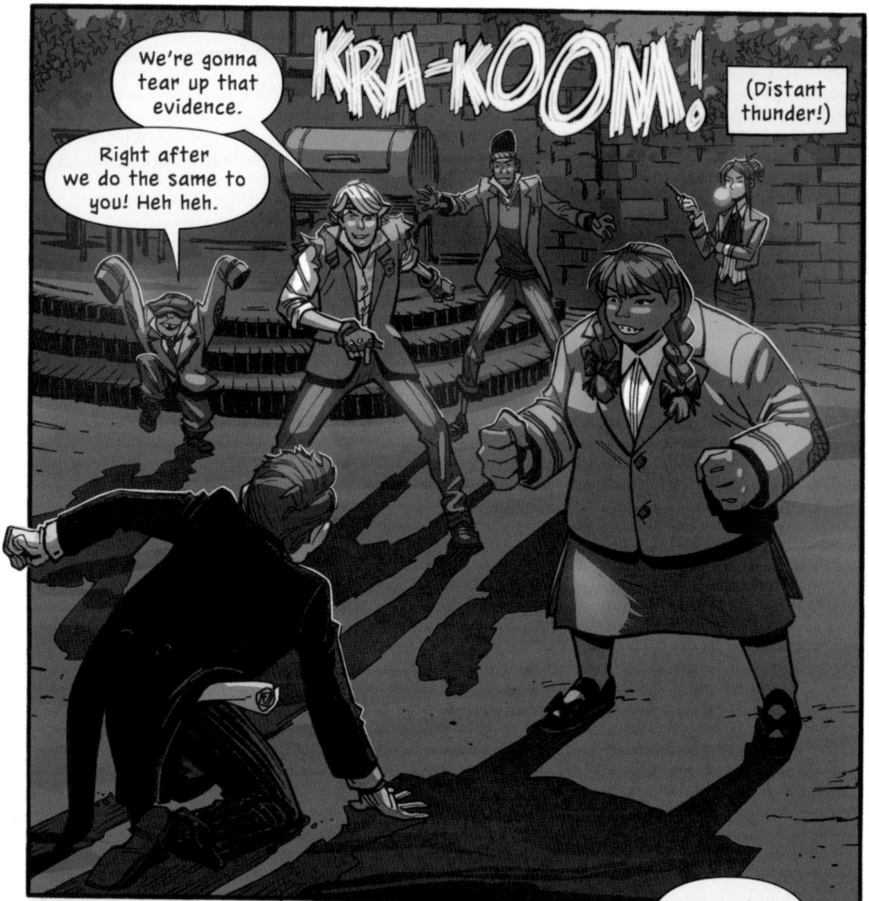
We're gonna tear up that evidence.
Right after we do the same to you! Heh heh.
KRA-KOOM!
(Distant thunder!)

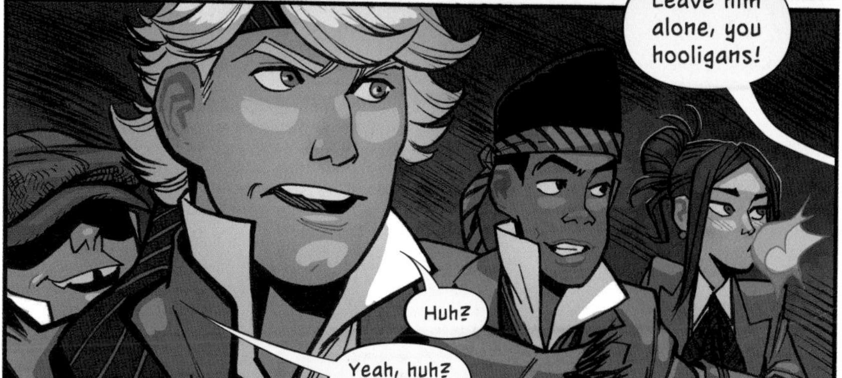
Leave him alone, you hooligans!
Huh?
Yeah, huh? Heh heh.

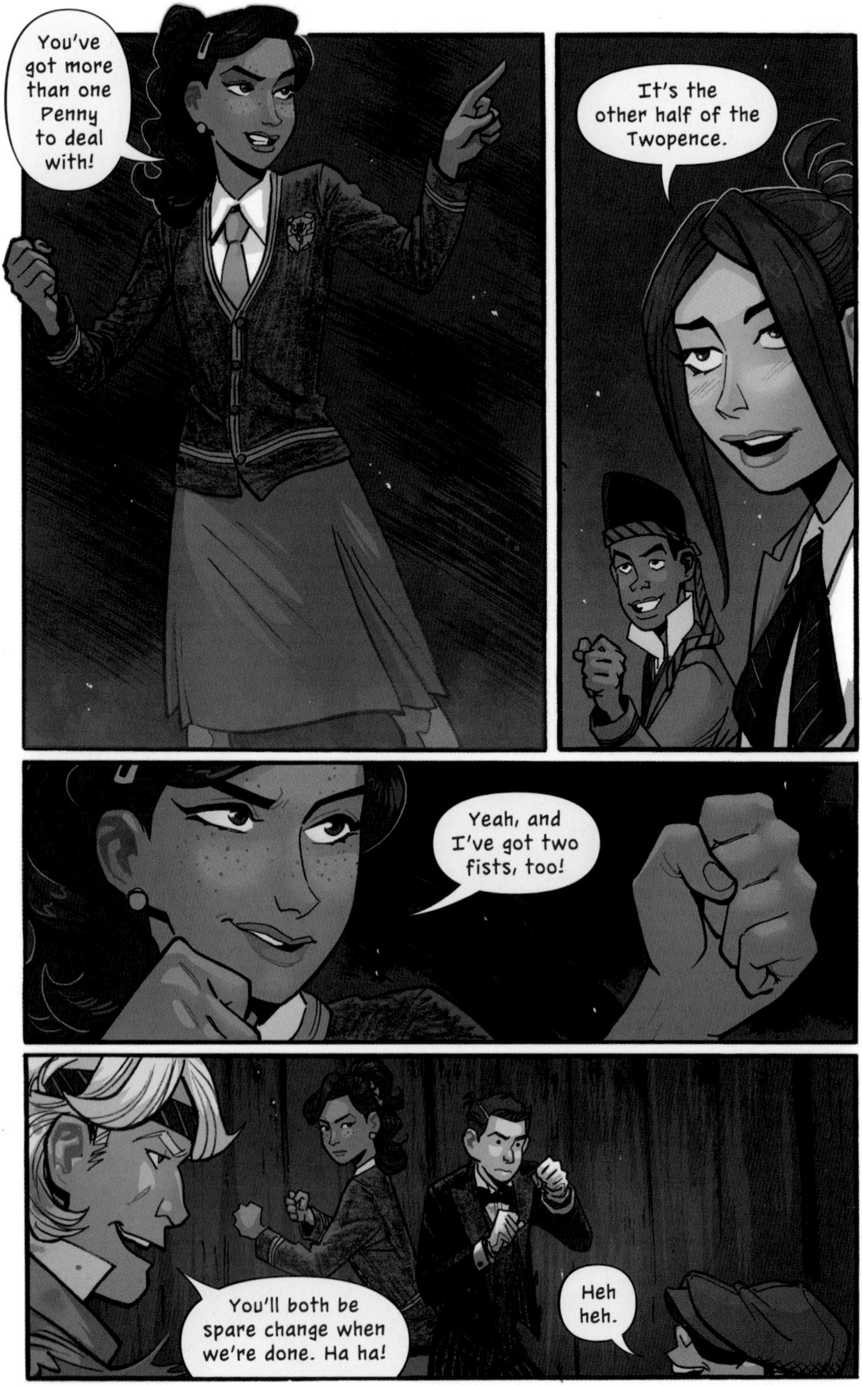
You've got more than one Penny to deal with!
It's the other half of the Twopence.
Yeah, and I've got two fists, too!
You'll both be spare change when we're done. Ha ha!
Heh heh.

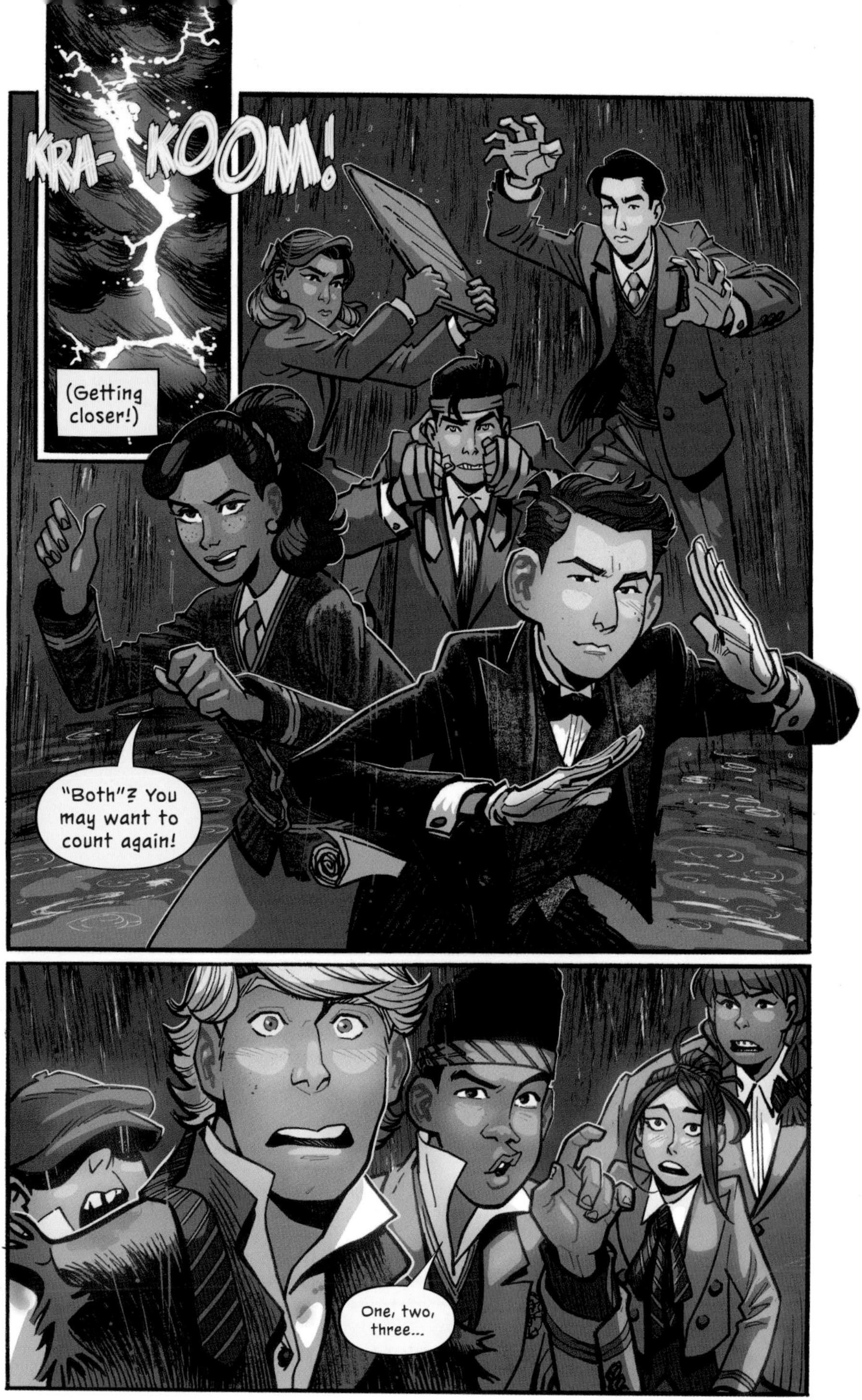
KRA-KOOM!
(Getting closer!)
"Both"? You may want to count again!
One, two, three...

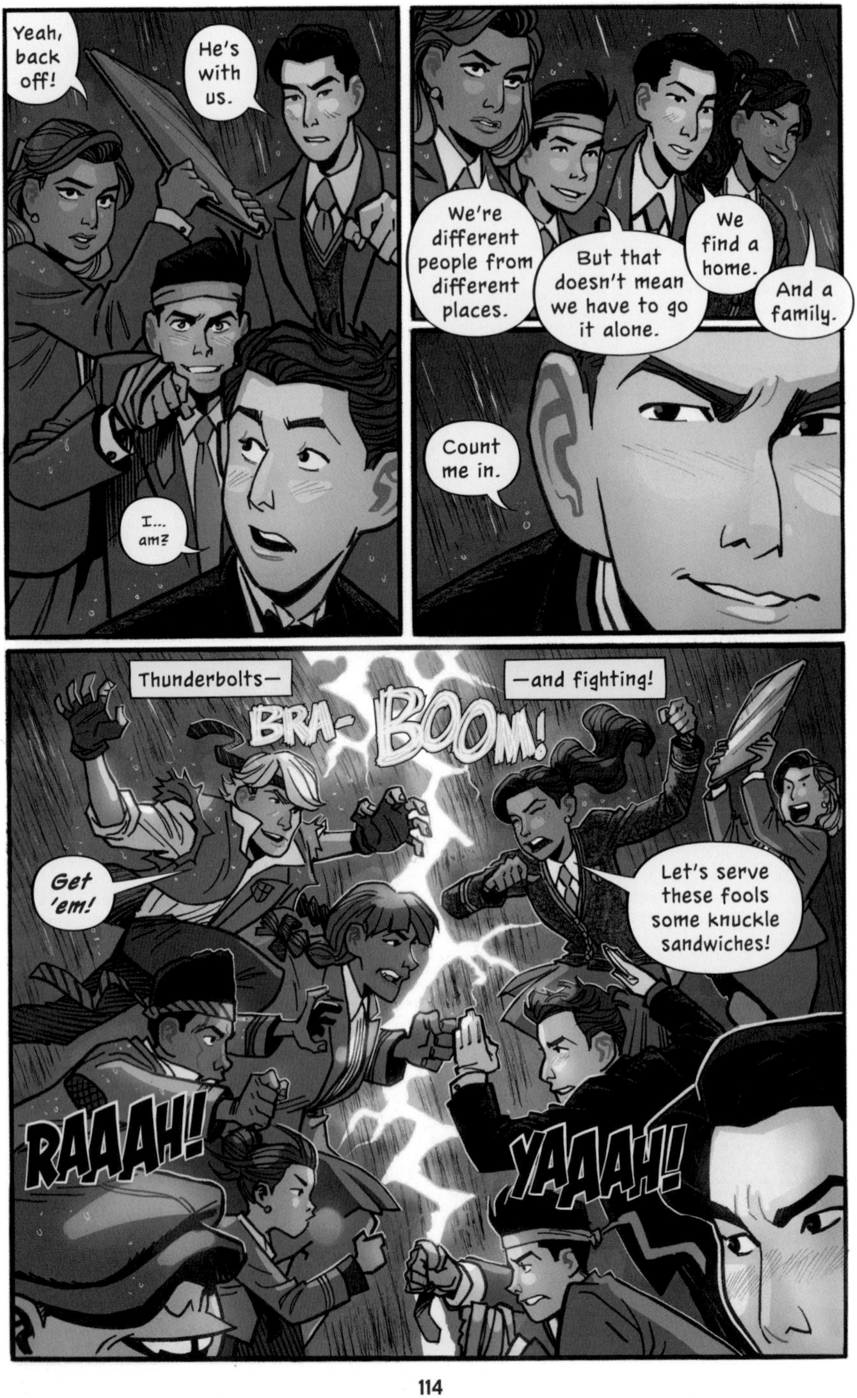

Yeah, back off!
He's with us.
I... am?
We're different people from different places.
But that doesn't mean we have to go it alone.
We find a home.
And a family.
Count me in.
Thunderbolts—
BRA-BOOM!
—and fighting!
Get 'em!
Let's serve these fools some knuckle sandwiches!
RAAAH!
YAAAH!

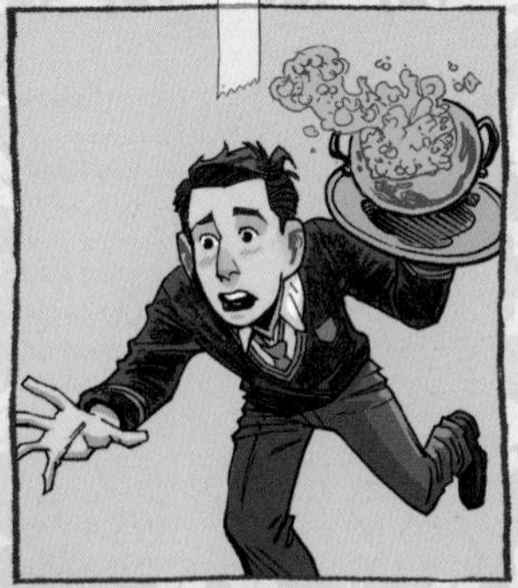

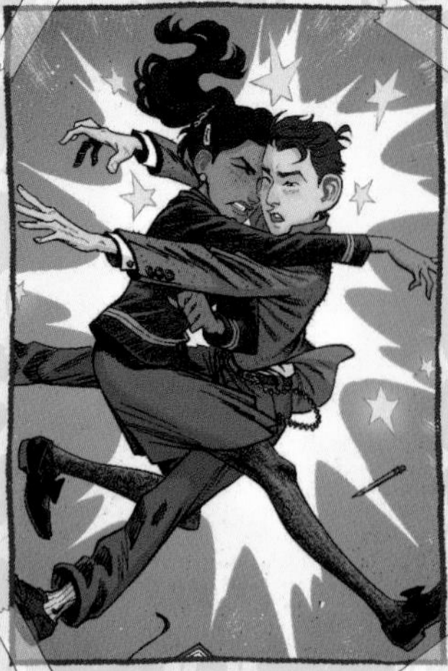

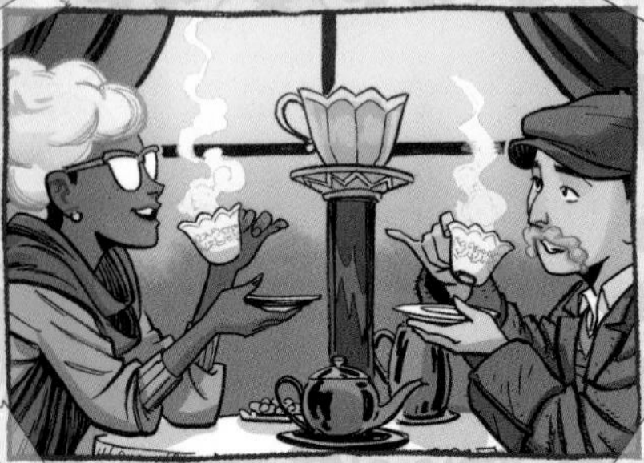

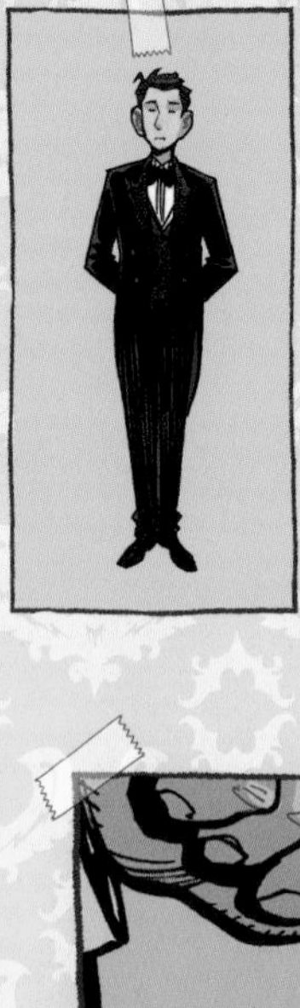

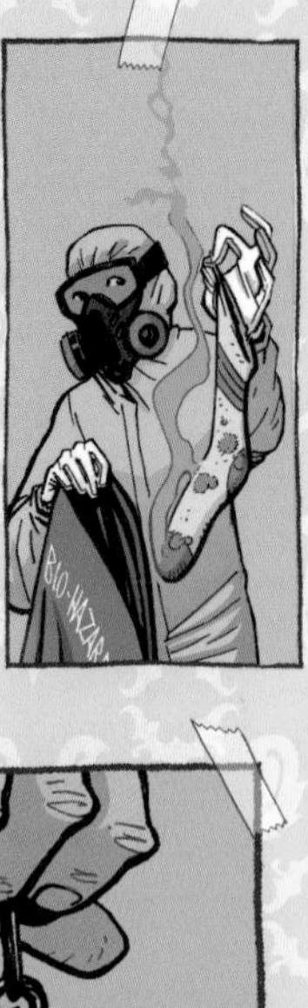

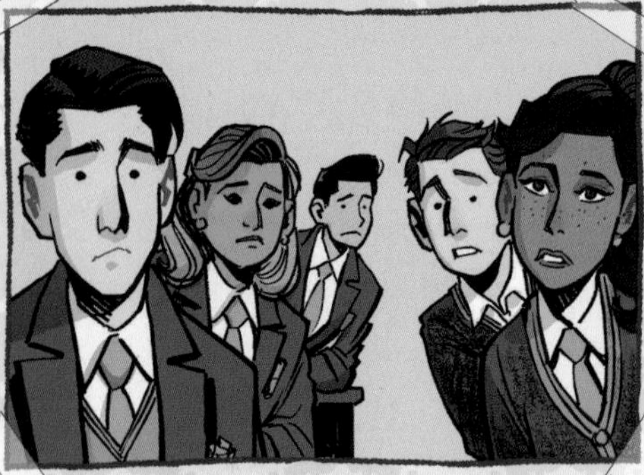

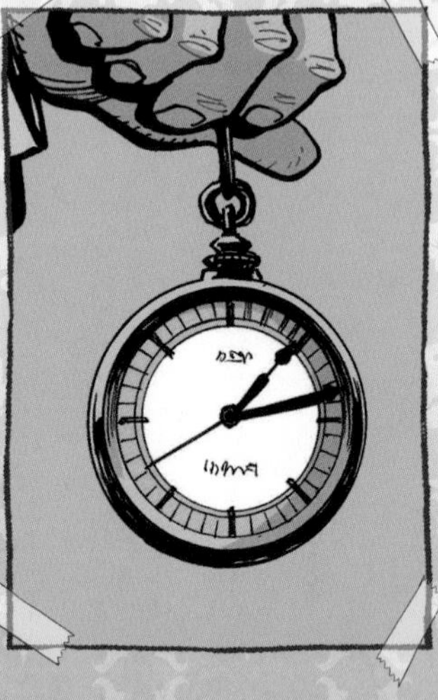

CHAPTER 10

Justice Is Served!

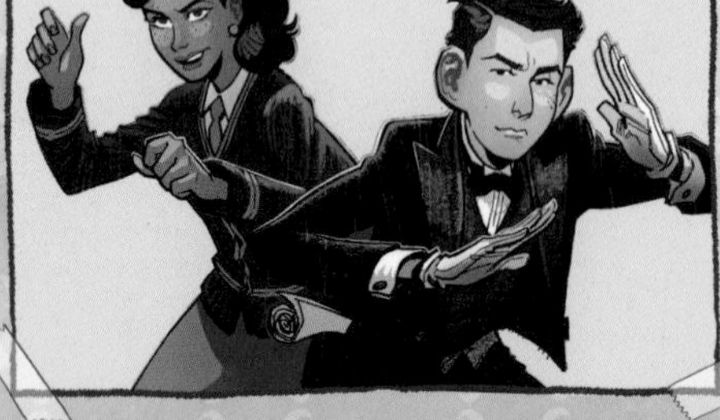

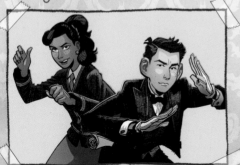

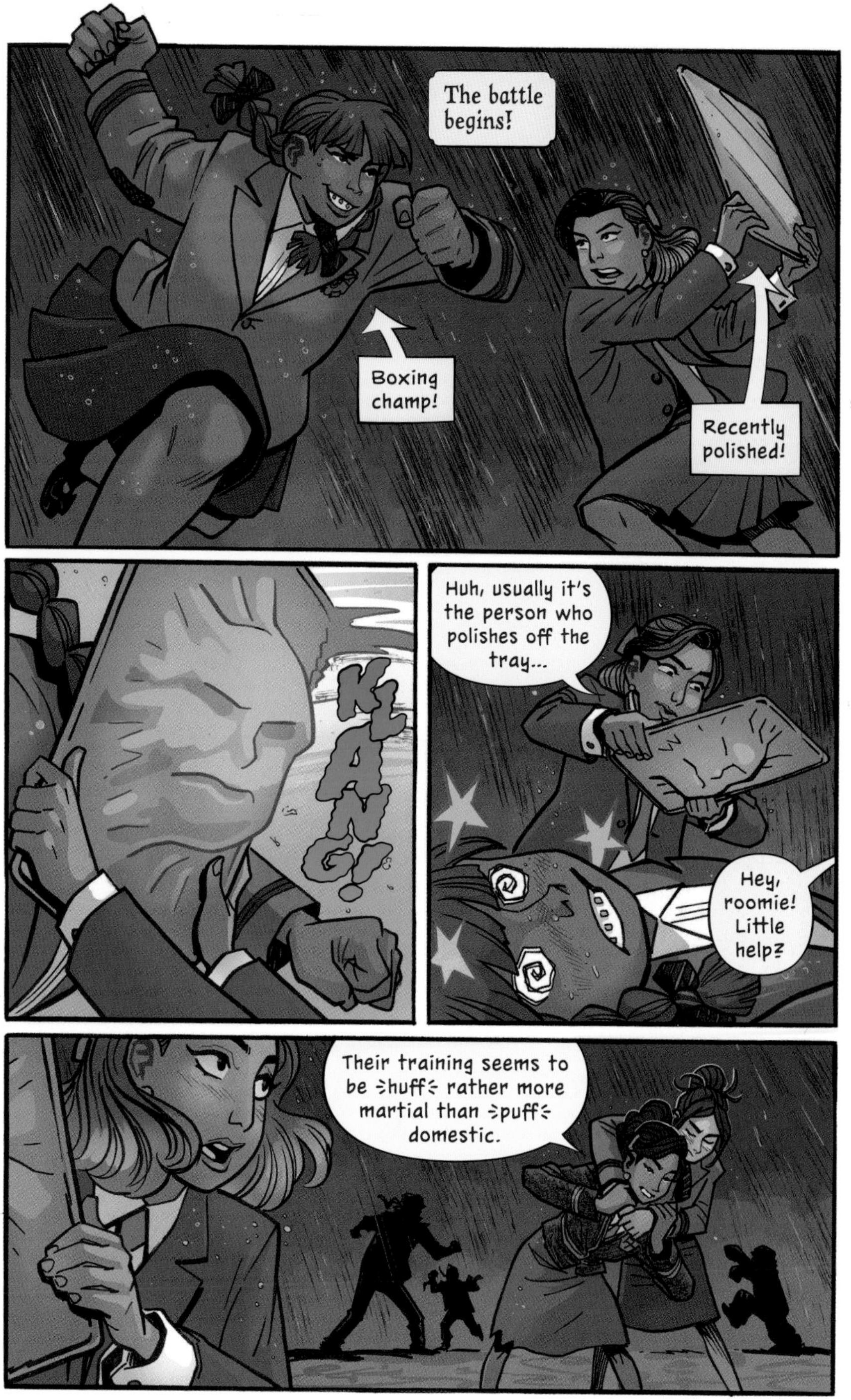
The battle begins!
Boxing champ!
Recently polished!
KLANG!
Huh, usually it's the person who polishes off the tray...
Hey, roomie! Little help?
Their training seems to be =huff= rather more martial than =puff= domestic.

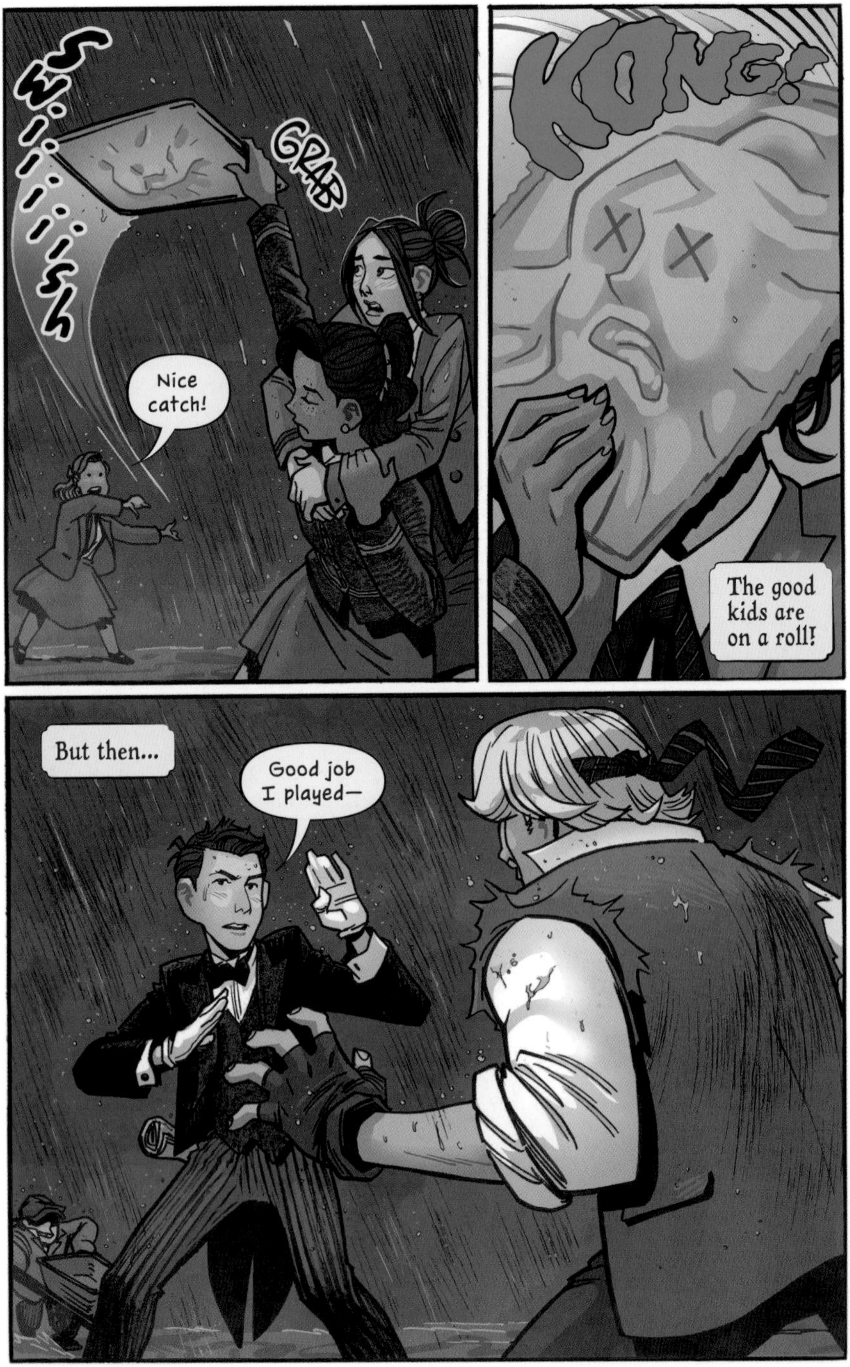
SWIIIIIISH
GRAB
Nice catch!
KONG!
The good kids are on a roll!
But then...
Good job I played—

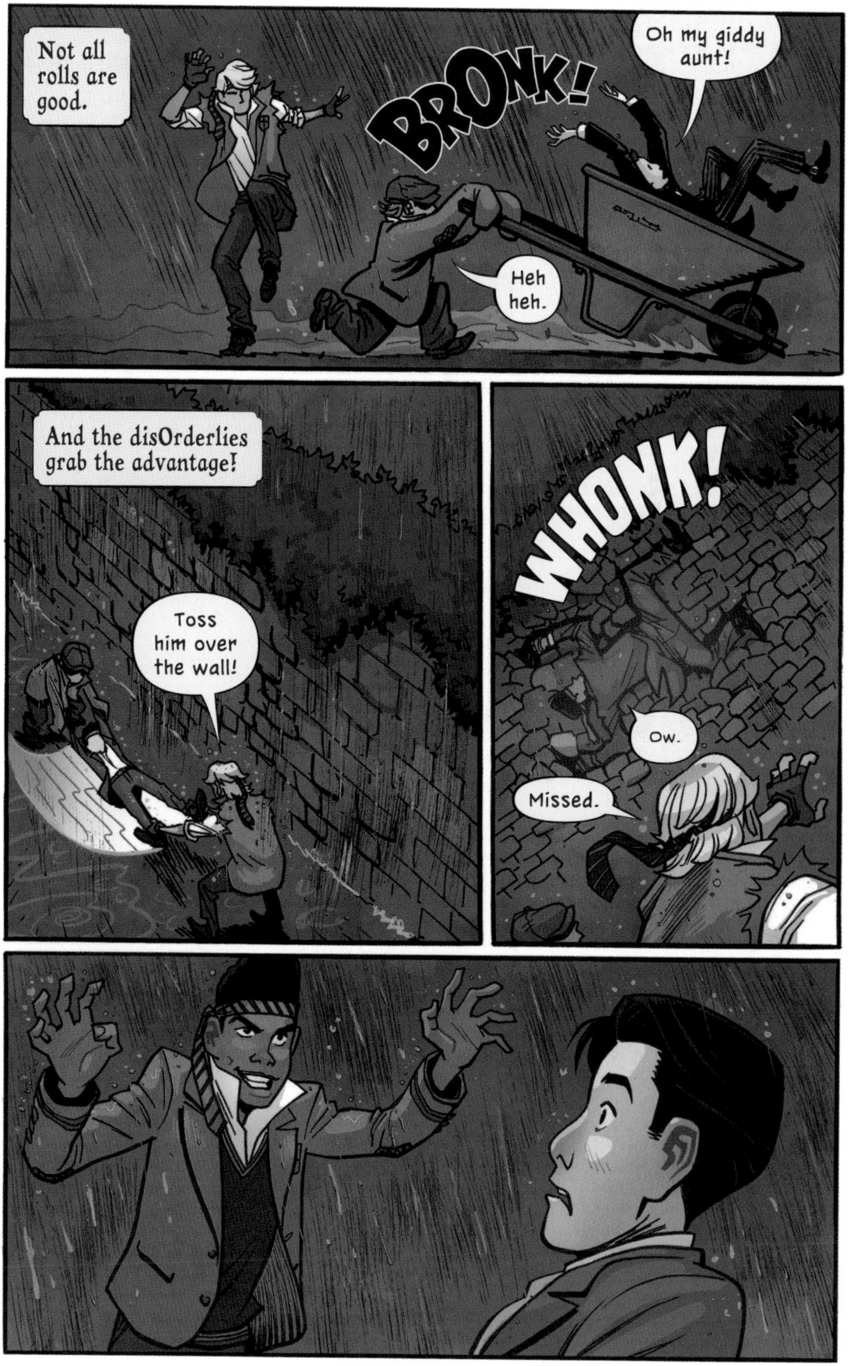
Not all rolls are good.
BRONK!
Oh my giddy aunt!
Heh heh.
And the disOrderlies grab the advantage!
Toss him over the wall!
WHONK!
Ow.
Missed.

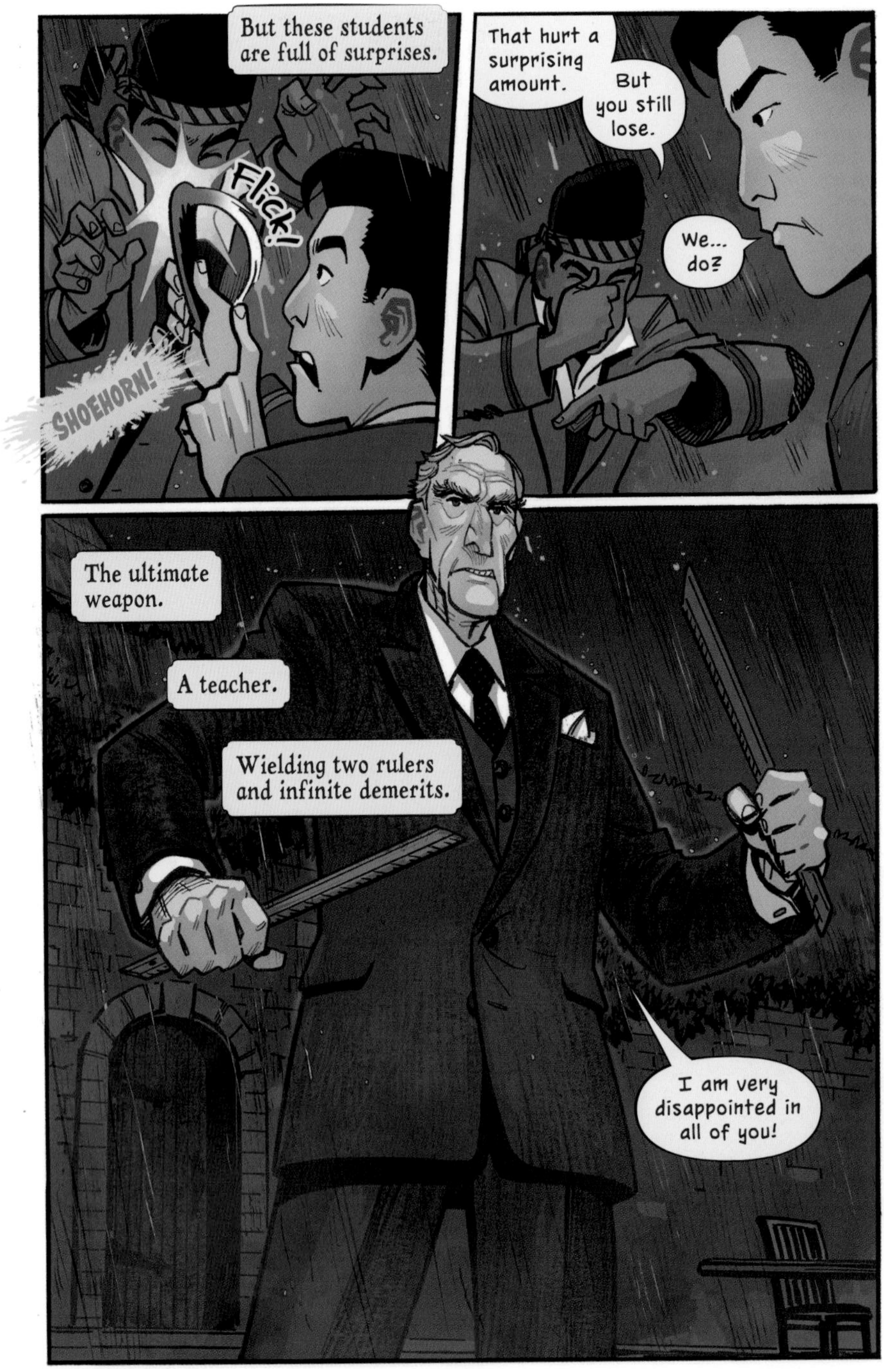
But these students are full of surprises.
Flick!
SHOEHORN!
That hurt a surprising amount.
But you still lose.
We... do?
The ultimate weapon.
A teacher.
Wielding two rulers and infinite demerits.
I am very disappointed in all of you!

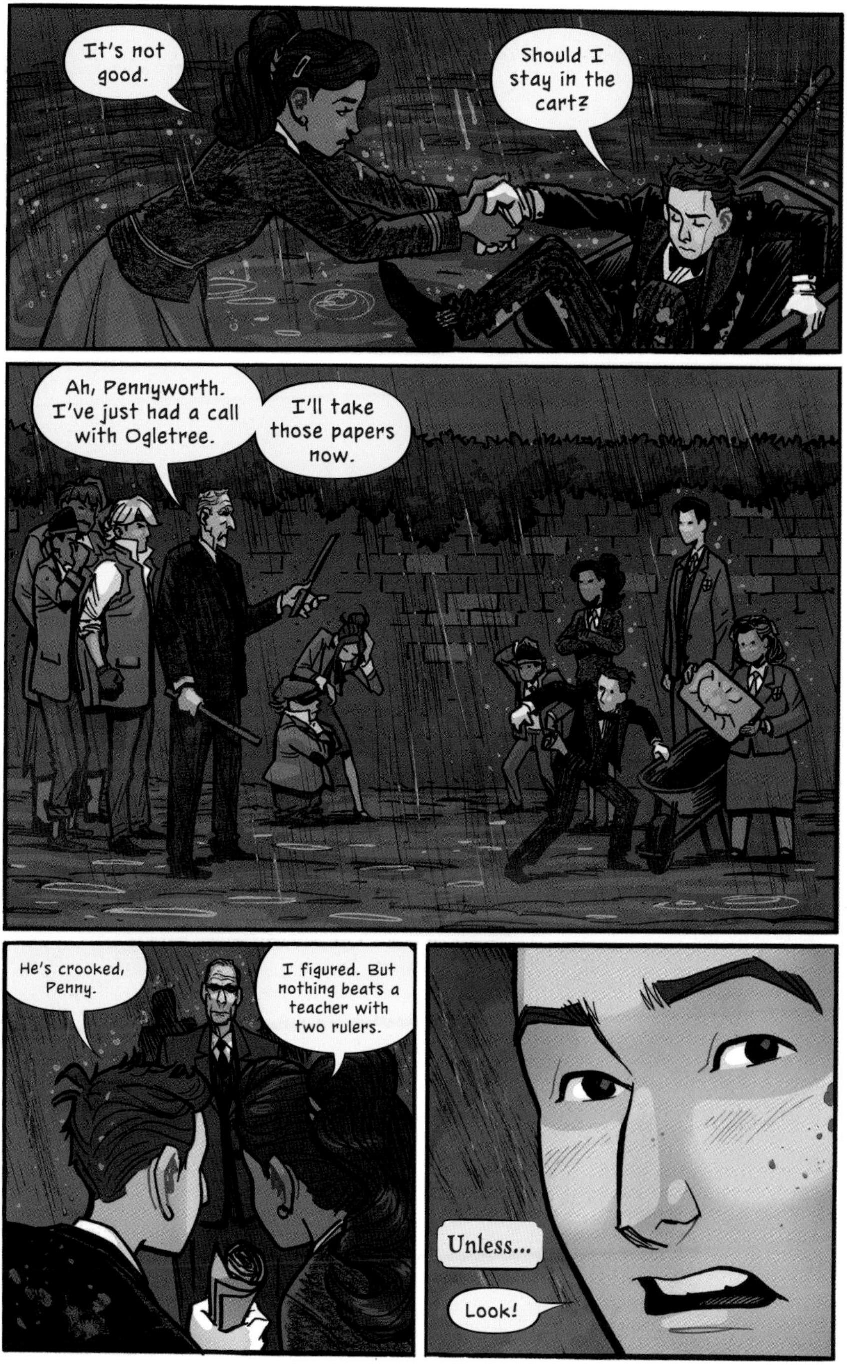
It's not good.
Should I stay in the cart?
Ah, Pennyworth. I've just had a call with Ogletree.
I'll take those papers now.
He's crooked, Penny.
I figured. But nothing beats a teacher with two rulers.
Unless...
Look!

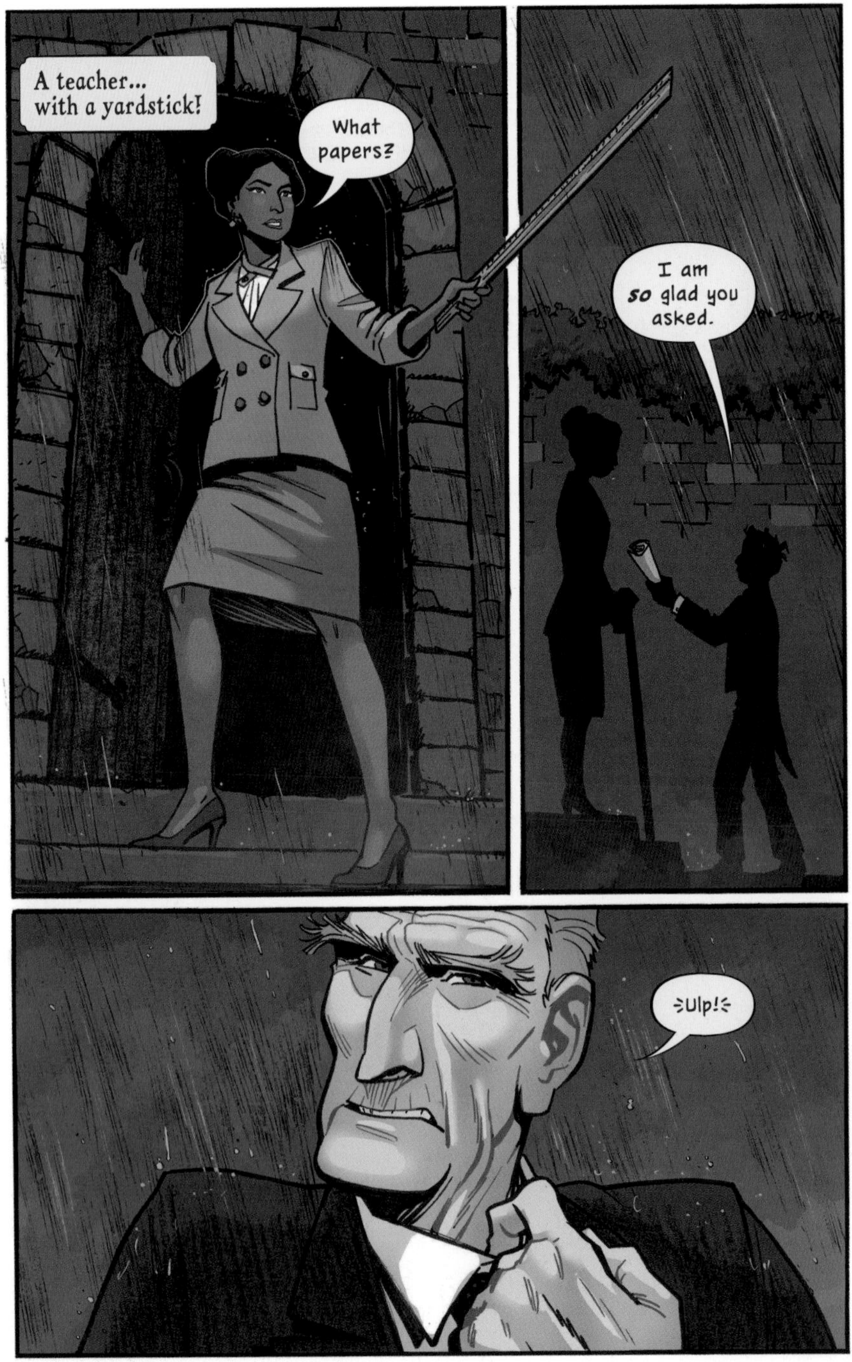
A teacher... with a yardstick!
What papers?
I am *so* glad you asked.
Ulp!

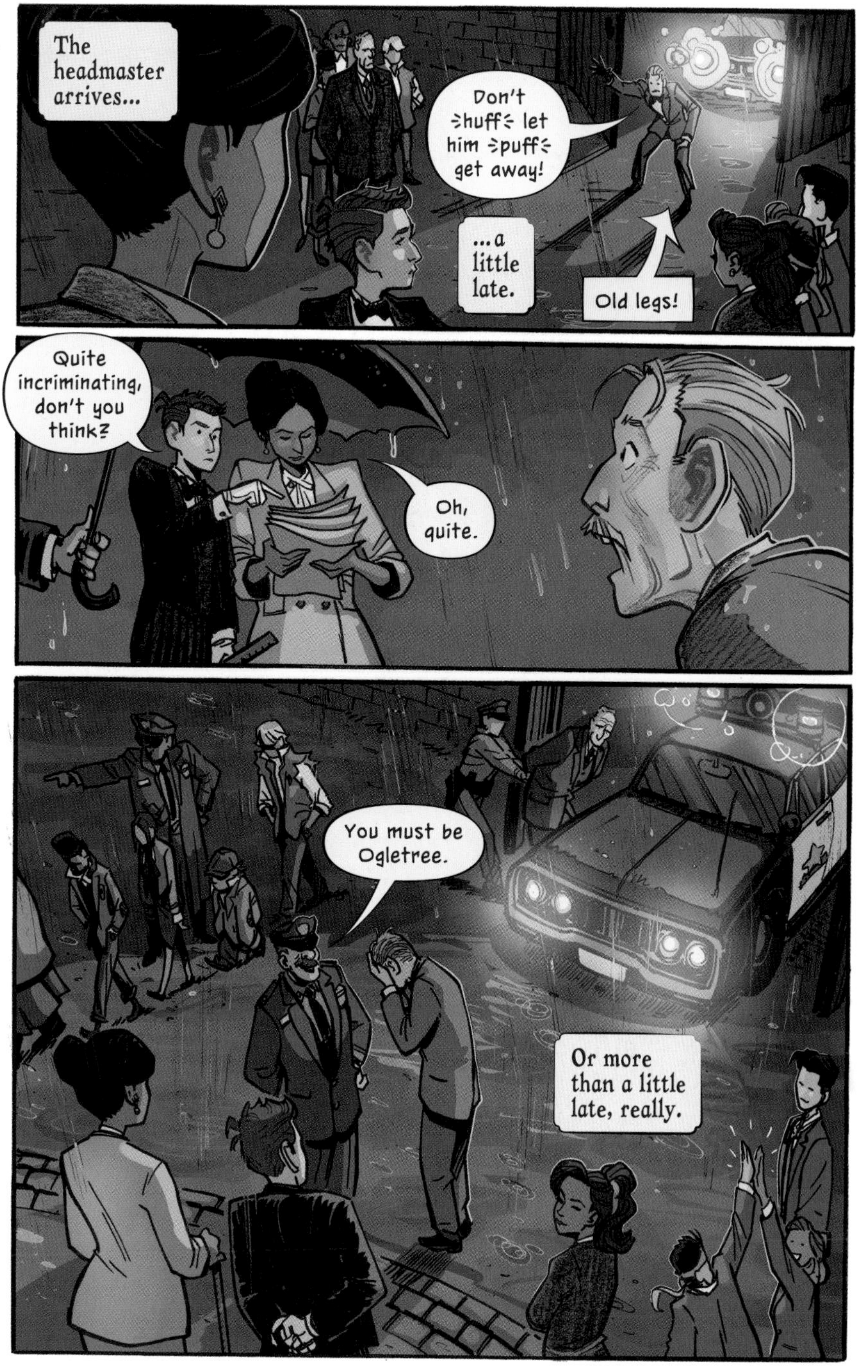
The headmaster arrives...
Don't huff let him puff get away!
...a little late.
Old legs!
Quite incriminating, don't you think?
Oh, quite.
You must be Ogletree.
Or more than a little late, really.

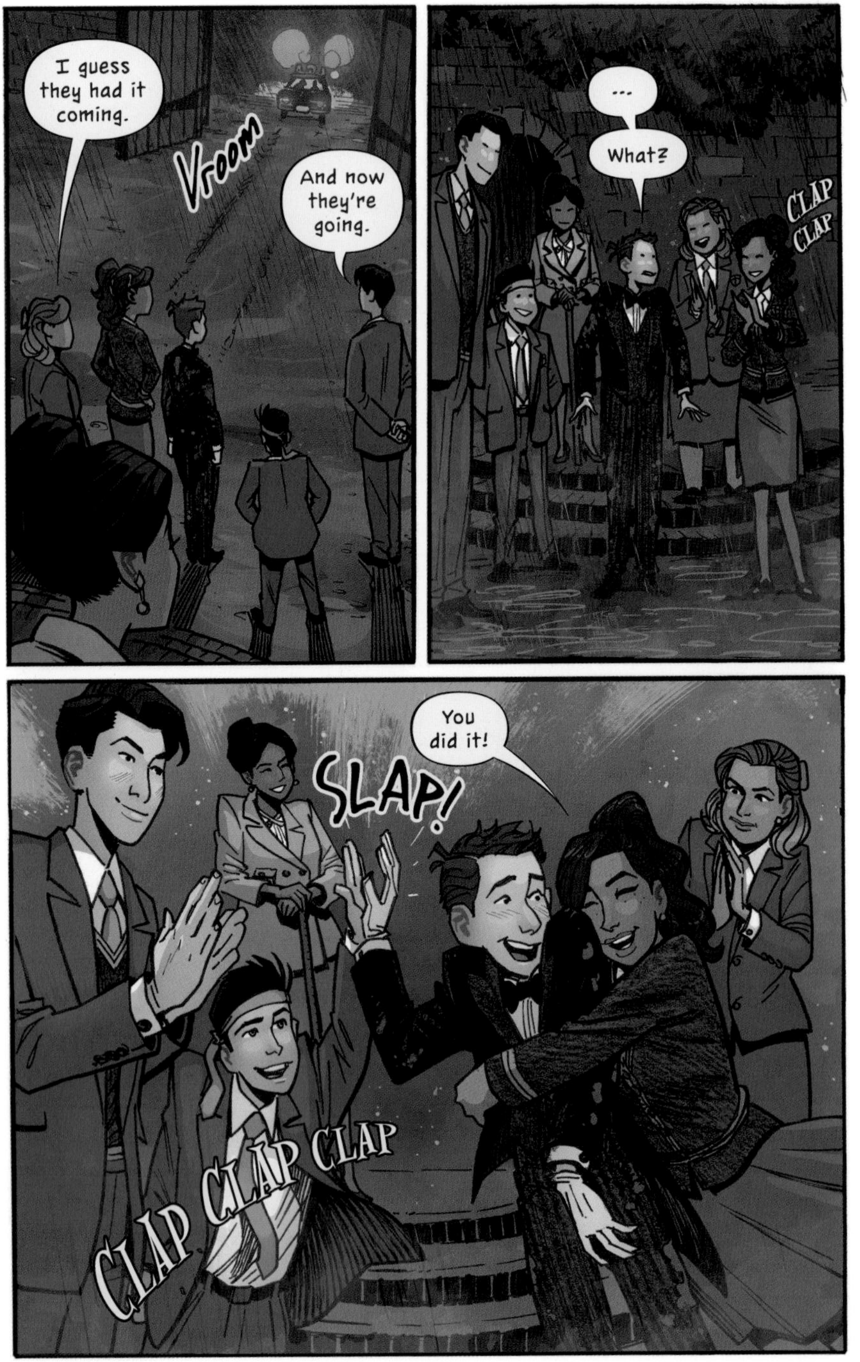

I guess they had it coming.
Vroom
And now they're going.
...
What?
CLAP CLAP
You did it!
SLAP!
CLAP CLAP CLAP

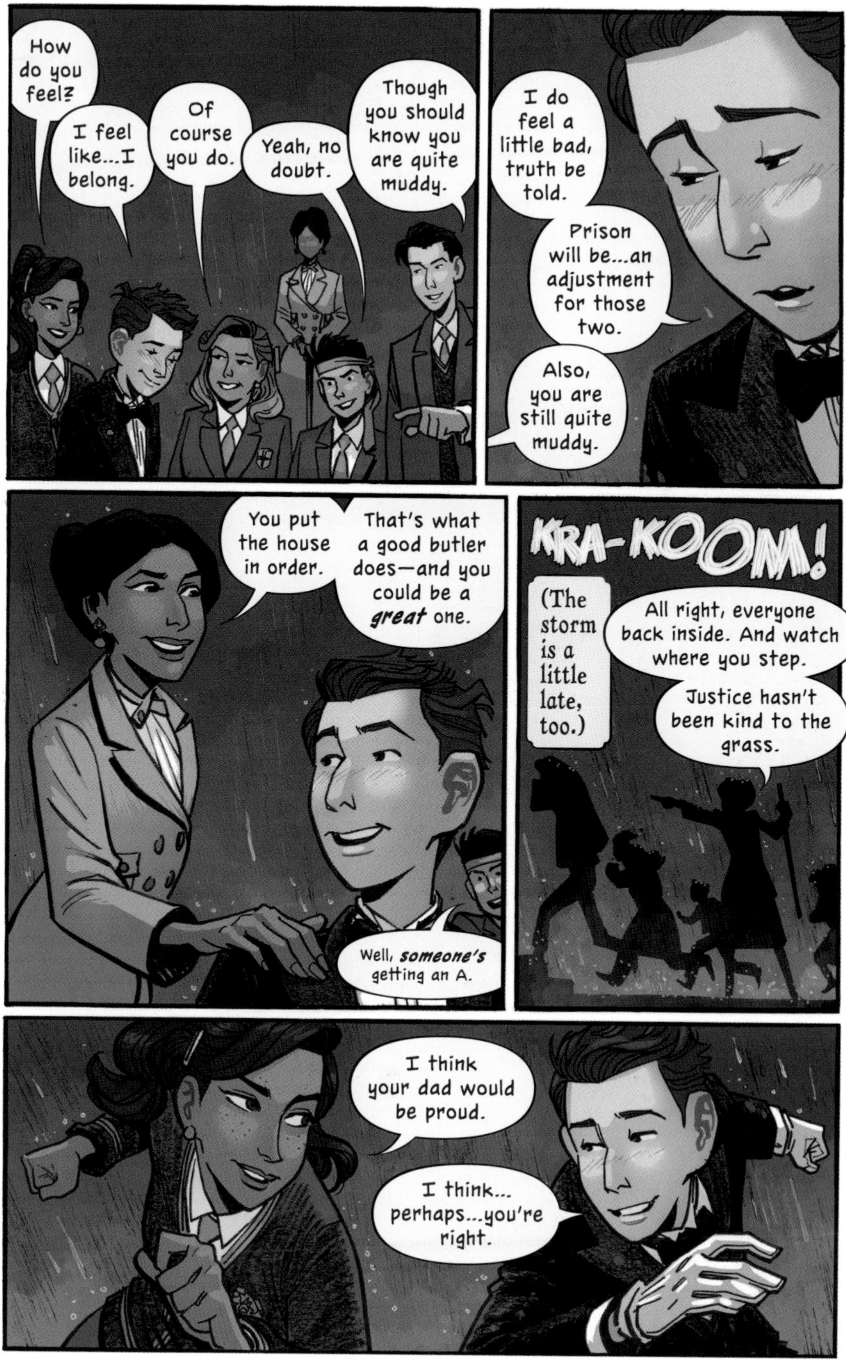
How do you feel?
I feel like...I belong.
Of course you do.
Yeah, no doubt.
Though you should know you are quite muddy.
I do feel a little bad, truth be told.
Prison will be...an adjustment for those two.
Also, you are still quite muddy.
You put the house in order.
That's what a good butler does—and you could be a *great* one.
Well, ***someone's*** getting an A.
KRA-KOOM!
(The storm is a little late, too.)
All right, everyone back inside. And watch where you step.
Justice hasn't been kind to the grass.
I think your dad would be proud.
I think... perhaps...you're right.

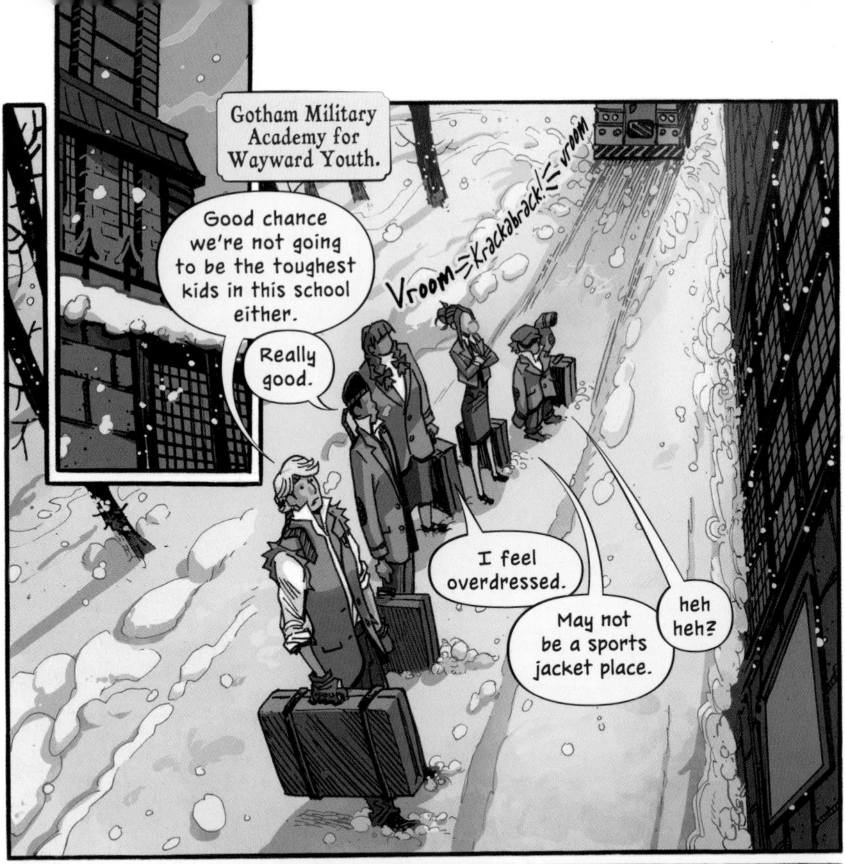
Gotham Military Academy for Wayward Youth.
Good chance we're not going to be the toughest kids in this school either.
Really good.
Vroom Krackabrack! vroom
I feel overdressed.
May not be a sports jacket place.
heh heh?

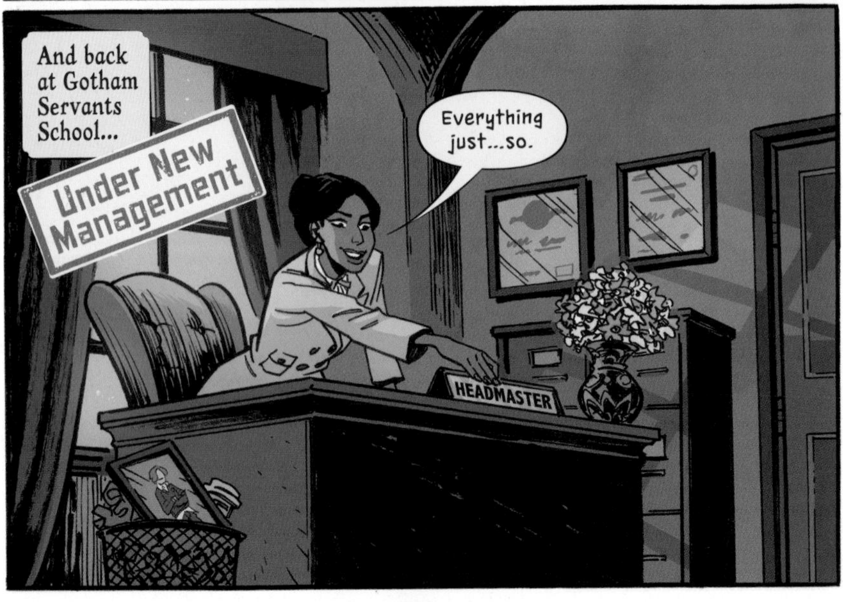
And back at Gotham Servants School...
Under New Management
Everything just...so.
HEADMASTER

CHAPTER 11
Chutes
and Liars

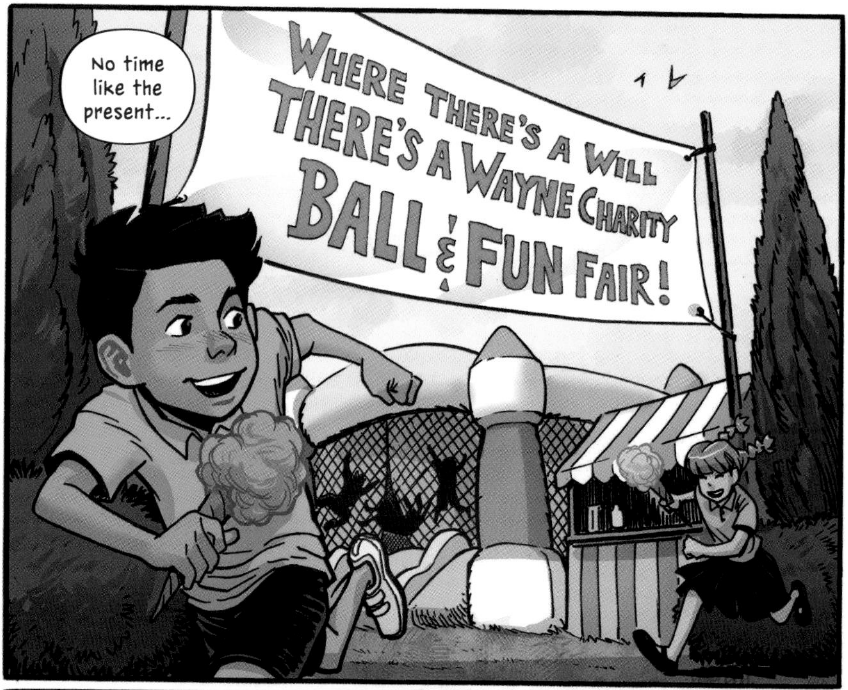
No time like the present...
WHERE THERE'S A WILL THERE'S A WAYNE CHARITY BALL & FUN FAIR!

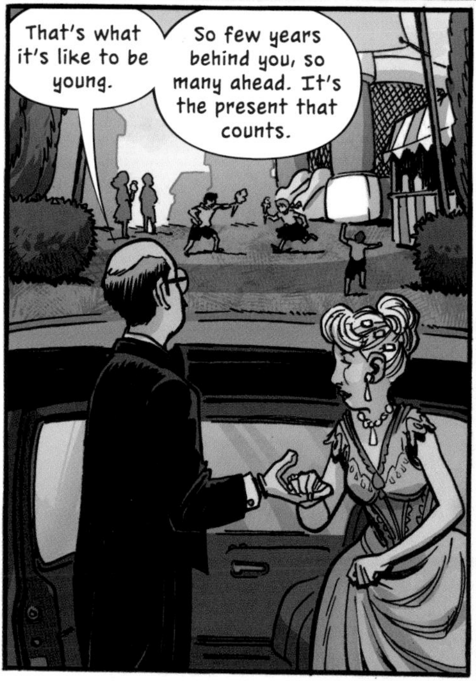
That's what it's like to be young.
So few years behind you, so many ahead. It's the present that counts.

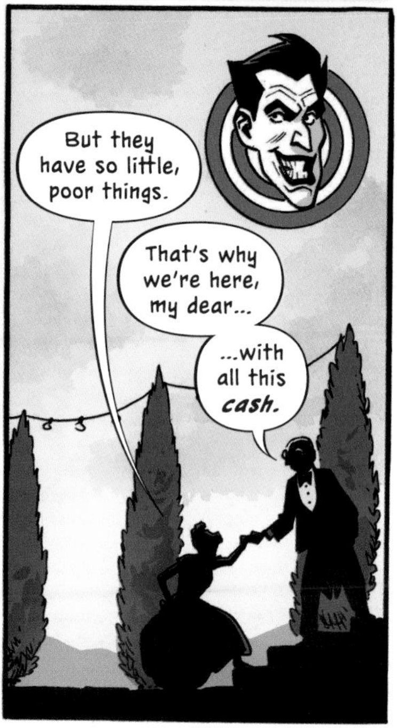
But they have so little, poor things.
That's why we're here, my dear...
...with all this *cash.*

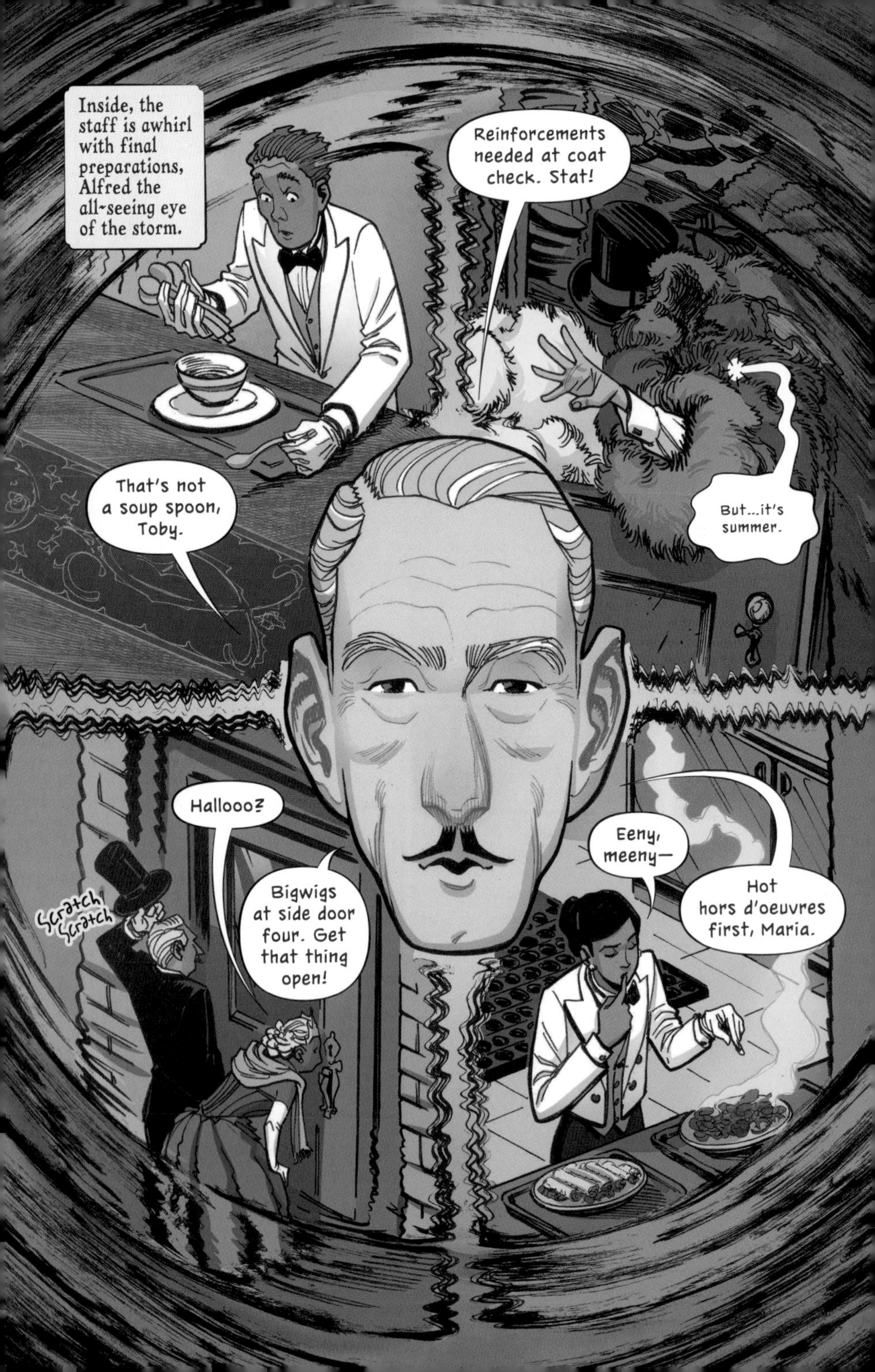
Inside, the staff is awhirl with final preparations, Alfred the all-seeing eye of the storm.
Reinforcements needed at coat check. Stat!
That's not a soup spoon, Toby.
But...it's summer.
Hallooo?
Bigwigs at side door four. Get that thing open!
Scratch Scratch
Eeny, meeny—
Hot hors d'oeuvres first, Maria.

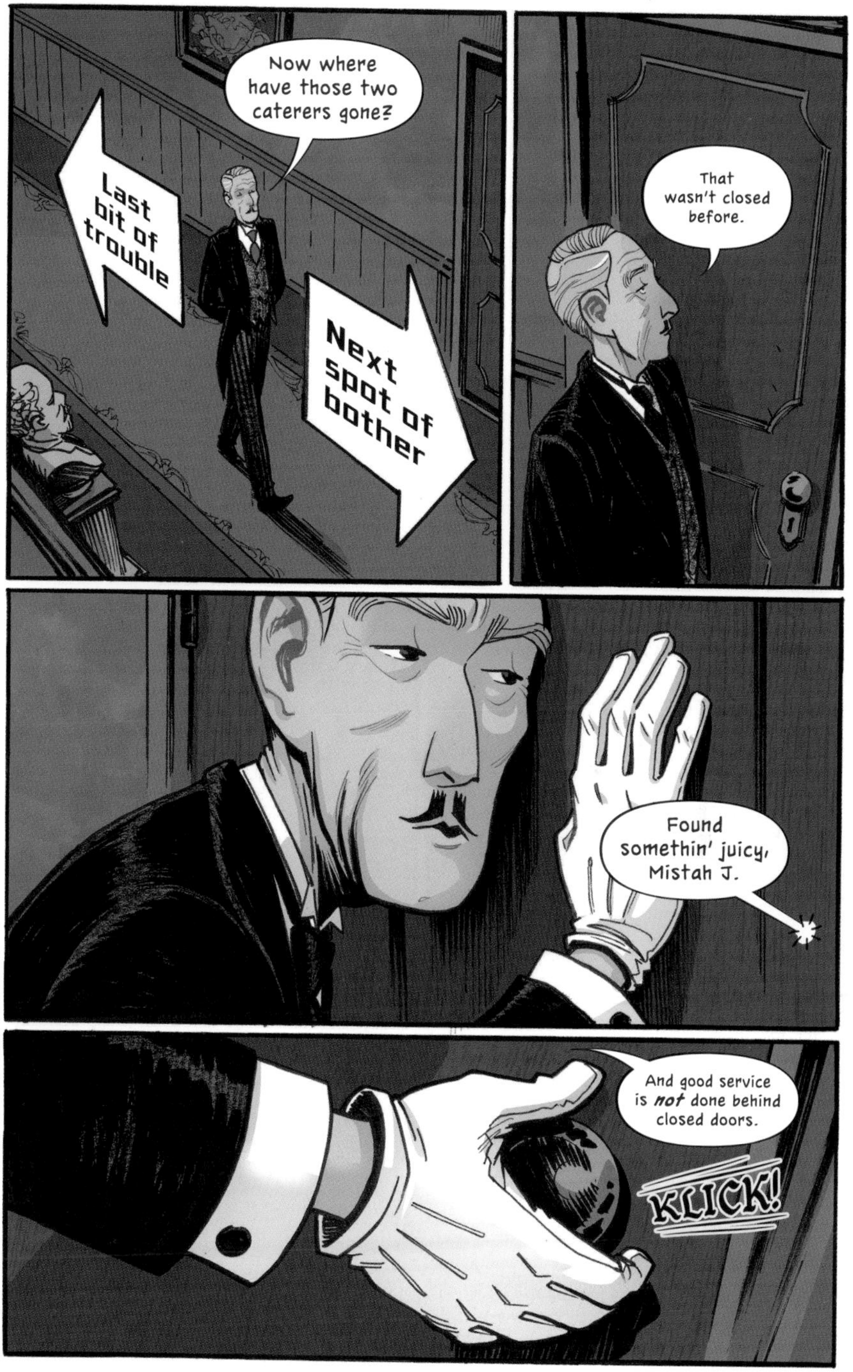
Now where have those two caterers gone?
Last bit of trouble
Next spot of bother
That wasn't closed before.
Found somethin' juicy, Mistah J.
And good service is *not* done behind closed doors.
KLICK!

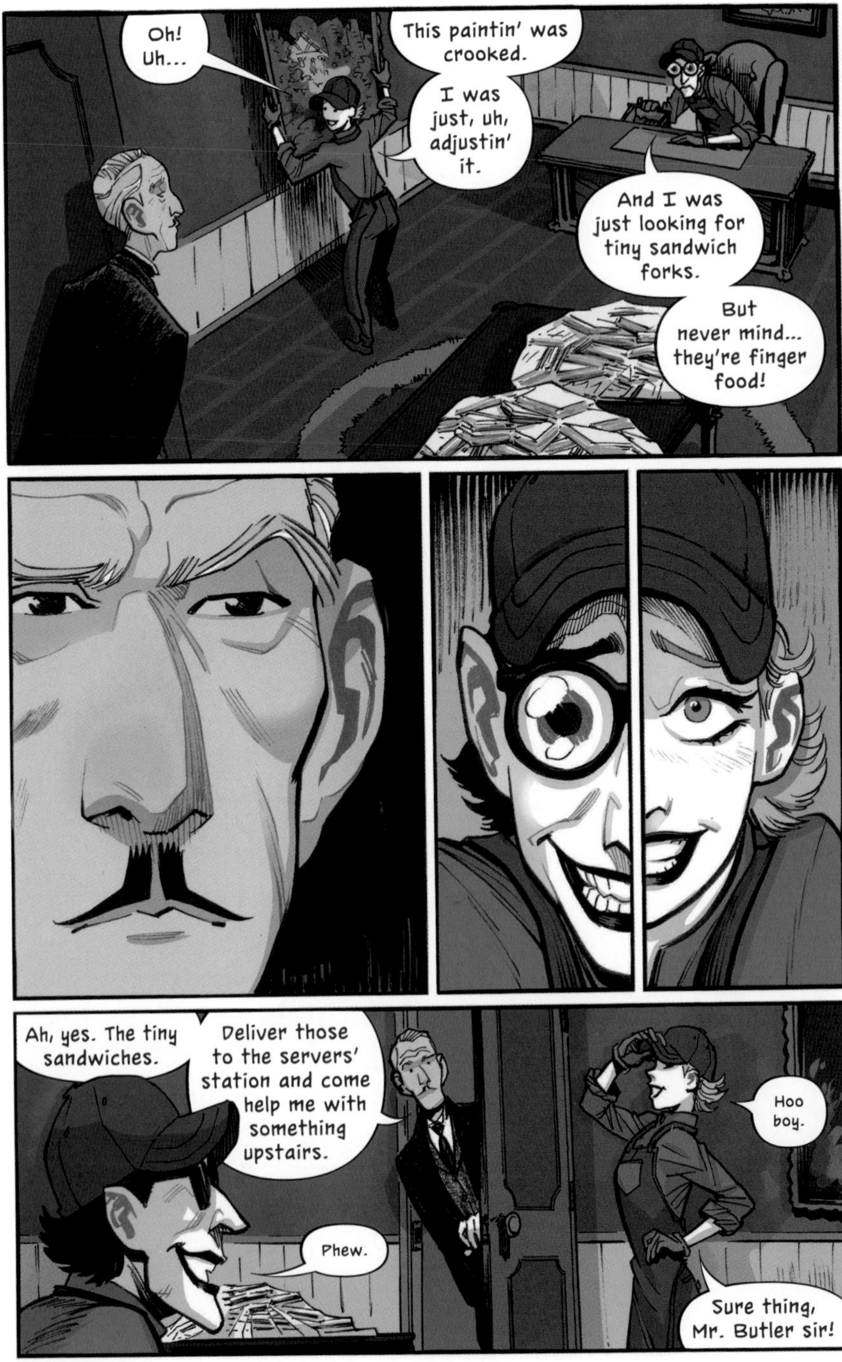

Oh! Uh...
This paintin' was crooked.
I was just, uh, adjustin' it.
And I was just looking for tiny sandwich forks.
But never mind... they're finger food!
Ah, yes. The tiny sandwiches.
Deliver those to the servers' station and come help me with something upstairs.
Hoo boy.
Phew.
Sure thing, Mr. Butler sir!

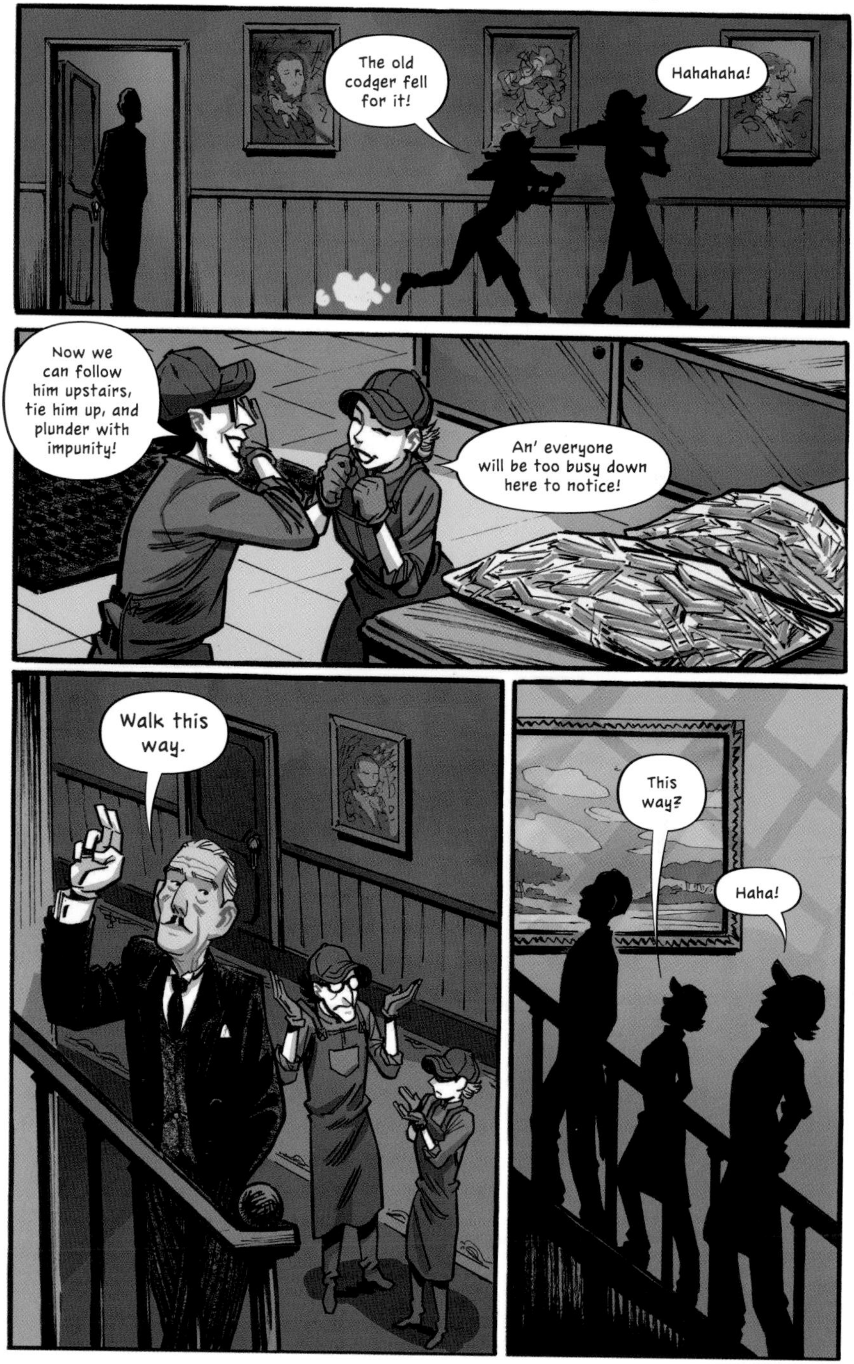
The old codger fell for it!
Hahahaha!
Now we can follow him upstairs, tie him up, and plunder with impunity!
An' everyone will be too busy down here to notice!
Walk this way.
This way?
Haha!

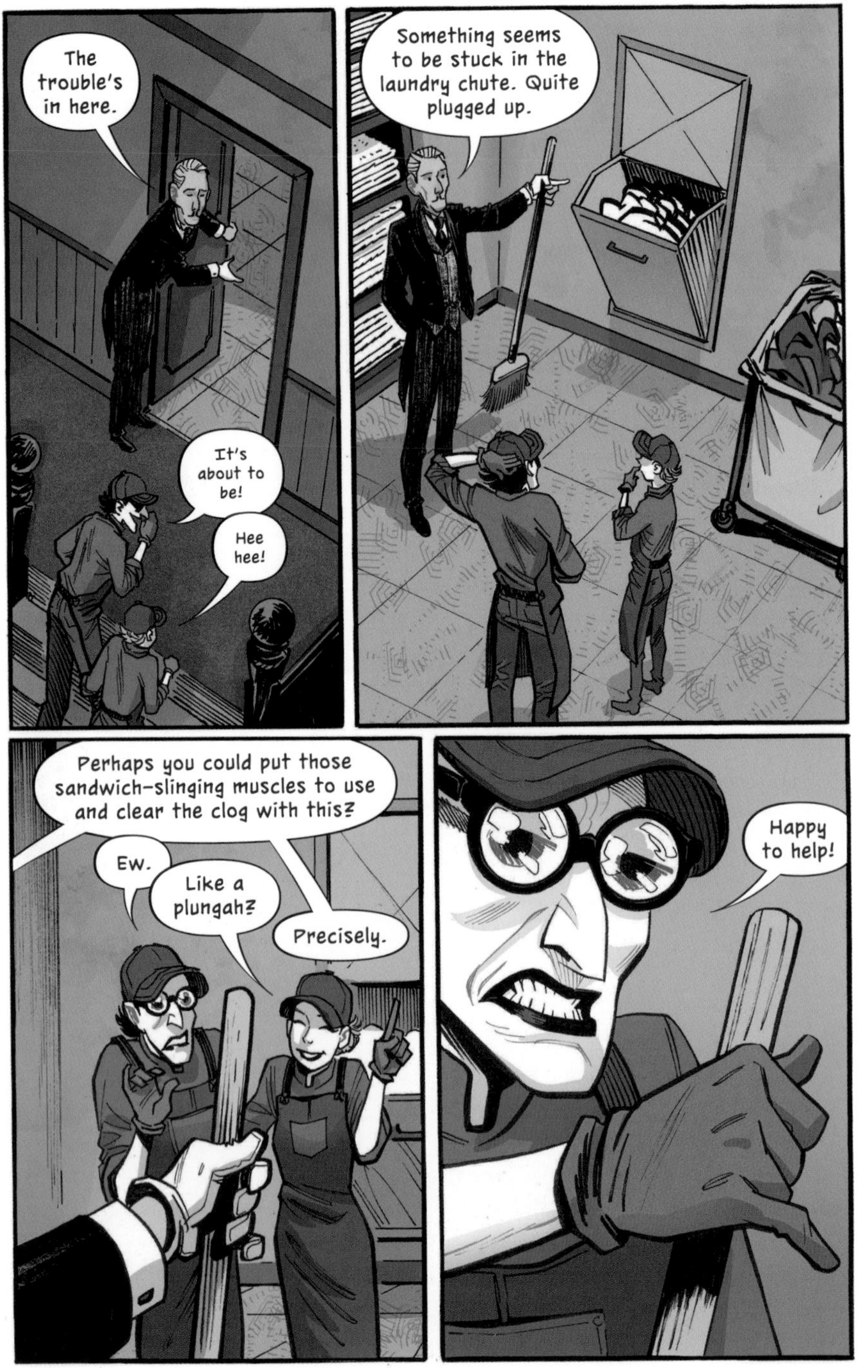
The trouble's in here.
It's about to be!
Hee hee!
Something seems to be stuck in the laundry chute. Quite plugged up.
Perhaps you could put those sandwich-slinging muscles to use and clear the clog with this?
Ew.
Like a plungah?
Precisely.
Happy to help!

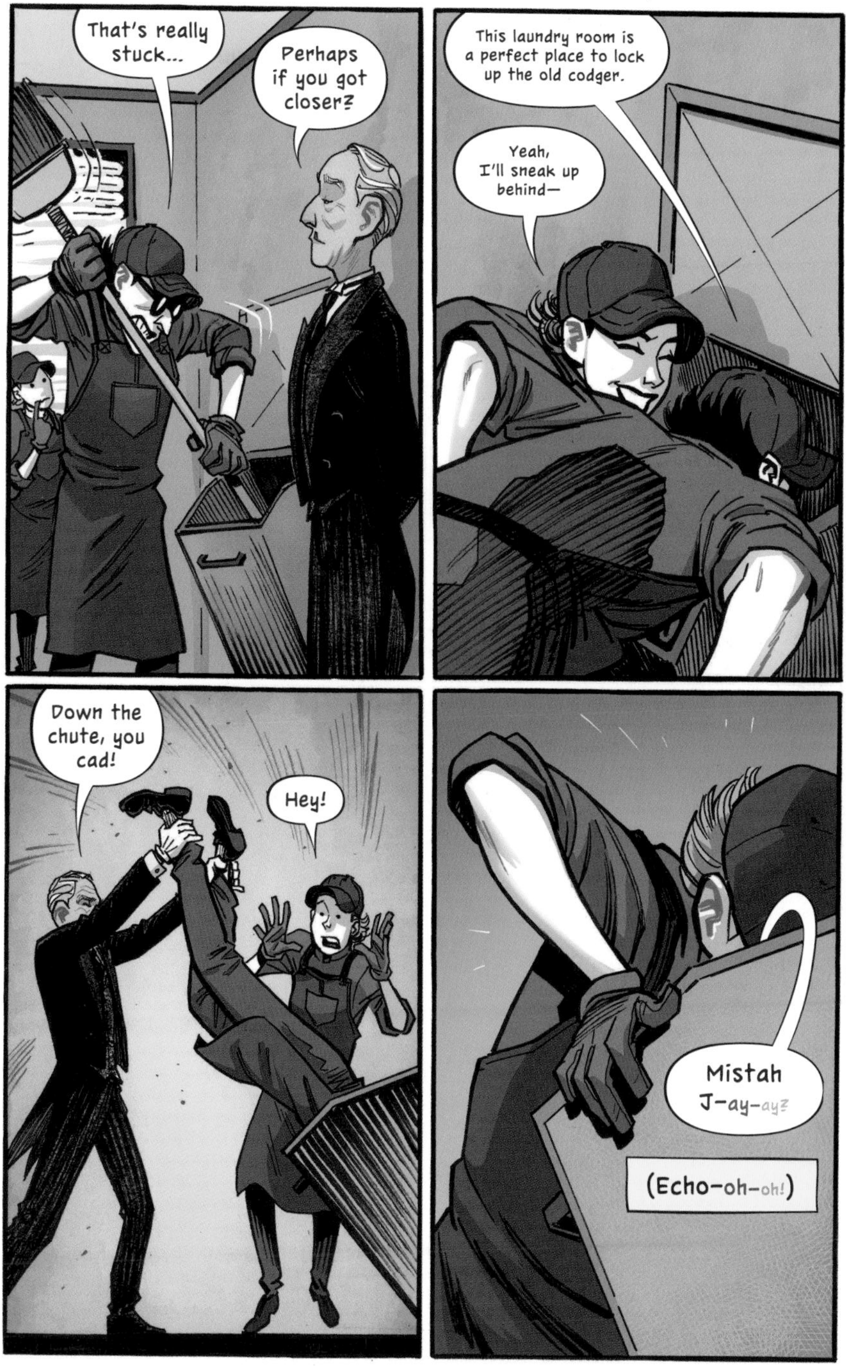
That's really stuck...
Perhaps if you got closer?
This laundry room is a perfect place to lock up the old codger.
Yeah, I'll sneak up behind—
Down the chute, you cad!
Hey!
Mistah J-ay-ay?
(Echo-oh-oh!)

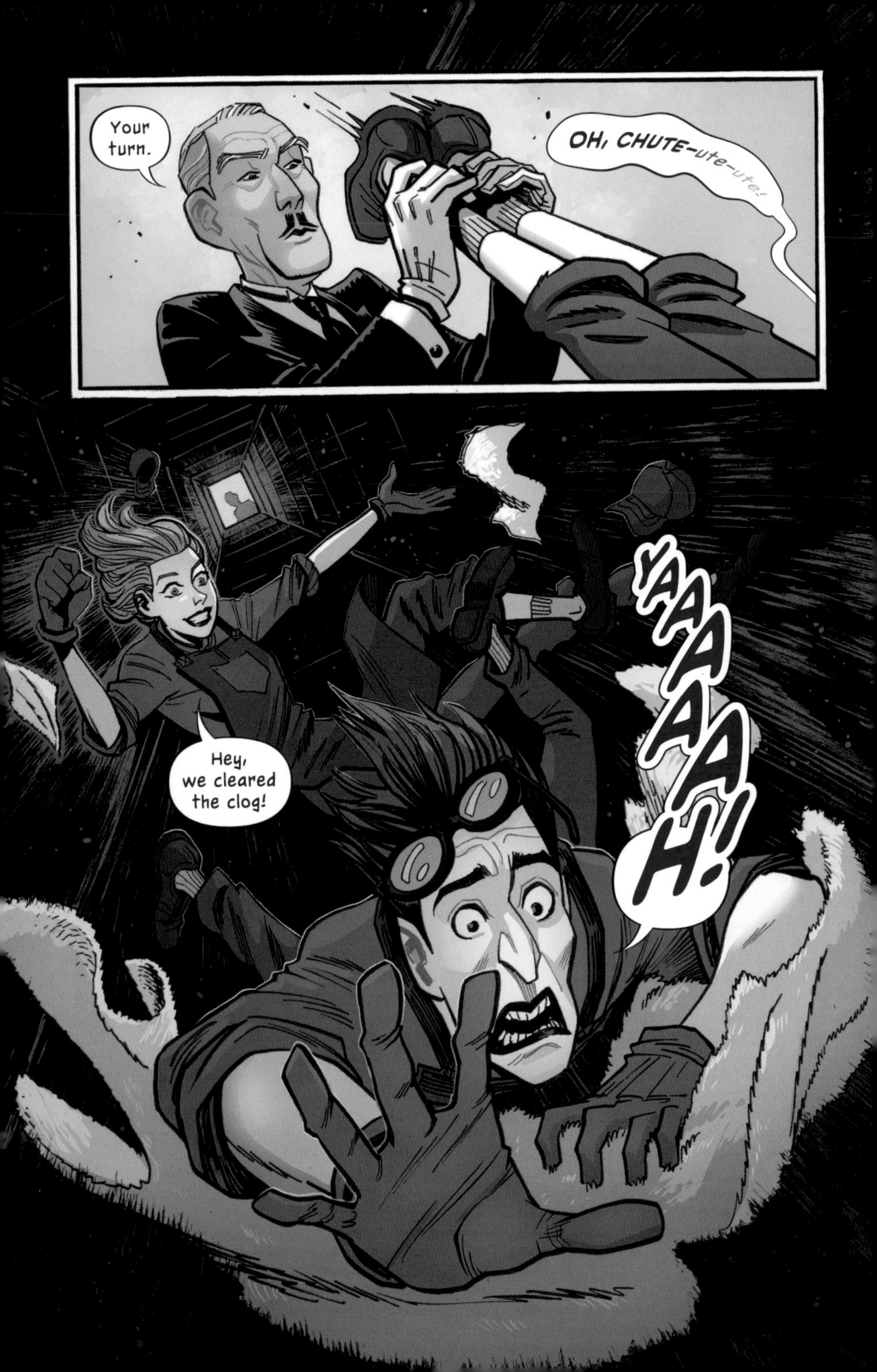
Your turn.
OH, CHUTE-ute-ute!
Hey, we cleared the clog!
YAAAAAH!

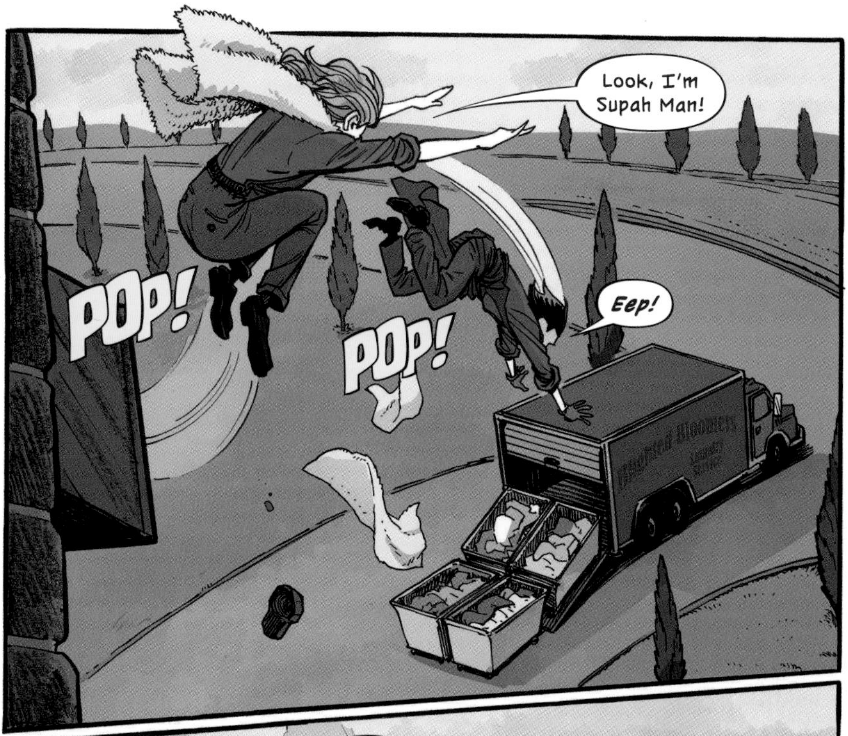
Look, I'm
Supah Man!
POP!
POP!
Eep!

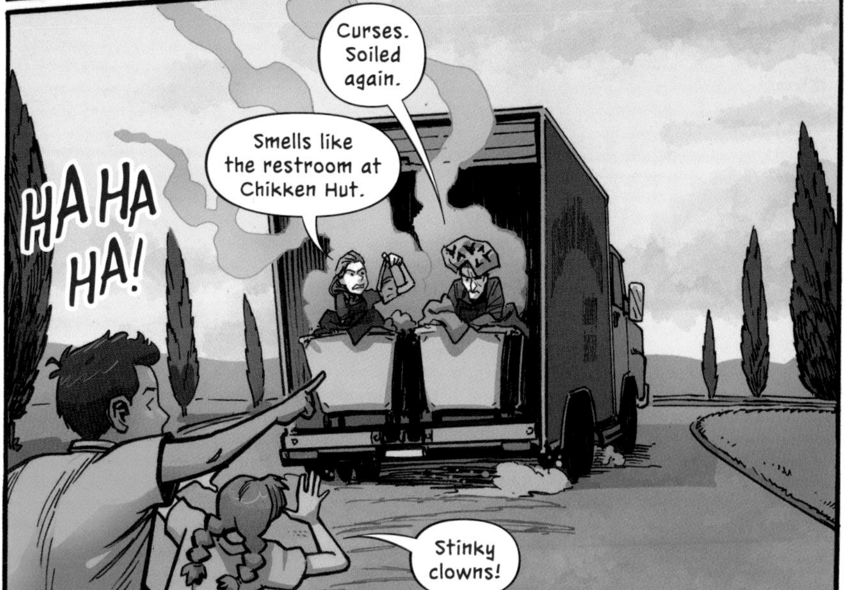
Curses.
Soiled
again.
Smells like
the restroom at
Chikken Hut.
HA HA
HA!
Stinky
clowns!

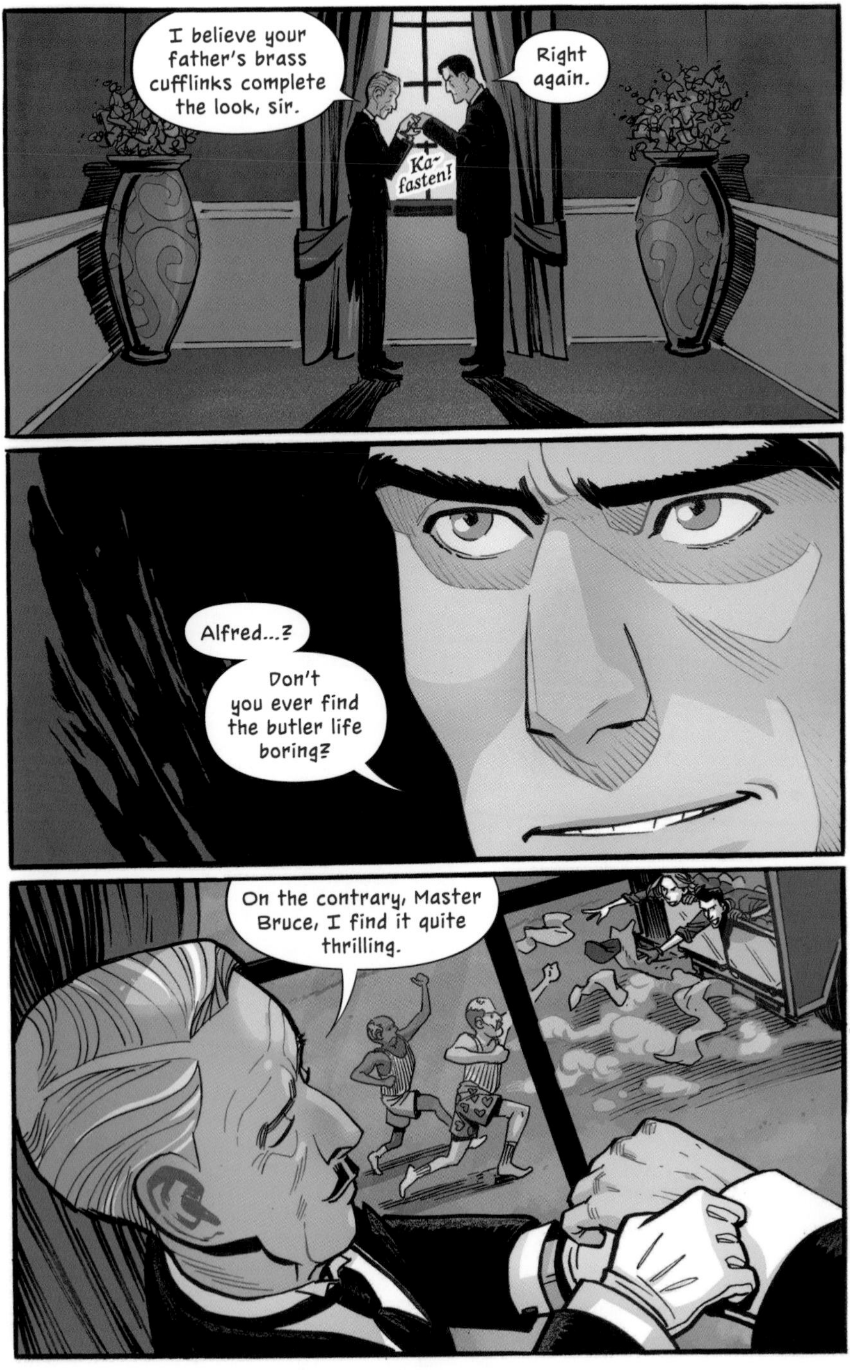
I believe your father's brass cufflinks complete the look, sir.
Right again.
Ka-fasten!
Alfred...?
Don't you ever find the butler life boring?
On the contrary, Master Bruce, I find it quite thrilling.

CHAPTER 12
The Final
Tally

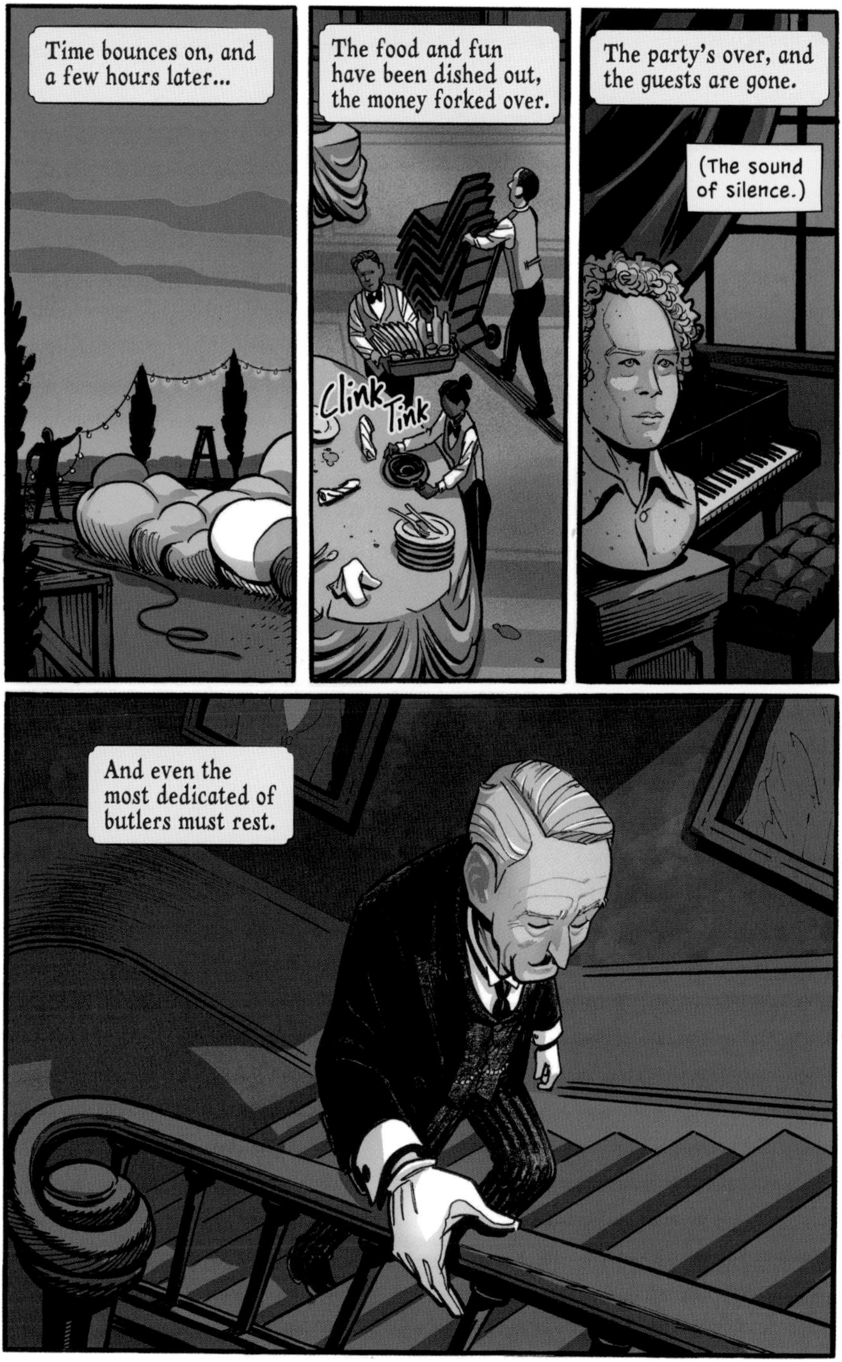
Time bounces on, and a few hours later...
The food and fun have been dished out, the money forked over.
Clink
Tink
The party's over, and the guests are gone.
(The sound of silence.)
And even the most dedicated of butlers must rest.

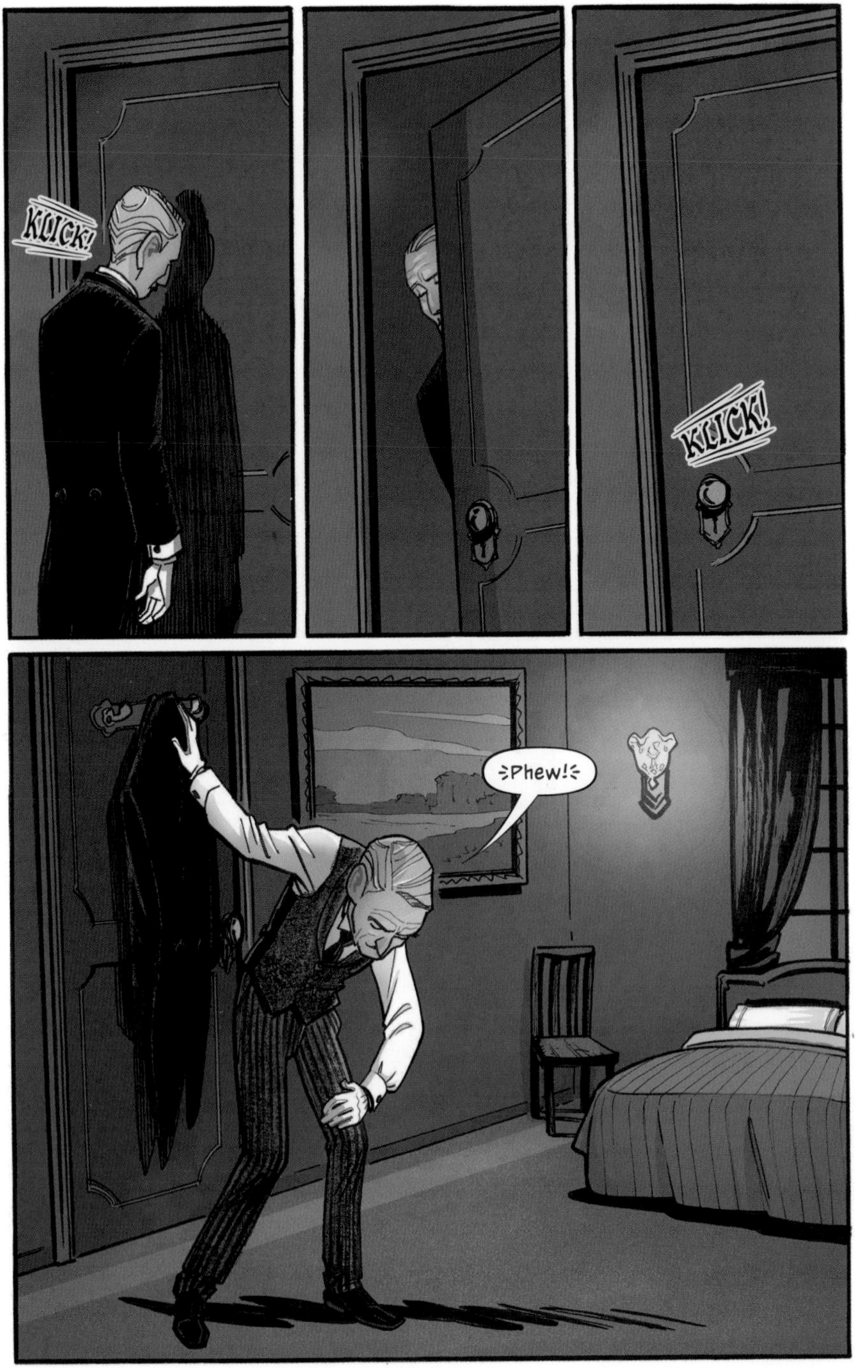
KLICK!
KLICK!
Phew!

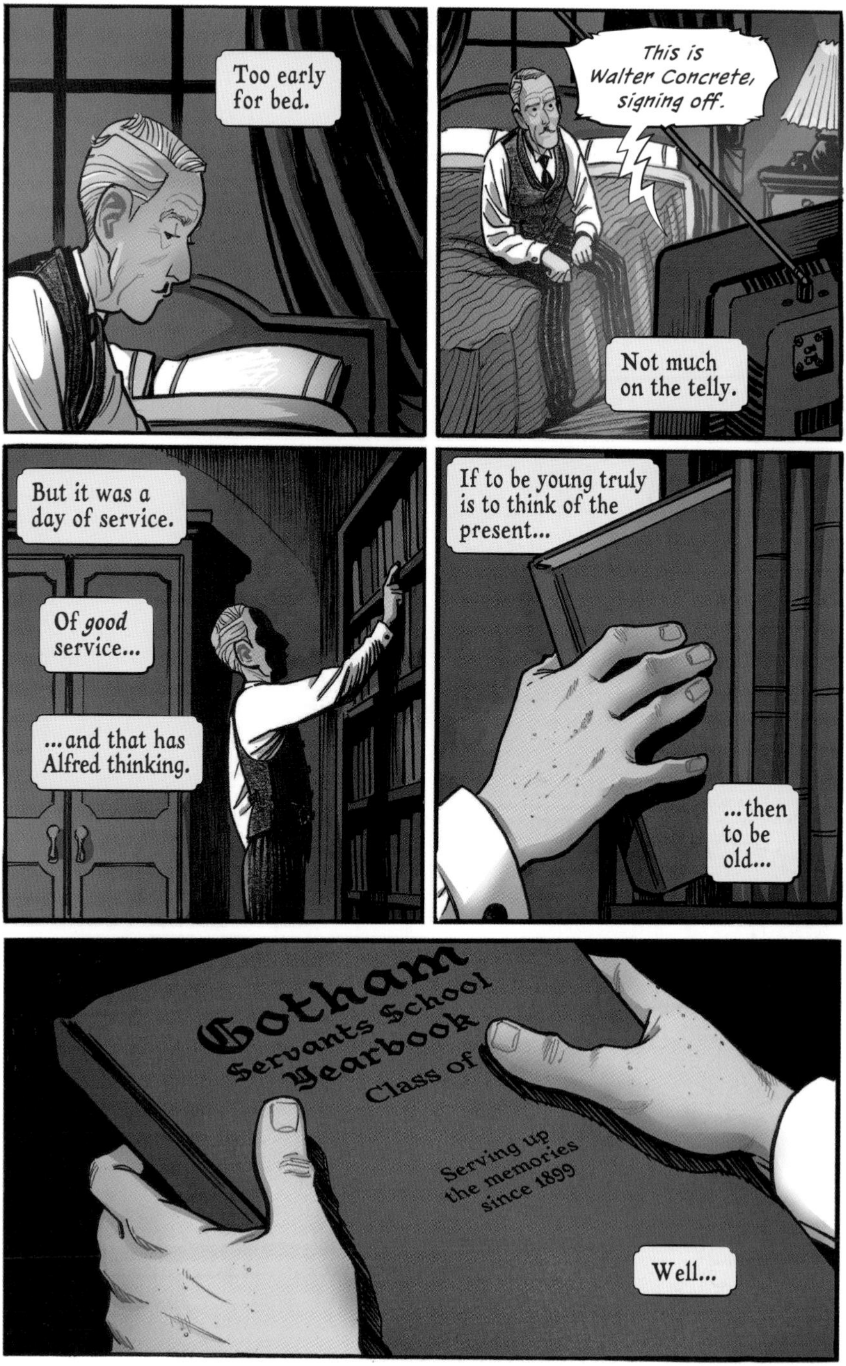
Too early for bed.
This is Walter Concrete, signing off.
Not much on the telly.
But it was a day of service.
Of *good* service...
...and that has Alfred thinking.
If to be young truly is to think of the present...
...then to be old...
Gotham Servants School Yearbook
Class of
Serving up the memories since 1899
Well...

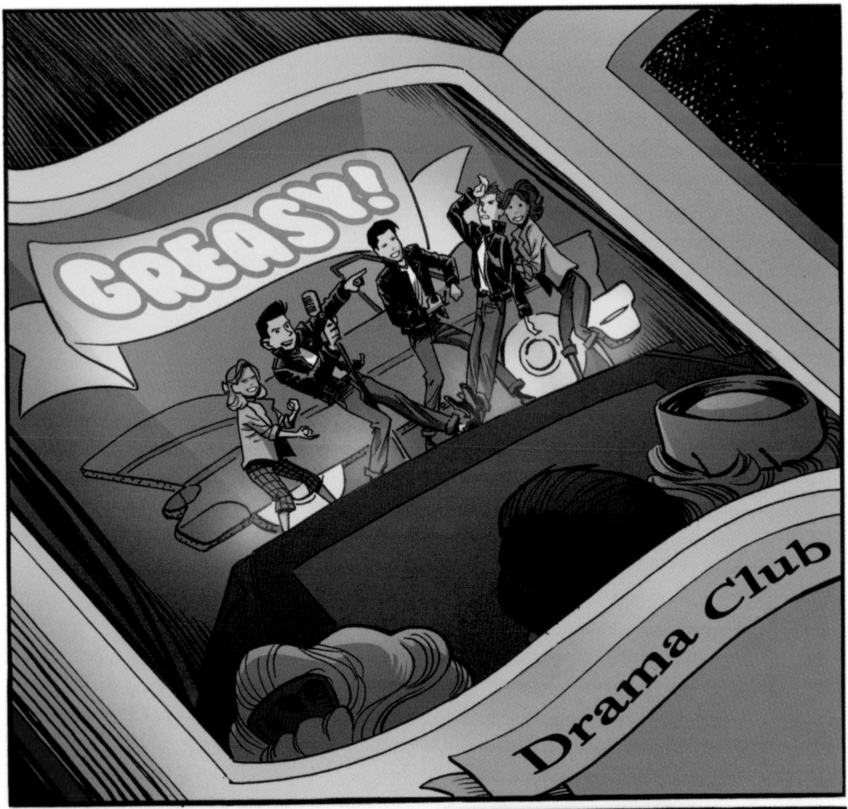
GREASY!
Drama Club

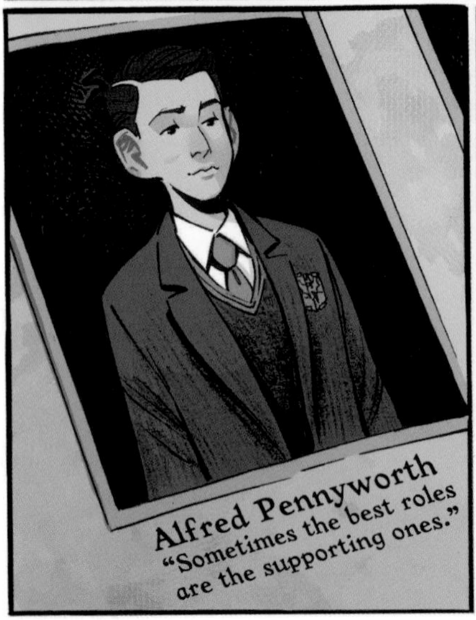
Alfred Pennyworth
"Sometimes the best roles are the supporting ones."

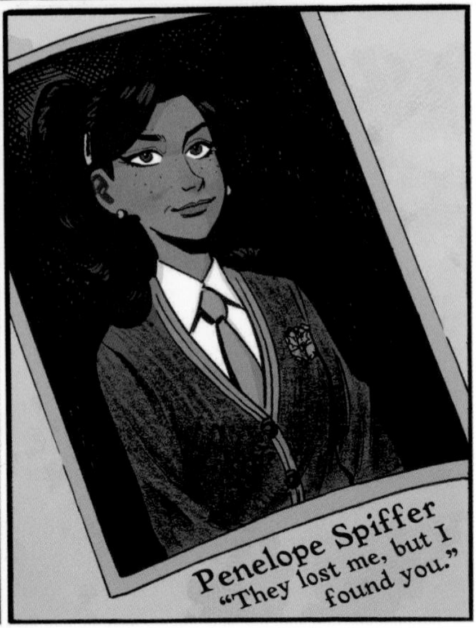
Penelope Spiffer
"They lost me, but I found you."

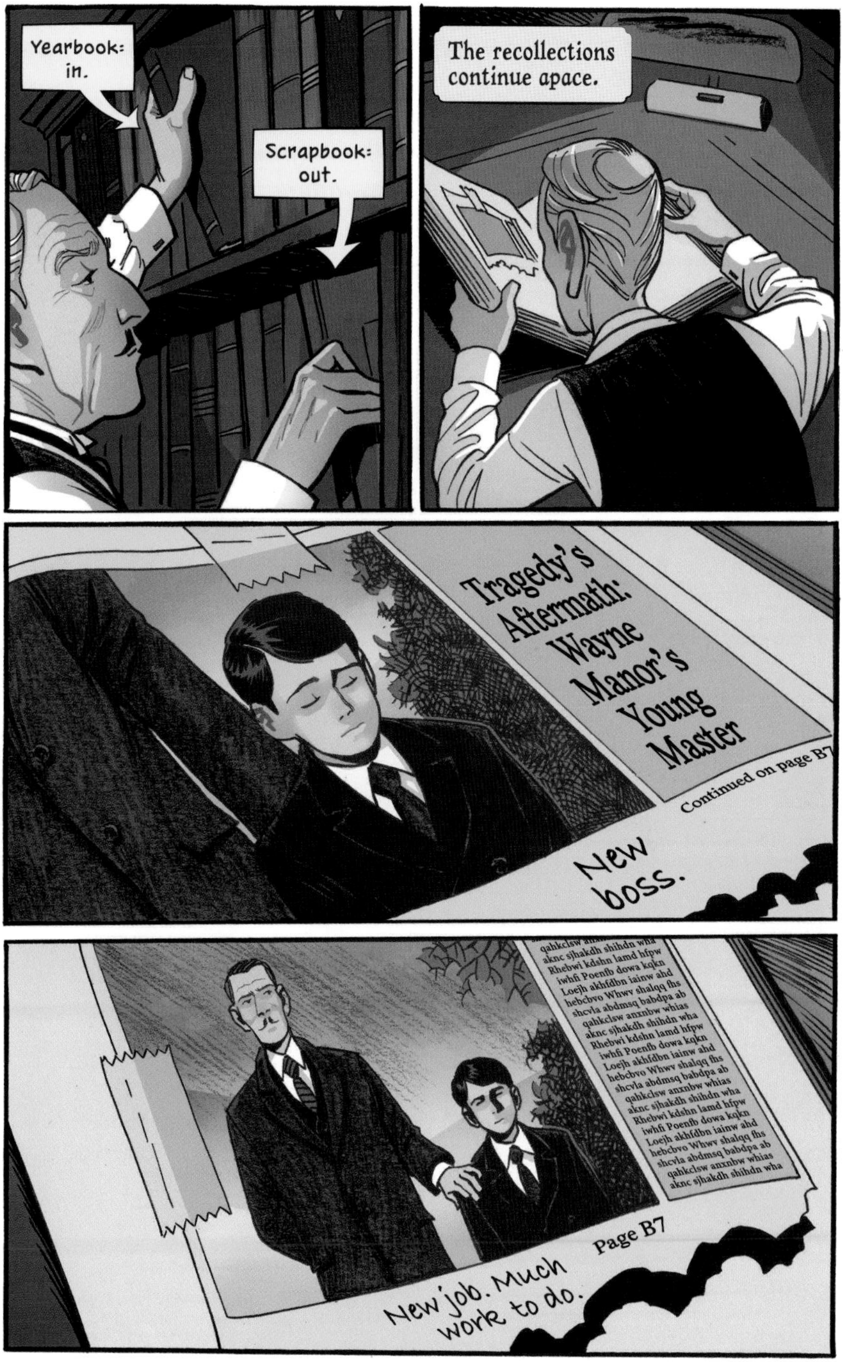
Yearbook: in.
Scrapbook: out.
The recollections continue apace.
Tragedy's Aftermath: Wayne Manor's Young Master
Continued on page B7
New boss.
Page B7
New job. Much work to do.

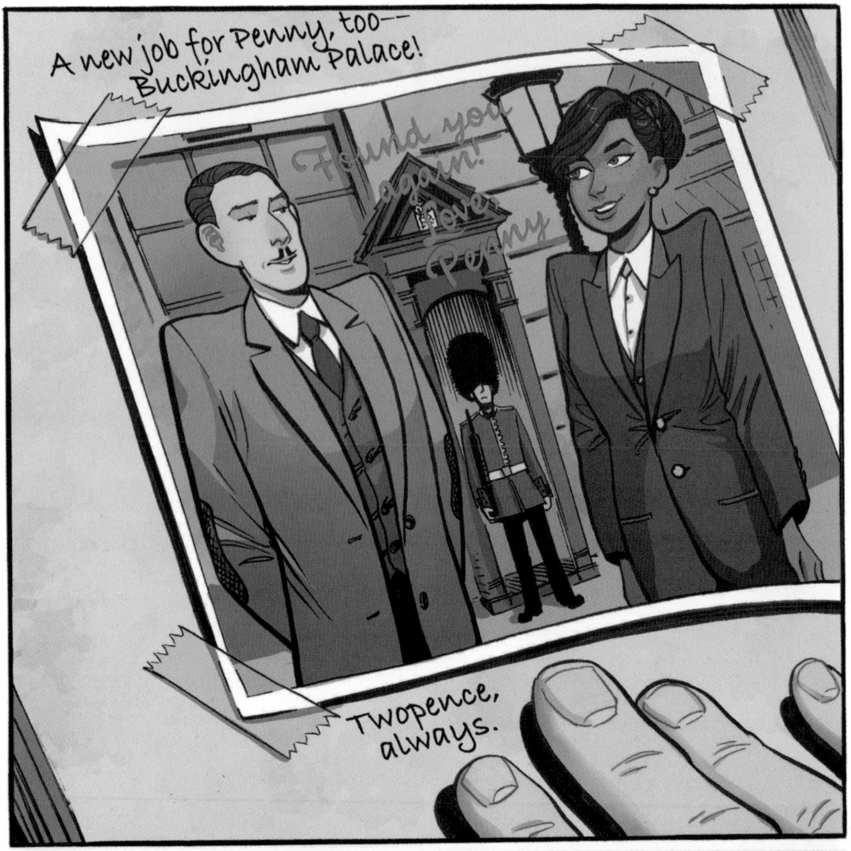
A new job for Penny, too--
Buckingham Palace!
Found you again! Love, Penny
Twopence, always.

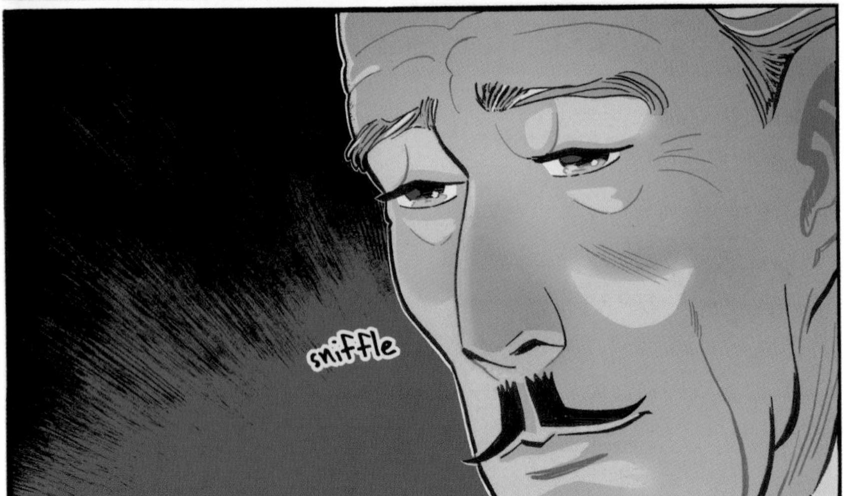
sniffle

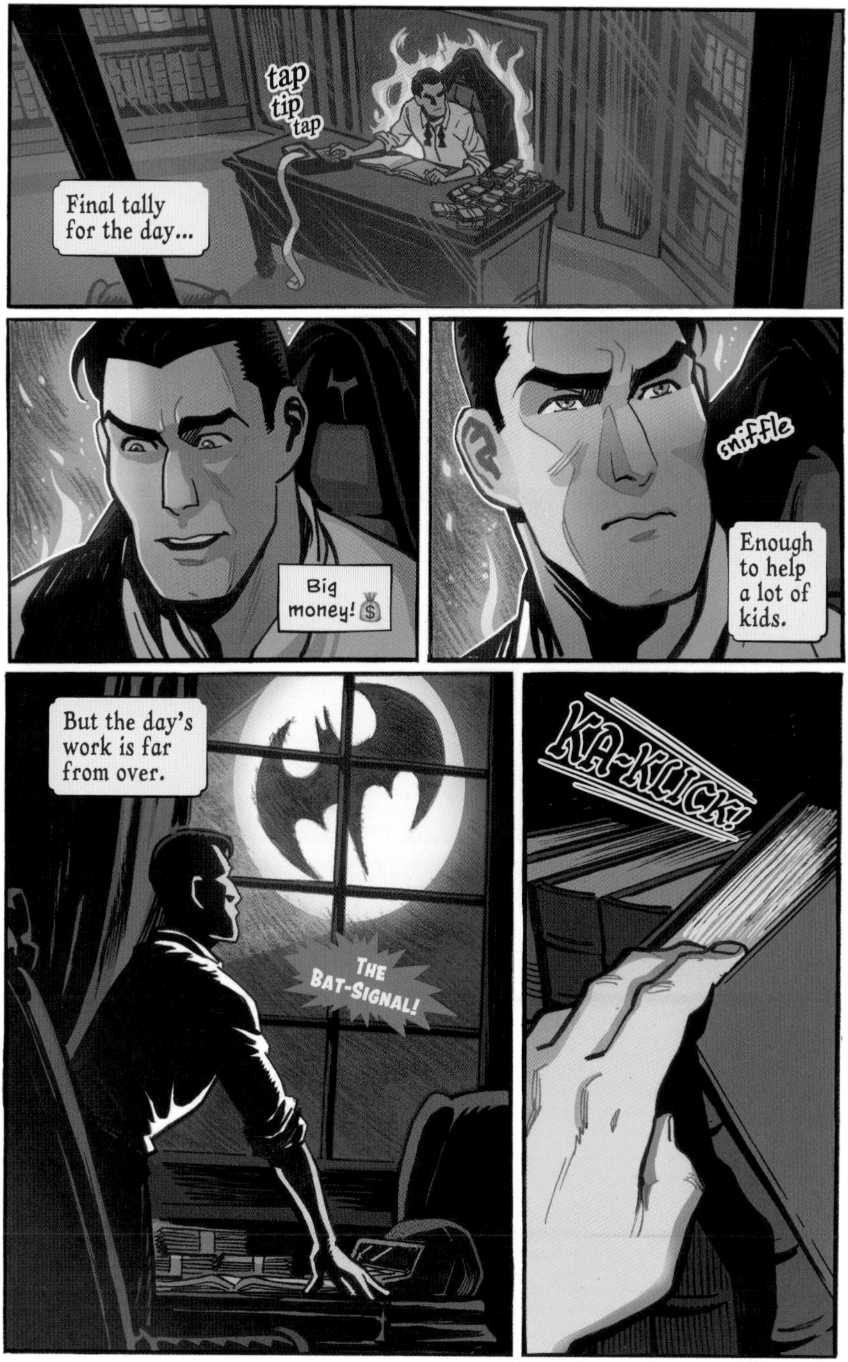

tap
tip
tap
Final tally for the day...
Big money!
sniffle
Enough to help a lot of kids.
But the day's work is far from over.
THE BAT-SIGNAL!
KA-KLICK!

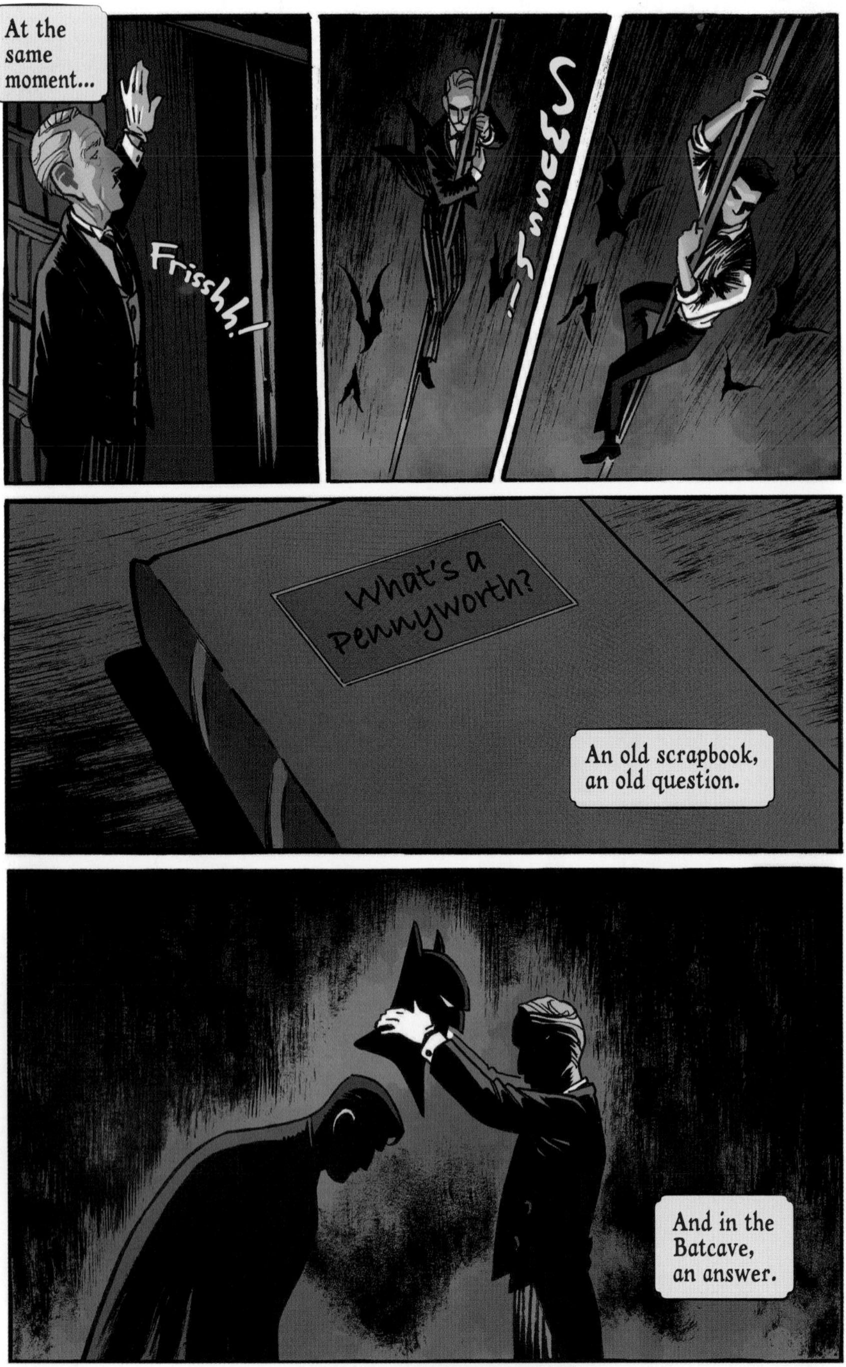
At the same moment...
Frisshh!
Swoosh!
What's a Pennyworth?
An old scrapbook, an old question.
And in the Batcave, an answer.

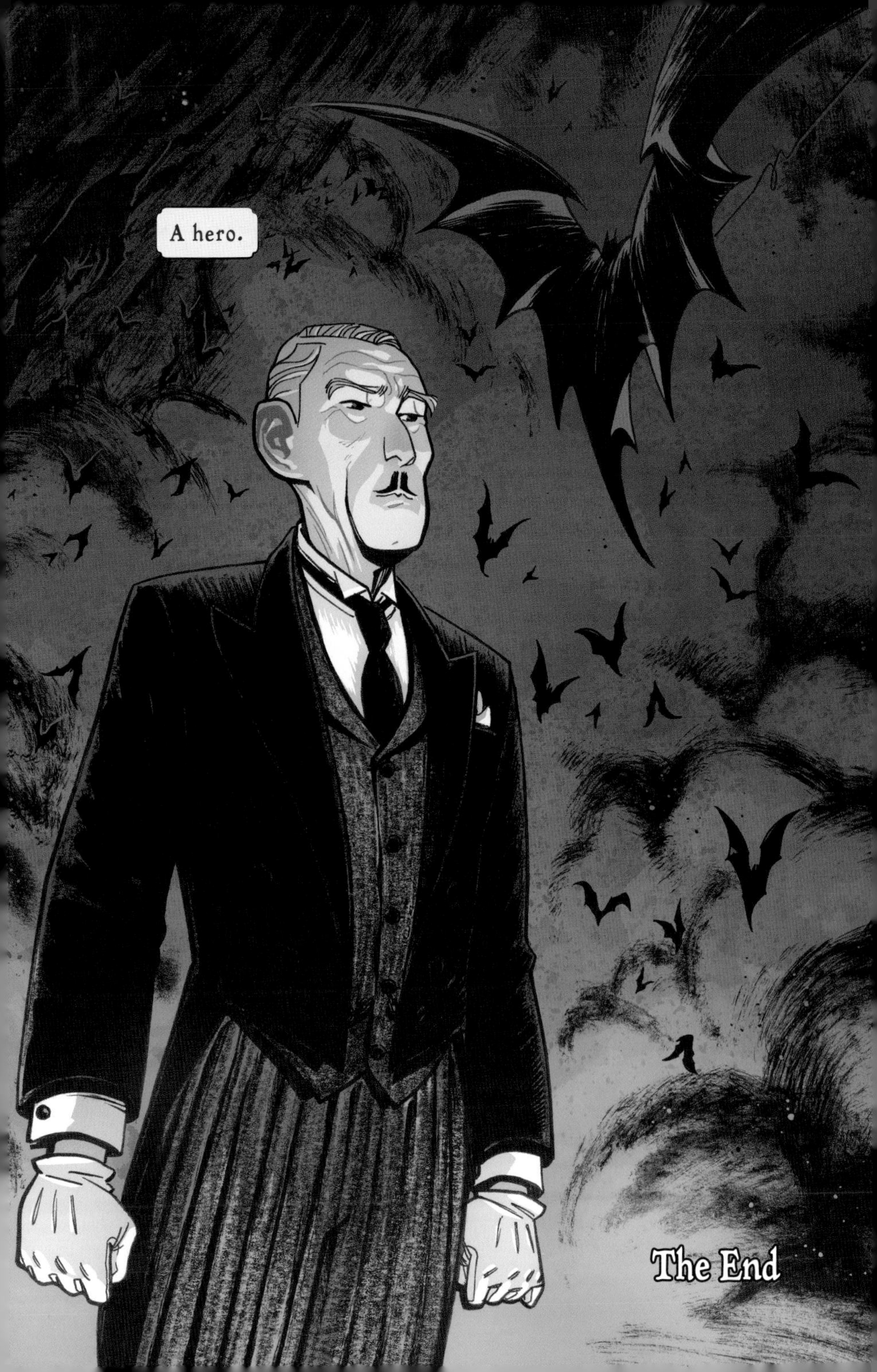
A hero.
The End

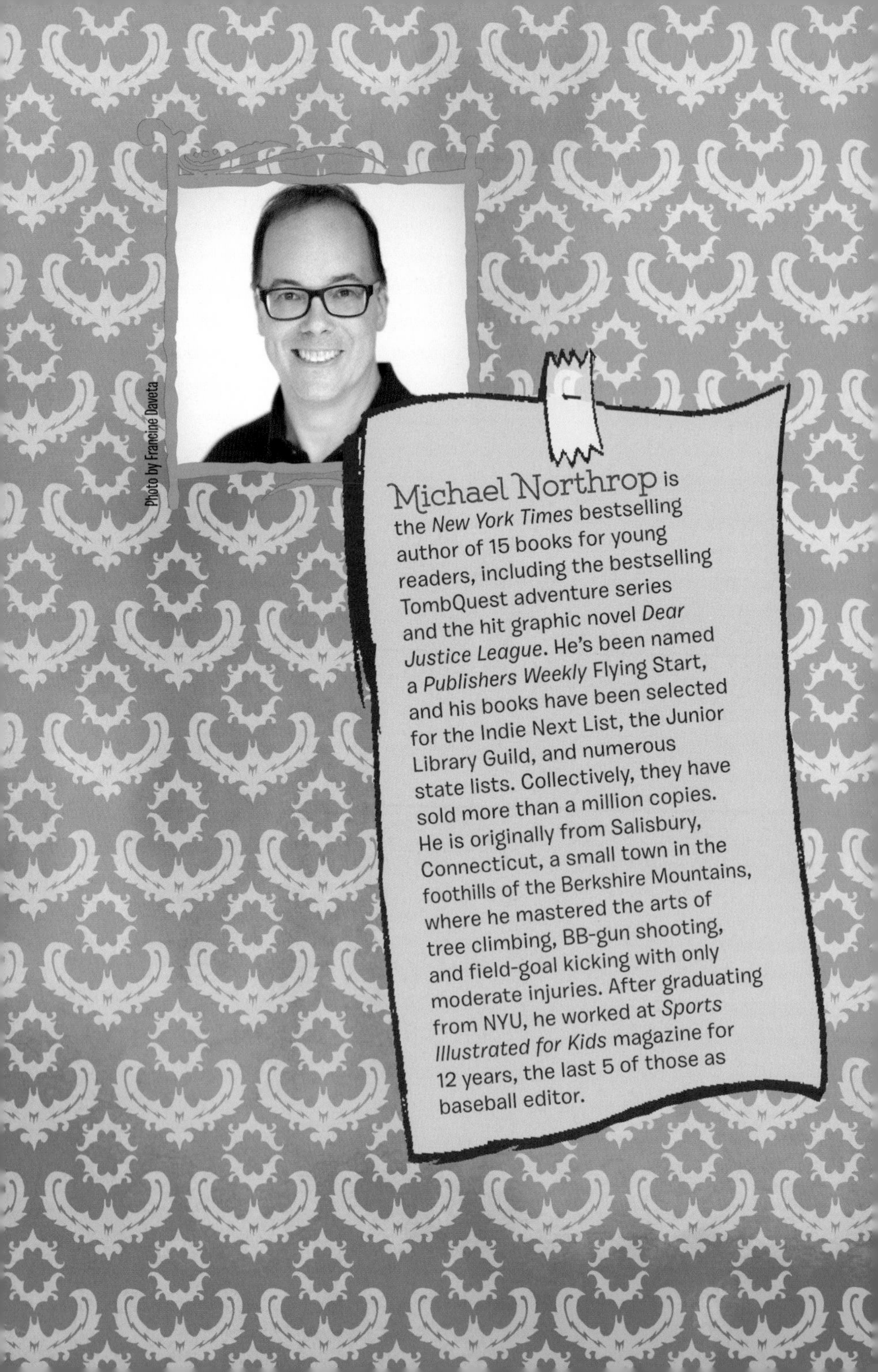

Photo by Francine Daveta

Michael Northrop is the *New York Times* bestselling author of 15 books for young readers, including the bestselling TombQuest adventure series and the hit graphic novel *Dear Justice League*. He's been named a *Publishers Weekly* Flying Start, and his books have been selected for the Indie Next List, the Junior Library Guild, and numerous state lists. Collectively, they have sold more than a million copies. He is originally from Salisbury, Connecticut, a small town in the foothills of the Berkshire Mountains, where he mastered the arts of tree climbing, BB-gun shooting, and field-goal kicking with only moderate injuries. After graduating from NYU, he worked at *Sports Illustrated for Kids* magazine for 12 years, the last 5 of those as baseball editor.

Sam Lotfi is the co-creator and artist of the supernatural thriller *Last Stop on the Red Line* from Dark Horse Comics. He was selected for the DC Comics Talent Development Artists Workshop in 2016 and has since worked on characters such as Superman, the Flash, Doctor Fate, Harley Quinn, and Secret Squirrel as well as the DC graphic novels *Zatanna: The Jewel of Gravesend* and *Anti/Hero*. Other works include Marvel/Icon's *Painkiller Jane: The Price of Freedom*, Dynamite's *Ash vs. the Army of Darkness*, 1First Comics' *Lark's Killer*, and covers for IDW's *Teenage Mutant Ninja Turtles*, *Micronauts*, and *Hasbro Heroes Sourcebook*. In addition to comics, Sam has worked on various animation and video game projects. He lives in Austin, Texas, with his lovely wife and their two adventurous boys. For more of Sam's work, you can follow him on social media at @slotfi and visit his website, samlotfi.com.

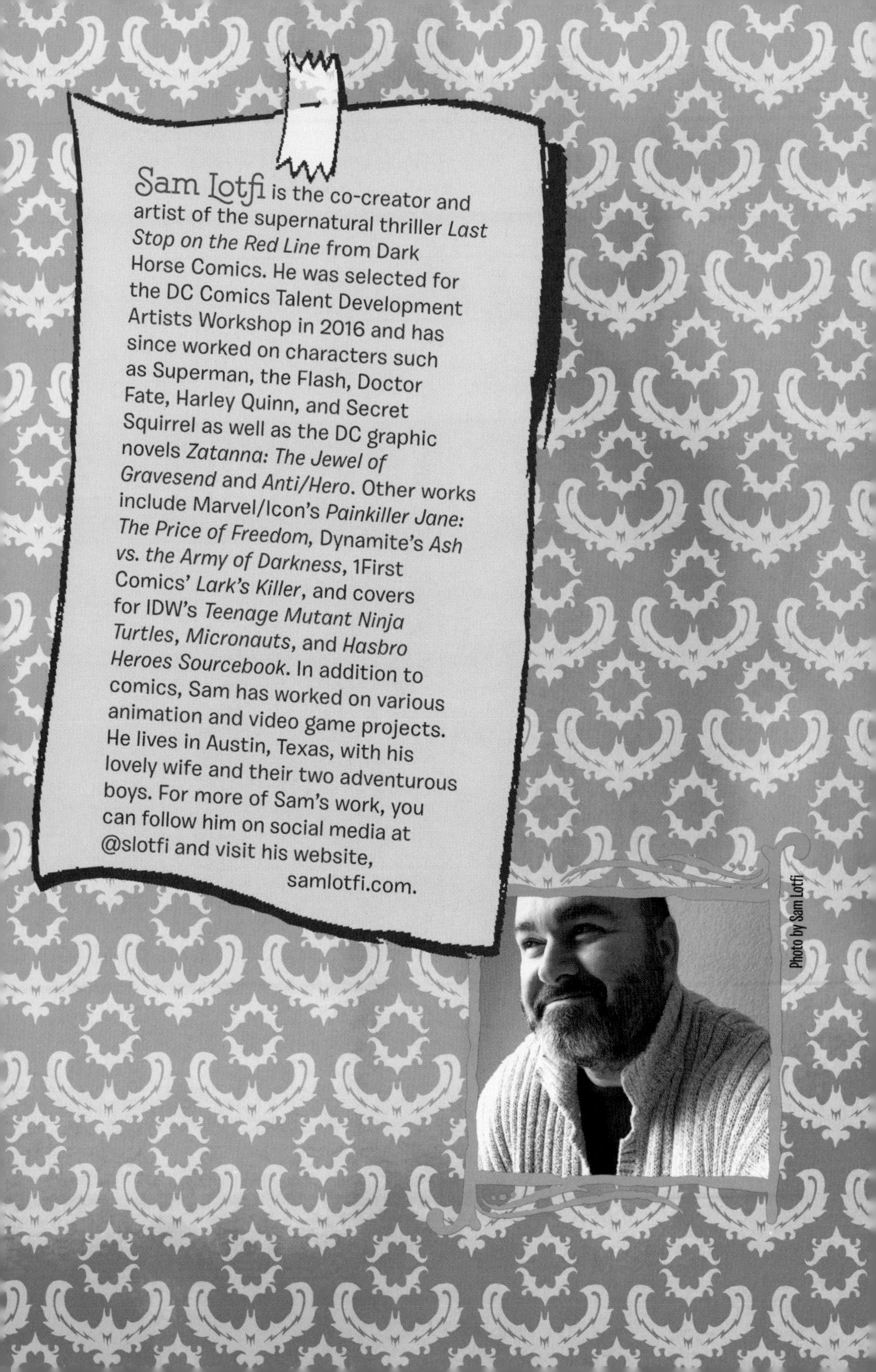
Photo by Sam Lotfi

Want more graphic novels from the writer behind *Young Alfred*? Keep reading for a sneak preview of his hilarious and charming stories about the greatest heroes in the DC Universe as they answer mail from their biggest fans—kids!

From *New York Times* bestselling author Michael Northrop, with colorful illustrations by Gustavo Duarte, *Dear Justice League* gives readers the inside scoop on everyday heroics, no matter who wears the cape!

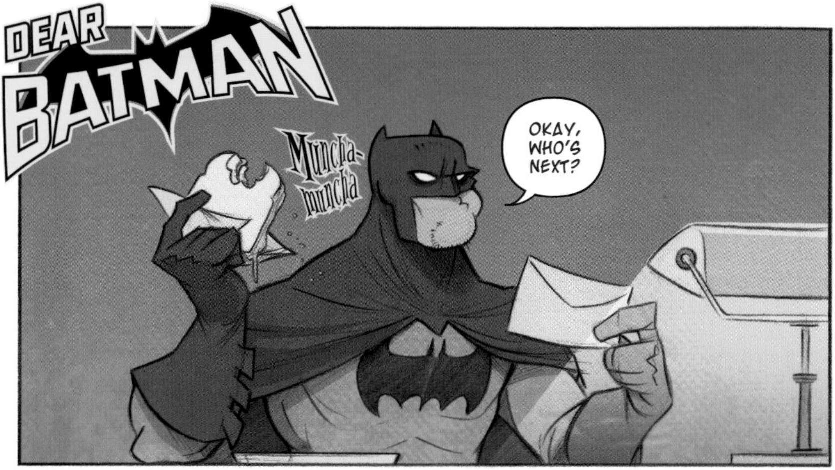
DEAR BATMAN
Muncha-muncha
OKAY, WHO'S NEXT?

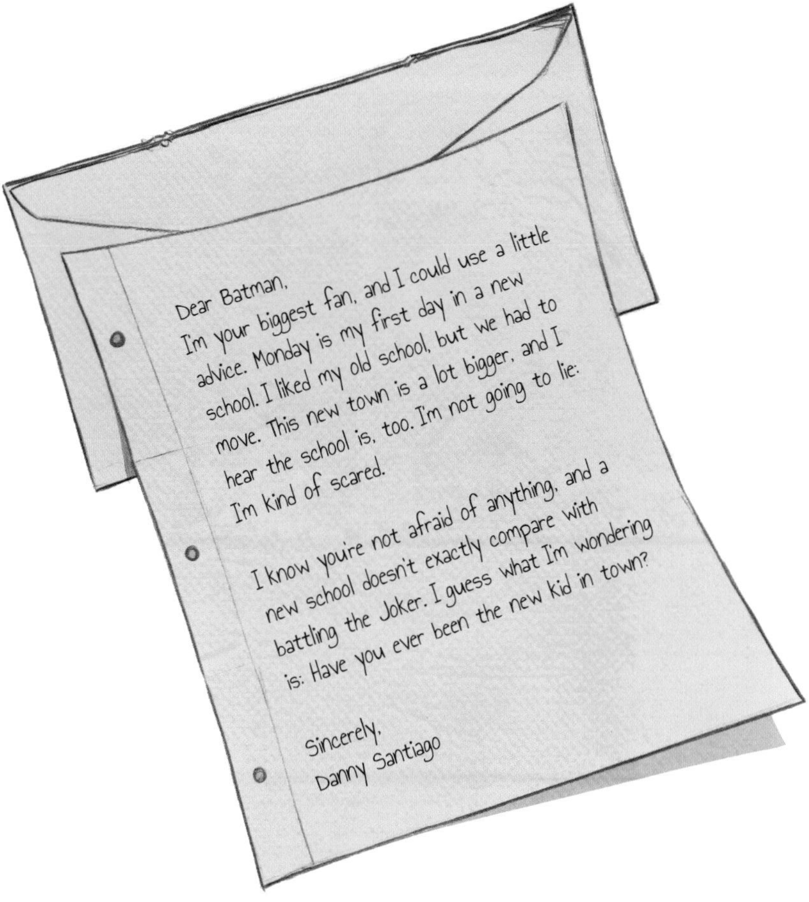

Dear Batman,
I'm your biggest fan, and I could use a little advice. Monday is my first day in a new school. I liked my old school, but we had to move. This new town is a lot bigger, and I hear the school is, too. I'm not going to lie: I'm kind of scared.

I know youire not afraid of anything, and a new school doesn't exactly compare with battling the Joker. I guess what I'm wondering is: Have you ever been the new kid in town?

Sincerely,
Danny Santiago

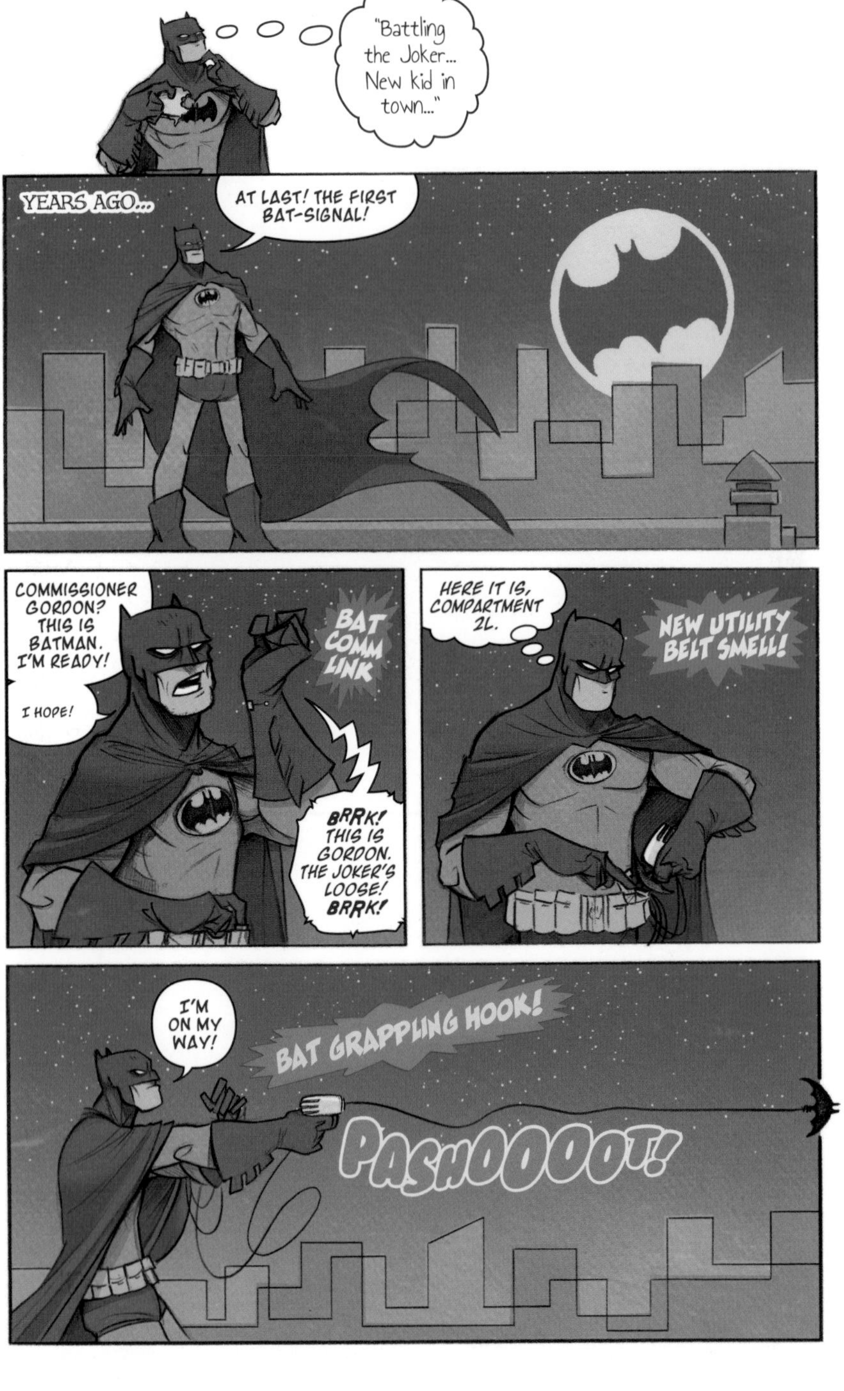
"Battling the Joker... New kid in town..."
YEARS AGO...
AT LAST! THE FIRST BAT-SIGNAL!
COMMISSIONER GORDON? THIS IS BATMAN. I'M READY!
I HOPE!
BAT COMM LINK
BRRK! THIS IS GORDON. THE JOKER'S LOOSE! BRRK!
HERE IT IS, COMPARTMENT 2L.
NEW UTILITY BELT SMELL!
I'M ON MY WAY!
BAT GRAPPLING HOOK!
PASHOOOOOT!

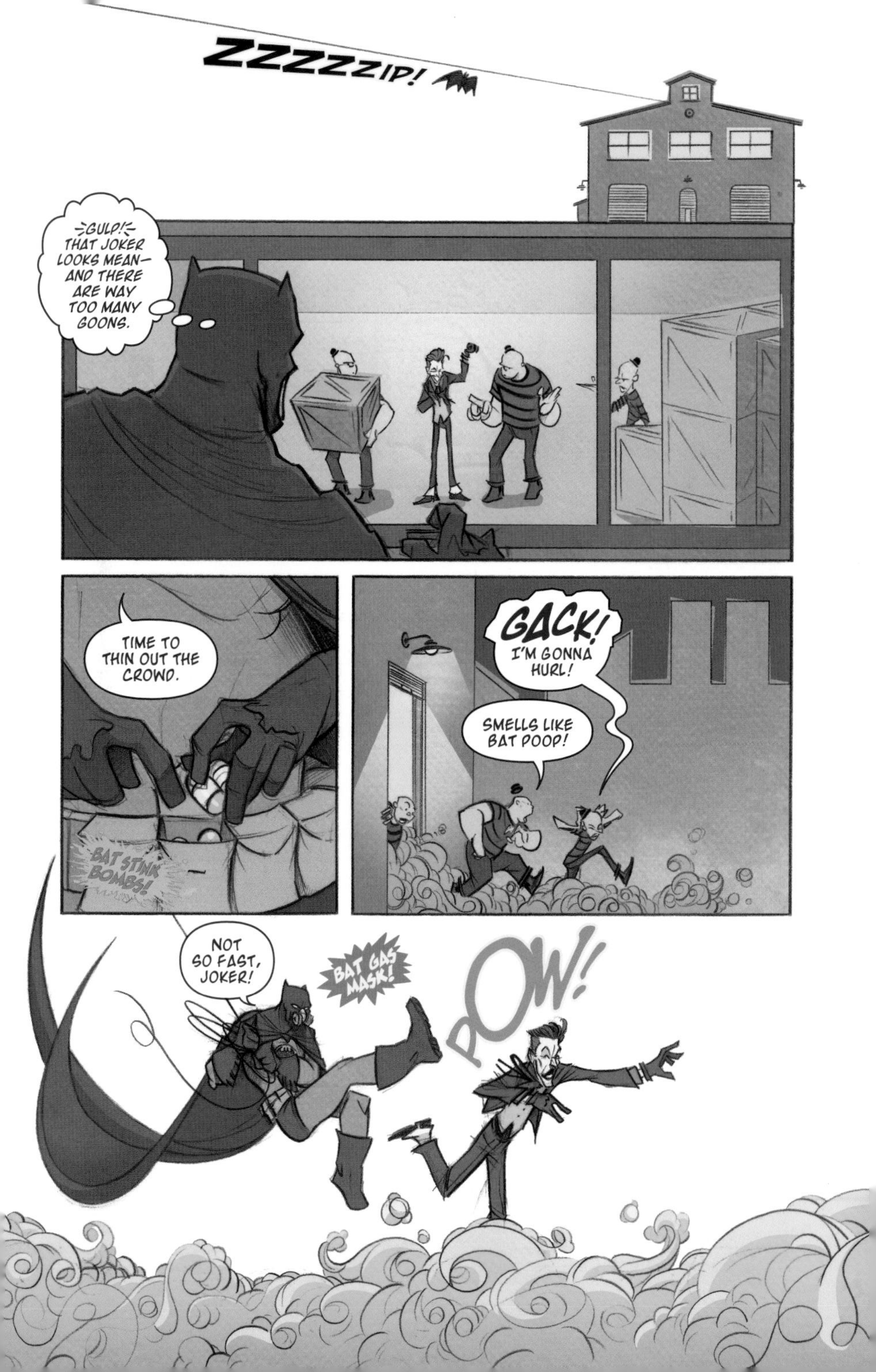
ZZZZZZIP!
≶GULP!≶ THAT JOKER LOOKS MEAN— AND THERE ARE WAY TOO MANY GOONS.
TIME TO THIN OUT THE CROWD.
BAT STINK BOMBS!
GACK! I'M GONNA HURL!
SMELLS LIKE BAT POOP!
NOT SO FAST, JOKER!
BAT GAS MASK!
POW!

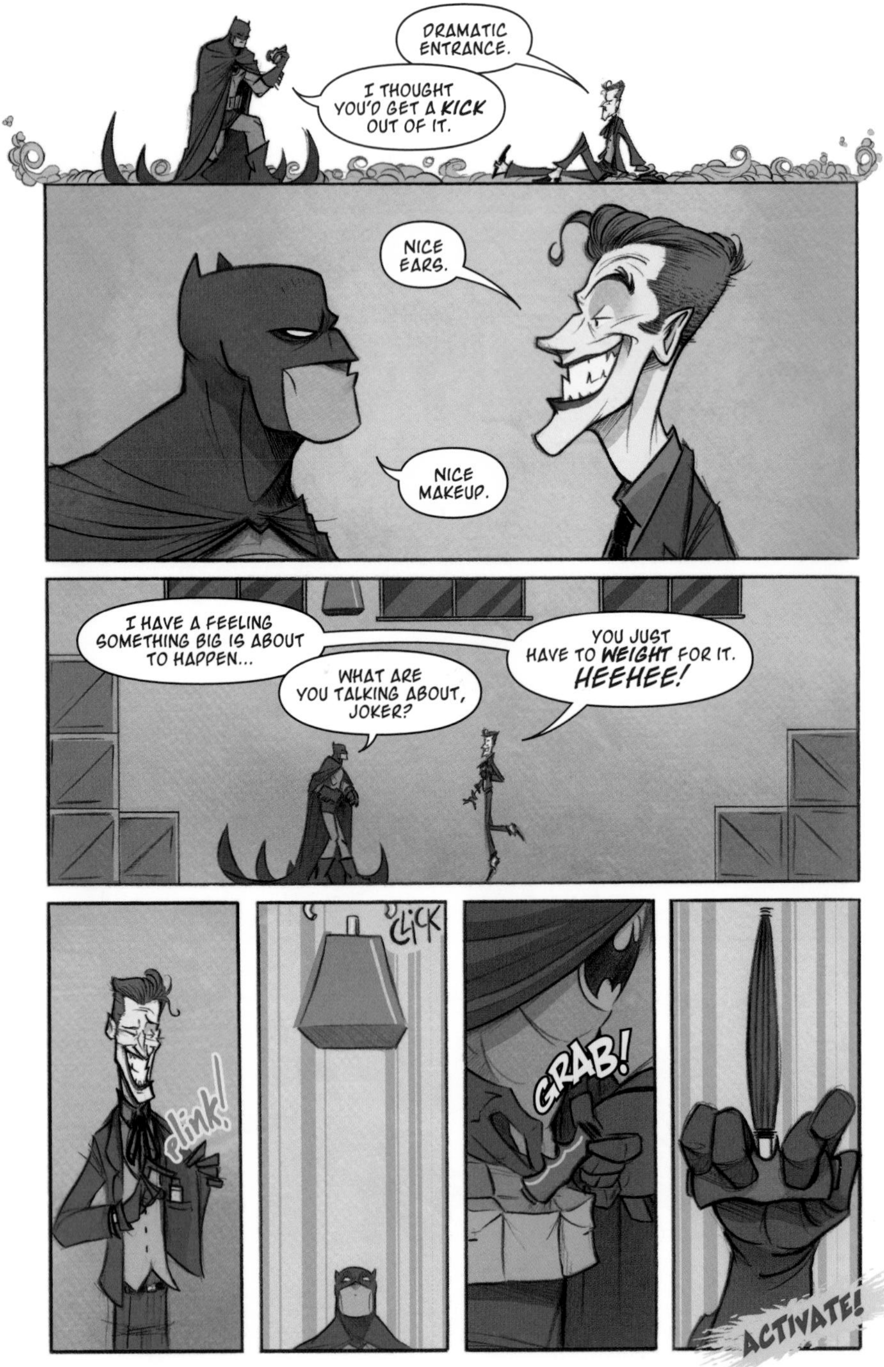
DRAMATIC ENTRANCE.
I THOUGHT YOU'D GET A KICK OUT OF IT.
NICE EARS.
NICE MAKEUP.
I HAVE A FEELING SOMETHING BIG IS ABOUT TO HAPPEN...
WHAT ARE YOU TALKING ABOUT, JOKER?
YOU JUST HAVE TO WEIGHT FOR IT. HEEHEE!
plink!
CLICK
GRAB!
ACTIVATE!

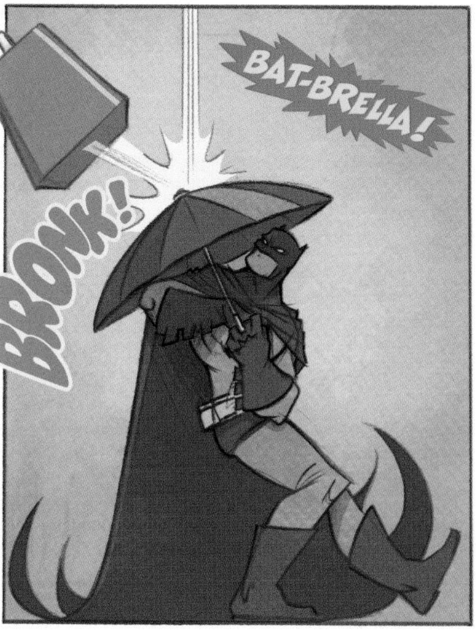
BAT-BRELLA!
BRONK!

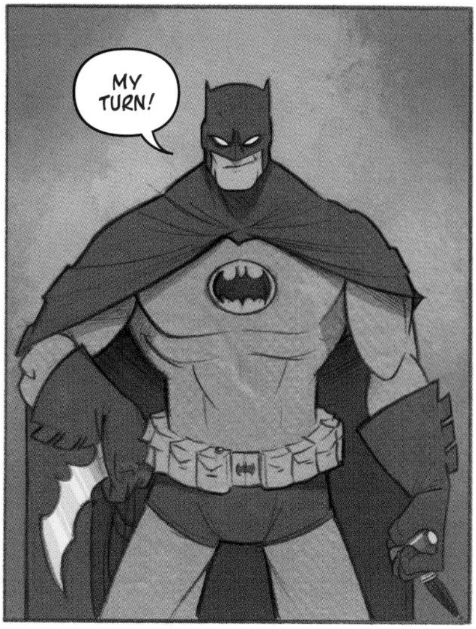
MY TURN!

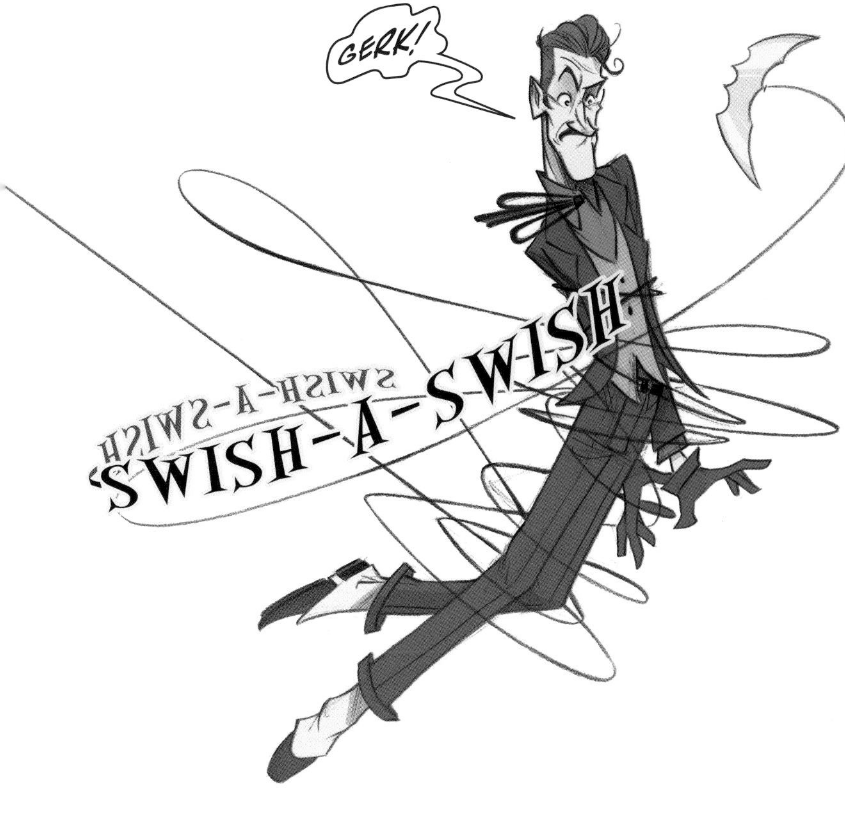
GERK!
SWISH-A-SWISH
SWISH-A-SWISH

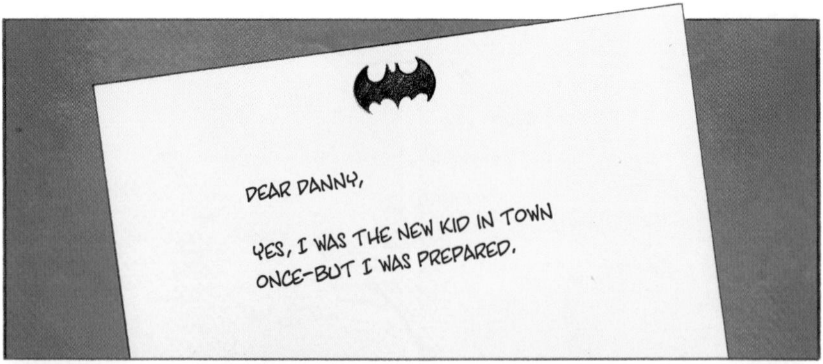
DEAR DANNY,
YES, I WAS THE NEW KID IN TOWN ONCE-BUT I WAS PREPARED.

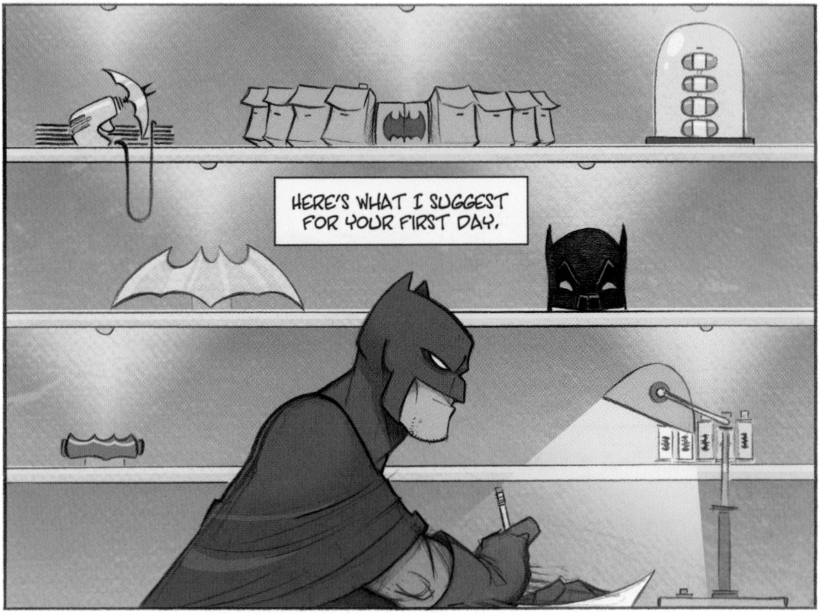
HERE'S WHAT I SUGGEST FOR YOUR FIRST DAY.

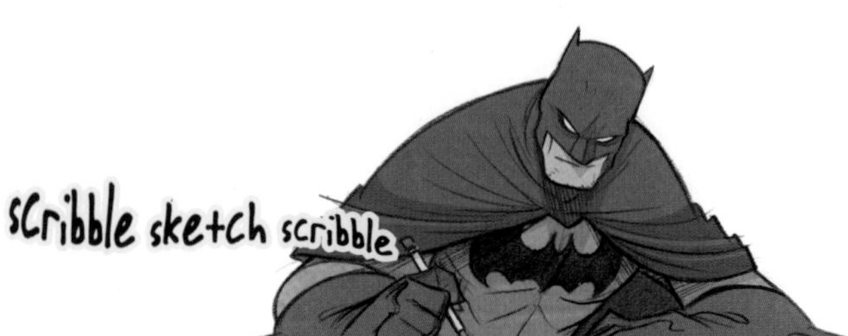
SCRIBBLE SKETCH SCRIBBLE

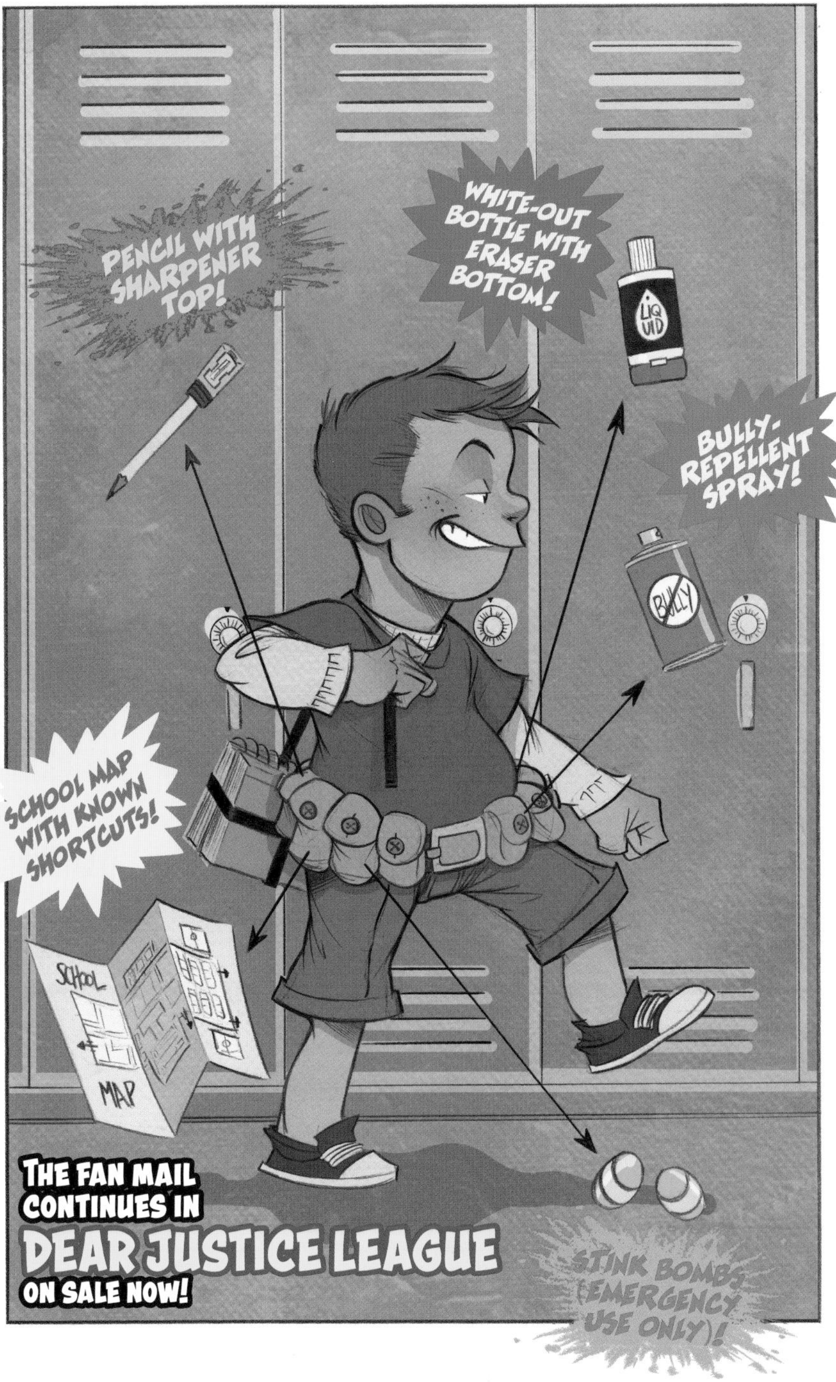
PENCIL WITH SHARPENER TOP!
WHITE-OUT BOTTLE WITH ERASER BOTTOM!
LIQ UID
BULLY-REPELLENT SPRAY!
BULLY
SCHOOL MAP WITH KNOWN SHORTCUTS!
SCHOOL
MAP
STINK BOMBS (EMERGENCY USE ONLY)!
THE FAN MAIL CONTINUES IN
DEAR JUSTICE LEAGUE
ON SALE NOW!

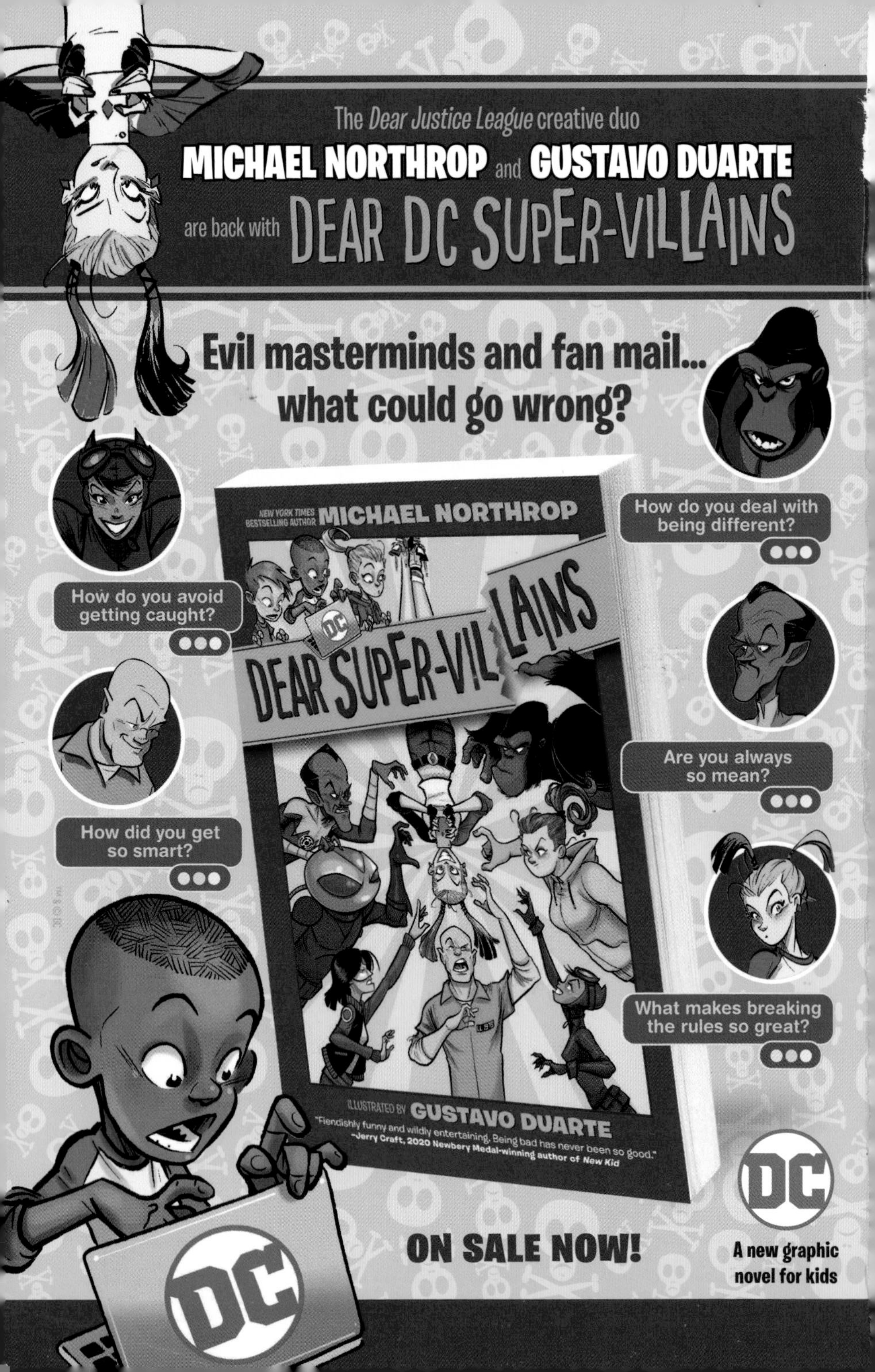

The Dear Justice League creative duo
MICHAEL NORTHROP and GUSTAVO DUARTE
are back with DEAR DC SUPER-VILLAINS
Evil masterminds and fan mail... what could go wrong?
How do you avoid getting caught?
How did you get so smart?
How do you deal with being different?
Are you always so mean?
What makes breaking the rules so great?
NEW YORK TIMES BESTSELLING AUTHOR MICHAEL NORTHROP
DEAR SUPER-VILLAINS
ILLUSTRATED BY GUSTAVO DUARTE
"Fiendishly funny and wildly entertaining. Being bad has never been so good."
–Jerry Craft, 2020 Newbery Medal-winning author of New Kid
ON SALE NOW!
A new graphic novel for kids